A SOLDIER'S PROMISE

A COMING HOME ANTHOLOGY VOLUME 1

COMING HOME SERIES

JESSICA SCOTT

THIRTY ONE FOX BOOKS

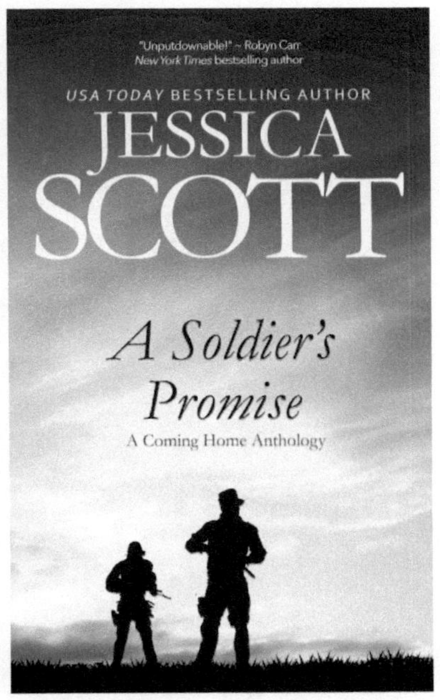

Welcome home...back to the place where everything is worth fighting for. Available for the first time in a box set, the first two books in the acclaimed Coming Home series from USA Today bestselling author Jessica Scott.

Because of You

Welcome Home - these are the words every soldier longs to hear after an endless deployment. But for Sergeant First Class Shane Garrison, there's no one waiting when he arrives back at Fort Hood, unconscious and barely hanging on. The IED that nearly took his life took something more important - something he's afraid he'll never get back.

Back to You

Dying has a way of changing a man. Ever since the day Army captain Trent Davila lost his life, he's been fighting the demons that haunt him from that terrible day. Time and again, he's left his wife and their two children behind as he's volunteered to put himself in harm's way until his wife had enough.

A Soldier's Promise
A Coming Home Anthology
Volume I

Because of You
Back to You

By
Jessica Scott

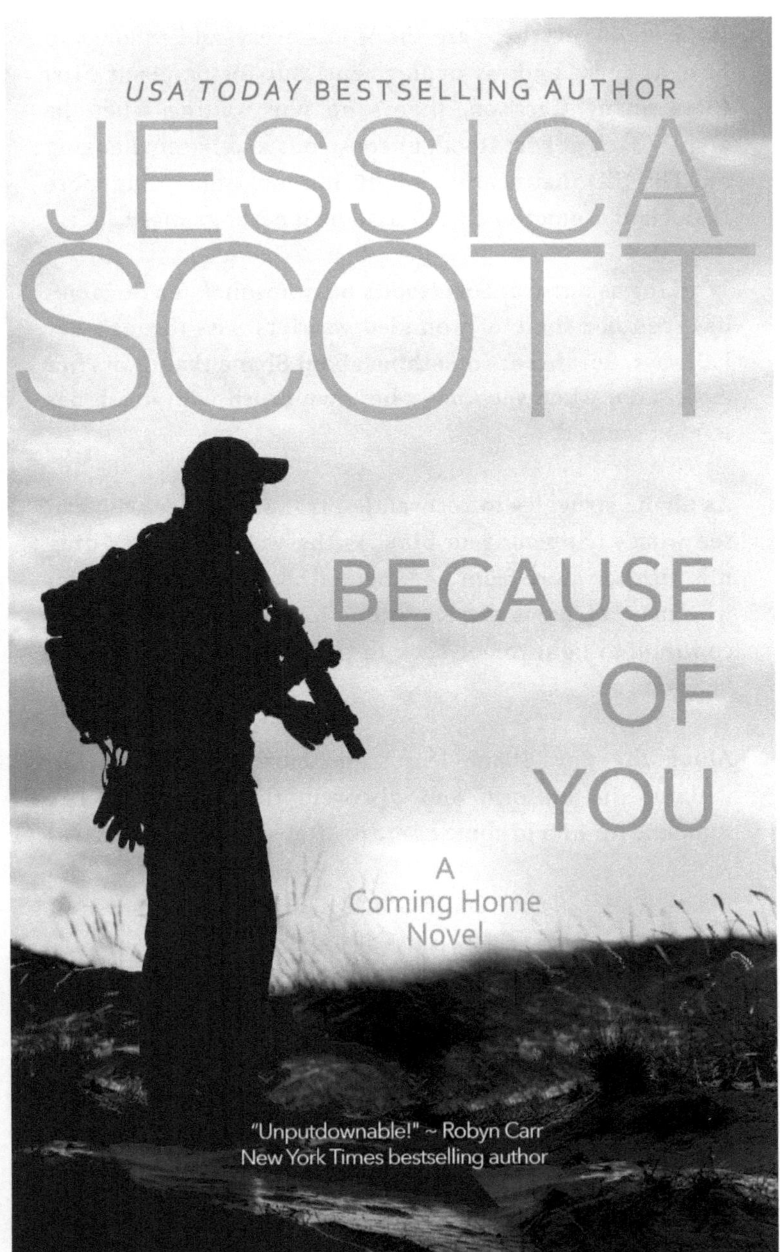

Because of You is a beautifully crafted, wonderfully emotional debut."~ **JoAnn Ross** *New York Times* **bestselling author**

Welcome Home - these are the words every soldier longs to hear after an endless deployment. But for Sergeant First Class Shane Garrison, there's no one waiting when he arrives back at Fort Hood, unconscious and barely hanging on. The IED that nearly took his life took something more important - something he's afraid he'll never get back.

Working as nurse at Fort Hood's busy hospital, Jen St. James has seen her share of wounded warriors pass through her hallways. But there's something about Shane that draws her close, even when she knows her own brush with death has left her scarred.

As Shane struggles to recover, Jen is the only one who can see what's happening to him. As the wounds of war drag him further away from healing and everyone around him who matters, Jen is there, pushing him, demanding that he continue to fight to get back to the only thing he believes he's good at.

Along the way, Shane learns the hard truth about life without the uniform and discovers that maybe, there's someone for him to come home to after all.

THE COMING HOME SERIES
Because of You
I'll Be Home for Christmas: A Coming Home Novella
Anything For You: A Coming Home Short Story
Back to You
Come Home to Me: A Coming Home Novella*
Carry Me Home*
A Place Called Home*
Take Me Home*
Homefront
After The War
Last One Home*

Note – these books are fiction. Any resemblance to real people or events is purely coincidence

Learn More At…
http://www.jessicascott.net
Follow Jessica on Twitter
Like Jessica on Facebook
Sign up for Jessica's Newsletter

Author's Note

The Coming Home series and Homefront series were originally published as separate series. I have rebranded them to get things organized as they were originally intended.

Come Home to Me: A Coming Home Novella* was originally published as part of the Homefront series

Carry Me Home* was originally published as Until There Was You as part of the Coming Home series

A Place Called Home* was originally published as All for You as part of the Coming Home series

Take Me Home* was originally published as It's Always Been You as part of the Coming Home series

Last One Home* was originally published as Find My Way Home as part of the Homefront series

To my husband, who smiled the first time he saw my name in print
To my mom, who instilled in me a love of books from as far back as I can remember

PROLOGUE

National Training Center
Fort Irwin, California

Sergeant First Class Shane Garrison knew that life wasn't fair. But after thirteen years in the Army, it still surprised him what a relentless bitch reality could be sometimes. He stood outside the tactical operations cell in the middle of the California desert and studied the legal-sized envelope he held in his hand. Everything out here was supposed to be a training exercise to prepare his men for their upcoming combat tour in Iraq. No one was supposed to get hurt. But they did anyway, and just like in Iraq, the wounded were sent on to the nearest hospital while their buddies were left behind to worry.

Noise raged around him—shouts, the constant crunch of boots on gravel, and the rumbling of the generators that powered the servers, radios, and—most important—the coffeepots that kept the war running at all hours of the day and night. There was no escape for him, not from the noise or from the fact that sometimes, life just sucked. He turned the envelope over in his hands. He didn't need silence to guess what was inside.

A shadow passed in front of him and Captain Trent Davila heaved himself up onto the hood of one of the command-and-control Humvees next to Shane. By regulation, when Trent had been commissioned as an officer several years earlier, they shouldn't have remained friends. Relationships were prohibited between officers and enlisted soldiers, but they'd gone through too much together over the years to let something trivial like Army regulations dictate the terms of their friendship.

"Any word on Morrell?" Shane finally asked when Trent didn't speak. The sun slid behind Tiefort Mountain, sending the desert sinking into darkness.

"Just came out of surgery. He's going to keep the leg." Trent cleared his throat. "That was real quick work you did, getting him out from under that Bradley track so fast."

Shane shrugged and spat into the dirt. "Just doing what Uncle Sam pays me for."

"Yeah, well, most people Uncle Sam pays wouldn't have known what to do with a guy screaming under a thousand-pound vehicle." Shadows cast by the headquarters' floodlights cut across Trent's cheeks as he nodded toward the envelope. "Anything good in the mail?"

"Divorce papers."

"Shit."

"Guess my wife decided not to wait for me to get back to make things official. Like I deployed to the National Training Center just to keep her from running off with her shiny new lover." He couldn't hide the bitterness in his voice. But he wasn't irritated over the fact that his wife had left him for another man. He was irritated because she'd made him feel like shit when he should have been having a cigar because Morrell was going to be okay.

He was hot, tired, and dirty from forty-five days in this California desert paradise. Before today, he'd wanted nothing more than to pack all of his soldiers off to their wives and girlfriends, and then go home to try to save a few mementos from his dying marriage.

Funny how five years of marriage had finally ended with a whimper, and the only thing he'd spent the day worrying about was whether one of his boys would make it out of surgery alive and intact. Trent's good news had sent that worry scrambling into the night, leaving only his failed marriage to occupy his thoughts.

Guess that had been part of the problem all along for him and Tatiana. He'd always been more focused on his men.

"Who pissed in your cornflakes?"

Shane sighed as Carponti strolled up. In any other unit in the Army, no sergeant would talk to his platoon sergeant or company commander the way Carponti did to Shane and Trent. For some reason, though, Shane let him get away with it. He was pretty sure it was because he'd never trained anyone who was better at infantry squad tactics at such a young age. Even in the middle of a firefight, Carponti would crack jokes while he maneuvered his fire team into position. He'd had Morrell laughing his ass off today as they'd carried him to the medical evac flight. Granted, the medics had Morrell so drugged, he hadn't known his own name, but still, Carponti had a gift.

"My wife."

"What, did she finally leave you? Good, now you can stop feeling bad about doing what you do best."

"Dickhead, I'm getting divorced. That's not exactly great news."

"Hell yeah, it is. Your wife has made your life miserable for the last five years. She's got her new man, you've got your freedom, and now I've got a designated driver whenever we go out to Ropers." Carponti hopped up onto the hood next to Trent. "And speaking of which, Ramirez turns twenty-one when we get home. We're christening him the first weekend we get back and it'll get you back in the saddle."

Trent snorted and choked on a laugh, and Shane hid his own wry grin. He'd love to go out with the boys, but contrary to what Carponti believed, it wasn't as simple as sign the papers, get your life back.

"He's right," Trent said, still chuckling.

"About which part? Christening Ramirez?"

"About getting your life back. No one should make you feel guilty for leading our boys. You're damn good at what you do. You make a difference and you know it."

Shane glanced over at his longtime friend. "Does Laura still understand? You're gone more than you're home. How many birthdays and anniversaries have you missed?"

"Laura gets it. She understands what we do."

Carponti snatched the papers from Shane's hand. "Laura sends cookies to NTC, unlike your wife, who sends this bull."

"Ex-wife," Shane corrected, and snatched them back.

"Put this crap away and let's go smoke a cigar. Morrell's going to be okay and that's worth celebrating."

"I'll catch up in a sec."

He pulled out the papers. *Tatiana Garrison, Plaintiff vs. Shane Garrison, Defendant.*

He stared at the formal letter, lit by the floodlights overhead. He knew the exact moment his marriage had stopped being anything but a farce.

It was the first time he'd missed her birthday. She hadn't understood that he'd had no access to a phone or the Internet. She hadn't understood that he'd spent that day and the next two days in the hospital with one of his boys, who'd been on life support after being hit by shrapnel. Oh, she'd pretended to be sympathetic, but she had never gotten over it, and Shane had paid for it every single day since.

Divorce.

He closed his eyes, shutting out the memory of when he'd first met her. He didn't want to remember the girl she'd been, or the fool he'd been, trying to explain to her why what he did was important.

No, right now he wanted to remember this moment. The moment he realized that he no longer cared about saving a marriage that never should have been in the first place.

The only thing in life he'd ever been good at was the Army. He'd been a shitty son and a terrible husband. He hadn't set out to be bad at either of those relationships. It had just turned out that way.

But he was a damn good infantryman. He had that going for him. His men needed their platoon sergeant focused and steady. He couldn't be the leader they needed him to be if he was mooning over a woman who didn't want to be with him. His hand didn't even tremble when he signed the papers, ending the farce and freeing himself to focus on what he was good at: being a soldier. His marriage was over. This just made it official.

At least now their constant arguing about money and time—two things Shane had been too busy fighting a war and taking care of his soldiers to care about—was over. Sorry, but when asked to choose between picking out sheets at Bed, Bath, & Beyond or teaching a young soldier to shoot at the small arms range, he would always choose the range. Maybe that wasn't fair to Tatiana, but it was who he was and she'd known that when she married him. Instead of trying to make things work, they'd done nothing but make each other miserable.

He tucked the papers back into the envelope and stuffed them into the cargo pocket on his uniform pants. Tonight, he wasn't going to dwell on something he couldn't change. Tatiana had made her choice a long time ago. No, tonight he was going to celebrate, and he wasn't going to let the end of his marriage crush the victory that surged inside of him. His men didn't need to know about his problems. He took care of them, not the other way around. Tonight, one of his boys was okay. Somehow, he'd made a difference.

And that beat the hell out of any bad news from back home.

1

____

Fort Hood, Texas

"What crawled up your ass?"

Shane shoved his last Ziploc bag of T-shirts into his Army-issued duffel bag and tried to smother his rising irritation. "What part of no don't you understand?"

Carponti—aka the most annoying soldier in Shane's entire platoon—picked up Shane's grey ACU pattern patrol cap and put it on, strutting around like he owned the place. Then he puffed out his chest and swung his arms wide, like a bad caricature of an angry gorilla. Sometimes Shane wished he didn't let Carponti into his apartment as often as he did. But Carponti had recently turned into a permanent fixture in Shane's after-duty life. Shane wasn't sure what that said about the state of his affairs. As if Carponti mocking him in the empty apartment wasn't enough of an indicator. "I'm Sarn't Garrison. I'm too badass to relax and have a good time."

"Piss off."

"Did your wife take your sense of humor in the divorce, too?" Carponti asked, flopping into Shane's chair. "Come on, man, it's just a few hours and a couple of beers. The whole platoon is going to be there."

Shane sighed and hooked his duffel bag shut, tossing it into the corner of his apartment near the front door. He flinched as the sudden movement stretched the fresh stitches that were holding two tiny holes in his abdominal wall closed. Carponti didn't know about Shane's recent brush with death and Shane intended to keep it that way. If Carponti wanted to believe the divorce was keeping him from going out, then so be it. But the truth was that Shane had been too busy, over the past five months, to dwell on the end of his marriage. Of course, he missed feeling like he had a home, but he couldn't lie to himself—Tatiana hadn't made their life together a home any more than he had. She'd been familiar, though, and he missed that. At least, that's what he told himself when he had time to think about it. So many of his guys were having problems in the lead-up to this deployment that Shane had barely seen the air mattress on the floor of the apartment they'd shared, let alone slept on it. And tomorrow he was leaving for good.

Shane shoved his body armor into a second duffel bag, then stuffed socks and more T-shirts into the gaps. It was a pain in the ass packing for deployment. It was easier just being deployed.

"The whole platoon being there is the problem. Makes it kind of hard to explain why the platoon sergeant is in jail with the platoon if you guys get too fired up tonight. Someone has to be around to bail your sorry asses out of Bell County tomorrow."

Carponti rolled his eyes and rubbed the back of his neck, serious for one hot second. "Look, just come out with us. You've been a real asshole since your wife left; you need to unwind, or we might just shoot your ass when we're in country for being such a dick."

Shane rested his hand over his heart and blinked rapidly. "God, I'm so touched by the depth of your concern. I can drink beer here. Alone. Quietly."

"Sissy."

Shane laughed and the feeling caught him off guard. If it had been that long since he'd laughed, maybe his wife *had* taken his sense of humor along with all of his furniture. He shook his head at Carponti's relentless nagging and finally surrendered. Under duress, but still. "All right, fine. But I swear, if a single one of you miss movement tomorrow . . ."

Carponti made the sign of the cross over his heart. "Promise. Let's go. I'm picking up Nikki on the way."

Shane stuffed his wallet into his back pocket and grabbed the keys to his truck. At least he didn't have to change. Killeen, Texas, didn't exactly sport any high-class bars. The place they were headed to, Ropers, was only moderately slimy, meaning that he wasn't likely to die of dysentery from the beer glasses and he was just fine in his T-shirt and jeans. They were clothes he didn't care if he ruined if—scratch that, *when*—he had to drag one of his soldiers out of a brawl.

Truth be told, he didn't have any problem with the boys going out. Shane just didn't want to watch them say good-bye to their wives and girlfriends, and it had nothing to do with his own divorce. Shane hated the knowledge that he might not be bringing everyone home to their families.

It was 2007 and they were deploying as part of the Surge to stabilize Iraq. He knew he would probably bury some of his men this year. He'd deployed too many times to entertain the naive hope that all of his boys would come back in one piece. He'd move heaven and earth to protect them, and it looked like that would have to start tonight, instead of tomorrow. He couldn't promise they'd all come home from the war, but they'd sure as shit make it to formation in the morning.

That much he *could* guarantee.

"Stop touching it."

Jen St. James jumped and dropped her hand from the edge of her blouse. "I wasn't."

She should have known Laura would catch her tugging at her clothes, which, with the addition of a triangular-shaped silicone form, now fit much better. And that was part of what made Jen uncomfortable. She wasn't used to her blouses hanging properly anymore. But she couldn't tell Laura that. It had been hard enough to convince her that she wanted to buy only one form and not the entire shop.

Laura couldn't seem to wrap her brain around the fact that Jen didn't need to feel sexy, that she wanted to be comfortable instead.

"Yes, you were. No one can tell and the more you play with it, the more horny GIs are going to check your boobs out." Laura raised her glass, and then lowered it. "On second thought, keep playing with them."

"Boob. Singular."

"You still have two. Just not a full set. And honestly, no one can tell. So please quit worrying and relax. You look amazing."

"Except for the silicone stuck to my chest."

"That no one can see. Here," Laura said, shoving a sweating green Heineken bottle into Jen's hand. "Drink. Don't argue. I finally got you out of the house to have a good time and damn it, I'm going to accomplish that mission if it kills me."

"You sound like a soldier," Jen said with a smile.

Laura took a pull off her drink. "I can't help it. I spend all day every day around soldiers. I'm bound to pick things up here and there."

It had been a long time since Jen had been around this many people. She felt the proximity of too many bodies, too much cologne and spilled beer. The smells bombarded her and reminded her of the life she'd had once upon a time. A time when she would have danced until dawn and then closed the night out with pancakes at IHOP.

Jen had not been inside a bar for more than two years, and she was no more comfortable today than she'd been the last time she'd been out when her ex had made a point of announcing to everyone in the bar that she had only one breast. So the fact that she was here was amazing in and of itself. The loud music, the crowd, and the GIs mingling with the wannabe cowboys was not an ambience Jen typically sought out. The smoke grated on her lungs but wasn't nearly as smothering in the seat she'd managed to snag at the edge of the bar. Still, anything was better than the sterile smell of the hospital, and she wanted to get back to feeling normal, really she did. Whatever normal meant nowadays.

Laura was the one saying good-bye to her husband for the fifth time in seven years. Jen was just here for moral support, so the least she could do was put her own demons to rest and have a good time. She lifted the beer to her lips.

"I can't believe you dragged me here," she shouted in Laura's ear over the din of Kenny Chesney.

"I can't believe I found a babysitter. Trent's whole company is here tonight." Laura smiled and nursed a Corona while Jen sipped on her Heineken.

"Shouldn't you be molesting your husband? He's the one leaving."

"I don't want to leave you hanging out here, teasing all these horny soldiers with your fake boob."

"Ha-ha-ha. My fake boob and I are just fine, thanks. And speak of the devil." Strong, wide hands slipped around Laura's waist, yanking her back. Laura tipped her face up to her husband's for a kiss and Jen offered Trent a mock salute with the tip of her beer.

"Will you please take your wife to dance?" Jen shouted with a smile.

"Gladly." Trent pulled his wife into some convoluted line dance, leaving Jen alone at the bar where she was quite content to watch everyone else and sip her beer.

She discreetly tugged at her blouse again. In a dark corner at the other end of the bar, a sensual flare of movement caught her eye. She looked closer and saw a couple kissing intensely, so engrossed in each other she couldn't say where one person ended and the other began, lost in the heavy scent of lust and liquor. She looked away, studying the green bottle in her hand. She wondered if she would ever again know what it felt like to have warm, rough hands move over her flesh.

Jen had come a long way, and it had still taken all of Laura's persuasive powers to convince her to buy the breast form. But it didn't mean that her scars no longer bothered her. She'd hesitated for a different reason. The round shape beneath her blouse now was just false advertising. She swallowed and pushed aside a brief flicker of melancholy.

Someone solid and heavy knocked into her and sloshed beer down the front of her blouse. A strong vise latched around her arm to steady her. She glanced up into the lightest grey eyes she'd ever seen. Grey eyes that she'd seen before but never this close. In the dimly lit bar, they looked almost silver.

Shane Garrison. A friend of Trent's. Jen had seen him around before, but had never actually spoken to him. He'd always seemed big, but up close he was massive. Black tribal tattoos twisted up both of his wrists, writhing up his forearms to disappear beneath the frayed edge of a green T-shirt. And who knew that bald could be so sexy in the right lighting? Had to be the rough jaw that did it.

"Sorry. You okay?" He leaned close to her ear so he didn't have to shout. Jen shivered as his breath brushed across her skin. He stood closer to her now than any man other than a doctor had in over a year. The heat from his body caressed her skin, and she could smell him, a mixture of spice and smoke and something entirely male. She swallowed and tried to find her voice.

"I'm fine. Thanks. This place is crowded." She knew better than this. She pulled her arm free and tugged the clinging blouse away from her skin, suddenly afraid that he would see the scars on her chest through the wet material.

As the words left her lips, someone jostled her into him again. He tried to steady her but she fell against him anyway.

Time hung suspended and she stood in this man's embrace, feeling protected and safe and deliciously unflawed. It was impossible to miss the hard angles of his body. For one brief fantasy moment, she imagined what it would feel like if this dangerous and sexy man lowered his mouth to hers.

But the fantasy faded as quickly as it had come and Jen stepped back into reality. A reality in which a man like the one standing oh-so-close to her was just being polite to a woman he had met in a bar. *Down girl.*

He lowered his mouth to her ear again. "Since I nearly crushed you twice now, can I buy you a drink?"

She smiled and sipped from the sweating green bottle. "I still have some of this one left. Thanks, though."

"Jen, right?" He retrieved his own beer. "Are you here with Laura and Trent?"

"Yeah. How did you know?"

"I've seen you around. How long have you known Laura?"

Jen ticked off numbers on her fingers. "Ethan is almost six, right? Almost six years. We met right after she had him."

A shadow flickered across his face and was gone before she could truly say she'd seen it. Instead of letting it go, she chased it. "What?"

"I've known Trent a long time. That's all."

Why would that make him sad? She wondered at the man who scanned the bar, splitting his attention between her and the crush of bodies on the floor. With each question, he leaned in close to her, sending a shiver down her spine. A shiver that chased away her awkward discomfort and, for one brief moment, made her feel whole and feminine. There had been a time when she would have acted on impulse and pursued this man, but those days were long gone.

"Yeah. Going away party and all that. Are you deploying tomorrow, too?" God but she loved how he smelled.

"Yeah." He took a long pull from his beer.

"For how long?"

He shrugged. "A year, with an option for fifteen months." She caught a glimpse of a black tattoo around the edge of his collarbone and wondered just how much of his body was covered by the twisting dark lines of ink. Tattoos didn't usually do it for her. She wondered at people who would permanently color their bodies. But on Shane, they worked. They worked well.

She sniffed and sipped her beer even as Shane shifted, resting one arm on the bar behind him and angling his body slightly toward her so that he could see the dance floor. Jen turned in time to see Laura dragging Trent away from the Copperhead Road line dance. They wove through the crowd, heading toward her, and Jen felt a sense of guilt creep up the back of her neck like a flush. Laura was spending too much time worrying about her—she should be focusing on her husband instead.

Trent's face split into a wide grin when he saw Shane. "Miracles will never cease. Carponti actually got you to come out?"

"Yeah."

"Jen, you didn't tell me you knew Shane," Laura said, twining her arm with Jen's.

"I don't. He bumped into me."

Laura leaned close, so that the men couldn't hear her. "Shane is one of Trent's platoon sergeants, but they've been friends for years. And he's divorc—"

"Not another word. Not one." It didn't matter that she'd been wondering if he was single. Her friend's words shattered her fantasy and brought reality into sharp, silicone-shaped focus.

Laura feigned innocence with widened eyes and a wicked smile that fooled no one. "What?"

"I know where you're going with this, and it's not even close to possible."

Laura shrugged, a smile painted on her lips, and danced away with Trent, leaving Jen alone at the crowded bar with brooding, sexy Shane. She sipped her beer and studied him. He was watching the crowd, his jaw flexing in the shadows.

What did it feel like to know that tomorrow he was going off to war?

2

———————

Shane sighed and looked out over the crowd, checking on each of his soldiers. He felt the little blonde shift against him and he leaned down so she wouldn't have to shout.

There was something hot about the way she tried to keep her distance, like she thought he might bite.

"You've known Trent a long time?"

Shane nodded, inhaling the clean scent of her hair as he leaned toward her again. "We were privates together in Germany." He looked into his beer. "Man, it's been almost twelve years. He's my commander now."

He enjoyed leaning close to her ear. She had adorable earlobes and—man, he was pathetic. He wasn't even supposed to be here tonight, let alone talking to a beautiful woman, and he was going to blow it by being melodramatic and staring at her earlobes like a psycho.

Laura and Trent embraced in the center of the dance floor, slow dancing to Lonestar, and a pang of longing stabbed him in the heart. He had never had that kind of closeness with his wife. Laura and Trent looked like they'd been made for each other, they always had. What did that kind of trust and comfort feel like?

"Isn't that weird with him being your boss now?"

Shane shook his head. "Not really. I don't put him in a position to make it awkward."

She raised her beer to her mouth, and his body tightened as her lips circled the green tip of the bottle. A bolt of clean, pure desire shot through him. He was no warrior monk by any stretch of the imagination, but watching her struck something different inside of him. Something he thought he'd shut down and buried long ago.

She smiled up at him. "That's nice of you."

"Nice is not exactly how most of my men would describe me." He snorted, taking a sip of his beer. So far, he'd managed to nurse his one beer quite well as the party went on around him. He didn't need to get distracted, no matter how sexy the distraction.

She leaned in and her breath brushed against his ear, stroking the skin of his neck. "Why would you say you're not nice?"

"I'm an infantry platoon sergeant. I say jump, my guys jump; they don't even ask where or how high. That doesn't equal nice." He sucked in a deep breath and found himself wishing he'd had more practice being, well, nice.

"I think you're being too hard on yourself." She turned and set her now empty beer bottle on the bar. "I'm going to run to the bathroom. Can you tell Laura if she comes back before I do?"

"Don't females usually travel in packs to do that?"

"I'm a big girl."

He watched her go, his blood singing with curiosity and something else. Just then, an elbow jabbed into his ribs, slamming right into the stitches he was doing his best to ignore. He didn't have to guess who the elbow was attached to.

"Will you cut that out?"

"Who is that and why are you mooning over her?" Carponti's speech was a little too smooth to be considered sober.

"I'm not mooning over anyone."

Carponti snapped to the position of parade rest, slapping his hands together at the small of his back and spreading his feet. He swayed a little from the force of the movement. "Roger, Sergeant. My mistake."

"Knock it off, asshole. I thought you were trying to have a good time tonight?"

"I am. I'm screwing with you, my number one pastime, Sarn't G."

Shane narrowed his eyes and studied Carponti, trying to decide if he was hammered. Anyone who'd been in the Army for a hot second used the shortened sarn't instead of fully pronouncing sergeant. He'd said it the right way, and without slurring, but that didn't mean Shane's suspicions about his level of intoxication were laid to rest.

Shane looked skyward, praying for a small dose of patience. Regardless of Carponti's smart-ass ways, he was a damn fine infantry-man. If he could ever get him to stop screwing off, he'd be one hell of a master gunner. But passing that course required studying and Carponti adamantly insisted he'd joined the Army to avoid anything remotely associated with school.

"Where's Nikki?" Shane asked, turning the conversation away from himself.

"The little girls' room." Carponti gestured toward the end of the bar, the same direction in which Jen had just disappeared.

Shane glanced over and his stomach tightened when he saw the one person who was more of a pain in the ass than Carponti could ever dream of being. Lieutenant Jason Randall—a thick-necked full bird colonel's son—looked like he was lecturing one of Carponti's boys near the latrine. Seeing it, too, Carponti stiffened. "Looks like Randall has his fan club with him," he said.

Shane shifted to get a better look at Randall's companions. "Isn't that the female clerk we've got in the motor pool now?"

"Yep."

"Wonderful. She's one of the few women serving in a maneuver unit and Randall is already leading her down the path of self-destruc-tion. He should know better than to hang out with enlisted."

"Pot meet kettle."

"I'm not a private and I knew Trent before he ever became an officer."

"Whatever. I don't care what he does or who he does it with." Carponti took a pull from his beer, then set it roughly on the bar. "Things are getting a little rough in here. I'm going to go over there to grab Nikki."

"I'll go with you." Shane finished his beer, following Carponti into the crowd, not so much to watch his back, but to keep his sergeant from starting any fights. Lieutenant Randall had a small group of soldiers—including the new clerk—who treated him like a god. Shane suspected it was because Randall's father was a brigade commander up at Fort Carson. No one in Shane's platoon was in

Randall's fan club, but that didn't mean Shane could give Carponti a pass if he hit him. Lieutenant Randall frequently assumed that Daddy's rank translated into Randall's authority. Add in the fact that he didn't listen to anyone, and that made him not only a dickhead, but a dangerous one. Officers like Randall got people killed.

Literally.

And the soldier Randall was currently chewing out belonged to Carponti, which meant he belonged to Shane.

Shane was determined that Randall was not going to ruin his boys' last night in the States, whatever it took. He just hoped Carponti wasn't as drunk as he appeared to be, because otherwise tonight just might turn into the fiasco Shane had feared—one he would have to explain the following morning. He waded into the crowd and started coming up with a good story for the sergeant major.

Well, Sarn't Major, what happened was . . .

JEN STOOD in front of the mirror, studying her profile. She tugged at her blouse, and then squared her shoulders, seeing a full, equal-shaped silhouette. Why couldn't she get used to it? She reached behind her to adjust the band around her ribs.

"Will you stop?" Laura said, stepping out of a bathroom stall. She moved to the sink to wash her hands. So much for going to the bathroom alone. And damn it, she'd gotten busted adjusting the form. Again. "You look great and the only one who doesn't seem to know that is you."

"I can tell."

"Knock it off and have another beer, will you?" Laura reached for her, like she was going to plump her breasts together. Jen dodged with a horrified laugh, but ended up stumbling into someone else. Someone else turned out to be a beautiful strawberry blonde with brown mascara smeared beneath her eyes.

"Sorry!"

"Nicole," Laura said at the same time. "Honey, what's wrong? Carponti hasn't been arrested again, has he?"

"Not if I have anything to say about it. If he costs me my job interview at CID, I'll kill him." Nicole offered a watery smile. "I just hate that he's leaving again."

Jen bit her lip, unsure of what to say or how to act. Surrounded by Army wives, she was seeing a sadness that was usually hidden behind smiling masks. She felt like she'd been granted access to a secret world, a special world filled with women like Laura, who spent as much time as single parents and deployment widows as they did with their soldiers. There was a deep discomfort in her as she watched Laura help Nicole repair her makeup, complete with emergency concealer and mascara.

"He'll never know you've been crying," Laura said, dropping the small cosmetics bag back into her purse. "We'll get together with the rest of the family readiness group. Just like last time. Make sure everyone's holding up okay."

"Okay. Let me go round up my husband before he *does* do something stupid." Nicole breathed deeply. "Sorry," she said, turning toward Jen. "I'm Nicole and I promise I'm not usually this melodramatic."

"It's kind of understandable," Jen said, but Nicole waved her comment off.

"Doesn't matter. Put it away and smile. I'll cry once he's gone." And with that, she dashed her fingers beneath her eyes once more and pushed through the door.

Laura leaned over the sink and checked her own makeup.

"How do you do it?" Jen asked her suddenly.

"Do what?"

"Act like Trent leaving is no big deal."

Laura shrugged, but her smile wavered, just a little—just enough for Jen to see through the facade. "It sucks. And I won't lie and say I'm not tired and frustrated and irritated, either. But I've got to hold it together back here so he can go do what he has to do to come home to me and the kids."

Jen didn't know what to say. Laura's strength and resolve awed her. Laura filled the silence with a smile.

"Come on. Let's go find Shane and Trent."

"Um, how about just your husband? Don't pawn me off on Shane. The last thing he needs right now is to have to babysit the resident basket case."

"How about you take care of him so he doesn't spend the entire night worrying about his soldiers. That man never relaxes. He needs a distraction more than you do."

Jen rolled her eyes and wished the thought of seeing Shane again tonight didn't send a tiny thrill through her. It didn't matter, anyway. Even if she was interested—which she wasn't—he wasn't available and neither was she.

He was leaving for Iraq. Tomorrow.

And she was damaged goods.

"Don't pawn me off on him," she said again.

"I thought I was pawning Shane off on *you*."

Jen backed through the door and for the second time that night, plowed straight into Nicole Carponti . . . and into in the middle of a tense, awkward conversation.

" . . . Nice to me, considering . . ." The guy running his mouth was dark and good-looking, but that didn't prevent his drunken sneer from ruining his looks. Nicole was braced, feet apart like she was ready to fight. Or run. Jen wasn't sure.

Laura's smile was tight as she stepped up next to Nicole. "Lieutenant Randall, I'm sure you must have Nicole confused with someone else. Someone who isn't married to a soldier in your company."

Jen's stomach pitched as her heart slammed against her ribs. It didn't matter that Laura knew the drunk. The smell of beer on the man's breath sent adrenaline pumping through her veins. Jen did not do confrontations. "Come on, let's go."

Carponti melted from the crowd and grabbed at Randall, shoving him toward the dance floor. "Get away from my wife, dickhead."

Everything exploded into sudden violent action all at once. Fists and elbows descended and sounds like meat being beaten thudded to the beat of Toby Keith's latest song. Chairs skidded across the floor and Jen found herself mesmerized by the absolute chaos bursting around her. She searched for a path through the melee, and then found herself pinned between a pillar and the dance floor, which churned now with bodies. Worse yet, she'd lost Laura and Nicole in the fray.

Everything turned to slow motion. She needed to get out of the way, but her feet suddenly felt like lead weights as Carponti and Randall grappled and stumbled toward her.

Strong hands yanked her hard to the right so fast her neck popped.

Shane. And ridiculous relief flooded through her, tingling over her skin.

He braced his hands on the bar on either side of her shoulders to keep from being jammed into her again. "Sorry. It looked like you needed a hand. You okay?"

The fight spun out of control around them, but at the moment, she was cocooned between his body and the solid wood of the bar pressing into her back.

His voice was warm and smooth over the uproar. "I'm going to drag Carponti outside and beat him."

She almost laughed at the mixture of resignation and irritation in Shane's voice. It sounded like he'd spent one too many nights saving Carponti from trouble.

It might have been half an hour or five minutes, but the next thing Jen knew, the crowd had parted and she was outside. She wrapped her arms around her belly and walked around Randall and Trent, who were arguing loudly in front of the soldiers and spouses who'd trickled out into the parking lot. Shane was busy stuffing soldiers into cars or cabs, depending on their sobriety level. Laura leaned against the hood of her car, next to Nicole, who had an amused look on her face.

"Is this how they always spend their last night in the States?" Jen asked.

Laura looked more like a centerfold than a mother of two who'd just escaped a bar brawl. Her friend was either halfway to well lit or furious. Or maybe a little bit of both. Jen couldn't really tell.

Nicole laughed and brushed her hair from her face, sending a whiff of smoke and perfume floating through the thick Texas night air. "It is for me. Vic is constantly pulling stunts like this." She shrugged. "I love him and I guess that doesn't come with a 'but,' you know?"

"Guess this is what I get for trying something different. The last few times Trent left, I was either pregnant or nursing, so no, bars weren't really an option." Laura's voice cracked, and with it, Jen's heart. She wasn't really close to any of these men, and yet, a sudden sadness welled up inside of her that she could not understand.

"If he's peeing in the bushes, I'm thinking this is the end of the night," Nicole said, as Carponti stumbled from behind a parked car, tugging at his zipper. Shane and Trent bullied Lieutenant Randall into a cab. "And hey, no one went to jail. That's always a plus."

Laura cracked a wry grin. "Looks like he's one of the last ones. Nicole, can you get Carponti out of here? I won't be able to get Trent to leave until all his boys are home."

"Sure. See you tomorrow morning?"

"Yeah. I'll be there."

Nicole snagged her husband and urged him toward their car in a backward waltz that was at once a drunken stumble and an erotic dance. The silence wrapped around them like the dark shadows at the edge of the parking lot.

"Are you bringing the kids tomorrow to see Trent off?" Jen asked.

"No." Laura's throat bobbed as she looked into the floodlit parking lot, her eyes settling on her husband. That single word nearly broke Jen's heart. She wrapped her arm around Laura, who rested her head on her shoulder.

"I should be used to this by now," Laura whispered.

"I don't know how. It doesn't get any easier no matter how many times you say good-bye."

Laura sniffed and straightened as Trent slammed the door of Randall's cab closed. "I don't say good-bye. I say see you soon."

Having shipped the last of the soldiers home, Shane and Trent finally approached them. Jen could see why Shane had stayed to mop up. He looked so different from Trent, whose black hair and wire-rimmed glasses made him look more like a warrior monk. Shane was pure fighter, all black ink and hard angles. There was no dichotomy to him, like there appeared to be with Trent.

"Ready to head home?" Trent asked, wrapping his arms around Laura's shoulders.

"Absolutely. You okay to get home, Jen?" Laura lips curled in pure wickedness. It took Jen all of two seconds to realize what she had in mind.

"Laura, don't you dare," Jen hissed as she scanned the parking lot, searching for a way out of her friend's scheme. She wanted to entertain her curiosity from a distance, not up close and personal.

Shane hooked his hands behind his back, looking more relaxed than he had at the beginning of the night. Jen frowned and for a brief moment, thought that he'd actually enjoyed himself during the fight. "Trent, take your wife home. And I better not see you at the gym before ten. I'll take accountability until First Sergeant gets there."

"Thanks, man. See you in the morning." Trent walked off, his wife's arm wrapped around his waist. Laura leaned back, shooting Jen a half-drunken, enthusiastic thumbs-up.

Jen felt a pang of sadness overshadowed by something else. A feeling both awkward and intense that sparked to life when she looked up at Shane. All at once, it struck her that she was alone with him in a dimly lit parking lot.

And she wasn't embarrassed or self-conscious or afraid.

For the first time in she couldn't remember how long, she felt a pang of desire that wasn't overruled by the constant heat of the scar on her chest. She let the awareness of her femininity coast through her veins, and she savored the feeling along with the man.

He was leaving for Iraq in the morning. She could hold on to this one moment.

What's the worst that could happen?

WHEN THE FIGHT had broken out, Shane had seen her standing in the path of the two fighters. He'd mentally urged her to move aside, but everything she'd done had only brought her closer to harm's way. Finally, he'd surrendered to instinct, and stepped in to move her to safety. Looking down at her now, at her hesitant smile mixed with a hint of expectation, he felt it again. The same emotion he'd felt earlier that night. The urge to protect. To shelter. It flickered to life inside of him, something long dormant unfurling inside warmth. The feeling staggered him with its simplicity and power. Had he not been leaving for Iraq in the morning, he might have taken that single step forward and closed the gap between them. She was temptation bundled with a nervous tension—a combination he found absolutely sweet.

"I don't bite," he said, stuffing his hands into his back pockets.

"I'm not worried. You're supposed to be one of the good guys, right?"

Shane chuckled quietly. "My men might disagree."

She narrowed her eyes and peered up at him thoughtfully. "That's the second time you've said that tonight. Why do you have such a low opinion of yourself?"

"I'm not nice. I'm effective. They're mutually exclusive in my world." Shane tried to keep the bitterness from his smile but gave up, surrendering to the truth with a sigh. She was easy to talk to. Something else he was out of practice with.

"Really? Is your world really all that different?"

"I'm a rifle platoon sergeant in a combined arms battalion. I was issued weapons, not baskets of flowers."

"Can you translate that to non-Army?" she asked.

"Infantry. I train my men to shoot things." Shane felt like an awkward teen, unsure of what to say or do.

"Ah. Much easier to understand." She tipped her chin. "But it doesn't explain why Laura has such a high opinion of you if you're such a bad guy."

God but he needed to be somewhere else. Anywhere other than talking to this particular beautiful woman. Laura would unman him over this if he so much as blinked wrong at Jen, let alone give in to the desire to move beyond small talk.

"Can I, ah, make sure you get to your car okay?"

Her mouth was curled in the sweetest half smile, like she couldn't quite figure him out. "Not going to answer?"

"Walking you to your car does not involve psychotherapy. At least, I didn't think it did."

She laughed quietly, the noise of the bar fading a little as they rounded the corner of the parking lot.

She paused and looked over her shoulder at him. A single beam of light slanted across her cheek and almost, he gave in to the urge to trace his thumb over her skin. When she froze, her lips parted just slightly, he stepped into her space. Not close enough to scare her, he hoped. He might regret this. But he wasn't going to spend the next year wondering what it would have been like. "Shit, I'm not good at this."

"Good at what?" Her face was bathed in shadows now, and she

rubbed her hands over her arms. He placed a hand on her shoulder, hesitating and unsure, but filled with a need he couldn't explain.

"I'd like very much to kiss you good night," he whispered, and felt like an urgent seventeen-year-old for even asking. But the moment her lips parted and she lifted her chin, just a little, he was done.

"I'd like that, too."

His breath caught in his throat as he lowered his mouth to hers. He hesitated, nudging her lips open before he curved his mouth over hers. It had been far too long since he'd kissed a woman simply for the sake of it. And now?

Now he felt like he was drowning in her.

A deep, hard ache rose within him. An ache that he would not, no matter how she might lean into him, satisfy tonight. Maybe in a year, if he came home, he might give her a call.

But for tonight, all he had was this kiss. This soft, yearning kiss that tugged at a passion within him that he'd thought long dead. Her sensual gasp against his tongue, the soft stroke of hers against his twisted up inside of him and made him want more, so much more than he could ever hope to have in a single night. He lifted his hand, brushing his finger over her throat, and felt her heart hammering against her skin.

Jen sighed quietly as Shane kissed her, afraid this was just a dream. The taste of him flowed through her, singing through her blood. And then? Then she kissed him back. She slipped her tongue into his mouth, tasting beer and mint and everything sensual and arousing about kissing a man. She burned, a slow fire for this man lighting through her veins.

For Shane.

There was a delicious ache inside of her and she held on to it, clung to it. His arms were strong around her, his skin hot beneath her fingertips. He shifted and pulled her closer, until she was softness and heat pressed against steel.

She sighed and leaned into him. He traced his fingertips down her spine, his hand warm and solid against her lower back.

He was hard and rough, surrounding her with his kiss, his body.

She tried telling herself this wasn't what she thought it was. But she'd never lied to herself before; she wasn't about to start now.

This man was attracted to her. *Her.*

She refused to argue with it, and instead gave herself over to the utterly arousing sensation of being desired. This was what she missed about her former life. That beautiful sensation of a first kiss, the delicious tug of first desire deep in her belly. She lost herself in his kiss, in the slide of his thumb over her back.

Arousal sang through her blood the moment his fingers brushed against the soft skin of her belly. She gasped softly at the power in his hands. His scent wrapped around her like spice and silk and urged her closer to something she hadn't allowed herself to crave.

HE FELT her soften a little more with each moment. Shane had never imagined this and he was completely unprepared for the strength of his own reaction. For once in his life, he surrendered. To the moment. To the taste and feel of Jen. Just Jen and the feeling of being wanted.

He wanted to hear her gasp again, to hear the sweetness of that sound and to carry the memory of it into the darkness with him. He slipped his hand up over the arc of her ribs, swallowing each gasp, each sigh as she reacted to his touch.

He was not prepared for her to stiffen.

He froze immediately, stilling his hand at the edge of her ribs. Her fingers flexed against his forearms and she eased away. Shane rested his hands lightly on her shoulders, even as he brushed his lips over hers again, determined to ease the sudden awkwardness, if not erase it.

"I'd hate for you to think I'm one of those easy girls," he said, his lips twisted in a grin. "You'll have to at least buy me dinner."

"I'll still respect you in the morning." She laughed, and just like that, the tension between them was gone. "It was really great seeing you tonight."

He cupped her cheek, her skin so incredibly soft beneath his rough hands. She was tender and beautiful, and for once he truly wished he had more time before he left. He'd never know if tonight could have led to something more. "You, too."

She blinked hard and Shane wondered at the sudden emotion he saw flicker in her eyes. "Be safe this year?"

"I'll do my best."

"You do that."

He kissed her then, sweetly this time, and he was intensely glad that she didn't stiffen or pull away. He hadn't ruined this precious moment after all. "Good-bye, Jen."

"Good-bye, Shane."

He swallowed the bite of hard emotion that lodged suddenly in his throat. She'd given him one hell of a memory to carry with him into the desert.

He'd hold the memory of that kiss with him even as he walked—willing and able—into a war. He'd volunteered to serve, but tonight, for the first time, he was walking away from something precious. Because of Jen, he had a reason for coming home.

3

Shane walked into the gym, taking in all the activity around him, trying to see how things were set up for this deployment. In the center of the gym, soldiers waited in line for medical approval in order to officially begin their season in the desert. Good times had by all. Reaching the bleachers, he dropped his assault pack on the bottom step, laid his M4 on the floor at his feet, and took a seat, resting his head on his forearms. For the first time in twenty-four hours he was able to close his eyes.

He never slept the night before deployment. The first time he'd deployed, he'd been too nervous to sleep and had crashed hard on the plane, waking up somewhere over Turkey. Last night, though, he'd lain awake for different reasons. His stitches had been throbbing like a bastard, and there'd been blood on the bandage this morning. He was doing his best to ignore that, though, along with the pain. He just had to make it through today without a physical and he'd be fine.

Shane sat fully upright, wincing as the sudden movement jarred his stitches. He looked around, hoping no one had noticed. To be deployed, a soldier had to be one hundred percent medically ready, and he did not want to give anyone a reason to suspect that he was not. No one knew that less than a week ago, while he was on vacation down in Corpus Christie, catching a few catfish, he'd had to make a quick side trip to the local civilian hospital. So far, he'd manage to keep anyone in the Army from finding out, and had kept it out of his official medical records. The way he saw it, his lack of appendix wouldn't be the problem getting out of here today. His *recent* lack of an appendix could, especially if Trent or Carponti found out, as they'd make damn sure he didn't deploy. They wouldn't do it out of spite, but rather worry. It was Shane's job to worry about the guys, not the other way around. He realized that Trent had the authority to make him stay behind, and Carponti had a big mouth. If Carponti knew, everyone else would, too . . . and that was not going to happen. Shane just had to grin and bear the pain. It wouldn't be the first time he'd stepped over the fine line between hooah and stupid.

The medical line was a final clearance that was damn sure going to stick it to him, and not in a good way. He overheard one of the nurses say "exam." Shit. A couple of the guys didn't come out from behind a white curtain looking too happy. He'd counted at least five that had been pulled off flights and they weren't even halfway through the line. He had to find a way to get on that plane without seeing a doc.

But more than just his stitches had kept him up last night. In truth, Jen St. James was the primary reason he'd had trouble sleeping. Even now, his body tightened at the memory of her kiss—Jen had given him a taste of what might have been if he hadn't been going off to war. Deployments were filled with long bouts of boredom and loneliness, punctuated by bursts of pure terror and an overdose of adrenaline. He had no idea how the wives and girlfriends who were left behind managed while their soldiers unplugged and shipped out. Well, he had an idea, but most of them didn't cheat like his ex had.

But he was a soldier and duty called. Being a soldier meant leaving behind the soft kisses and warm beds. It meant toughing it out in the heat, dirt, and sand for the guy next to you. It took a special kind of woman to wait for the wars to be over.

He might not have someone waiting when he came home, but that kiss was going to keep him company through the long nights of his deployment. It would give him something good to think about when the weight and responsibility he carried got a little too heavy.

Shane shifted on the bleachers, tensing as his stomach clenched and pain burst through his gut. He should have been more careful last night while trying to keep the fight between Randall and Carponti from getting out of control. It was never a good thing when sergeants felt like they could take a swing at an officer, especially an officer in his company. And Randall was just petty enough to complain to Trent about Carponti's insubordinate conduct. Never mind that Randall had hit on Carponti's wife. That little fact would likely be left out of the report.

Nearby, the gym's main door slammed open, hushing the dull noise of the crowd as everyone turned toward the boom. Shane looked up as Carponti strolled in, his arm draped around his wife's shoulders. Shane narrowed his eyes as they stumbled toward him. "He better not still be drunk," he mumbled beneath his breath.

Shane had no idea how Nicole put up with all of Carponti's antics, but she did. It looked like neither of them had slept. He was happy to see that there was laughter in Nicole's eyes—so much better than the tears he'd seen in the other wives. Carponti had a wife who'd stood by him no matter how many times he went off to war. He was one of the lucky ones. Shane glanced around at the myriad of couples saying their last farewells, wondering how many of the wives and girlfriends would be here when they returned. And wasn't that a cheerful thought.

Nicole peeled away from her husband and ducked into the bathroom. Meanwhile, Carponti strolled up to Shane, dropping his assault pack next to him on the bleachers. "What's got your panties in a bunch?"

As he dropped his gear on the floor, Carponti removed his patrol cap, and Shane damn near choked on a laugh. He'd shaved his red hair completely off except for a tiny patch on the top of his head.

"Is that supposed to make you look tough?" Shane asked, covering his mouth with his hand.

Carponti shrugged and slid his hand over his ghost-white scalp. "You're just jealous because I can still grow hair and yours has long ago surrendered the field to old age."

Shane scowled. "Are you drunk?"

"Nope, cold sober. Wish I was still at home in bed with my wife, though. But no. Not drunk." His grin spread across his face as he plopped down next to Shane, elbowing him in his stitches. "Watch out, here comes the sergeant major and oh, he looks so happy to see you."

Shane and Carponti both stood as the major approached.

Carponti raised his voice several octaves as he imitated a deliriously happy teenage girl, as Shane, once again, wished that annoying people in charge wasn't one of Carponti's favorite pastimes. "Morning, Sarn't Major. Did you bring a pillow and a blankie for the flight?"

Shane shoved Carponti behind him as he assumed the position of parade rest, hands folded at the small of his back, his feet spread. Sergeant Major Giles didn't laugh at Carponti's smart-ass remark. A smirk didn't even dent the creases in Giles's hard-lined face. He glared, pinning Shane with a hard look. Light glinted off his smooth scalp.

"Want to explain what happened last night?" Giles stopped in front of them, his feet braced shoulder-width apart, thumbs hooked on his belt loops.

"Nothing that I'm aware of, Sarn't Major," Shane said, mentally willing Carponti to keep his mouth shut while at the same time hoping that Nicole would hurry back from the bathroom. If Carponti's wife was there with them, maybe Sarn't Major wouldn't rip them new assholes...

It wasn't like Shane and Carponti hadn't been grilled by the Sarn't Major before. There was a period right after the last deployment when every single one of Carponti's team had been arrested. All at once. Shane had managed to keep them from being thrown out of the Army. Barely. And just his luck, his bullshitting skills were asleep at the moment.

Sergeant Major pulled out a can of dip and slapped it between his thumb and index finger then stuffed a wad between the side of his cheek and his teeth. "So there wasn't an assault on an officer last night at Ropers?"

"Well." Shane cleared his throat. "There's a lot of confusion about what actually happened..."

Giles jabbed a finger toward Shane's chest, cutting him off. "Save your tap dancing for the commander. Did anyone get arrested?"

"No, Sarn't Major."

"Good. So explain to me how you're the only platoon sergeant who hasn't cleared the medical section." He folded his arms over his chest and jerked his head toward Carponti. "Along with this delinquent."

Shane cleared his throat, praying Carponti would keep his mouth shut for a few more minutes. "Must have slipped my mind, Sarn't Major."

It was a banner day that Sarn't Major didn't eviscerate him over that lame-ass excuse. Giles jabbed his thumb over his shoulder toward the medical line.

"Now" was all he said before he moved off to some other hapless bastard. "You, too, smart-ass."

Shane swore beneath his breath as they walked over to the medical line, leaving their weapons with Ross, one of Carponti's soldiers. Carponti, eager to get the process over with, elbowed his way in front of him. Something tore deep beneath the muscles in Shane's abdomen and white pain blocked his throat.

"That was the worst excuse ever."

When Shane felt he could talk he said, "We didn't have to see the battalion commander, so it worked, didn't it? And thank you for keeping your mouth shut."

"I'm not stupid," Carponti responded. Shane shot him a look that suggested otherwise. "I'm fully aware that assaulting an officer isn't a good way to start my deployment."

Shane laughed, folded his arms over his chest, and scanned the line, seeing many familiar faces. Several guys had their noses buried in books but most of them were just talking trash and throwing insults at one another as the line inched forward. There were a half dozen nurses in blue smocks, poking and sticking the men with last-minute anthrax and smallpox and a dozen other vials of mysterious crap ending in x.

A mass of soldiers stood in several lines, obscuring the view, but every so often he'd catch a glimpse of what was happening at the front of the lines. Each soldier stepped forward, and removed his Army Combat Uniform top, then rolled up the sleeves of his tan undershirt. Some would hold on to their weapons, others would hand them to a buddy before they went under the needle. Then he'd hand the nurse his records and wait to see how many needles were involved in this little medical party.

Maybe he could bluff his way through the line. He'd banked on there not being medical processing today. Looks like he'd been wrong. He *had* to skip a full-blown medical exam. The minute the nurse saw the bandages taped to his belly, he'd be well and truly fucked.

Most of the guys stood in silence as the nurse reviewed which shot —or shots—they needed. Shane grinned as one of the soldiers tried to convince his nurse to falsify his records so he wouldn't have to get smallpox. It didn't work. It never did. Shane scanned the crowd, trying to formulate a plan.

The nurse at the front of his line caught his attention just as she raised a needle over a soldier's biceps. Shane's skin prickled with recognition as pale green eyes looked right past him and back to the soldier she was about to inject.

Holy. Shit.

Jen St. James.

JEN BIT her bottom lip as she reviewed the medical chart in front of her. She searched for composure as she swabbed the GI's shoulder. When she'd been asked to fill in for another nurse that morning, she had known there was a distinct possibility that she would see Shane again, but she hadn't really counted on it . . . Now he stood just two soldiers away from her and she had no idea what to do next.

He was even more incredible in broad daylight, and that was saying a whole lot, because he'd been pretty damn impressive last night. His tan T-shirt stretched across his chest like a second skin, making his shoulders look wider than they had last night, and she could see the outline of his dog tags beneath it.

Shane's friend stepped right up, instantly recognizing her. "Hey, aren't you Laura Davila's friend from last night? I'll have your child if you let me skip the smallpox vac," Carponti begged. "I will make Shane send you pictures of his—"

Suddenly Shane's palm struck him on the back of the head and Carponti's freckled face went from grinning to groaning. Carponti stumbled forward and nearly collided with Jen before he caught himself.

Shane covered his mouth and coughed, and she couldn't tell if he was laughing or horrified. "Sorry about Carponti, ma'am. We don't let him out to play very often."

"That's all right." Jen held out her hand for Carponti's ID card.

"The animals have to be let out sometime," she added, with a lightness she hadn't felt a moment before.

Shane leaned toward her and her breath caught in her throat, his familiar scent wrapped around her. She wanted to ask him what soap he used, because, damn, he smelled good. Then he spoke, his voice low in a conspiratorial whisper, and she forgot all about how good he smelled when his voice reverberated off her skin. "If you could make this hurt a little extra, that would be great."

"I'm standing right here," Carponti whined. "And just a reminder, I know where you're going to be sleeping for the rest of the year."

Jen tried not to laugh at his antics while she quickly injected him with the vaccine and then covered the puncture with a bandage. "Keep it covered for the next ten days and don't leave the bandage laying around."

"So putting it on Sarn't G's bunk is probably a bad idea?"

"Um, yes." She stamped Carponti's record and handed it back to him. "Good luck this year."

"I don't have to sign anything?" he asked, looking over at a soldier signing some orange form.

"No. You're just getting vaccinations. He probably needs an exam." She paused. "Take care, okay?"

Carponti moved off to the next station as Shane reluctantly stepped up to the medical station. She fought the tiny curl of her lips at seeing him again. It was a ridiculous reaction. But it felt good.

"Hi," he said, breaking the heavy silence between them.

"Hi." It was another moment before she held out her hand. "Do you have your records?"

His jaw flexed. "No. The clinic lost them."

"Oh. I can pull them up here if you give me your ID card." He handed it over and a moment later, Shane's medical history flashed on the screen. "You missed your last exam. I can't clear you until you have a periodic health assessment."

"Can't you do that?" Shane said.

She shot him a baleful look that said he should know better. "I can do the exam, but it has to be validated by a doctor. And no, you can't skip your predeployment health screening. Unless you want me to get fired," she added.

"I'm healthy as an ox." He stepped closer, so close she had to tip her head up to look at him. Last night, he'd dipped his mouth, just a little, and she'd met him halfway. "If there's any way you can get me cleared today I'd really appreciate it . . . I need to deploy."

Jen then looked up at the man who had shielded her at the bar last night. At the man who, for one breathtaking, soul-blinding moment, had made her forget her own scars and inhibitions and made her feel sensual and beautiful and whole. She wanted to help him, but there were rules, very strict rules that could get her fired. Rules that invoked patient privacy and fit-for-duty standards. Too many commanders had bullied soldiers onto planes who weren't fit to deploy. Broken legs or broken spirits, it didn't matter, it was the commander who held the final vote. The tight rules were there to keep soldiers who weren't healthy off the planes and out of combat until they were fully healed. Some never were. But it was the soldier who begged to deploy anyway, even though he wasn't physically ready, that really tore at her soul.

She looked up at the unspoken plea staring back at her from concrete-grey eyes.

"I'm going to jail for this," she murmured. She raised her voice, just a little. "Sergeant Garrison, would you step over here, please?"

Jen motioned for him to follow her behind the white curtain, not missing the wary expression on his face. Last night he'd looked at her like she'd hung the moon. Now? Now he looked at her like she might be the enemy.

"I need to take your vitals. Sit there." She pointed at a chair then pulled out the blood pressure cuff, wrapping it around his arm. His skin was hot and smooth beneath her fingertips; the black tattoos writhed up his arm and disappeared beneath the cotton sleeve. She looked anywhere but in his eyes as she slipped the stethoscope beneath the cuff and listened to his heart. As she pumped up the band, his strong, solid heartbeat thumped in her ears over the hiss of air as she counted silently. Her gaze drifted down again to the outline of the dog tags pressed against his . . . wait a second. Beneath the soft tan cotton of his shirt, a small square outline caught her attention.

"Shane, what is that?" She glanced at the area in question.

He tensed, suddenly immobile. Totally still. No movement. No sound. The kind of still that her patients became when they were getting ready to lie to her.

"What?" he asked, avoiding her gaze.

"That lump beneath your T-shirt."

"Cut myself shaving," he said, but his voice was tight.

"You shave . . . your chest?" Jen asked weakly. She knew some guys did. She just never understood why.

"Bad joke?"

Forgetting his blood pressure, Jen tugged at the edge of his shirt, revealing a white bandage, stained with blood. Turning, she grabbed a pair of gloves and pulled them on, then quickly eased back the bandage. "That's more than a shaving cut." She finally met his gaze, confronting the emotions she'd tried to avoid. The torrent inside of her was nothing compared to the intensity looking back at her. Tiny flecks of green tinted the blue-grey of his eyes. Lines creased the skin beneath them and she very suddenly wanted to get as far away from him as she could. That or smooth her fingers over those lines after she asked him for the one thing she doubted he'd give her. The truth. "These are surgical incisions. Did...did you have surgery?"

He swallowed, his jaw flexing, and looked away. The muscles in his neck visibly tightened. He breathed hard, his nostrils flaring. Finally, the answer ground from his lips. "Appendix."

Jen held her breath as she moved his shirt and saw the blood seeping around the edge of the bandage where she held it against his skin. This was a recent appendectomy. Really recent. What the hell was he thinking? She pulled the bandage off, and inspected the sutures. At least it had been laparoscopic surgery. Small wounds, one on his left side, the other at the base of his navel. The other bandage was still partially hidden by the rest of his T-shirt and the waistband of his pants. She reached behind her for a clean bandage, but Shane snagged her wrists.

"Please keep this quiet, Jen. I know it looks bad, but really I'm fine. If I need to sign something to get you to agree to let me go, I will, but I'm asking you to pretend you didn't see this."

The silence grew and still she didn't speak as she pulled her wrists free and replaced the bandage. Finally, she looked directly at him, refusing to look away from the plea in his eyes. "Let me see your other stitches."

Shane lifted the rest of his shirt free from his pants, revealing his hard stomach, covered with a dark swirl of hair. Another white patch stood out against the dark hair at the bottom of his navel. And just like before, a bright red splotch of blood seeped through.

"Oh, Shane," she whispered as she reached and peeled the bandage back from the incision. Fortunately, it wasn't as bad as she feared. The stitches hadn't ripped, just stretched enough to leak. With an alcohol pad, she wiped the blood from the clean-shaven skin around his wound. She tried not to notice warm, smooth heat radiating from his skin. Thankfully, it was the warmth of a healthy male, not the intense heat that suggested infection. Gently, she pressed a clean bandage over the stitches. "They're not ripped, but they easily could have been."

Sighing, she looked up at him, immediately noticing that his cheeks were clean-shaven, in stark contrast to the night before. Hidden behind the white curtain, a barrier had grown between them. A wall made of two blood-soaked bandages and a missing appendix.

She swallowed and studied him closely, hating her next words. "Shane, you can't deploy today. You're days out of surgery. Technically, you should be on convalescent leave."

"Obviously, I'm not. I'm here and I'm getting ready to get on a plane for an eighteen-hour flight to the sandbox. With. My. Men." He never raised his voice, but the intensity ratcheted up with each word.

He *was* serious. He was trying to deploy. Today. "You could die."

"Jen, I'm going to run combat patrols in northern Baghdad. I figure my odds are fifty-fifty at best anyway."

She took a step backward and folded her arms across her chest. "I'm sorry. I can't let you deploy. The risk of infection alone . . ."

Shane stood and stepped into her space, close like he had been last night only this time his voice was low and rough. Ragged. "Do you know what it feels like to have a kid die on patrol because his squad leader did something stupid? Something you could have prevented if you'd been there? Jen, this is the Surge. The last big push to try and stop the violence and stabilize Iraq. This is going to be worse than any year since the supposed end of combat operations. Don't send my men to war without me. Please, Jen."

"You won't do a damn bit of good if you're laid up with an infection." She tried to step back, away from the intensity in his words, the plea that was in his voice. But she didn't. She'd never seen this kind of concern before.

"Then I won't get an infection. Tell me whatever I have to do, whatever pills I have to take to prevent it, and I'll do it." He glanced around, like he was searching for something, then he picked up a syringe to help him make his point, holding it in the palm of his hand. "You wouldn't send the guys over there without their shots, right?"

She tried to take the syringe from him and he closed his hand over hers. Jen shook her head and tried to free her hand.. "Shane, that makes no sense and has nothing to do with you, but no, of course not. They need the immunizations to stay healthy."

He squeezed her fingers beneath his and grinned down at her, his eyes warm like they'd been last night. "Think of me as part of their stay-healthy plan." He slid his fingers over the back of her knuckles, the gesture too familiar and too enticing all at once. The grin was now gone, the plea back in his eyes. "Don't send my men without me. Please."

"You're not God, Shane. You can't control who lives and who dies."

"No, I can't, but I can make a difference."

"You really believe that? Enough to risk your life?"

"Yes, I really do. There is nowhere I would rather be than at the center of the fight with my platoon."

Jen swallowed and looked away, finally pulling her fingers free. "I don't understand you," she whispered. He was willing to risk everything to deploy. He wanted to get on that plane with stitches that were barely healed, putting his life at risk . . . not that the war didn't do that all on its own. "Why do you want to go so badly?"

"My boys need me." He lifted his free hand, like he was going to reach for her, then dropped it abruptly, squeezing the fingers he still held. "Don't make me leave them. Not now."

"You could die."

"That's going to happen anyway. It's just a question of when." He tucked his hands into the waistband of his pants. "I'd rather die doing what I love."

She turned away, staring at the form she'd need to sign in order for him to deploy. She couldn't shake the feeling that she was about to make a tremendous mistake, one that was potentially illegal and certainly unethical. But with one stroke of her pen, she gave him her blessing.

Shane sighed with relief. "Thank you."

Jen poked her finger in his chest. "Don't thank me. Anything happens to you, I'm responsible. And you still need your flu shot."

He smiled down at her, but there was no gloating in his eyes. Only a quiet victory. "You're not God, Jen."

"No, but I am responsible for my patients," she replied.

He tucked his shirt into his pants, a faint smile at the corners of his lips. "Then you understand me."

She shouldn't have been surprised that Shane didn't read the form she handed him. He simply scribbled his name where she indicated. A sense of gloom settled around her heart. He rolled up the sleeve that had slipped down, baring his arm for the immunization. "Poke away."

She swabbed his skin and when she positioned the needle on his biceps, he caught her gaze one final time. "Be careful. I'm fragile."

Jen stared at him for a moment. His eyes glittered in the bright light. The sides of his mouth twitched. She looked at his wide chest, his heavy arms and rough hands. Fragile? Her lips quivered as she tried to hold back her response and failed. She covered her mouth with the back of her gloved hand and *laughed*.

Shane couldn't remember the last time he'd made a woman really laugh. Not like this anyway, this full-blown laugh that sent a smile creeping across his own lips. He'd meant to make her smile, to ease the regret he saw in her eyes. But this? This laugh was its own reward.

Jen wiped her eyes and answered his smile with her own. "I'm sorry."

"Glad I could help." He slid his fingers across her knuckles and over the back of her hand, his fingers lightly circling her wrist. "Thank you for this," he whispered.

She finished with the shot and looked away, hoping he didn't see the moisture filling her eyes. She stood there for an impossible moment, realizing that she had violated her ethics for a man she would probably never see again, knowing it was the wrong thing to do. It didn't matter that he was a friend of Laura and Trent's. He'd come into her life for a brief moment and made her *feel*.

"Shane?"

"Yeah?" He paused where he'd shrugged into his uniform top.

Jen wanted to say something. To tell him to be safe, but what good would it do? He was the guy who ran toward the burning building while everyone else ran the other way to safety. "Never mind."

Instead, she held on to the one final moment she'd have with him before he left for the only other place on earth hotter and more dangerous than hell. . . .

Iraq.

IT WAS time for roll call. Jen finished cleaning up her station and walked along the edge of the gym floor, skirting the massive formation. Near the door at the far end, a sergeant called out names, one at a time. A loud "hooah" or "here sarn't" rang out as the soldier grabbed his gear and moved into formation.

Laura waved at her from the bleachers, where she sat with the girl from last night, Nicole. As she approached, she noticed that Nicole's eyes looked red, but she wasn't going to mention it. It wasn't her place.

Jen threaded her arm through Laura's and scanned the crowd, looking for a familiar face. She knew Laura was doing the same. Near the back edge of the formation, Shane stood next to Trent and Carponti. Carponti was telling a story that took a whole lot of movement. She smiled and wondered just how much the young sergeant got away with.

Jen didn't miss the fact that Laura's eyes were also rimmed with red and swollen. She leaned her head on her friend's shoulder.

"It's his fifth deployment in seven years," Laura said. She sniffed and wiped her eyes. "I don't understand how he ends up constantly deploying when there are others who haven't gone once."

"How are the kids holding up with everything?" Jen asked, unable to find anything comforting to say.

"You mean other than not knowing their daddy? They're fine. These days they're more comfortable being left at day care than spending time with Trent. It's mostly older kids who have trouble with deployment. Mine are still young. But Ethan's starting to have problems. Crying for Trent when he gets mad at me. Stuff like that."

"Is that why you didn't bring them?" Nicole sniffed.

"No. I didn't bring them because it's too hard on Trent. It prolongs the pain. He needs to focus on getting the job done, not on the kids clinging to him until the last minute."

"Isn't that harder on you?" Jen asked.

"Not really. I'm used to it at this point."

Nicole sniffed again as she searched for something in her purse. "You make it sound so easy. I hate that Vic is leaving again. I felt like shooting him in the foot so he couldn't deploy."

Laura covered her face with her hands as Jen rubbed her back. "I can't keep doing this."

Pulling a fresh pack of tissues from her purse, Nicole handed one to Laura. "Vic promised me this'll be the last one. He's going to ask for an ROTC assignment or something else that will let him be home for a while."

"Good luck with that," Laura said, swiping the tissue beneath her eyes. "I hope it works for you. I'm starting to suspect that Trent's happier when he's deployed."

Jen blinked back her surprise. It was the first negative thing she'd ever heard Laura say about her husband.

"I hope this year goes by quickly and is uneventful," Laura said. "I don't think I can handle another bad year like '04."

Jen frowned, squeezing Laura's hand, and answered the question in Nicole's eyes. "The year Trent died." It wasn't a question.

"Yeah. Trent was hurt bad and someone screwed up and ruined my life for almost two days. I got the whole casualty notification and everything. He called a day and a half later." Laura bit her lips together. "I thought I'd gotten him back. Guess I was wrong."

The sergeant major moved to the front of the formation. "Detachment, atten-*tion!*"

The answering cry of the unit's motto "Death Dealers!" echoed off the rafters and thundered through Jen's chest.

"Right, face!" As one, the entire formation pivoted and turned to the right. "File from the right, forward, *march!*"

The rest of the formation stood still as the first file of soldiers began marching from the gym. Jen squeezed Laura's hand as Trent started to march toward the door. Shane looked up, and their eyes met over the top of the crowd. He mouthed a silent thank-you before he turned and marched from the gym without another glance.

Oh joy. Lucky her, neither Nicole nor Laura missed the gesture. "What was that?" Laura asked.

"What was what?" Jen said, fidgeting with her ID badge. She tried and failed to keep the tiny smile from the edge of her mouth.

"That?" Laura asked, pointing at Shane's retreating back.

"Nothing."

"Oh really? You saw that, right, Nikki?"

"I have no idea what you're talking about," Jen insisted.

She wasn't sure why she had lied. She bit her lip, remembering last night's kiss, and how Shane had chased away her nervousness and self-consciousness, leaving her with a lingering ache in her belly. Maybe it was the fact that, last night, she'd felt like a real, whole woman for the first time in over a year. It was something she was still absorbing, still trying to figure out, and she wasn't ready to share it with the group and have it dissected.

"Nothing my foot. I saw that, too," Nicole said. She quickly glanced at her watch and jumped up. "Oh man, I've got to get to work." She rushed down the bleachers, waving good-bye over her shoulder, leaving Jen at Laura's mercy.

"Okay, it's just us. Spill."

Jen clenched her keys and smiled. "Nothing. He walked me to my car, I went home. *Alone.*"

"Uh-huh," Laura said in a tone that clearly called her bluff, as they got up to walk to their cars. Jen said it again. "Nothing happened. He was a perfect gentleman."

"Ha, now I know you're lying," her friend said, as they stepped into the bright Fort Hood sunlight.

"Why do you say that?" Jen asked, curious, then clicked her remote to unlock her car.

"I've known Shane since he and Trent were nineteen. Let's just say he's done some growing up."

"Once again, care to elaborate?"

"Ha, so you are interested!" Laura shook her butt in a victory dance. "I knew it."

"Knew what?" Jen asked, palming her keys.

"That it was just going to take the right person to push you out of your comfort zone."

"Shane didn't push me anywhere," Jen said. "And a guy like him isn't going to cure what ails me." She just wished Laura would drop the whole conversation, *now*.

"Scars heal, Jen. But your boobs don't make you a person."

"Can we not talk about this right now? Hell, you've got Shane checking out my boobs and being the Great Penis who will save the damsel in distress. I've talked to him twice. Reality check?"

Laura choked on a laugh. "I'm so going to tell him you called him the Great Penis."

"Laura . . ."

"I'm kidding. I'll tell Trent. He'll get a kick out of that. Seriously, just admit that you went out and had fun when you didn't think you could."

"I admit it." Jen rolled her eyes, smiling. "Are you happy now?"

"See, we're making progress." Laura glanced at her watch. "I've got to get going, too. Come by the house this weekend. I'm hosting a family readiness group meeting and I could use a hand with the kids."

"Sure." She paused and decided there was no better time than the present to ask. Might as well get the harassment over with. "Do you have their address?"

Laura cast her a sideways glance. "Sure, why?"

Jen swallowed the lie. She couldn't admit to Laura that she wanted to check on Shane because she had medically released him. *Hey, I just sent one of your friends to his potential death and I wanted to keep tabs on him and make sure he didn't actually die. Nothing big.* She shrugged and tried for a nonchalance she did not feel. "I'd like to send the guys a care package or something. What do guys like when they're deployed?"

"Porn and junk food."

Jen realized by the look on Laura's face that she must not have hidden her horrified expression very well.

"What? I'm married to him. Though Trent has never specifically asked for porn—"

Laura got in her car and slammed the door shut, cutting off whatever she was saying.

Jen got into her car, too, and sat in her driver's seat for a moment, thinking about Shane as she watched the last bus pull away from behind the gym. Had she made the right call? Was she doomed to spend the rest of the year worrying about the man she'd sent to war? It would serve her right.

She shouldn't have cleared Shane to deploy today. But the need and the loyalty in his eyes when he'd asked her to let him go had touched her deeply. No one had ever shown her that kind of loyalty before, and to see a man willing to risk his health to stand by his men was compelling and something unique that she did not understand.

And heaven help her, she'd sent him to Iraq.

4

———————

Four Months Later
Taji, Iraq

Shane closed his eyes, and prayed. For a man who wasn't particularly religious, that said a lot. He was running on little more than faith and caffeine and a hell of a lot of adrenaline and he was just about out of caffeine. He'd known this deployment was going to be bad. He'd had no idea how bad. Shane and his boys had been going full throttle since they'd transferred authority and taken over their battlespace. Patrols had been running every sixteen hours around the clock and they were getting hit every goddamned time they rolled outside the wire. They didn't even have a decent place to crash after patrols. They were stuck sleeping in the middle of a wide-open hangar bay, bunks packed in next to one another.

His men were tired and there wasn't a damn thing he could do about it. Frustration clawed at his heart. He had to do something. He had to figure out how to stop, to slow the train down, because it felt like his men were heading for a wall and had no brakes.

Something heavy landed on his gut, forcing the air from his lungs. He balled up and waited for his lungs to relax to make room for more air as magazines, envelopes, and a box scattered over his stomach and onto the bunk with a flutter.

"Mail call," Carponti said.

Shane hardly ever got mail, and when he did, it tended to be junk. He squeezed his eyes closed and prayed for patience.

"Really, Carponti? Was it that fun dropping crap on my guts?"

"Ah, yeah. Why else would I have done it?" Carponti sank into the bunk next to Shane's. "LT Randall is looking for you by the way."

Shane rolled his eyes and swore as he sat up, throwing a stray magazine at Carponti's head. Shane hated the fact that Randall's father had been able to get him into West Point. There was no other commissioning source on earth that would have made him an officer otherwise. But he had to watch what he said to Carponti because Carponti was as likely to tie the lieutenant to the turret of their Bradley fighting vehicle's main gun as not. If Shane went to jail, he wasn't going because of one of Carponti's stupid pranks. "What now?"

"Inventory or something," Carponti said with a shrug. "Can you please go see him so he'll stop nagging me every time he sees me? Why isn't he talking to the platoon leader, anyway?"

Shane tossed his mail into a pile and sat up. His platoon leader, Lieutenant Miller, and Lieutenant Randall, the company executive officer, were officially not speaking, but Carponti didn't need to know that. At least, he didn't need to hear it from Shane. It would end up scribbled all over the Port-a-Potty walls, and that wouldn't do anyone any good. Randall would just cry about it and then the first sergeant would make the guys paint over the graffiti in the hundred-and-twelve-degree heat. He'd laugh, but he'd still make them paint. No matter how many times it happened. "Him and LT Miller are having a disagreement."

"Well, shit, can't they stop bickering like first graders and act like adults? Why doesn't Miller tell Randall to pound sand."

"Sergeant Carponti!"

Carponti's face went completely blank at the sound of Randall's voice echoing across the bay. Shane narrowed his eyes and studied his sergeant. His expression was pure innocence.

"What did you do?" Shane asked.

"Nothing."

"What did you supervise?"

Carponti sniffed and his mouth twitched. "Nothing."

"What did you see happening and not stop?"

"One of the troops drew a new picture of the LT on one of the latrine walls." Carponti's face broke into a shit-eating grin. "It's really a work of art. You can completely see the freckles on Randall's nose and everything."

"Carponti . . ." Shane fought the urge to laugh. Last week, Randall had been the subject of a particularly off-color demotivational poster that had made the rounds. Something about being the officer in charge of killing fun.

"It's got a camel and a water bottle and . . ."

Randall stalked up, his face flushed. He looked like he'd been trying not to run. "Sergeant Carponti, I don't appreciate your attitude. If I find out that you're behind this . . ."

"Behind what, LT?" Shane asked as he stood up, stepping between Carponti and Randall. "What can I do for you?"

"You can start by teaching your sergeants some basic customs and courtesies."

"And you can stop trying to sleep with their wives. So I guess we're at an impasse."

For a brief moment, Randall looked like he was going to argue, but he apparently remembered that Shane was a hell of a lot bigger than he was. And the last time the lieutenant had run his mouth, Shane had ended up explaining to the battalion sergeant major how Randall had run into the end of his fist. Course, Trent didn't know that and Shane planned on keeping it that way. As his company commander and his friend, Shane did his best not to put Trent in untenable positions. So long as he didn't cross the line with this particular lieutenant anymore, Sarn't Major Giles had agreed to keep it quiet, which would keep it from the battalion commander, which would keep it from Trent. Shane had no idea *how* Sarn't Major was keeping Randall from running to the battalion commander or his father, but that wasn't Shane's problem.

Keeping Randall and Carponti from getting into it in the middle of the bay was.

Shane called on every ounce of patience he could and simply waited for the lieutenant to continue. As Trent's friend, he owed him no altercations. Unless, of course, they couldn't be avoided. Lieutenant Randall was rapidly pushing him to the couldn't-be-avoided phase.

"I don't need the executive officer to take charge of my troops' training," he said again, deliberately not using any form of address. He looked into Randall's flushed face and couldn't resist the urge to poke at the LT. Trent was going to kill him but what the hell. Randall needed an attitude adjustment, big time. "Pretty sure your job is to get us toilet paper and paper clips?"

"Sir. You can call me sir or lieutenant or LT Randall. But if you can't be bothered to act like a professional, then it's easy to see why your soldiers don't, either."

He took a step toward the edge of the bunks, forcing Randall to either stand toe-to-toe with him or back up. Randall backed up. "Lieutenant, I've got two boys on their way to the hospital in Germany from last night's attack. I've got a mission brief in fifteen minutes and I haven't slept in forty-eight hours. I don't have time to stroke your wounded ego. Find someone else for that. So get on with it, or get gone."

Randall flushed and swallowed. Shane was starting to hate that nervous habit of his. He really was.

"I need the sensitive items report before you leave on patrol tonight," Randall said, looking down at his clipboard like it held all the secrets of the universe.

"And yesterday I needed parts ordered for one of my fifty cals. Guess which one got someone hurt?"

"I can't control the mechanics or the armament repair teams. There were other priorities more important than your weapons and trucks."

"Really? Because I checked with the motor sergeant and he said he never got the maintenance report that I turned in. To you."

Randall pursed his lips and clicked the cap on his pen. "I can double-check on that. But I need the sensitive items report."

"I already submitted it through Lieutenant Miller."

"I don't have it and I can't find Miller."

Shane rolled his tongue over his teeth and started counting to ten, buying himself some time before he jumped down Randall's throat and ripped out his spleen. He made it to three. "I could really give two shits about what's going on between you and Miller. I gave him the report; he knows when it's due. If you two can't act like adults and stop dragging the troops into your pissing contest, I'll do it for you. But your incompetence has cost us time and blood, so my patience with you is running remarkably thin. Go find him and get the goddamned report yourself. And if I find out that you deliberately failed to get my equipment fixed because you wanted to get even with my lieutenant, I will personally nail your ass to the wall."

Randall's jaw flexed as his nostrils flared. "So that's how it is?"

"I think I made it pretty clear."

The LT lifted his chin and walked off. Not quite stomped, but it was a close thing.

Carponti snorted and a full-blown laugh wasn't far behind. Shane's temper finally snapped. "This isn't funny. He's not doing his job and people are getting hurt."

"Not the first time."

"And it probably won't be the last, either, unfortunately. Did you check on Osterman like I asked?" Shane sat back down on his bunk, pulling out his weapons cleaning kit.

Carponti sobered visibly. "Yeah. He's already in Germany and he'll be back in the States by morning."

"And?"

"He's stable, but he lost the leg."

Shane shoved his mail out of the way and rubbed his eyes as soul-crushing agony wrenched his guts. Osterman's accident was just a tragic fucking mistake. They'd expected an easy path to the compound where their target had reportedly holed up, but what they'd gotten instead was a complex attack. And Shane had led the team into that goddamned choke point. The intel had shown a clear path through the village, but the militants had piled up burning trash and tires and created a funnel that Shane's platoon had to either push through or turn and avoid and end up missing their objective. They'd pushed through the kill zone and captured the high-value target, but not without a cost. And it was too goddamned high for an intel mistake. Shane could do better. He'd get reports directly from brigade. He'd scrub the reports himself if the damned staff couldn't do their jobs.

But none of that would help Osterman. Shane could move heaven and earth to get correct intelligence reports, but it would still be too damned late for Osterman. He breathed deep and met Carponti's gaze. He couldn't change yesterday. He had only today to make a difference.

That didn't stop the regrets, though.

"Fuck."

Carponti looked down at his hands and was silent for a long moment. "Yeah."

~

"Laura, what's wrong?" Jen approached her friend, who was directing a soldier's wife toward the elevators.

They stood in the middle of the hallway of the Army medical center where Laura had spent the morning checking on a couple of wounded soldiers who had come in from Trent's battalion. Laura worked for Trent's brigade family readiness group. She often told Jen that the position was a thankless one. Some in the military considered the wives to be a small insurgency. Many times, the spouses felt ignored and maltreated by the military, who they felt didn't care about their soldiers. It was Laura's job to mediate between the two opposing forces and help the spouses take care of their own issues while getting the officers in charge to bend a little and care more about the wives' challenges. And it was because of some dedicated spouses that soldiers weren't charged travel days when they went on leave from the combat zone along with dozens of other quality-of-life improvements.

Jen didn't know how Laura balanced it all but she did. One of her duties as the family readiness group adviser was to check on the wounded and make sure they weren't swallowed up by the medical system or forgotten by their unit. Not everyone had a family to come in and run interference between the hospital administrators and the docs.

That's where Laura and the rest of the family readiness group came in—all of them were volunteers. Laura's was the only paid position. And asking a volunteer to sit with a family member who'd just lost a loved one . . . it was the hardest thing you could ask someone to do. Especially if that someone knew the next knock could be on their door.

But today, her focus was elsewhere. She was checking on the wounded that'd just been flown in from Germany, doing her best to ensure that the officers and the wives all had the same information.

Rumors could be deadly. But Jen was willing to bet that the soldiers' recent arrival was not the main reason for the distracted look in her friend's eyes. In the months following Trent's departure, Laura had been relatively silent about her husband and that wasn't like her. Laura *always* talked about her husband.

Laura pressed her lips into a flat line, a shadow of her normal smile. "That obvious?"

"Spill," Jen said, as she threaded her arm through Laura's, and started leading her toward the small coffee kiosk near the hospital's main entrance. There were exactly five tables and six chairs and, happy day, two chairs were empty. It wasn't really a place designed for comfort or confessions, but then again, a caffeine fix required neither. "And it's my turn to buy therapy coffee."

Laura attempted to perk up at the mention of her favorite food group. "Thanks, but I think it's my turn, isn't it?"

"Not with that look on your face it isn't."

They sat tucked into a corner table, far from the crowd. Laura fiddled with her coffee stirrer while Jen waited for her to speak.

"I haven't heard from Trent." Her voice cracked ever so slightly. "I always hear from him."

Jen leaned forward and squeezed her hand. Laura was the strongest person she knew and part of her strength was in trusting her husband. Trent's constant deployments had taken a toll, but Laura had always bucked up. That was because Trent had always kept in touch. If she was worried, she had reason to be.

The thought left a deep disquiet in the pit of her stomach. "What do you mean?"

"He called last week, right? And the entire conversation was all about work. He didn't ask about anything back here. I know he's busy and has a ton of responsibility, but he always asks how I'm doing. It's not that I need to talk to him about everything back here, but it helps that he always asks. Jen, he didn't even ask about Ethan or Emma. He didn't crack any jokes. He sounded exhausted and just hung up after a minute. This isn't like him."

"This is the Surge. We all knew this time was going to be different." Jen heard the hollowness of her own words as she struggled to defend her friend's husband. But sometimes she wondered what they did over there, twenty-four hours a day, seven days a week.

"Jen, don't make excuses for him. I know what he's doing, and it's not calling home. There is *always* time to call home. Hell, he called me right after a big fight in Najaf last time, just to ask me how my day went. It's like he's shut off or shut down. He never does stuff like this." Laura rubbed her hands over her arms. "I just don't know what's wrong. I can't fix it if I don't know what's wrong."

Jen stayed quiet, not sure what she could say to make things right again. Until her husband was home—permanently—nothing would be right in Laura's world.

Laura released a hard breath and leaned away from the table. "The last thing I want is to put pressure on him. I know how hard it is for him as a commander. He's got a hundred and eighty soldiers that he's responsible for. But something is wrong, Jen, I know it in my heart."

"Any idea what?"

Laura looked away. "I have no clue."

"Can you tell him that? Tell him you need him to call home more, just to talk? It can't be that bad over there, can it?"

"What kind of wife would I be if I finally get him on the phone for more than five minutes and I give him shit about not calling home enough? Gee, honey, I know you're getting blown up and all, but I need you to let me complain about the lawn mower breaking last week." She lifted her coffee cup, then set it back down without taking a sip. "I can't do that."

"So what are you going to do?"

"You mean other than cry on your shoulder? Not much I can do."

Jen reached for her hand and squeezed. "Let me take the kids off your hands for a day. Or something. Why don't you go to the library or relax or just take some time for you?"

"Because . . ." Laura closed her mouth. "I might. Sorry. I shouldn't be taking this out on you."

Jen laughed. "Um, pretty sure I owe you a meltdown or two. I dumped a whole lot on you when I was sick and my family didn't bother to come down."

"Yeah, well, the least I could do was be there when they wouldn't.

Your family sucks." Laura tucked her hair behind her ear and finally smiled.

"And look on the bright side. At least you have hair when you're giving me shit." Jen smiled, still sometimes amazed that she could joke about what had happened to her. At least about some of the stuff. And it felt good to laugh. To be able to sit there and find something funny about the loss of her grandmother and her own brush with death. Anything was better than focusing on the missing pieces.

"Great, thanks for that memory. Just where I wanted to be right now."

"At least it made you laugh."

"Yeah, it did. I just miss him so much," Laura said. "I'm so damned tired of being alone." She smiled sadly. "I told him a couple of weeks ago that he'd been replaced by my vibrator. You know what he said?"

"I don't want to know."

"Send pictures."

Jen snorted coffee out through her nose. It burned and her eyes filled up as she tried to choke it back down. "Way too much information. Really."

Laura's laugh echoed through the small coffee kiosk, prompting several odd looks from those around them. "Man, you should have seen your face. Priceless, truly priceless."

"Feel better now? I'm going to be smelling coffee for the rest of the day, thanks."

Jen turned at the sound of running footsteps to see Nicole rushing toward them, a panicked look on her face. She stopped at the edge of their table, breathing hard, her keys clenched in her hand. "Have you heard?"

"Heard what?" Laura sat up straight. Focused. Attentive. This was the Laura Jen knew so well.

"There are posts on the battalion Facebook page saying Vic's whole platoon got hit."

All the color drained from Laura's face and she went deathly still. Jen's own skin went cold as she stood. "I'll see if we have any information on the hospital manifest yet. I'll be right back."

"I'm heading to the battalion headquarters," Nicole said. "I'll meet you over there."

Nicole was gone before either of them could answer and Jen

rushed to find any information she could. Since Jen worked in the hospital on base, she kept an eye on the incoming personnel from Iraq, giving Laura a heads-up whenever she could. What they did wasn't technically illegal, but it worked when the regular systems were too slow. Not a single soldier from Reaper battalion had been lost in the medical system, and they weren't about to start now.

"One of Trent's soldiers." She glanced at the sheet, just to make sure she didn't make a mistake. "Aaron Osterman."

Laura's eyes instantly watered, but she brushed the sudden emotion aside—a reaction that unfortunately came from too much practice. Jen knew she should be used to Laura's stoic calm, but it still amazed her. Laura cared and cared deeply for the men in her husband's company and, by extension, those in the other companies that made up his battalion. Jen didn't know how she coped with so many notifications—of deaths, of injuries—over the years. Each one took a toll. Each one had to remind Laura that Trent had almost been one of them. All men Laura had known, whose wives she'd helped support after their husbands' deaths. How did she do that after she'd come so close to losing Trent herself?

In the back of her mind had to be the fear that someday Trent's name could be on that list again, like it had been those horrible thirty-six hours early in the war. Jen would have to ask her how—why—she still did what she did with the families after what happened to Trent. But now was not the time.

"What are we looking at?" Laura made notes in her ever-present green notebook.

"Burn trauma and lower extremity trauma."

"When's he coming in?"

"Tonight." Jen frowned. As hard as it was to break the news to family members that their soldier was wounded, it was so much worse to see wounded men and women sitting alone, day after day, week after week when no one showed up to check on them. Jen knew exactly how they felt, but it didn't make it any easier. Which was another reason why she helped Laura. Every little bit helped. "Do you know if anyone *is* coming?"

"Yeah. I just sent a text back to battalion and checked our notification rosters. Becky Fitzpatrick. Fiancée," Laura said, scribbling notes. "Okay. I'll brief the rear detachment commander that we've got things taken care of here." Laura shouldered her purse and stuffed her notebook back inside. She squeezed Jen close before she headed toward the door. "Thanks. For everything."

Jen waited until she was alone to let a guilty relief prickle over her skin. Shane was safe. She hadn't gotten the chance to know him well, but she still held her breath every time she saw a casualty report. The relief she felt for her friends' husbands was real, but in a secret part of her heart, she was glad Shane's name hadn't crossed any of her lists.

SHANE SAT on the edge of his bunk and stared at the floor. He bounced one leg constantly, needing to exorcise the caged frustration churning inside of him. Goddamn, he couldn't remember the last time he'd been so amped up with nothing to do with the energy.

He cradled his forehead in his palm, needing to shake the deep foreboding twisting in his guts. Five nights ago, Jennings had been shot. Three days before that, Wallid had been wounded, but he'd returned to duty with nothing more than twelve stitches and his second Purple Heart. He was still in the fight.

Too many of his boys were walking around with Purple Hearts from being wounded by the enemy or with Combat Action Badges for engaging the enemy. Damn but he wished battalion would send some more soldiers into his sector. His platoon was on edge, overworked, and undermanned, with a battlespace that required two companies' worth of infantrymen. He had sixty men, but needed more like two hundred to clear and hold the real estate they'd been assigned. He rubbed his hands over his face and forced the dread down into a tight box.

A small, flat-rate U.S. Postal Service box poked out from beneath his bunk, partially hidden by his ancient, green sleeping bag. He had forgotten about it. Curious, he reached for the box, turning it until he could see the address label. *Jen St. James.*

A slow smile spread across his lips. He hadn't expected this. She'd kill him if she knew how sick he'd actually gotten after landing in country. His platoon had been on the range, verifying their battle sight zeros and making sure they could actually hit what they shot at before heading north, and he'd been balled up on his cot, sweating and shaking and puking so hard he thought he'd crack bone.

But he wasn't about to tell her any of that. He pulled his knife from its sheath and sliced the box open with a flick of his wrist. Shane swore softly as he dug through the white foam and a billion packing peanuts scattered on the floor.

Buried beneath the Styrofoam was a small, vacuum-sealed bag of brownies, a couple of boxes of salted almonds, beef jerky, and a small envelope with *Shane* scrawled on the front. He felt kind of stupid, but the smile wouldn't leave his lips as he flipped her letter open.

Dear Shane,

I hope its okay that I asked Laura for your address. When she mentioned you didn't get a lot of mail, I thought this might cheer you up. Of course, she recommended that I send porn and junk food, but I don't know you well enough for that. At least, not the porn part. I hope you like the junk food, though, and that the brownies made it all right. Several of the wives swear that vacuu-sealing them is the way to go. Will you let me know?

Anyway, I just wanted to drop you a note to let you know I hadn't forgotten about you. In truth, I haven't—

"Carponti didn't sign you up for another dating with herpes care package, did he?"

Shane stuffed the letter back into the box like a guilty teenager as Trent walked up to him. "Nah, just another random care package from a support-the-troops organization. Jelly beans and magazines and sunscreen."

He nudged the box beneath his bunk, hiding Jen's address. Something about the brief, distant contact with Jen had struck a chord with him, and he wanted to keep it private.

Trent blew out a hard breath and sat down on Carponti's bunk. Carponti would have kittens if he found out Trent had violated the place where the magic happened—nightly—with the woman of his dreams. Nicole apparently enjoyed sending her husband dirty letters.

Briefly, Shane considered telling Trent what he might be sitting in then thought better of it. It was purely speculation and trash-talking on Carponti's part, and to be honest, Shane just didn't want to think about it. Damn, but he missed having a space of his own.

"I suppose you're here about Randall?"

"Who else? I'm not really in the mood to deal with this bullshit. His or yours. So what happened this time?"

Trent looked tired. More tired and beat down than Shane had seen him in years. He wasn't sleeping, that much Shane knew. He often saw him up at night, pacing outside the company tactical operations center or crouched over his laptop on the other side of the bay at three a.m. The Surge was more brutal than anyone had expected. Shane and the other senior leaders in the company all pulled their weight and tried to mitigate Lieutenant Randall's incompetence. He was unreliable at best, untrustworthy at worst.

"Randall and Miller are fighting again. I don't care why but I'm tired of playing mediator between whoever Randall has pissed off this week. You need to squash it. The troops are starting to notice and infighting isn't what you need right now. No one does."

Anger flashed in Trent's eyes, quickly followed by fatigue. "I'm aware of everyone's responsibilities. But I'm at a loss about what to do about it. Because in fourteen years, I've never run into something like this."

"Two lieutenants not getting along is nothing new." Shane nudged the box farther beneath his bunk and started lacing up his boots.

"Believe me, that I know. But I don't trust him. And that's a bigger problem than you neutering him in front of the troops."

"Why don't you trust him?" Shane had put the lieutenant in his place. And yeah, soldiers had seen it. So what? This was the infantry, not elementary school. Feelings got hurt. Suck it up. But he didn't say any of that to Trent. Preaching to the choir and all that.

"I don't know. If I did, I'd already be talking to the battalion commander about finding a replacement. I can't articulate why. And if I can't define the problem, I damn sure can't find a solution for it. The boss damn sure isn't going to let me fire someone on a whim."

Shane studied his longtime friend and, not for the first time, wondered at the heavy load of worries Trent carried as an officer. Things had been so much simpler when they'd been sergeants together back at Fort Benning. "Pal, this is a tough one, but if you don't trust him, you need to deal with it, sooner rather than later. I can

tell you why I don't trust him, but that's not enough to go to the boss
with. He's going to get somebody else killed." Shane stood and heaved
his body armor over his head in a single movement. "This crap gets
heavier and heavier every year. You coming tonight?"

"The alternative is prying lead out of your ass," Trent said,
handing Shane his Kevlar helmet. "And not on this mission. I've got to
go see the equal opportunity adviser."

"For what?" There was a time when the equal opportunity
program had been value added, designed to teach tolerance and bring
harmony between the races and the genders. Now, though, it seemed
like it was just another way for disgruntled troops to complain when
things didn't go their way.

"Some bullshit. Don't worry about it."

Shane shrugged and fastened his gear around his torso. "Look,
Trent, I think Randall is screwing up the maintenance. Parts aren't
getting ordered. I've still got two deadlined weapons systems. I can't
prove it. But it might be something worth checking out."

"All right. I'll look. You dropped this," Trent said, reaching down
and picking up a brown, legal-sized envelope.

"Well, crap." The warmth he'd felt from Jen's note flickered and
died as he saw yet another sign that life was going to hell in a hand
basket.

"What is it?"

"Love letter from my ex-wife, probably." Shane tossed the envelope on his bunk and then shoved it beneath a couple of magazines.
"I'll deal with it later. I've got to troop the line before we roll tonight."

Trent snorted and followed him out. "You keep saying that, and
she's going to clean you out."

"I don't have shit left she can take. And I've changed my direct
deposit account information three times already, but the Army can't
seem to get the money into the right account. I'm flat frigging broke
until I get my happy ass over to the finance battalion and get this
fixed." Shane secured the Velcro straps around his waist, then
checked his weapon and ammo.

"You shouldn't have let her leave with everything." Trent clapped
him on the shoulder with a sigh.

"Yeah, well, I'm just glad she's gone. As soon as I get finance to get off their ass and fix my pay, that part of my life will be done. There's nothing else she can do at this point."

They walked outside into the bright orange and red and pink sunset and Trent shook his head. "Famous last words, brother. Famous last words."

5

———————

The bright red sun crept over the Baghdad skyline as the dawn call to prayer echoed across the city. Shane scanned the road ahead, watching the trash that lined it for hidden det cords leading back to improvised explosive devices, and was silently amazed that he could hear the *adhan* over the rumble of the engine. His chest tightened as his armored Humvee approached the overpass. *Not today. Come on, you motherfuckers. Cut us a break. Just this once.*

He looked up at Private Adkins, whose head stuck out of the machine-gun turret, ready to grab him if he didn't duck down behind the defilade. Shane held his breath until they passed beneath the bridge. His lungs burned until their up-armored Humvee was in the clear and then he let his breath out in a *whoosh*. He wished they'd hurry up and get more of those new blast-resistant vehicles that big Army kept talking about. For now, the armored Humvees were the best they had, especially since his platoon was two trucks short because of that stupid Lieutenant Randall.

No matter what happened, Shane was determined to keep his own fears deeply buried, like the IEDs hidden across Iraq. He had told Jen he could make a difference. He'd believed his own bullshit then. Now, four months into the Surge, he wasn't so sure. Six men from his platoon alone had already been sent home with injuries, and the overwhelming failure to stop any of them from getting hurt ate away at his soul.

Shane's stomach knotted as his driver, Specialist Howell, swerved around a dead dog, in case the carcass hid a deadly IED. Sweat trailed down his spine as they rounded the corner, approaching the soccer stadium.

Once there had been professional FIFA soccer games held there. Now fresh dirt barely covered the latest bomb crater. It was like the locals didn't want to waste money repairing something they knew was going to be destroyed again. *Please, not again.*

The thought of losing another man to an IED made Shane's bladder tighten. His platoon had been hit the last three times they'd rolled off the base. The mission had been a success and they'd captured their high-value target, but his men knew better than to relax despite the relative lack of resistance they'd run into. The sun slid higher into the sky, casting an eerie red tinge onto the buildings, amplifying the already sweltering heat.

As if his thoughts had tripped the det cord, the earth exploded and a volcano of concrete and dirt mushroomed beneath the Humvee in front of him. The blast overwhelmed the roar of the engines. Time froze as the explosion launched the truck into the air. It slammed into the field, grinding to a halt fifty meters away. Flames shot out from the wrecked front end.

Shane's blood slammed through his body, priming it for action. Training kicked in as his body reacted purely on muscle memory. Fear? He would deal with it later. Right now he had to secure the site, get the wounded out of the kill zone, and recover the downed vehicle.

Howell slammed on the brakes as the blast wave rocked their armored Humvee. Small arms fire tinked off the armored shell like deadly hail. They needed suppressive fire before they could determine the shooters' positions.

"Adkins! Get that fifty rocking suppressive fire at three o'clock. Howell, give LT Miller fifteen seconds to call this up, and then call it in for him!"

"Looks like LT Miller just got his cherry popped!" Adkins called down as he shifted fire with the heavy machine gun.

"Watch your mouth and pay attention," Shane shouted back. He doubted Adkins heard him. He couldn't hear himself think over the thunder of the big gun blasting overhead, the reverb slamming against his breastbone.

Shane jumped out of the still rolling vehicle, dropping the radio mike and raising his weapon in a single fluid movement. His gut spasmed as his men dismounted, too. But then quiet pride took over as the fire team leaders, Carponti included, ran through the react-to-contact battle drill quickly and efficiently. Shane directed the security positions to better control their position, then got the recovery team set to maneuver once they controlled their sector.

"Enemy contact from the front and left. Security established on the left. Unknown status of wounded in Bravo Thirty-Two," Shane called out as he rushed past Carponti and assumed a tight kneeling position and returned fire on a second-story window. Shane rushed passed him as the replay came over the radio speaker behind him. "Air weapons team will be inbound in ten minutes."

"Shit, they'll be dead in six," Carponti muttered under his breath.

Shane swallowed hard and kept moving. He didn't need Carponti to tell him that. He violently suppressed the paralyzing fear that slithered into his chest and tried to grip his heart. Carponti was being serious. He was never serious, unless the shit and the fan were making babies.

Shane glanced around, not seeing the lieutenant. Shit, he hoped the LT wasn't sitting in the truck pissing himself. Which was just as well if it meant Shane would be leading the assault team to recover their boys. "Okay, first squad needs to lay down suppressive fire. I'll take second squad to recover our boys," Shane shouted down the line of troops, catching acknowledgment from his squad leaders.

Carponti relayed orders to his own fire team leaders over the pounding thunder of the fifty-caliber machine guns. Shane knelt and laid out suppressive fire as one of his boys shifted his position to get behind a mound of dirt. Where the hell was LT Miller?

Carponti shot Shane a thumbs-up—his men were ready to move.

Shane scanned the area and spotted the LT, standing near his vehicle, the radio handset pressed to his ear. LT Miller was three months out of Infantry Officer Basic Course and, from the looks of it, currently scared shitless. He'd spent his first two months in theater on the staff as a battle captain, writing up after-action reports. Nothing on the staff had prepared him for the chaos and smoke and uncertainty of the battlefield. It was a different ball game when the fire really burned, the inbound rounds were deadly, and the blood wasn't a moulage training aid.

Miller's eyes were wide, his face a mask of fear and panic. His mouth opened and closed as he tried to get coherent words past his lips. He held the radio handset near his ear. Miller should have been the one calling in the reports, but from the looks of things, the kid wasn't hearing anything from the tactical operations center, or from the rest of the platoon for that matter. He damn sure wasn't coherent enough to call in a report, let alone lead the recovery operation.

Shane took a deep breath and wondered—not for the first time—why the Army, in all its wisdom, put inexperienced young lieutenants in charge. Shane snatched the LT by the collar of his body armor. He pulled him in close, so that only the wild-eyed kid could hear his next words.

"Calm down, LT. The men are watching you."

Miller's eyes scanned the tight defensive formation of their vehicles, unable or unwilling to make eye contact with him.

Shane briefly contemplated the consequences of slapping some sense into Miller. Instead, he jerked a thumb over his shoulder. "Security is set. I'm taking second squad to retrieve the wounded in that vehicle."

Miller's eyes skittered around the battlefield and Shane swore. "*Look* at me, Lieutenant," he commanded. Miller finally locked eyes with Shane. "The longer we stand in the kill zone, the bigger the target on our collective asses gets. We're not getting air support soon enough—we're on our own for this one."

He watched Miller take a deep breath. Then another. And then he watched with satisfaction tinged with pride as the cherry LT grabbed his balls and started commanding his platoon like he'd been trained to do. Shane's men fell into the maneuver positions, and Shane rushed with the retrieving element to pull their boys out of the truck, and God willing, no one would be hurt. At least not bad enough to get sent home.

Rounds landed with sickening thuds and sent up sprays of dirt and dust as they crossed the field.

"Damn it, Carponti, get down!" Shane demanded as Carponti jumped on top of the burning vehicle, and tried to wrench the heavy door up and open. It didn't move. Carponti peered into the armored ballistic glass instead.

"I can't get this fucking door open. Try through the turret! Ross!"

"Get off the fucking—" A hiss whizzed by Shane's head and he hit the dirt. Facedown, his helmet absorbed the blast concussion as an RPG exploded a hundred feet away.

He looked up in time to see a second rocket nail Carponti square in the chest. Shane's heart slammed against his ribs as he shouted Carponti's name. *No explosion.* Goose bumps raced across his skin as he rushed around the truck. Carponti was struggling to sit up, choking as he tried to catch a breath in the thick smoke. Shane grabbed him by the collar of his body armor and dragged him away from the fire.

"Why don't you ever listen!" Shane's voice carried the chaos. "Are you okay?"

"The boys back at the FOB are never going to believe this shit." Carponti was either laughing or coughing, Shane couldn't tell. He didn't have time for relief.

"Get your ass around this truck and lay down suppressive fire. Then, you're going back with the MEDEVAC."

"Bullshit!" Carponti propped himself up, raised his weapon, and fired at an insurgent running across the field. One shot and a body slammed into the dirt. "There's nothing fucking wrong with me!"

"This isn't a choose-your-own-adventure game," Shane yelled back. "For once in your life you are going to fucking listen to me. Now shut the hell up and help the LT prepare the nine line."

He didn't hear what Carponti muttered as he rushed low across the field back to the truck where LT Miller was alternating between talking on the radio and firing his weapon.

What the fuck was taking the air weapons team so damn long? Shane sucked in a deep breath, forcing his lungs to release the tightness in his chest as Tully and Branyan dragged Ross out through the turret. He coughed and tried to help, but everything moved in slow motion. He'd had his bell rung, that was for damn sure.

Another volcano of debris and dirt exploded a hundred feet away. The heat blasted Shane's face and he'd never been so glad he had on his ballistic glasses as right then.

As he went down, he saw his men hit the dirt, faces buried, arms tucked beneath the armor that protected their torsos. Two of his platoon's medics fell across the bodies of the wounded, shielding them from the blast. Something burned, like someone had sliced into his legs with a red-hot blade.

"Damn it, that's what I get for fucking listening! Sarn't G!" He heard someone shout from very, very far away. His last thought was that Jen was going to be pissed at him for getting hurt.

Then the world went black.

JEN SURVEYED the lobby near the emergency room entrance. Damn but she'd be glad when the new hospital was built. Sometime in 2012, or so they said. If the wars were still going on then, it was going to be sorely needed. The old lobby was too small, and the emergency room inadequate for the sheer size of the population the hospital was expected to service. And don't even get Jen started on Labor and Delivery. For what was arguably the busiest maternity ward in the nation, the number of beds was appallingly inadequate, but somehow, women rarely gave birth in the hallway. Across the way, Nicole waved and then focused back on the nervous wife in front of her.

"I'm sorry. We're still getting conflicting reports," Nicole was saying as Jen approached. "We think we know who's coming in, but we're just not sure."

There was a flight of soldiers due in today, and Jen was part of the team responsible for getting them processed and triaged. Some would be easily treated. But others would need to go directly to surgery. Controlling the chaos around the soldiers' arrival was part of her job. Laura and Nicole had been among the first to arrive when word got out that Reaper battalion soldiers were among the wounded. Over the last few months, Nicole had become part of the fabric of her life, so much so that she didn't remember what life had been like before they'd been friends.

She needed to add three new names to Nicole's list, then scrub it against Laura's to make sure they matched. It was all admin until the wounded actually arrived.

Nicole held up her finger as she pulled her phone out of her pocket. "Vic? I am so glad to hear your voice."

"Ask him if he can get us a confirmed list of who's on the manifest," Laura said. She walked up from the edge of the crowd that seemed to be growing. So far, they were tracking only five soldiers en route. "There's five passengers, but only three names."

Nicole nodded. "Laura wants to know if you've got a list of—oh my God." Her eyes filled, spilling tears down her cheeks almost instantly. She staggered and Jen caught her before she fell. Together she and Laura guided her to a chair. "No. Don't get on a plane. I'll call Mom. I'll be there tomorrow . . . I'm not freaking out, damn it. I'm coming. So don't argue . . . I love you, too."

Nicole flipped her phone shut and stared at it for a long moment. When she moved, it was like she snapped back, ready for action. "I've got to go. Vic's hurt. He's in Landstuhl in Germany."

"I'll drive you to the airport," Laura said. "What happened?"

"He wouldn't tell me, but he's heading in for surgery." She shook her head in response to Laura's offer. "Everyone needs you here. My mom will help get me on a flight." Laura pulled Nicole close and for one brief sliver of time, she lost her strength again, breaking down with a quiet sob. Jen rubbed her back, biting back her own sadness to be strong for her friend.

After a moment, Nicole straightened, but her lips quivered as she struggled to pull everything back inside. "I gotta go."

Jen wanted to say something, anything that could offer her friend comfort. But before she could think of the right words, Nicole was gone. She looked at Laura. "How does she do that?"

Laura smiled sadly. "She's married to Carponti. I imagine that takes a different kind of strength." She took a deep breath. "We've got work to do."

She was right, but that didn't make anything easier about today. Today was personal. It always hurt bringing the wounded home, but this? Knowing some of the wives in the waiting area made this so much worse.

The wait was the hardest part. Jen hated seeing the wives and mothers and fathers lingering in the lobby, waiting for the ambulances that would bring their loved ones from the airfield to the hospital. The chalks from the airfields, the convoy of ambulances and police escorts, were always rushed and urgent. It was critical to keep control of the chaos as the soldiers arrived and were processed.

A little boy, no more than four years old, was crying for his breakfast, leaning against his mother, who was huge with a new pregnancy. He'd jammed his fist in his mouth, and his eyes were bright with tears as he sobbed quietly. Jen knelt in front of the little boy's mother, who looked panicked and exhausted all at once. "Can he have a Nutri-Grain bar?"

The mother nodded, relief sparkling in her red and swollen eyes. The boy wasn't the only one stressed out. Jen squeezed her hand briefly. "What's your husband's name?" Tears mingled with fidgeting and the air hung thick with the tension of the unknown.

"Caspers. Private John Caspers," she whispered, and the urgent hope in her voice broke Jen's heart.

"John is scheduled for immediate surgery."

Mrs. Caspers's face fell and she held on to her son as he chewed on the blueberry bar. "Will he be okay?"

She wanted to say yes. Oh, God, how she wanted to say yes and give Mrs. Caspers the certainty she yearned for. "I don't know. We'll do our best."

Tears leaked out as Mrs. Caspers rested one hand on her belly, the other clutching her son.

Releasing a tense breath, Jen turned toward Laura, the calm in the eye of the storm. She was handing out baskets of basic personal hygiene items to family members for their soldiers, who would arrive in borrowed clothes at best or tattered uniforms at worst. She'd been on the phone constantly since she'd arrived at the hospital, making arrangements at the Fisher House and other lodging facilities for families who'd just arrived and needed somewhere to stay.

Jen's hands clenched around her clipboard as she glanced at her watch. She released a breath and focused on something she could control. "How many families have been notified?"

Laura checked her list, frustration creasing between her brows. "All but the families of the two who haven't been identified. I mean really? We're seven years into two damn wars and we still can't manifest wounded soldiers properly? How hard is it to count soldiers when they're all high on painkillers?"

"Any word from Trent?"

"Not a damn thing."

Jen wished she could have ignored the biting hurt beneath Laura's words. But she didn't have time to even offer sympathy, because that very minute the ambulances pulled into the drop-off area in front of the emergency room. Conversation froze as Laura shuffled the waiting families back, clearing a path for medical personnel.

Two men climbed out of the second ambulance under their own steam. Jen's throat tightened as their wives, both looking no older than high school seniors, rushed up to them. One of the men had his arm wrapped in a bandage that was six inches too short. The other sank into a wheelchair almost instantly, but not before his wife nearly knocked him over.

One of the nurses guiding a gurney shouted, bringing everyone's attention to the wounded soldier under her care. "Blood pressure's dropping over here!"

Jen raced to the side of the gurney. Blood seeped through a bandage on the kid's thigh. He couldn't have been more than nineteen years old. The kid's screams echoed through the waiting room.

They needed to stop the bleeding or he'd be dead in minutes.

Jen rushed over, applying pressure in the middle of the choreographed movements of the emergency team. She ran with them, keeping her hands pressed to the wound until the trauma team took over and they pushed through the automatic doors that swung wide to let them through.

"Got it from here, Jen. Thanks." The dark-eyed surgeon met her gaze. "Go wash your hands."

She held her hands up. Blood smeared over her palms. Reality crashed over her. Blood. Exposure.

Jen walked toward the stainless-steel sinks but turned when the door to the OR swung wide and two nurses maneuvered another gurney back to the operating room. She froze, stunned into absolute silence.

Shane.

He was wrapped tightly in grey thermal blankets. An IV bag hung from a solitary stainless-steel pole, the tube ending at the juncture of plastic, tape, and black tattoos. Thick straps snaked around his torso, hips, and legs, securing him to the gurney. Jen couldn't see if he was breathing on his own or not. The medics wheeled him back to surgery as Jen just stared, unable to resolve this image with the man she remembered.

Her heart bled for him as the door closed behind the second surgical team.

Oh shit. Laura. Jen quickly washed her hands and rushed back to the emergency room waiting area. Laura was no longer calm. Tears streamed down her friend's face and her breath came in quick, short gasps. "You saw him?"

Jen nodded, her own heart breaking even as she folded Laura into her arms. For once, her friend wasn't the strong one. Jen didn't have the right to be upset. Shane wasn't hers; she shouldn't care enough to cry for a man she barely knew.

So how could she explain the tears spilling down her own cheeks?

SOMETHING SHIFTED, like plastic sliding against linoleum, and Shane had the sudden sensation of being watched. The feeling pulled at him, urging him out of the haze of the drugs and the pain of his memories. From somewhere far away, an echo of something burned his skin.

The morphine that deadened everything inside of him made thinking difficult. He closed his eyes, wishing he could drown out the buzzing in his head and sink back to sleep. Sleep was good. Nothing burned when he was asleep.

Her face was fuzzy, but he could make out the vague shape of a woman. *No . . . Anyone but her.*

Shane turned his face away, denial tearing at this soul. She couldn't be here. Not now.

"Shane? Can you hear me?"

He groaned and covered his face. At least he attempted to. His right arm was too heavy to lift. He squinted hard and saw the fuzzy outline of a cast.

Shit.

He started taking inventory of his available body parts. At least the ones that would respond. He couldn't feel a thing from his waist down and he damn sure wasn't about to look. He was horrified that he might see an empty space where his legs should be.

Shane dragged his good hand over his face and pulled himself out of the despair that threatened to pull him back under. He blinked several times, trying to clear his vision. Disappointment threatened to choke him.

"Shane?"

Jen stood at the edge of his bed, near his hip. Her image kept fading in and out of clarity but during a single moment of lucidity, he saw what he'd been afraid of written across her face. Great. Fucking sympathy. Just what he wanted.

"The fixators holding your legs together are going to hurt for a while." Her voice was soft, like a pillow after a hard day. "You need to tell us so we can stay ahead of the pain."

Fury sparked to life inside of him, crashing through the haze of drugs. "Do I look like I'm in fucking pain?"

He was used to the way his men reacted to his temper. But Jen? She simply folded her arms over her chest and stood near that damned sheet, watching. Waiting.

"You don't have to be an asshole."

Shane couldn't look at her. Not again. He couldn't bring himself to look up at her and see pity staring back at him. "I'm fine."

"No, you're not."

He turned his face away, unwilling to look into those dark eyes and see the remains of himself reflected back at him. He heard the tink of glass against a tray, and something hot crawled up his arm. Fuck, more drugs. Which meant sleep. It was a reprieve from the incessant dreams of fire burning around his platoon while Shane could do nothing but watch his men burn. He didn't deserve the reprieve. The pain was his punishment for fucking up and getting hurt.

The drug slithered through his veins, wrapping around his brain like a warm blanket fresh from the dryer. He hated it. He didn't want to feel, didn't want to think. He just wanted to drop into that hollow morphine cloud and sink straight to hell where he belonged.

Maybe then the burning failure in his heart would stop bleeding out.

$$6$$

Four days had passed since Shane had arrived. Four days of silence and avoided looks and hostile body language. He barely ate. She wasn't sure if he slept. But the silent treatment he'd offered her didn't match the reports from the rest of the nurses. The reports of violent outbursts. Of thrown medical equipment. But whenever she was in the room, she'd been treated to nothing but stone silence. So when Jen heard a loud crash from her perch at the nurses' station, she knew exactly where it came from. She rushed toward the noise, doing her best not to outright run. She shoved the door to Shane's room open as the crash cart slammed into the stainless-steel sink. Blood welled from the open IV puncture wound and dripped down his arm.

Shane's face was contorted, a battle between determination and pain tearing across his hard features. The veins in his forearm bulged against his black tattoos as he tried to maneuver himself into the overturned wheelchair wedged beneath the bed rail.

"Shane!"

Silence hung heavy and thick as he froze. He lifted his gaze. *I'm not nice.* She hadn't believed him when he'd told her that. Holy crap, had she been wrong.

The muscles in Shane's neck corded tight. For a moment, she was sure he would ignore her and drag himself farther out of the bed.

Time hung suspended. His jaw pulsed and he gripped the rail as a wave of pain shuddered through his body.

"Don't touch me."

Jen took a deep breath and approached the bed. "Let me help you."

She edged closer to the wheelchair, standing close enough that if he lashed out at her, he'd easily connect. His fist balled on the chair and though she hated herself for it, she flinched. Wounded or not, if Shane hit her, she wouldn't be getting up.

"Please, Shane. Let me help you."

His arm shook. He didn't look at her, but he finally nodded. Just a quick jerk of his chin, but it was enough. She stepped closer, wedging herself beneath his good arm. "On three. One." He braced against her, using his casted hand to awkwardly grip her shoulder. "Two." She planted her hands on his ribs and chest. "Three."

Together they pushed, rotating Shane back into the bed. Silence hung in the room like a day-old corpse. She picked up the chair and moved it out of the way. Then she gathered up bandages and a fresh IV.

The threat of violence and risk of injury safely past, her hands shook in a delayed reaction to the fear. She sucked in a deep breath and steadied herself.

Finally she turned, and what she saw stunned her. His hand covered his face and she could see the strain in the lines of his neck and forearms. Her heart ached to see him hurting so badly. He still didn't respond. Her fingers trembled, but still she reached for him. He jerked when her fingers brushed his skin. She applied a gentle pressure, and drew his arm away from his face. He surprised her when he didn't resist her, didn't pull away. Pain echoed in every spasm of his muscles. She applied pressure on the former IV site, cleaning the blood with her free hand. Once the bleeding slowed, she wrapped medical tape around his elbow, securing the bandage in place. She finished cleaning the blood from his arm, then prepared a new IV.

He didn't move. He was absolutely still as she worked. She felt his gaze burning into her.

"What hurts?"

He looked out the window, his jaw pulsing as he ground his teeth. "Everything." His voice broke over the whisper. He massaged his temples with his thumb and index finger. "I don't want any more damn drugs and I want this fucking tube out of my dick."

"We can't take the catheter out because you've got seventeen stitches holding your guts inside of you. So unless you feel like picking your spleen up off the floor because you want to be stupid, the quote fucking tube stays."

He glared at her then, but remained silent. She swallowed and stepped closer to the bed. "There's no shame in using the drugs to get through this. They're a tool, like anything else a doctor uses."

"I can't think." He scrubbed his palm against the new beard covering his jaw. "I don't trust myself on them."

She rested her hip against the rail. He looked away and Jen saw a hint of despair replace the anger and pain in his face. The shift was so sudden, so without warning, and so utterly heartbreaking that tears sparked behind her eyes.

"Fine." His sudden acquiescence surprised her.

"I'll be right back." He didn't acknowledge her statement but she squeezed his hand before she left anyway.

She'd never seen him in so much pain, not even when he'd first arrived. The strain in his voice hurt. She injected the drug quickly into his IV, then she reached for his hand. He didn't pull away. She stroked his knuckles until his fist was no longer tense. Then she threaded her fingers with his and waited in the silence with him, his big, rough hand resting in hers.

The tension eased back as the narcotic took hold, binding to the pain. The lines around his mouth relaxed, and his neck muscles visibly loosened. His fingers stayed linked with hers, though, strong and steady. She looked down at that hand she held and wondered at her fascination with this man who was capable of such naked determination.

"Better?" she asked. He nodded slowly and squeezed her fingers lightly before unthreading his hand from hers. "How's your head?"

"It's killing me." He rubbed his forehead between his eyes. There was no force behind his words. None of the violence that had been there just moments before. Was he giving up? She didn't need him climbing out of bed on his own, but this? This was somehow worse. She blinked rapidly then poked him in his chest, in the soft flesh between his pec and his shoulder. He turned his face quickly and scowled at her.

"Hurting yourself isn't the way to get out of the hospital."

A slow flush crawled up his neck and Jen almost took a step backward, anticipating an outburst. Almost.

Shane didn't explode. Instead, his words came out quiet, the anger behind them barely concealed.

"You have no idea what it's like to sit here and not be able to do anything for yourself. So don't talk to me about healing when I'm just another warehoused GI."

"You're hurt. You need help. "

His eyes flashed and he leaned up, getting right into her face. His voice was a low growl, deep in his throat. "I don't *want* help. I don't need your help. I *want* to get fixed and get back to Iraq."

She jammed her finger into his chest again. "You do need help, you're just too stubborn to accept that the invincible Shane Garrison needs it. It's not the end of the world."

"This is your idea of help?" He slammed his fist against the rail of the bed. "Keep it and get the fuck out!"

She didn't argue with him. She'd lost the one tattered edge of momentum she'd had. She left, and felt his rage burning holes in her back as she shut the door quietly behind her.

JEN'S HANDS shook and she balled them into fists until her nails bit into the skin. That had gone well. If by well, she meant utter failure. She closed her eyes as she calmed down, trying to remember how she'd felt when she'd been heaving on the bathroom floor after chemo. Thank God she'd had Laura. Her friend had cleaned up the mess and helped her into bed. And she'd stayed by her side all night.

Just like Shane, Jen hadn't wanted to hear that she needed help. Laura had stuck with her through those terrible times, even though she had been eight months pregnant with her second child and Trent had again been deployed. Jen had protested, but Laura had stuck. And when Jen's brother had served her with legal papers contesting their grandmother's will, Laura had still stuck.

Jen pushed away from the door of Shane's room, and the

unpleasant walk down memory lane. Just then, Laura walked down the hall, like she was walking out of Jen's memories. She looked exhausted and was carrying a large, colorful tote that doubled as a purse. Shane's injury had capped off a month filled with bad news. Laura looked tired and Jen knew she wasn't doing well. No one was. The Surge was taking its toll on all of them.

"Have you heard from Nicole? How's Vic doing?"

Laura's somber expression cracked into a genuine smile. "Making jokes. He's taking her down to Italy before they head home. Listening to Nicole, you'd think he did no more than stub a toe instead of lose a limb."

"Well, that's good, right?"

Laura offered a one-shouldered shrug. "I think so." She sighed and gripped the tote beneath her arms so tightly her knuckles showed white. Her gaze drifted over Jen's shoulder to the door behind her. "How's Shane?"

Jen puffed her cheeks out and let some of her exasperation show. "Do you want the truth or do you want me to lie to you?"

"Oh, the truth sounds like much more fun," Laura said dryly.

"He's a pain in the ass."

Laura laughed out loud, then quickly covered her mouth with her hand. "Sorry. That's more of a relief than you know."

"Any ideas on how I keep him from ripping his IV out every five minutes? You know him better than I do." She was willing to take suggestions at this point. Anything would be better than feeling this helpless and out of ideas.

Laura shrugged and tugged her hair from her face. Jen frowned and looked a little closer. Had she been crying?

"Hon, you should be able to relate to where he's at right now better than anyone. You didn't talk to me for weeks when you first got sick. I had to practically drag you to the spa at gunpoint to get those toenails under control."

Jen snorted and covered her smile with the back of her hand. "Oh God, I'd forgotten about that."

"Just don't let him do anything stupid, okay? I'll be here as much as I can for him, but you're here every day. And I don't know how much they'll let me up here if I'm not official, you know?"

"Huh?"

Laura looked away. "I'm resigning as the battalion family readiness group leader."

"What's going on?" Jen tucked her hands into the pockets of her nurse's smock.

Laura shifted the bag to her other shoulder. "Nothing. I don't think I'm being a very good FRG leader. I can't take care of my own husband, so how can I help the other wives? So I'm stepping down."

"Does Trent know?" Jen asked cautiously.

"Don't know. I emailed him. Haven't gotten a reply, though."

"He's still not talking?"

Laura shook her head, biting her lips together. "And the rumors are damn near killing me."

"What rumors?"

Laura shook her head. "They're not important. I'm just so worried and I can't help because he's not talking. And all the rear d commander says is that Trent will call when he can."

Jen slipped her arm around Laura's shoulders and rested her head against hers for a moment. "I wish I had some way to make it better."

Laura sniffed and pulled away. "Yeah, well, it's my husband who's being a shit. I'll deal. You, on the other hand, need to deal with Mr. Crankypants in there for me, okay?"

She snorted and headed to the nurses' station. "What am I supposed to do? Show him my scars? Hey, pal, check this out. I can totally relate to how you feel?"

"That's so not funny." Laura managed to laugh and look horrified all at once. "But hey, you never know, right?" Her tote buzzed and she fished around until she pulled out her phone. "It's Nikki."

Jen's eyes widened. Carponti's warped sense of humor might just be the thing to kick Shane in the tail and get him out of his funk. "How soon are they coming back?" Jen whispered.

"Huh?"

"Tell Nicole to get her and Vic back here. Shane needs him."

Laura narrowed her eyes. "Hang on, Nikki. Jen, are you sure?"

"Yeah. I am."

It was a risk. A big one considering that Carponti was still healing from his own injuries. But right now, it was a chance—the only one she had.

A QUIET KNOCK on the door penetrated the fog in his brain. He wished the damn nurses and doctors and well-meaning volunteers would leave him the hell alone. He didn't want company. He didn't want the neat little hygiene kits they left or the cheap underwear that wouldn't fit over his freakish legs even if he had been interested in getting dressed. Which he wasn't. Getting dressed implied that he was going somewhere. Which, again, obviously, he wasn't.

He didn't answer the quiet knock, hoping that if it was a visitor they'd leave. The friggin' docs and nurses were in his damn room at all hours of the night and day. Not that he slept much. The drug-induced haze he lingered in couldn't really be called sleep. So when the door to his room pushed open, he sighed and slammed his head back against the pillow and fought the urge to throw the remote control at whoever was walking in now.

"Wow, Jen wasn't kidding."

He glanced over sharply at Laura's familiar voice. She stood near the door to the bathroom, her hands gripping the handle of the tote tightly. Her gaze flicked down his body, surveying the damage and he bristled but remained silent. Barely.

He hated this part. Each time someone he knew walked into the room, they didn't see him, they saw his injuries. He felt like he was just another freak on display, and now knew exactly how he'd made others feel every time he'd glanced away and thought, thank God it wasn't him.

He swallowed and tried to think of something civilized to say. But he wasn't feeling civilized and despite Laura's being a good friend, he didn't want her company.

Unless . . . "You don't happen to have a coat hanger in there, do you?" he asked.

Laura frowned and shot him a funny look. "Why?"

"I will have your children if you'd straighten one out for me."

"What are you talking about?" She approached the bed then, his remark breaking through the barrier that had kept her away from the bed.

"My fucking arm is itching like crazy." He tried to shift his arm inside the cast but it didn't move and the creeping sensation of something prickling up his skin crept higher.

"I wish I'd thought to bring some." She shrugged. "Sorry."

Shane sighed and tossed the remote onto the sheet next to his hip. "You're no help."

"You really are in a sunny mood, aren't you? You could try being a little bit less of an asshole, you know." Laura shifted the tote higher on her shoulder and folded her arms over her chest.

"Laura—"

"I'm just giving you a hard time." She swallowed as her voice cracked. "You scared the shit out of me."

She bit down on her lips and looked away.

"Ah, hell, come here." He lifted his good arm and she accepted the peace offering, hugging him gently before pulling away. "Sorry," he mumbled.

"Yeah, well, it's not like this is Disneyworld." She swiped beneath her eyes. "Are you okay?"

He shrugged. "Peachy."

"I thought we covered this don't be a dickhead stuff already," she said dryly.

"Yeah." He tried to smile. It was weak but it was there. "We did."

"So, anyway, I brought you some clothes. I don't know when you'll be out of the bed or anything but, well, as sexy as that hospital gown is, I'm sure real clothes might make you feel a little more, I don't know, normal?"

He glanced down at the cast covering his left arm. "Not likely. But thanks."

Silence greeted his sullen response but he couldn't make himself apologize. Laura was a friend. She'd gone out of her way to come see him and bring him clothes. And how did he say thanks? By being a douche bag. Trent was going to kick his ass when he saw him next.

"This isn't the end of the world," she said quietly, her palm warm against the exposed skin of his forearm. "And I know this is the last thing you want to hear, but I'm glad you're okay."

"Look, Laura—"

"Don't argue." She squeezed his arm gently, then let go. "I've got to get going. I know this sucks but I meant it. I'm glad you're okay." She sniffed and set the tote on the floor between the chair and the bed. "The clothes will be here if you change your mind."

Finally he looked at her and saw the tears shimmering in her eyes. "Aw hell, Laura, don't cry."

She shook her head and covered her mouth. "I'm not."

"Bull."

"Busted." She rolled her eyes and smiled weakly. A faint buzzing filled the silence and she tugged the cell phone out of her purse. Something thawed around his heart when her eyes lit up, just a little. "Trent?"

She motioned to the door and rushed into the hall. He hoped the call didn't drop but in the hospital, it was likely. The door shut behind her, leaving him alone in the silence once more.

He closed his eyes and wished he could have made conversation. Asked about the kids, about the wives. About anything so he wouldn't have been such an asshole. But then again, that was what he was good at.

He scoffed. What he *had* been good at. Now? Now he was . . . he had no idea.

But he damn sure wasn't a good friend and wasn't much of a soldier anymore, either. He looked down his body at the dingy white cast and the sheet covering the skeletal frames around his legs.

What the hell was left?

7

____

Three weeks since he'd been shipped out of Iraq and he was just as useless now as he'd been when he'd first arrived. The only difference was now, he was slightly less stoned and every single nerve burned with energy, both real and imagined. He looked down at his right arm as an itch crawled up his wrist toward his elbow. He shuddered, unable to do anything to stop the sensation —it felt like a spider was crawling over his skin.

Nurse Ratchet had confiscated the coat hanger he'd transformed into a scratching stick.

Bitter helplessness tasted like sand in his mouth. He scrubbed his hand over his face, wishing like hell he could shave. That he could take a piss by himself. That he could do *anything* other than sit here.

He was stuck. Between the pins sticking out of his legs and the stitches holding his abdomen together, the cast on his right arm and the tube sticking out of his dick, he was a damned invalid. He clicked through the channels searching for anything related to the war, but all anyone was talking about was some pop star's latest stint in rehab.

He was going fucking insane.

The door to his room slammed opened and Shane glanced over, expecting to see one of Nurse Ratchet's pals.

Shane's mouth fell open, but no sound squeezed past the knot in his throat. He barely recognized the man who walked into his room. His face was covered with a bushy red beard, his dark red hair grown out and slicked back in some Irish version of the Fonz. He'd let his hair grow out of that stupid red patch months ago, but this? This was ridiculous. Cold shock crawled up his spine when he saw Carponti's bandaged arm. Several inches too short.

Holy fuck.

Carponti strolled in like he didn't have a care in the world and flopped into the chair that was reserved for visitors. Except for Laura —who visited him regularly despite his less than charming attitude— it had gone basically unused since Shane had arrived. Not that he wanted company anyway.

Reclining in the chair, Carponti kicked his feet up on the edge of Shane's bed. "You're still in the hospital? Legs get blown all to hell and suddenly you can't walk. What the hell is the Army coming to?"

Shane finally thought to close his mouth, then struggled to smile at his best squad leader. The last time he saw him—"You survived that explosion?"

"Nice to see you, too. Asshole," Carponti said with a grin. "You tried to send me out on the MEDEVAC. I ended up dragging your heavy ass onto that bird instead."

Carponti continued, oblivious to Shane's silence. "Is this what you've been doing for the past month? Sitting back here relaxing? And you still have all your limbs? That is such bullshit! Put a Band-Aid on that shit and get your happy ass back over to the sandbox."

"What are you on?" Shane was reasonably certain Carponti had lost his mind.

"Me?" Carponti's eyes widened in pure innocence, an expression that was both familiar and unsettling. It meant he was into something. Something bound to get Shane's ass in a sling one way or another. "Nothing. Well, nothing much." He held up his bandaged arm and waved it around like a flag. "Check this out. Makes buttoning up shirts a whole new adventure. The only thing that sucks is that sometimes my fingers still itch. And the docs don't have a pill for that. At least not one that works."

Shane could barely form a complete sentence as deep disquiet crawled over his skin. "When did you get hit?"

"Couple of days later. There was another IED because there always is, right? My arm got pinned in between one of those heavy armored doors, and the truck. By the time they got me out, the arm was pretty much dead. So the docs over in Germany did a quick little nip and tuck and sent me on my way." Carponti was chomping on mint gum, like a Valley girl at the mall. "Boy, I'm sure glad they didn't stop my combat pay right away. I took Nikki shopping in Italy so she'd stop hovering over me. Man that woman can *shop*."

Shane struggled to smile. To do something other than gape at his friend. The guy had lost part of his arm, and he made it sound like nothing.

"CID gave her leave?" Shane asked, struggling to pull his thoughts together to form at least one coherent thought. Carponti had swaggered into the company tactical operations center about four months back, bragging that his wife was now a full-time investigator at the Fort Hood Criminal Investigations Division and that everyone had better watch their asses. He'd had a feeling that Carponti hadn't been kidding when he'd mentioned it to LT Randall.

"Yeah. She's working gangs in Killeen and the Central Texas area with the feds. Man, you'd be shocked at how many gangs send guys into the military. They try to buy people off, too, especially armorers and guys with access to weapons repair parts. You'd be amazed at what she can't tell me."

Shane struggled to keep up with Carponti's stream-of-consciousness dialogue. Damn it, but his brain was clouded. Carponti continued, oblivious. "We thought we'd lost you. But I knew it was going to take a whole lot more than a couple of bombs to knock your disgruntled old ass off the planet."

Finally, Shane's thoughts cleared as his lips cracked into an awkward smile. "I'm only five years older than you, dickhead."

"I rest my case. So anyway, when are they sending you home?"

Shane didn't want to talk about home or his lack thereof. His mom had been more of an incubator than a parent. His dad? Well, he assumed his dad was one of the random truckers his mom had pretended Shane didn't know about. And he'd closed out his apartment when he'd deployed, never dreaming he'd need to have a place to stay before the end of the tour. No, home was the last thing Shane wanted to think about.

Carponti was fine, cracking darkly inappropriate jokes as always. Suddenly that was the most important thing in the world to him. Why was he freaking out if Carponti wasn't?

"I have no idea. Who else got hit?" Who else had he let down when he'd been taken out of the fight?

"Adkins broke his arm in like four places, but he pissed and moaned so much the docs let him stay. He's riding the rest of the rotation out in the orderly room, but he's happy because he's still with the boys."

Shane's smile slipped more firmly into place. The knot around his heart loosened. Just a little. It was so good to hear Carponti's voice. To hear about his men.

"How's Captain Davila doing over there?"

Carponti's jaw slowed on the gum and his gaze went a thousand miles away to the Iraqi desert. "He's holding up, I guess. There were rumors flying around that someone in our battalion had killed some Iraqi civilians. Bad shit, any way you shake it." And he flipped the switch, and was instantly back to his chipper self, chomping away at the gum. "But you're back here sitting around staying stoned and getting fat, so what do you have to worry about?"

Brett Michaels wailed about wanting nothin' but a good time from Carponti's phone. Carponti glanced at it, then dropped it back into his pocket. "Hey, man, gotta run. Wife's downstairs. Have you started physical therapy yet?"

"No. Not till this thing comes off." Shane lifted his casted arm a few inches off the bed. The itch was getting worse.

"Oh, yeah, well. Anyway, I'm going to be in here every day at nine. So anyway, I'll see you around, okay? Hurry up and get back to work, will ya?"

He swung open the door and Shane heard a loud, "Oh, hey, Jen."

Jen came walking back in, wheeling a portable blood pressure machine. She barely glanced in his direction, her movements quick and efficient. Shane cleared his throat, trying to tamp down on the emotion churning inside of him. Still, his words came out more gruff than he intended. "How the hell did Carponti know I was here?"

Jen wrapped a blood pressure cuff around his arm, waiting as it inflated. "I figured if anyone could annoy you enough to get moving, it would be Vic."

Shane stared at her, blinking slowly, unable to hide his surprise. He searched her face, stunned to silence. She'd rounded up the one soldier who could be counted on to be a pain in Shane's ass. It was something Shane would have done to get his guys motivated. "You did that?"

"Yeah." She smiled faintly and finally met his gaze. The uncertainty he saw there shamed him. "I thought having Vic around might help."

She finished taking her notes, then headed from the room before Shane could find the words he needed.

The words to thank her.

8

———————

Shane was being quiet. Too quiet. She didn't think his silence could be explained by the recent infection in his abdominal wound, even though the infection and subsequent antibiotic treatment had drained him, physically and mentally. He was still getting fluids pushed through the IV that should have been stinted days ago.

No, Shane's silence convinced Jen that she'd made a horrible mistake that had nothing to do with physical medicine. Maybe bringing Carponti hadn't been the right decision after all. Since he'd shown up several days before, Shane hadn't said a word—to anyone. Hadn't thrown her out of the room. Hadn't tried to rip his IV out. He'd sat and watched her, intently. She left like a rabbit entering a wolf's den every time she went in to check his vitals and to make sure the infection hadn't spread to the fixators holding his legs together.

It made it worse that she'd been working the night shift this past week. She was alone, or mostly alone, with him on the floor. The other patients weren't any more mobile than he was. And so she sat at the nurses' station and studied his chart, wondering if the risk she'd taken had been worth it.

His vital signs were stable. So far, there were no signs of further infection, but that didn't mean anything. One wrong move in caring for his injuries and they might find themselves fighting a drug-resistant staph.

Shane still had miles to go before he was out of the bed and moving around on his own. One leg was less damaged than the other, but that didn't mean that he'd be walking on it anytime soon. He needed time, the one thing he wasn't willing to accept he needed. She glanced toward the door of his room from her seat at the nurses' station. He was awake. She could hear him flipping through the channels on his TV from down the hall. He didn't sleep much. She wondered if that was something new or if he'd always had insomnia. She looked down at his chart again. Time to take his vitals once more.

She couldn't take back her decision to bring Carponti to see him. She'd been so wrong it wasn't even funny. She'd have to apologize. It wouldn't make it right, but she needed to do it all the same. She took a deep breath and held it, waiting until her lungs burned to release it. Then, she walked into the darkness.

Gunshots reverberated off the walls, echoing in the dim light. Brilliant explosions pierced the darkness and for a brief moment she thought he was playing a video game. It only took a moment before she realized he was watching the History Channel.

"Not very comforting late-night viewing," she remarked from the doorway.

He turned and looked at her, his expression dark and unreadable in the dim light. The shadows cut across his cheeks, giving him a harsh look. "Interesting though. For my line of work."

She worried her bottom lip between her teeth. He clicked the remote and turned down the sounds of battle. "Look, Shane, I'm sorry."

"For what?"

"For Carponti. I thought bringing him here would help you realize that being hurt wasn't the end of the world. I didn't mean to upset you or make you worry more."

He shook his head slowly. "You didn't. You did exactly the right thing."

"Then why have you been so quiet since he was here? You haven't said two words to—" She was going to say *to me,* but she stopped herself. "To anyone."

The muscle in his jaw worked for a long moment. The silence broken only by the occasional round of gunfire from the television. "I hate it here. I hate being broken and useless and dependent on every-one." Finally he looked at her. "I need to get back to my team."

What could she say to that? She stopped at the edge of his bed. The rails were up, his legs concealed as always by a blanket. She could see the outlines of the fixators that held his bones together. But it was his eyes that held her. Dark and shadowed, the torment not masked by the drugs that kept his pain at bay.

"Some of your team is here. They need you, too." She didn't know if it was the right thing to say. She searched the depths of his soul in those dark grey eyes, looking for the man who'd pulled her out of the middle of a bar fight. Who'd kissed her and made her feel like a real and sensual woman if only for a moment.

"I don't know where to start." The confession ripped from his throat.

"Start by giving yourself time to heal," she said quietly. "Then you can get back in the fight." He looked at her sharply and she smiled. "I'm trying to learn to speak your language."

A faint smile broke the edge of his lips. "That's not infantry. But it's a start."

Shane watched as Jen scribbled on his chart and he braced himself as she prepared to clean the fixator pins on his legs. He watched her move, trying to find a way to bridge the chasm that stood between them. He missed the easy connection they'd had on that night before he'd deployed. And at the medical processing the next morning, she'd been so strict and so completely sexy. She'd told him to sit that day and he'd sat. Being on the receiving end of her directives had been one hell of a turn-on. He'd never been one to entertain fantasies but he knew he would never look at a nurse's scrubs the same way.

He'd been entranced when she'd run her fingers over his stomach, changing the bandages on his appendectomy incisions. Watching her now, she was a study of quick efficiency and professional distance. She was also sexy as hell. That much hadn't changed.

Then there was nothing but pain. It felt like she was pouring molten lava on open wounds. The fire spread from his flesh into his bones, and traveled through his veins. It was as close to physical hell as he could imagine getting without actually being dead.

He gripped the bed rail with his one good hand and ground his teeth to bite back a groan. It might have been a scream. It was the second time the pins had been cleaned that day and it made him seriously reconsider his stance on pain medication. A good dose of morphine straight into his vein would work wonders right now. Hell, he'd take a shot in the ass at the moment. His jaw popped and he was sure he'd snapped bone. If this was what it took to keep infection at bay, amputation might not have been such a bad idea. It probably would have hurt less.

"Almost done," she murmured, more to herself than to him. He latched on to her voice like a dying man following a white light.

Maybe if he hadn't been such a dickhead, he could have asked her to flash him before she started. Or give him a kiss. Yeah, one kiss from Jen would make everything better. He sucked in a hard breath as she adjusted one of the pins.

He'd had a brigade commander once who said hope was a weak word.

Shane could relate to weak right about now. And hope, fragile though it was, was all he had. The hell retreated in waves as the pain rolled back, slowly lessening. He'd have to find a way to ask her about that kiss. Maybe after the fire stopped burning and he could see straight again.

"You can breathe."

He forced out an exhale. He hadn't realized he'd been holding his breath in until Jen had pointed it out. He rubbed his hand over his chin again and tried to focus on anything other than the pounding echo of pain running through his veins.

He stopped when he noticed the stillness in the room.

Jen looked up at him as she gathered her supplies, a quiet calm in her light eyes. "I could shave you, if you want."

The hesitation he heard in her words nearly broke him. He'd done that. Damn it. He had to fix this.

But the offer was too good to pass up. No matter how tentative the olive branch, he was going to take it. Now he just needed to find a way to make up for being a complete douche bag.

He swallowed and nodded and took one more thing from her even though he'd given nothing in return.

She disappeared into the bathroom, and when she came out a moment later, she was carrying a steaming towel folded in a basin of equally hot water, a can of shaving cream, and a razor. She adjusted his bed so that he reclined almost flat and arranged the towel over his jaw and cheeks. He tried to take a deep breath and failed. Every time he inhaled, all he smelled was vanilla and strawberries.

"I don't have any clippers. This might pull on your beard a little."

After a moment, she pulled the towel off his face. She palmed the can and squirted shaving cream into the center of her hand. She stroked her palms over his face, rubbing the heavy cream into the crisp hair along his jaw. The tips of her fingers ran down his neck, spreading the blanket of foam. He couldn't remember the last time anyone had touched him with such gentleness. Warmth bloomed inside him, cracking the hard shell around his heart. She tugged at him. He wasn't used to that. People in his life left. But not Jen. She was here. Day in and day out.

The silence was absolute, except for the faint crackle of shaving cream swelling across his cheeks. She scraped the razor over his skin, removing his beard, one slow, short stroke at a time.

He couldn't breathe. He tried to swallow but his mouth was filled with dust. He stifled a groan, the pleasure at simply being touched nearly unbearable.

"Did I hurt you?" Her voice was barely a whisper in the silence.

He closed his eyes and shook his head, wishing he didn't feel such an intense need for her to put her hands on him again.

He wouldn't betray the simple intimacy between them by making this more than it was.

But it didn't stop the want. In his mind, he let the fantasy take over. He would slide his hand up her waist, slowly, feeling that cool blouse beneath her scrubs crinkle under his touch. He'd rest his hands against her ribs and feel the rise and fall of her breath beneath his touch. In his fantasy, she wouldn't stiffen or pull away; she'd allow his hands to stroke over her skin. He wanted to hear her quick intake of breath and to know that he was the one who made her gasp.

Their eyes would meet. That perfect mouth would part just a little. He'd give her a little tug. His hand would rest just at the bottom swell of her breast as her lips opened against his. He'd nibble on that plump bottom lip like he'd seen her do so many times, and his tongue would stroke over her bottom lip and slip into her mouth. She'd be soft and warm and wet and she'd taste of mint, like she had that night at Ropers. Her tongue would dip out to touch his and he'd groan at the sensation.

"Shane?"

He opened his eyes. His heart pounded in his throat. Her face was a breath above his. She wiped the last of the shaving cream from his cheek. He licked his lips and swallowed, unable to moisten his mouth.

His fingers curled around her forearm, catching her hand and holding it to his cheek. Her fingertips rested at the edge of his still damp jaw. He stared up at her, time suspended. Her eyes darkened in the low light. Her pulse throbbed visibly in her throat. And in the stillness, she moved. A simple caress. Her thumb slid against the edge of his cheek.

Her lips curved with a hesitant smile. But beneath it was an edge of sadness that touched his soul. She pulled away, leaving him alone. And in the empty room, Shane ached and wanted more. She'd cracked something open, this beautiful nurse who touched his heart with her kindness, and he didn't know what to do with what she stirred in him.

JEN SIGHED HEAVILY and rested her head against her steering wheel. She wanted to hide from what she'd done. And worse, what she wanted to do. The emotions inside of her were no longer limited to worry about Shane's wounds. Now a warm desire wrapped itself around her like a satin ribbon and drew her closer to what was sure to be a mistake of epic proportions.

He would have kissed her. And heaven help her, she'd have kissed him back, and allowed herself to pretend for a brief, intense moment that she was capable of feeling for this man. In that moment, she hadn't cared about the bright pink scar on her breast. She hadn't heard her own voice in her head, calling herself a freak. And she hadn't let herself think of all the reasons why this wasn't right—that he was her patient, and she was the one who had let him deploy.

She'd simply felt his hand, and craved his touch like a starving woman.

She felt edgy. A need pulsed within her, threading through her veins like raw heat. His quiet groan whispered through her memory. She walked into her house, exhausted from her shift, but alive with energy from the way he'd looked at her. She'd felt desired. Needed.

Jen covered her face with one hand. Why had she let things go this far? She was his nurse. Not that that particular detail had kept her professional with him so far. It was all rapidly spiraling out of control. And what was worse was that she wanted it to. She was so unbelievably out of practice in this arena, it was pathetic.

What was she going to do? She was still responsible for his medical care.

She needed to try to get her feelings back into the little box where they belonged instead of twisting inside of her all day. She longed to talk to Laura about all of it, but she was determined to deal with her issues by herself for once. Jen smiled. And, knowing Laura, she would've probably just given Jen hell for not taking the lead and kissing *him.*

She rolled her shoulders, wincing as she hit a stiff muscle. A hot bath would end her night on the right note.

She opened a bottle of water and rested it on the black granite countertop in her kitchen. She pulled a breakfast burrito out of the freezer and popped it into the microwave, unable to keep her mind from drifting back down the road to the hospital. To Shane.

She'd really never been objective with him. It was time, at least, to stop deluding herself about that. She'd tried to see him as a patient when she'd checked his stitches at the SRP, but she'd failed then, too. Had he been just another soldier, she would have red-stamped his file and sent him to the head doc. Instead, she'd let his impassioned plea sway her.

Just like today. She hadn't stopped him from reaching for her. She'd let the heat from his simple touch soak through her skin and touch her heart.

She left her shoes by the fridge and padded up the carpeted stairs into the bathroom, enjoying the soft fabric beneath her feet after a night treading on the hospital's hard tile floors. She started filling the old-fashioned claw-foot tub. Steam filled the room as she dropped her clothes into the hamper. She turned her back to the mirror and began unbuttoning her blouse.

For a brief moment, she imagined Shane's fingers on her blouse, plucking the buttons free. His knuckles would brush against the curve of her breast. She stopped that fantasy before it got past the first button. She wasn't getting naked with him. She knew what he would see . . . How could he get past the scar blazing across her chest?

Jen paused and looked down at her hands, frozen on the tiny white buttons. She glanced over her shoulder at her reflection, at the blond curls sticking to her cheeks in the steam. Her fingers trembled as she turned, slowly, facing herself in the mirror. One by one, she pushed the rest of the buttons open, revealing the sensible cotton bra she wore.

She swallowed and reached behind her to unfasten the hooks. She deliberately kept her gaze on her chest, on the bra.

Shane kept his legs covered. Since he'd been admitted, she hadn't once caught him looking at his own injuries. She wondered if he'd ever looked at them. She had her doubts. She knew how hard it was to look at her own missing pieces. After all this time, her hand was still shaking at the thought of what she was about to see. She braced herself and pulled her bra away. The silicone form flopped to the floor with a splat, but she didn't bend to pick it up.

This. This was what she avoided.

The scar had long ago faded from angry red, but it still held her gaze. The raised pink scar and the indent in her skin where her nipple had once been cut across her chest like a jagged ravine through a field. The stark contrast between the swell of her right breast and the jagged, hollow left. Her other breast, still full and round, still with a perfect pink nipple, stood in the shadow of that scar and the missing flesh.

How long had she been hiding from what she was? The silicone mound gave the illusion that she was still a whole woman. Who had she been trying to fool?

No one but herself.

She pressed her lips together as she stared, her arms at her sides. Tears burned behind her eyes, but she blinked them away. She had convinced herself that she was fine. That focusing on everyone else's problems would make her own disappear.

She turned away from her image in the mirror and stepped into the thick bubbles in the tub, relieved when the scar sank beneath the vanilla-scented foam. She closed her eyes and rested her head back against the cool, hard edge, letting the heat work itself into her tired muscles.

Maybe it was time for her to stop kidding herself. If she couldn't see past the ragged scar running across her chest, how could she expect anyone else to? She closed her eyes, releasing the hard knot surrounding her heart. She was alone, and the scar bothered her. But when Shane had touched her today, when his rough hand had pressed against her skin and his eyes had held her captive, she hadn't felt the burn. She'd felt nothing but desirable. She felt his skin beneath her fingertips again. The clean, crisp scent of the shaving cream mingled with his skin. His touch had been rough and strong but gentle. It was the gentleness that had surprised her.

Yes, she'd told herself he was just another patient, but she'd been deluding herself. And the truth was, a tiny seed of hope dared to believe that Shane might really be different. That she might be able to set aside her own inhibitions with him and simply *be*.

She hadn't dared to feel anything for anyone since she'd gotten sick.

With Shane, all she did was feel.

And it hurt like hell to know that he might reject the real her.

9

---

er back was to him. Jen's pale skin glowed in the candlelight and he wanted so badly to stroke his hand over the soft curve of her hips.

He wanted to savor this. This first touch. This first caress. He couldn't believe she was really here. That she was naked and glorious and all he had to do was reach out and touch her.

His hands embarrassed him when they shook as they hovered over her shoulders. She shifted and tipped her head to one side, exposing her neck. He glanced over her shoulder to the mirror in front of them. Her arms were crossed over her chest. He closed his hands over her forearms, enveloping her. It was her eyes that caught him, huge and dark in the velvety blackness. They captured him.

Her lips parted as he leaned in to nuzzle her neck beneath her ear. He could almost taste her. Closer. Until his teeth scraped across her skin. She shivered and her eyes fluttered closed as the sensations rocketed through them both.

He tugged at her hands and urged her to lower them with a slight pressure. She resisted.

He frowned and turned her in his arms even as she pulled away.

Shane woke with the feel of Jen's skin on his lips, the dream ending abruptly. He turned his eyes toward the door. He'd been waiting for her, he realized suddenly. Waiting for Jen and missing her as the days ticked by and she still hadn't returned.

He wanted to see her eyes warm when she saw him. See her mouth turn up into that soft smile. It was a simple thing that he wanted. Just her.

But it had been nearly a week since he'd almost kissed her. A week he'd spent watching the door, waiting for that familiar smile and not seeing it. A week he'd spent wondering how the hell he was going to fix things this time. He wanted to ask the other nurses where she was. But he had kept quiet, not wanting to spark anything in the rumor mill.

He replayed the memory of Jen's kiss from that long-ago night and the memory of her touch from that dream. And having her close, her body heat warming his flesh. Even though it had only been a dream, the want had nearly crushed him.

The door slammed open and Carponti strode into Shane's room. His heart pounded against his ribs with renewed urgency. Any pleasure that lingered from thoughts of Jen crumbled as Carponti approached and plunked a netbook on the tray near Shane's shoulder.

"Were you raised in a barn? Quit slamming the damn door," Shane growled. It annoyed the hell out of him that he jumped every time Carponti banged the door against the wall, but he'd be damned if he was going to confess that to Carponti. He'd never hear the end of it.

"Quit being such a sissy."

"What's that for?

"Check your email. The guys are bitching at me about you not answering any emails."

"They need to be more focused on running missions."

Carponti shrugged. "The new platoon sergeant is a douche bag. They miss you."

"Which is even more of a reason for them to focus on their jobs instead of worrying about me."

"Holy crap, quit whining. Damn, did they take your balls off in surgery?"

Shane stared at Carponti openmouthed. Carponti raised both of his eyebrows, taking a long pull from a ginormous travel mug. "What?" he asked.

Silently, Shane reached for the netbook. "How do you work this thing?"

"Ah, power button." Carponti reached across him and pushed the little round button. He gave Shane a funny look. "How the hell did you shave with your left hand?"

"Shouldn't I ask you the same thing?" Shane shot back, taking in Carponti's recently shorn cheeks.

Carponti snorted, and whatever he'd been drinking shot through his nose. "Ha-ha, dickhead. So that's how it is? Make fun of the one-armed guy?"

"If the shoe fits." But Shane's grin matched Carponti's. It felt good, shooting the shit with his friend, even if he didn't want to tell him that Jen had been the first to shave that god-awful beard. "One of the volunteers gave me an electric razor."

"Yeah, well, let me tell you how great it is to jerk off with my left hand. Feels like someone else is doing it."

Shane choked on a laugh and opened his email. "Did not need to know that. Really."

"You brought it up."

"Great. Thanks. Now I need brain bleach to get that tortured image out of my head. I swear to God, if I dream about that tonight, I'm killing myself."

Carponti laughed out loud and sat down in the visitor's chair, kicking his feet up on the edge of the bed like he always did. Shane let out a low whistle.

"Lot of messages?"

"A hundred and forty-three."

"Best get to typing."

Shane shook his head and started with the oldest message first. He rubbed his hand over his mouth. He couldn't find any words at the moment that would fit past the blockage in his throat. "Man, did you know that Adkins had a baby boy?"

Carponti nodded. "He didn't get home in time for the birth. Named him Shane, though." His grin was absolutely wicked. "I would have thought that meant you'd boned his wife, but apparently he just thinks a lot of you. Can't imagine why," he mumbled as an afterthought.

Shane blinked rapidly, turning his face back toward the computer and away from Carponti. He'd never hear the end of it if his eyes started watering. Instead, he changed the subject. "How's Osterman?"

Carponti didn't answer for a long time. "I went to see him when I got back from Austin yesterday. He's having a real bad time."

"Define bad time," Shane said warily.

"Just . . . bad. Look, worry about yourself for once. I'll worry about Osterman. But get your ass out of this bed so he can see that it's possible to get hurt and get better. He doesn't believe me when I tell him that losing a limb isn't the end of the world." Carponti looked down at his shortened, bandaged arm. "Can't imagine why I don't have more credibility with him."

Silence hung in the air between them for a moment as Shane continued to read his emails. The next email was from Trent and Shane read it out loud, needing to change the subject. "Get your ass back to work and find out what the fuck is going on with LT Randall and the Rear D. The little bastard won't respond to my emails." Shane frowned and glanced at Carponti. "Randall's back on rear d?"

Carponti leaned forward, setting the travel mug down on the floor. "Oh, you're not going to believe this crap. They sent him back to interview all of us about the missing sensitive items."

"What missing sensitive items? I turned that report in to LT Miller before we rolled outside the wire that night." Shane scrubbed his hand over his eyes, trying to remember if he'd done an inventory before they'd left. He had to have. He never rolled without conducting his precombat checks.

"Yeah, well, apparently not. The company is missing a couple of night vision optics and an M4."

"What?"

Carponti shrugged and leaned back in his chair, taking a large draw from the cup. "Yep. It's a real big deal. Has Captain Davila's nuts in a vice, too. Hence the reason Randall is back in the States. So far the hospital staff has been keeping him out of here, but I'm sure he's just dying to see you since you two were such BFFs before and all," he said dryly. "At least I can avoid him."

Shane snorted and stared up at the ceiling for a moment. He was going to have to deal with the annoying lieutenant if and when he made his way to the hospital. "What happened after we got sent home, man?"

"I don't know, but it's better that Randall's back here. At least here he can't get someone killed." Carponti laughed suddenly and Shane gave him a sharp look. It was always a bad sign when Carponti made that sound, but Shane couldn't help the slow smile that spread across his own face. "Randall is better at Intimidating Shout in the World of Warcraft than he is at doing his job."

"Huh? What the hell is World of Warcraft?"

"Online role-playing game. Like Dungeons and Dragons or something. Randall is like a level seventy-six or some godlike level. It's all he does. Other than annoy the shit out of all of us, that is."

Shane grinned and fired off a reply to Trent that he'd do what he could to figure out what was going on as soon as he got his happy ass out of the hospital. Shane wanted to ask after the rest of the boys but Carponti pushed abruptly to his feet.

"I've got to run. You can borrow the netbook, but for the love of God, answer your damn emails."

If only everything were as simple as Carponti made it seem sometimes. His former platoon was going to shit. His legs looked like they were held together with chicken wire and hundred-mile-an-hour tape, and he'd run off the one good thing he still had in his life. He was still reading through his emails when the door slapped open. Shane looked up, hoping the weeklong drought of no Jen was over. Instead, his week took a turn for the even worse.

Lieutenant Randall stood in the doorway.

10

———

There were places that Jen had avoided since her illness and department stores were high up on that list. So when Laura and Nicole browbeat her into going shopping for a girls' day, Laura at least should have known better. Instead, her so-called stalwart friend had joined forces with Nicole and coaxed, prodded, and pushed until Jen had agreed to meet them at the Arboretum for lunch and a makeover, followed by shopping for underwear, or as Laura called them, visual aids. Jen really didn't want to know why she'd said visual aids in the same sentence as Skype. She loved Laura like a sister, but she still didn't want to picture her friend naked in front of a webcam.

Jen didn't want a makeover or new underwear. Lingerie. Whatever. Truth be told, she wasn't entirely sure why Laura was going for any of the above right now, either. Her husband wasn't due home on midtour leave for another couple of months and they still weren't talking.

So Jen sat in the parking lot of Austin's Arboretum and waited for Laura and Nicole to arrive, feeling her scar pulse against her bra. She was surrounded by luxury cars and women who were dressed to the nines just to get their nails painted. It was times like these that she wished she owned more than capris and T-shirts. She sighed. At least her toenails were painted.

Nicole and Laura pulled up and parked next to her. They'd gone down to the hospital in San Antonio to visit a couple of guys in the burn center and had asked Jen to meet them in Austin for a pilgrimage to their favorite holy land. As her friends stepped out of the car, Jen immediately noticed that they were both dressed to blend in significantly better than Jen. She groaned as she reluctantly left her own car. This was so not going to be fun. As if she could read Jen's mind, Nicole narrowed her eyes at her and said, "You could try to look like you're going to have a good time."

Jen offered a faint smile. "This isn't something I'm used to doing."

The pretty redhead looked scandalized. "Are you serious? Sephora is like Mecca. Next you're going to say you don't like chocolate." Jen didn't answer and Nicole's mouth fell open. "You can't be serious."

Jen couldn't help but laugh. "I like it, it's just not a *need*."

"Are you sure you're a girl? I mean, you're not crazy about Sephora and you don't have an emergency supply of chocolate."

Jen laughed. "Last time I checked, anyway."

Laura, who'd been digging through her purse for lip gloss, finally looked up at them with a smile. "So, what's first, faces or toes or undies?"

"Did you really just call them undies? What are you, four?" Nicole raised her hand. "I'm voting faces. I need a new look, especially now that I'm home more with Vic." She rolled her eyes. "He keeps threatening to trade me in for two twenty-two-year-olds."

Jen gaped, shocked and certain that Vic Carponti had indeed said these exact words. To his wife. "That's awful."

"Like any twenty-year-old would want him," Nicole said, with a laugh.

"Yeah, well, at least he's home," Jen said. "How are you holding up, though?" She threaded her arms into both Nicole and Laura's, and let herself be led into Sephora.

"I'm okay. I think if Vic were taking things worse, I would be, too, but he's hanging in there." She quirked a smile. "He says that it sucks, but at least he still has the rest of the equipment he needs. Oh, shiny." Nicole broke away, plucking a shimmery gold nail polish from a display.

Jen decided she didn't really want to know just what other equipment Vic might have mentioned. She eased into the mood of the moment and relaxed with her friends as they each had makeup applied. There was pleasure enough in watching them enjoy themselves, and it was fun to see them transformed beneath the skilled hands of the makeup artist. But her thoughts kept drifting an hour down the road to a hospital bed back at Fort Hood. She needed perspective on all things Shane. She'd wanted to go in and check on him, but she'd forced herself to stay away. It didn't hurt that she'd been attending a conference at Brooke Army Medical Center in San Antonio for the past week, too.

That didn't stop her from thinking about him, though. Or remembering the strength in his touch. Every time she stared into those dark grey eyes, she felt a warmth twine through her veins, making her achy. Needy. Making her want something far, far out of reach.

"Your turn. Shelly is doing your makeup." Laura gripped Jen's hand and tugged her toward the hot seat.

Jen pulled back. "Really, I'm fine. New makeup isn't in my budget."

"Oh bull. You do nothing but work at the hospital. You're getting a new look if I have to hold a gun to your head."

"I have a hard enough time keeping my patients from pledging their undying devotion without walking in looking like I'm ready for a TV spot," Jen said with a smile. She didn't need new makeup, didn't want it.

"What are you talking about?" Laura asked, as she pushed Jen into the chair. Shelly, a cute girl with a blond pixie haircut and in a black smock, immediately began removing the little makeup Jen did have on. Shelly's makeup was tasteful, not overdone, and she hoped she'd keep a light hand with Jen's new look.

"Nothing," Jen replied. "It's just that sometimes, some of the patients get nursing mixed up with stronger emotions."

"Like . . . ?" Nicole urged, leaning over Laura's shoulder to spread a pale coral gloss over her lips.

"Like one guy offered to marry me. This was after I changed his bedpan for two months running."

Nicole covered her smile with her hand. "Are you serious?"

"Honey, being a nurse is nowhere near as glamorous as it looks on soap operas. Bedpans are not sexy."

"That's all I need to know," Nicole said, before vanishing down an aisle of bright eye shadows.

Laura stayed where she was, and watched Shelly work. "You need to do girl stuff like this more often," she said twirling a new lip gloss between her fingers.

"For who?"

"For you."

Jen swallowed, then rolled her eyes to the ceiling as Shelly patted concealer beneath them. "I'm fine."

"You're a terrible liar."

She barely saw Laura move but the next instant, her longtime friend was standing right behind her, looking intently at her reflection in the mirror. "That scar is not who you are."

"Can we change the subject away from my boobs, please? What prompted this spending spree, anyway?"

"Nicole needed to get away from Vic for a little bit. She's trying so hard to hold it together for him, she's not taking care of herself." Laura shook her head before she backed away, pulling a tester tube of dark red lipstick from a display and running it over the tip of her middle finger. "This color is called Harlot. Really?"

"I thought Vic was doing okay?"

Laura smoothed the wine-red color over her lips, rubbing them together as Nicole disappeared down another aisle, cradling at least twelve different-colored boxes in her arms. Laura waited until she'd vanished again then swiped a Q-tip across the tip of another tube. "You're the trauma expert. You tell me if he should be acting like there's nothing wrong with him after losing an arm."

"Maybe he really is doing okay," Jen suggested. She closed her eyes as a brush descended toward her eyelids. She knew how she'd reacted to losing a piece of herself. But was her reaction the norm, or was it an example of what not to do? Maybe Carponti had really adjusted to his new reality and had chosen to get on with it. Maybe instead of worrying about his nonreaction, Nicole should have been grateful he'd moved on to the next phase of his life with little difficulty. Did Vic Carponti know more than she did about getting on with life after a serious injury—even though his was so fresh that it still required bandages?

"What do you think?"

She opened her eyes and looked in the mirror to examine Shelly's handiwork. Light gold dusted her eyes, now lined with soft brown.

She smiled and for the first time in what seemed like forever, she liked what she saw.

Maybe it was time she took a play from the book of Carponti and embraced the life she had.

~

"I HEAR you're harassing the hospital staff," Randall said by way of greeting.

"Nice to see you, too." Shane was never in the mood to deal with this particular lieutenant, but today, his tolerance was at an all-time low. He had a hard enough time maintaining his military bearing around Randall when he *wasn't* immobilized in a hospital bed. Seeing the man plucked a cord on Shane's last nerve. He glanced down at the IV in his arm and wondered briefly if he could get some additional morphine so that he could punch the little prick and later claim that he'd been under the influence. Course, that would involve Randall coming close enough for Shane to reach him, and then standing still long enough for Shane's one working fist to connect. He almost laughed at the direction of his thoughts. Carponti would be proud.

"So I'm sure you know why I'm here," Randall said, walking in like he owned the room. Shane prayed for patience. Or divine intervention. He wasn't in a position to be picky.

"Enlighten me."

Randall ran his tongue over his teeth before he pulled out that damned clipboard of his from beneath one arm. "Sensitive items are missing from your platoon. Since you never bothered to finish your reports, the CO sent me back to find out what happened." Randall looked down and read off a series of serial numbers. "When is the last time you physically saw these items?"

Anger sparked inside of Shane with each passing number. He was hurt, his men were hurt, and this arrogant son of a bitch stood here, reading off serial numbers like the equipment was the most important thing in the world. Serial numbers Shane recognized from having read them off multiple times a day every single day during the deployment. Serial numbers Shane couldn't have cared less about at the moment. "Have you visited any of our men since you've been home?"

Randall frowned and studied the clipboard. "I haven't had time since I've been back. Someone had me barred from the visitor's list. I had to go all the way to the deputy hospital commander to get access."

Shane coughed into his hand. Barring Randall was something Carponti would do. He caught himself wondering how the young sergeant might have pulled that one off. Not that he was going to confess his suspicions to Randall.

"Do you even know how many of our troops are back here?"

Randall's eyes narrowed as he studied Shane. Shane answered for him.

"Three."

"I know. I have the names right here," Randall said, tapping the paper with the end of his pen.

"You need a clipboard to account for three soldiers? Really? And that's acceptable to you as an officer? We're talking about equipment versus troops, asshole. You can replace it."

"I told you—"

Shane held up his hand and the lieutenant turned a brilliant shade of apoplectic purple. Shane leashed his temper, barely. His words came out tight and tense. Close to the breaking point. He deliberately kept his voice low. "Do you even care that we've got wounded troops back here? Or is everything always about what's important to you?"

"We can get more people. Equipment has to be manufactured, shipped—"

Shane exploded, grabbing for the lieutenant, who was just out of reach. "You self-centered, arrogant, son of a bitch! These are people's sons and daughters!"

"Sergeant—"

"Out! If you've got a problem with that, *sir,* I recommend you contact Captain Davila downrange. Because I am not talking to you and my men are not talking to you. Not until they are out of the hospital and well enough to deal with your bullshit. Go play fucking Nintendo or whatever, but get the hell out of this hospital."

"If you'd bothered to do a simple inventory, you and your *men* wouldn't be in this situation, Sergeant," Randall said, using sergeant like it was a derogatory slur of the worst sort.

"Out. Now."

Randall lifted his chin and Shane wished, oh, God, how he wished, he could take the smirk off the lieutenant's face. Permanently. "I'll be back. And when I come next time, I'm bringing the MPs. You will answer my questions, Sergeant. Wounded or not."

The door slammed like a gunshot behind him and Shane's heart pounded against his ribs. He leaned back and closed his eyes, taking slow deep breaths and praying for calm.

Trent had to be out of his damn mind sending his executive officer back here. For this? There had to be more to the story. Shane slammed his fist against the railing, frustrated and impotent. What the hell was going on downrange?

11

───────

Jen paused outside Shane's door, and hesitated for a brief moment before knocking softly. Shane's muffled voice came through the door and she pushed it open.

She didn't know how he would receive her, but she wasn't prepared for the glow in his eyes when his gaze landed on her. His entire expression softened, then instantly, the shields were back and he was the rock-hard Sergeant First Class Garrison again.

"Hi," she said quietly as she stepped into the room.

He studied her without speaking for a long moment. Too long. Jen fought the urge to squirm beneath his scrutiny. She felt the makeup against her skin and wanted to scrub the new blush from her cheeks.

"How are you feeling?" She moved closer to the bed, and pulled his chart open. She was pretending to update herself on his status, but she really just needed something to do with her hands.

It had been a week since she'd shaved him. A week since his lips had hovered a breath from hers. A week since something deep and primitive had awoken in her, refusing to be ignored. She thought she'd imagined the intensity of her emotions. She'd been wrong.

"You've been gone."

She stopped short at the possessiveness of his tone. That dark and needy something shifted and stretched inside of her again. The kiss they'd shared had been a lifetime ago, but she suddenly felt the desire to do it again. So much for perspective.

"You look different." His voice was low. Edgy.

Heat crawled up her neck. "Is that a compliment where you come from?"

She watched him flush, noting the lack of stubble lining his jaw and his newly shaved head. It made him look rough again, but no less appealing. Then she saw the electric shaver on the counter and suppressed a brief flicker of disappointment. Guess she wouldn't need to shave him again, after all. She didn't know what to do with the sharp regret that came with that thought.

He cleared his throat and rubbed his jaw. "Sorry. I, ah, was wondering where you'd been."

She watched the way his free hand picked at his hospital gown, wanting to step closer to him. No matter how good it felt being in the same room as him, he was a patient, and she knew better. Even if he professed his undying love, she knew his feelings were all tangled up in gratitude. And she needed to be professional. She snorted softly. Yeah, right.

"So, things are looking good. When's the last time someone talked to you about your chart?" she asked, looking up at him. A lot had changed in a week. There was some questionable bone setting in his left leg but his right leg was knitting together nicely.

His silence unnerved her. He sat back in the bed, simply watching her. His expression could have been carved from Kevlar, but for the vein bunching in his neck. His eyes were dark and searching and she felt exposed beneath his gaze.

"I'm sorry." His words were quiet, barely audible.

She tipped her head and returned his scrutiny. "For what?"

"Making you uncomfortable." He sniffed. "Contrary to popular belief and recent demonstrations, I don't generally behave like an asshole."

"What are you apologizing for? Yelling when you first got here? Shane, that's all part of this. You were in pain. Thank you but your apology isn't necessary."

"That's not what I'm apologizing for. I ran you off after—last week. I didn't mean to . . ." He looked away and swallowed. "It's nice seeing a friendly face. Other than Carponti."

Jen couldn't quite get her mouth to work. Her throat closed for a moment and she set the chart down. She smiled, letting some of the warmth his words inspired show through. "I wasn't avoiding you, Shane. I was in San Antonio for training at the burn center."

She'd never seen him truly embarrassed. Now she knew that there was nothing sexier than seeing this man blush. His tan skin turned a deep shade of pink as her words hung between them. She couldn't resist the grin that broke through as she leaned on the edge of his bed. "It has to be hell on your ego thinking you almost kissed a girl and she didn't come back for a week, huh?"

His lips parted a little as he tried to figure out what to say. She rested her palm against his forearm, felt the heat from his skin.

"I wouldn't avoid you, Shane." She cleared her throat, hiding the thought that avoiding him was *exactly* what she'd been doing this last week. A whole lot of good that had done her. She'd come straight back to the hospital to check on him. He shifted then, catching her hand and holding it to his chest. Beneath the cool cotton, she could feel his heart, strong and steady.

"I didn't mean to make you uncomfortable."

"That's sweet of you to say," she whispered. The sensation of his palm against her skin sent heat spiraling through her belly.

"I'm not sweet."

"Charming?"

"No."

"How would you describe yourself then?"

"Useless." He swallowed and looked away, dropping her hand abruptly. She instantly regretted teasing him. "Can we change the subject?"

"Oh, Shane." The words were out before she could stop them and instantly, his anger was back. She shut him down before he could even launch. "You're not."

"What would you know about being so friggin' useless you can't even wipe your own ass?" His voice was a growl now. The quiet moment between them was gone, replaced by awkward insecurity and his own, glaring anger directed at just one person.

Himself.

She folded her arms against her chest, barely noticing that her scars didn't pulse against her skin. "Well, since you brought it up, how would you like to get your cast off?"

HE WAS GETTING his cast off.

Cold relief prickled across his skin. He'd had broken bones before. Hell, his right arm had been broken three other times in his life. With two arms, he could maneuver his Franken legs out of the bed. With two arms, he could go to the bathroom by himself. The first order of business would be getting that tube out of his dick. Immediately wouldn't be soon enough.

Jen moved with practiced efficiency as she set the cast removal tools down on a tray near the bed. He enjoyed watching her. He would have to be dead not to appreciate the curve of her hips against her pale cotton scrubs.

She turned back to face him, pulling on her gloves. Shane felt the memory of the soft brush of her lips against his, the slide of her tongue in his mouth. He looked at her now, her smile all soft and sexy, and wished she would come close again. His new favorite smell was strawberries and vanilla.

Damn, he was pitiful.

"Ready?"

Finally, he nodded. "Yeah."

She squeezed his shoulder and fired up the saw. It was slow work as she ground the lines down his biceps then circled his elbow. The cast came away in pieces, upper arm first, followed by the lower. When she'd peeled away the last piece of plaster, Shane flexed his arm for the first time in weeks.

Back and forth. Up over his head. He threaded his fingers together and stretched as warmth spread inside him. His arm was stiff and sore. But whole. He made a fist, opened it again, his muscles stretching and protesting the now foreign movement. He felt weak. Weak but whole. It was a start.

He looked down at his two hands, turning them to look at the veins running beneath his skin. He felt like a new man with both arms free. Like some of the weight that had dragged his soul into the depths of depression was finally lifting. He looked up again and caught Jen watching him. Her gaze softened as heat unfurled in Shane's belly.

"What?" he asked.

"You should see your face."

"That bad?" He tried to lighten things up. He tried to direct her attention anywhere but at him. Because try though he might, he couldn't shake the feeling that this was too good to be true. To finally have both hands free. To be able to take care of himself. To lose some of that damned dependence he'd been forced to live with.

It had to be a dream.

"Shane?"

"Hmm?"

"You stink."

He looked at her like she'd suddenly grown two heads. His sudden laugh surprised them both, most of all Shane. His breath caught in his throat. He went deathly still. "Are you volunteering to help me clean up?"

"Don't get excited," she said dryly. "It's my job."

"Okay. Yeah." Excited wasn't quite the right word, but he wasn't about to correct her.

Jen moved around the room, setting things up for a sponge bath. As badly as he might want a shower, it wasn't possible with all the pins in his legs. And the thought of her sliding her hands over his skin was damn tempting, too. Her fingers wet and warm slipping down his chest, across his shoulders. It was the stuff of fantasies.

Maybe if he hadn't kissed her all those months ago, the thought of her touching him wouldn't be such a big deal right now. Maybe if he didn't know her taste, hadn't felt her hand resting on his stomach as his lips traced hers, heat wouldn't be trailing down his body and settling someplace very obvious. Until now, someone else had always taken care of that. Today, Jen gathered together the soap and towels. Today, Jen poured water into the basin. His body was tight with a new tension coiling through his blood.

Today, Jen was going to bathe him.

The thought was torture. Pure, blissful torture.

"You're going to need to take this off," she said, flicking her thumb over the hem of his T-shirt.

He didn't answer. Shy was not a word he'd normally use to describe himself. But damned if he wanted to take his shirt off at this moment. Hell, he spent most of his time surrounded by men, half of whom went native when they were deployed or in the field. So why did the simple act of removing his shirt—something he could now do by himself thanks to free hands and a stinted IV—cause his mouth to go dry?

It was fear. Fear that he could say or do the wrong thing and crush this fragile thing growing between them.

He wanted to feel her fingers on his skin too badly to screw this up.

He lifted the shirt over his head, wincing as stiff muscles protested. She didn't move for a long time. What was she seeing? The black tribal lines that were tattooed across his chest and down each arm? Or was she noticing the scars interwoven with those black lines, some of them fresh enough to still be red gashes in his flesh.

He waited, watching her watch him. Finally, he closed his eyes, needing to regain control of the riot inside of him.

It was a long moment before she moved. Her feet shuffled against the tile. Then he felt it. The tiny brush of her fingertip over the half-inch scar at the base of his belly button.

The scar where the docs had gone in and taken out the appendix that had damn near killed him. The more recent wounds that were still knitting together were larger. More raw. But her fingers found the old one, the one that she had found before.

He jumped at her touch and she yanked her hand away. He was faster, though, and he grabbed her hand in his. All at once the heat was gone from her eyes, replaced by something else he knew all too well. "Don't. Don't blame yourself for sending me."

Her throat bobbed. "I could have kept you here. You would have been angry, but you would have been safe."

He gripped her hand tighter. "And someone else would be sitting here instead. Someone who might have had kids who loved him or a wife who actually gave a damn about him. It's better this way."

She didn't respond. Shane refused to release her hand. That simple human connection felt so right and it was the only thing anchoring him to this moment.

"How can you say that?"

"Because it's true."

"It's not true. You have a family, right?"

He snorted. "My mom's an alcoholic who spends all her time in truck stops up in Kansas, and I have no clue who my father is."

"There are other people who care about you, Shane," she whispered.

"Not really." He sniffed. "The one person who was supposed to care gave up, too. It's better this way," he repeated, as though saying it again would make it true.

He waited for her to speak, but she didn't. Instead, she reached for the sponge and Shane braced himself for the shock of cold water. The other nurses never managed to keep it warm, but when Jen dribbled the water over his newly released shoulder, he was surprised to find it not just warm, but hot.

A bath was a shameless excuse to have her hands on him. To feel her cool fingers running over his skin through the warm water.

He closed his eyes. Her fingers slid across his back and heat followed her gentle touch. She slipped the washcloth up his neck and he shivered.

"Sorry. Thought the water was warmer than that." She hadn't even started on his chest yet.

"It's fine," he managed, not wanting her to take her hands away for any reason.

She studied him quietly for a moment, then traced her hands down his chest, her fingers running over the maze of scars that marked his skin. Each one of them represented a failure. He hadn't been quick enough to keep Zublow from dying on the battlefield. He'd been too arrogant to wait for air support before he tried to rescue Widget. He hadn't pulled Ross from the kill zone fast enough. Somehow, the weight of those failures seemed a little less heavy as she ran her soapy hands over his skin.

She adjusted the bed and had him sit all the way forward so she could spread towels beneath him. She leaned across him, the heat from her body radiating into his, and dragged the warm, wet cloth down his jaw. He closed his eyes, enjoying the warm caress of her fingers on his skin. *Bathing patients is a normal thing for a nurse to do.* He clenched his fists, his lungs suddenly tight. He was jealous. Jealous that any other man had ever had her hands on him.

He captured her hand, rubbing her wet fingers between his. "Jen—"

He didn't care that she was a nurse and he, her patient. He wanted *her*. This beautiful, stubborn woman who touched him and made him feel like a man instead of an invalid. Her heart-shaped mouth was so close. Her lips parted.

Warm water dribbled down his chest, cooling as it slid over him. He stroked her palm, making small circles with his thumb. Her mouth drew him and held him mesmerized. Just one taste and he'd let her go.

Neither was prepared for the door to slam open like a cannon. Or to see Carponti staring at them like he'd just found Jimmy Hoffa's body.

IF JEN HAD EVER WISHED she could disappear, now was that moment. Carponti's grin was as wide as the Cheshire Cat's. Had he walked in on anyone other than Jen herself, she might have laughed with him. Instead, she felt like a guilty teenager.

"I'll, ah, wait outside," Carponti said, jerking his thumb over his shoulder. For the first time since Shane had known him, he didn't slam the door.

It took Jen all of a hot second to realize that Shane still had her hand captured against his chest. She was starting to enjoy this habit he was developing. A little too much.

"Shane—"

"Don't pull away. Please."

"Then let go."

She could feel his heartbeat beneath her palm. Strong and steady, she could imagine her cheek resting there instead. Just lying still and listening to his heartbeat. It was such a small desire.

She was hot and she was bothered and she needed to escape from Shane before she exploded.

"Thank you. For everything." He looked like he wanted to say more, but she stopped him. She didn't bother to fight the blush that crept up her cheeks.

"It's the least I can do." She smiled slightly. "Let go. Vic is outside waiting and you're almost naked."

He shook his head and refused to let her hand go free. "You're amazing, you know that?"

"That's nice of you to say." The moment was gone. She looked at him now, and just saw a patient who was grateful to regain a little more of the life he'd had before he got hurt. She tugged her hand free and cleaned up the remnants of his bath.

SHE DREADED the thought of leaving the room and walking by Vic Carponti. She kept her head down when she finally did leave, and she refused to make eye contact when she passed him in the hallway. Her hand burned where it had rested against Shane's chest. She balled her fist as though she could capture the memory of Shane's heartbeat inside of it.

It took all of ten minutes for her cell phone to ring.

"So I hear you gave the patient a happy ending to his bath?" Nicole asked.

"That was fast." Jen sighed. "Would it do me any good to lie?"

"Nope."

"Well, I'll say this, Carponti certainly has an active imagination."

"Ah, so something did happen. I knew it. Spill." The glee in Nicole's voice was contagious. Not so much so that Jen wanted to actually have this conversation, but still.

"Nothing happened. I took Shane's cast off. He was a little overwhelmed to have both of his hands back."

He had been more than overwhelmed. He'd been stunned into silence, and the way he'd looked at her, she'd have thought she'd conquered space instead of just cutting off his cast.

For that brief moment, Jen had forgotten about the scar slicing across her chest. For that brief moment, she'd felt desired and beautiful. She'd believed him when he told her she was amazing.

Reality had a way of crashing down on her, though—of reminding her that Shane would be leaving the hospital one day. How likely was it that he'd want anything to do with her after that? He'd probably just find someone else.

"Nicole, will you stop? Nothing happened."

"Uh-huh. Obviously I'm going to have to beat it out of you. I'll be at your house for dinner tonight at six p.m. sharp. I'm bringing food and Laura."

"Nicole, it won't kill us if we don't get together tonight. I'm tired."

"Honey, I might kill one of the neighborhood kids if I have to stay in another night. Besides, Laura needs a break."

"What's your husband doing?"

"Apparently he has duty, so he'll be sitting at a desk all night."

Jen sighed, unable to generate a single good excuse for why she wanted to beg off girls' night. "Would it help if I said I had laundry all over my living room?"

"No."

"Not letting me out of this, are you?"

"Nope." She could practically hear Nicole's grin through the phone. "I'm going to ply you with alcohol to get the details about Shane."

Jen rolled her eyes again. "*Nothing* happened."

"Uh-huh." They hung up and Jen tried to come up with a rational explanation for what Carponti "thought" he'd seen. Maybe she could suggest he was on drugs.

She was so screwed.

12

———

"Where's a good place to hide a body around here?" The door slammed open like a gunshot. Shane held his breath and waited for his heart to stop slamming against his ribs. Carponti stood at the foot of his bed, his face red beneath the beard he refused to shave. Again.

"Who are we killing?" Every six months or so, Carponti lost his cool. The guy might be a smart-ass but he was just as quick to get pissed off as he was to laugh. The problem was that he was less diplomatic than Shane. Which wasn't saying much at all.

"Randall. He just cornered me at the duty desk and tried to question me about the missing equipment."

"Doesn't sound like a reason for killing him."

"He accused me of dereliction of duty. Hell, I'm not even supposed to *be* on duty." Carponti snorted. "He can derelict my balls."

Shane tried not to laugh. "Did he read you your rights?"

"He started to, but I walked off. " Carponti paced the tiny space, his thumb tapping against his thigh. "I'm just covering for one of the guys as a favor so he can take his wife out for their anniversary. Because, you know, we haven't all missed out on enough of those over the years."

Carponti sank into the visitor's chair. Shane watched how he cradled his bandaged arm against his stomach. Other than that one subtle movement, he seemed completely fine. "What do we do about that damned lieutenant?"

"I don't know. I don't trust him. I never have. And I can't get ahold of Trent—Captain Davila—downrange to find out what's going on." It frustrated him to no end that every time he tried to dial the number of Trent's orderly room—the military equivalent of an office—he got a dead tone. Shane knew the number worked. At least, it had before he'd been evacuated out of theater and shipped home. Why was there such complete silence from Trent downrange? He knew the whole battalion couldn't be in blackout communications for this damn long, so the lack of contact was driving Shane to distraction.

"We need to figure it out, though, because the little weasel said he wants to find Osterman."

"Osterman isn't in any condition to be hassled by Randall on a good day. Unless he's getting his head straight? Is he in combat stress therapy or anything?"

"Not that I've seen. The kid just mopes through his physical therapy sessions. He sits and stares at his bandaged leg like it's the end of the world or something." Carponti held up his arm. "It's not. At least he doesn't have to learn to jerk off with his off hand."

"Second time you've mentioned that." Shane choked back a laugh. "I still don't care."

"You should be sensitive to my feelings. It hurts that you don't care about my problems," Carponti said, faking a wounded expression.

"Focus on the matter at hand."

"Oh, ha-ha-ha." Carponti chucked a towel at Shane, who slapped it down. "Since there aren't any good places for hiding bodies around here, do you have a better plan for dealing with Randall?"

"You tell him you'll talk to him but reserve the right to invoke your Article Thirty-One rights at any time. Keep copies of everything that you give him. I wouldn't put it past him to forge a sworn statement. I told Trent he might have been falsifying the sensitive items reports."

"Really?"

"Yeah."

"Plot thickens, huh? What's up with officers these days? They don't make 'em like they used to." Carponti kicked his feet up onto the edge of Shane's bed.

Shane reached down and shoved them off. "Guys like Randall are the exception. They don't make it much further than captain, and that's a good thing."

"Ah, you're forgetting that Randall's daddy is a brigade commander up at Fort Carson," Carponti said, propping his feet up again. "But anyway, changing the subject. What's up with you and Jen St. James?"

Here we go. "How do you know her?"

"Score one for avoiding the question," Carponti said, making a tick in the air. "She's a friend of my wife's. Apparently, they're doing some bizarre female thing tonight over at Jen's house because I'm on duty."

"What kind of female thing?" He captured a mental image of Jen leaning into a mirror, swiping lip gloss over her bottom lip. His body tightened and he shifted. He didn't need Carponti to think he was giving him a hard-on.

"No idea. Toenails or something. My point, however, is this—if you don't spill the beans, I'll get the info from my wife."

"Look, she's just doing her job. There's nothing to tell." That had to be the worst dodge in history, but maybe he'd get lucky and throw Carponti off the scent. He didn't want to dig into his personal life right now. Or ever.

"That didn't look like nothing," Carponti commented. Shane grunted and turned the TV on. Of course, Carponti smelled weakness. Fuck. "And the fact that she's cute as hell doesn't hurt, does it?"

"That's got nothing to do with it."

"Sure. You haven't had sex in how long? I mean, your wife moved out almost six months before we left. Your dick has to be pretty pissed at you right now. Have you even—"

"My dick isn't any of your business. My personal life isn't, either. Drop it."

"Well, aren't we touchy." Carponti stood and stretched. "Guess I'll just have to get the story from my wife." He made an exaggerated yawn. "Later."

Carponti was gone before Shane knew it, leaving him with uncomfortable thoughts of Jen and his dick. Damn it, why did Carponti have to plant that visual? He did like her. His imagination was having his way with her at the moment and he closed his eyes, needing to banish the images from his brain. He was going to hell for the way he was thinking about her now.

Because his imagination had her naked, her hips spread across his lap as she rode them both over the edge and into paradise.

~

"I'VE GOT THE WINE," Nicole announced, as she walked into Jen's living room and sank into the old couch that Jen refused to throw away.

The brown-and-white-striped sofa had been the most comfortable place for her to sleep when she'd been recovering from chemo. Laura had tried to convince her to get rid of all the things even remotely associated with her sickness, but she'd refused to part with the couch. She was funny that way.

"The two weeks a year my in-laws relieve me of my parenting duties are the only grown-up time I get." Laura sank into the couch next to her, curling her feet beneath her. "I think I love my in-laws more than my husband sometimes. What are we watching?"

"*Sweet Home Alabama*. I'm on a Reese Witherspoon kick right now and if Vic has to sit through one more showing of *Legally Blonde,* he swears he'll divorce me." Nicole wandered back into the kitchen barefoot to grab some wineglasses, and started pouring a glass for each of them.

"Really?"

She shrugged as she handed out the drinks. "No. I never complain when he wants to watch *Dune* for the thousandth time, but every Reese Witherspoon movie ever made? You'd have thought I was cutting off one of his limbs."

Jen, who'd just taken a sip of her wine, choked. "*Dune*?"

"Oh, not the remake. The original version. He calls one of his lieutenants a Harkonan."

Jen laughed and wished she didn't know that calling someone a Harkonan was just like calling them a Napoleon. Only significantly less flattering.

"Which lieutenant?" Laura asked.

"Which one do you think?"

"Randall?"

"Got it in one." Nicole snapped her fingers, and sipped her wine. Jen was suddenly aware that both of her friends were staring at her. Waiting.

"So I take it Shane liked the new look?" Laura said finally.

Heat crept up her neck. "I don't suppose it would help if I pretended not to know what you're talking about?"

"Nuh-uh. Nice try, though." Nicole shook her head and cupped her chin in her palm. "To hear Vic tell it, you were dry humping with the door wide open. I figured he was exaggerating."

Jen opened her mouth to speak, but Laura cut her off before she'd even drawn a breath. "So you were in a compromising position today." Laura's eyes widened. "Can we define compromising? You weren't in his lap or anything, were you? 'Cause I would be really impressed if you *were* in his lap."

"No. Nothing that exciting." It was so much more than that. How could she explain the delicious sensation of his skin beneath her fingers? Or the strong, steady beat of his heart against her palm? "It's just he . . ."

It wasn't just desire or lust. It was as intense as it was private. It was something more. At least it was to her.

"He . . . ?" Laura prompted.

"His emotions are just all mixed up with gratitude because I've been taking care of him. That's all."

"That's not what Vic says he saw," Nicole said. She tipped her wineglass up and drained the contents, then topped it off.

"Vic walked in on the tail end of a bath," Jen snapped. "Not so unusual in my line of work."

"Touchy, aren't we?" Laura studied her over the edge of her wineglass.

"Can we just start the movie? Nothing happened."

"But something would have if Vic hadn't interrupted," Nicole said.

Exasperation crept into Jen's voice. "I don't know. Why is this such a big deal?"

"The big deal, m'dear, is that you've been acting like the world ended when you got sick," Laura said. "The fact that Shane has broken through your shell is significant progress. I might just have to give him some pointers on how to get you into bed." Her eyes sparkled wickedly and Jen threw a pillow at her, even as a laugh escaped.

"Are we watching a movie or not?"

Laura filled up Jen's glass. "A toast first. To you."

"To taking chances on the good guys," Nicole said.

Jen stayed silent, clinking her glass with those of her friends. She was taking a chance. A small one. Even if it led to nothing, the feelings Shane inspired inside her were worth holding on to.

They broke up Nicole's Reese glom and decided on *City of Angels* instead. It wasn't long before Jen blinked back tears. Meg Ryan's character sat in a stairwell, constantly replaying the decisions she'd made in surgery, wishing she could have somehow saved her patient. She didn't know an angel stood in front of her. Even if she *had* known, she still wouldn't have stopped feeling guilty. Jen sipped her wine. It was all too easy to picture Shane sitting in that stairwell, arguing with the angel who had taken one of his men. Demanding that the angel take Shane instead.

She remembered what he'd said about his mother, how she wasn't really in his life. Had anyone ever worried about Shane the man, rather than just Shane the soldier? What had his injuries done to him emotionally? Had he even considered what the rest of his life would be like? And what if he never healed enough to return to the fight? Would he accept a life behind a desk instead of leading troops? What would that do to a man like him? As Jen fell into sleep that night, she wondered if he was capable of loving anyone aside from his soldiers. Could he ever devote his life to something other than his men?

He raced toward the burning vehicle at a dead sprint. One of his boys was pinned beneath it, struggling to break free from the approaching flames. As Shane closed the distance, he saw that the soldier's arm was stuck, wedged between the door and the Humvee. He kept running, but until he closed that final gap, he couldn't see who was trapped through the smoke.

The soldier turned toward Shane, revealing his face.

Carponti grinned in Shane's direction. "Hey, Sarn't G! Watch this!" Carponti grabbed his M4, his arm suddenly free, and put the barrel in his mouth—

Shane exploded awake, every vein in his body throbbing in time with his racing heart. Carponti's blood burned against his brain and Shane gouged his fingers into his eyes, trying to scrub the horrible sight from his memory. Shame threatened to choke him when he saw that his fingers were trembling.

Carponti. Why the hell was he dreaming about Carponti? What was wrong with him?

The door to his hospital room slammed open. "Speak of the devil," Shane muttered as Carponti strolled in, his bandaged arm held against his stomach.

"What the hell are you doing asleep at this hour? It's past lunch. Get up. We're playing spades." Carponti slammed a deck of cards onto the little rolling table that was positioned next to Shane's bed, and lowered one of the bed's rails. "You can move those sorry excuses for legs or I can, but I'm sitting down."

"Don't be such a dickhead." Shane frowned. If there was any hint that his dream held even a fragment of truth . . . Hell, what could he say? *Hey, man, you okay? I know you lost an arm and all—* He seemed fine. So why couldn't Shane convince his subconscious that he was? "In case you forgot, these things are still a pain in the ass to move."

"Boo hoo. At least you've still got ten fingers and ten toes. Well, somewhere in there anyway. Ready?" Carponti positioned his good hand and his bandaged arm against Shane's hips.

It wasn't like moving his legs was something new. Daily, the nurses and physical therapy interns came in and moved them for him. Lifting, stretching, and sending brilliant, exploding pain radiating throughout his body. But if the hell of therapy meant he didn't get any blood clots or more infections, so be it. They kept saying his legs were healing, but it wasn't fast enough for Shane. He wanted out of this goddamned bed and back on his feet. There was too much work to do and he wasn't getting any of it done sitting on his ass.

Together, they lifted Shane's legs gently and eased them over, creating space for Carponti to sit. Shane hissed in a breath and held it, bracing for the pain that would come from moving his legs. For once, Carponti wasn't a bull in a china closet.

"You can't play spades with just two people."

"Sure you can. You just lack imagination." Carponti pushed the deck toward Shane. "I haven't figured out how to shuffle the deck, though. You're going to have to do that. No cheating."

Shane spread the cards out between them, dividing the deck in half. Carponti swore as he struggled to pick up the cards Shane had tossed toward him. "Shit, this was a terrible idea," he muttered.

"Here." Shane pushed the cards into a stack and handed them to him. "Other than not being able to shuffle cards, how are you doing with all of this?" Better to name the elephant than beat around the bush.

Carponti shrugged and began peeling one card at a time off the top of the deck. "I'm fine. Nicole is kind of freaked out about the whole thing. But shit, it's not like my dick got blown off. I'd probably have killed myself if TC hadn't made it home."

"TC?"

"Thundercock."

"Who the hell names their own dick Thundercock?"

"My wife. I'm lucky like that."

Shane choked. He couldn't even pretend he'd taken a drink of water. "You lost a hand and you're worried about your dick?"

"Sure. I mean, we could cuddle all day long but if I didn't have my dick, she'd probably end up fucking the UPS guy."

"Nicole would never do that to you," Shane said. He picked up the cards and flipped them together. The sensation of the cards slapping against his fingertips was something simple. Something real.

Something Shane had taken for granted.

"This sucks." Carponti swore and laughed as some of the cards fell out of his hand. "We should take a picture of the two of us and send it back to the guys. Two fucking gimps trying to play cards. They'd laugh their asses off." He slapped an ace of spades on the table. "Besides, I know Nikki would never cheat on me. I was simply pointing out that the important equipment made it home."

Guess that was the end of that sensitive moment. Shane took the hint as relief prickled over his skin. "Does she still like her job with CID?"

"She loves it. They have her working on some missing weapons cases here on base. CID thinks it's linked with organized crime out of Dallas and she has to work with the feds, but she's doing great."

Shane sighed, glad that Carponti was talking at least a little bit. "How're you sleeping?"

Carponti shrugged and swore as he dropped two more cards onto the sheet covering Shane's legs. "I don't. At least not well. They gave me some pretty powerful sleeping pills, but if I plan on waking up the next morning, I can't take them . . . Not if I've already taken my pain pills. I almost made it through the entire series of *Sopranos*. Only a few episodes left."

Shane scratched his neck with the cards. "I haven't slept for shit since I've been home, either. Fucking nightmares." He couldn't tell Carponti about his horrible dream. Just the thought of whispering the dreams out loud sent a creeping sensation down Shane's spine. A fleeting shadow trailed across Carponti's eyes. Just a hint and then it was gone again.

Shane frowned as he said, "How much *do* you sleep a night?"

"Couple hours at a shot. It sucks because I'm always drifting off right as it's time to get up for PT. And Nikki won't let me miss a single appointment."

Once upon a time, PT had meant physical *training* to them. Now that acronym stood for physical *therapy*. He used to enjoy PT, running down Battalion Avenue, the rhythmic sound of cadence vibrating off his ribs as formations ran by. Now? Now PT was just one more thing to endure. One more thing that had changed in both of their lives. Silence stretched between them as they sorted their cards.

Carponti tossed his hand onto the table, face up. "You were right, this was a stupid idea. I'll bring checkers next time. Maybe Connect Four or Chutes and Ladders. Remember that game? I ought to be able to manage that."

Shane shrugged and tapped the cards together, returning them to their box. The image of Carponti with the rifle barrel in his mouth burned against his retinas. The words were out before he could stop them. "Are you talking to someone?"

"What's there to talk about?" Carponti frowned, his mouth pulling down into a tight line beneath the red beard as he took the cards from Shane.

Shane dragged his hand over his face. "You know, about adjusting and all that."

"That's really rich coming from someone who hasn't gotten out of bed in six weeks. I thought you knew me better than that." Irritation snapped across Carponti's face—sudden anger clouding his features. He threw the pack of cards at Shane's chest. "Fuck you. Psychoanalyze someone else."

The door slammed behind him, leaving Shane alone with the awkward embarrassment of his thoughts. Maybe he was the one who needed to talk to someone. Who was he kidding? He *was* having a hard time. Nothing in his life had prepared him to be so dependent on others. He'd fended for himself for as long as he could remember because his mom hadn't been there for him at all. Shane had joined the Army when he'd been a senior in high school, leaving behind the trailer park and all of his mother's random men.

Even in Ranger School when he'd broken his leg, he hadn't really been dependent. Being forced to sit out on the training had sucked, but it hadn't been anything like this, where he needed help taking a piss. Oh wait, he couldn't do that because of that fucking tube they insisted on leaving in his dick.

He grunted and scrubbed his face with his hand, the stubble on his chin itching like there was no tomorrow. "Oh fuck."

He'd forgotten. How the hell had he forgotten that his catheter was coming out today? He had deliberately avoided thinking about what came next. Oh, he wanted the damn tube out of his dick, but the part where Jen wrapped her hand around his cock and . . . No, he couldn't think about that. Please let it be someone else. Somehow it would be less humiliating if it was a complete stranger handling his goods.

He closed his eyes as the image took form in his mind, the faintest hint of fantasy attached to it. His blood was pounding. He was afraid to look down and see if he'd pitched a tent in his pants. Between the drugs and the catheter, he wasn't even sure he could get an erection anymore, but he damn sure didn't want to test that theory today.

He could deal with this. It was just a medical procedure, right? No big deal.

It was a very big deal.

Because Jen wasn't just some nurse. At some point between their long-ago kiss and her constant tending to him, she'd stopped being just a nurse and had become something so much more. She was someone he missed when she wasn't around. Someone he wanted to wrap in his arms and protect. He couldn't pinpoint the moment it had happened and there wasn't a damn thing he could do about it. He had nothing to offer. No home. No way to find one until he was out of the hospital. Hell, he couldn't even walk on his own.

It didn't mean he didn't care.

It just meant she was even more off-limits than she'd ever been before. It also meant he needed to find a way to get things back to being strictly business. Even though that was the last thing he wanted.

He closed his eyes and tried to remember how she'd looked that day in the gym. The day he'd convinced her to let him deploy. Funny, he could try all day long, but he couldn't remember how she'd looked. All he kept seeing was her now. Her sparkling green eyes, her soft blond hair.

Her soft hands and gentle touch.

He groaned and glanced at his lap. Guess that mystery was solved. He was rock hard.

Just in time for a knock on the door.

Shit.

13

______

J en stopped outside Shane's door and wiped her hands on her scrubs. Today he was getting his catheter out—bringing him one step farther on the road to recovery. Unfortunately, she was going to have to be the one to do it . . . and the task loomed before her like a giant . . . the thought of anything giant turned her thoughts in a decidedly unprofessional direction. She'd avoided Shane's room for as long as possible, but now it was time.

She hadn't been able to stop thinking about touching him. She'd woken abruptly last night from a dream about him. Bedpans and catheters were not, as a rule, sexy in any way, shape, or form. But in her dream, she'd lowered the sheet that covered his legs to find him aroused. And things had gone further than she'd ever dreamed of going in real life.

The thought of his penis in her hand had nothing at all to do with medicine and everything do to with Shane. She tried to think of it as a simple medical procedure. Except that it wasn't just any penis. It was *Shane's* penis she'd be holding. And she was going to have her *real* hands on his *real* flesh as soon as she stopped being a chicken and walked into his room.

She'd intubated him all those weeks ago, and hadn't had any difficulty then. There was something more intense, more difficult about touching him now. She tried to relax, but her stomach kept twisting into knots as she walked into his room. Nerves and something else.

Something *more* that she was afraid to acknowledge. His expression was tense even as his lips formed a pained half smile. She nodded in greeting as she set the catheter kit down and laid out the equipment. He was a big man, and she needed to get him positioned properly for the procedure.

"After this, we're going to start getting you outside for fresh air and regular exercise. The docs are reviewing your file, but you should be ready to go home in a few more days, tops." The muscles in his neck were corded tight, and his jaw was set. He turned his face toward the window. She deliberately avoided looking at his lap, but that didn't stop the heat from crawling across her cheeks. Damn her subconscious for planting that suggestive seed in her mind.

"Are you okay?" He turned toward her, and something in his dark gaze made her breath hitch. He'd looked at her like that once before. Just once, when he'd held her palm to his chest.

She wanted him to touch her again. She could admit that to herself, even if she'd die before saying it out loud. She sighed softly, and her body trembled with awareness of Shane.

"Is this going to hurt?" His words were soft and thick, and they slid across Jen's skin like warm cream. He cleared his throat.

"It'll probably hurt for a few days," she said. "Maybe a little burning. But we'll manage it. Just like we have been." Small talk when she was edging dangerously close to a full-blown panic attack? Great. Her cheeks burned hot, and she sucked in a deep breath. She could do this.

Yeah, right.

"Guess this would be a bad time for dick jokes?" he said weakly.

Any words she might have said got stuck in her throat. She tried to smile, but didn't quite manage. Instead she cleared her throat.

"Okay, so here we go." She washed her hands in the sink, and refused to look at him as she snapped on first one blue latex glove, then the other.

She could have sworn he groaned as he covered his face with one hand and nodded. She placed a sterile pad on his lap, looking only as much as was necessary to get it into place. She positioned the second sterile pad that would encircle his genitals and unsnapped one side of his hospital gown. He may have started wearing T-shirts yesterday, but pants were still out of the question until . . . well, until the catheter was out. She pulled back the pad covering his lap, prepared to pull his penis through the opening, clean him, and remove the catheter.

Shane's body had other ideas.

She cleared her throat and felt her cheeks flame even hotter. He'd been flaccid and barely conscious when she'd inserted the catheter. He was fully erect now. . . . The medical fact that this probably had nothing to do with her didn't stop a slow burn of warm heat through her veins. A simple procedure had morphed into something else with so much more. . . .

His very real erection stood in the room between them, like an unwanted uncle at the family reunion.

"Shit," he mumbled. His face was bright red. It must have matched hers.

She couldn't do this with him erect, even though she knew it was medically possible. She couldn't *touch* him. Not like this. Not with her dream pounding through her brain in time with the beat of her heart. She cleared her throat again and wondered why it was suddenly so hard to swallow.

"We have a couple of options. We can wait. I can get some ice water, or you can, um, thump it a couple of times to make it stop."

"Can't you just get it over with?" The sheer horror on his face was almost enough to make her laugh. But the urge to touch him consumed every ounce of her willpower.

She nodded and bit both lips, hoping the pain would distract her from the desire singing in her blood. He covered his face again as she reached for him.

Heat pulsed through the thin material of her gloves. His erection was solid and heavy and her hand only covered a portion of him.

In her dream, she had slid her bare hand down his erection in a slow stroke. Liquid heat rushed between her thighs even as she stomped on the fantasy and focused on the task, ahem, at hand.

She'd never had so much trouble removing a catheter in her life. She drained the sterile fluid that kept the catheter in place. Then she peeled the tape from his abdomen that had secured the tube. She finally pulled the tube free and covered his lap. His erection forced the sterile cloth into a tent.

Jen left him to adjust his clothes. She didn't think she'd be able to do that right now without torturing them both. She needed to put space between them before she burst into flames.

There was a medical explanation for his body's reaction. It had nothing to do with her.

But a whisper of promise slid behind her as she left his room.

What if it did?

14

Jen needed coffee. Her shift ended in exactly three minutes and she needed to escape. The floor. The patient in room twenty-six. And more importantly, the patient's penis. She flushed as she ordered her coffee and tried to think of anything that didn't involve Shane's dick. Five hours had passed since the "incident" and still she flushed at the barest thought of it.

She looked up as the hospital's main door swung open. Nicole smiled and leaned against the kiosk's tiny counter while Jen dumped sugar and creamer into her coffee. Her smile was positively wicked and Jen groaned, bracing. She couldn't know. Could she?

"I hear Shane had a small erection problem."

Jen muffled a horrified laugh, releasing some of the tension that was wound up inside of her. "How did you hear about that?"

"Vic caught Shane thumping it earlier today."

Jen closed her eyes as her face flamed hot again. She hadn't found the courage to go back into his room for the rest of her shift, and the idea that Carponti had caught Shane thumping it *hours later* meant . . . she didn't really want to think about what that might have meant. Maybe he was just an easily aroused kind of guy. "Can we not have this conversation here?" Jen asked as she tucked her hair behind her ear.

"Can't think of a better place to have this conversation. Except maybe a locker room." Nicole sighed and rubbed her forehead with her index finger, as though she was trying to relieve a headache, her words lighter than her mood. "Okay, so there's a reason I'm here that has nothing to do with Shane's penis."

"Nikki, what's wrong?" Any lingering worry or anxiety faded in the face of her friend's very real struggle to get the words out.

Nicole cleared her throat after a long moment. "So, Vic has all these pills, right? He has like six different bottles of pain pills, two sleeping pills, and one or two for anxiety or something. All kinds of good stuff."

She followed Nicole outside toward the stone benches and away from the crowded tables. Jen stirred her coffee in silence, her own problems seeming distant and trivial as her friend spoke. Nicole searched the ceiling for the rest of her words.

"I sometimes catch him lining up his bottles and mumbling to himself. I can't keep track of everything he's supposed to take because he won't let his doc give me any kind of schedule."

"And you need to know what he should be taking to keep him from messing up a dose?"

"Bingo." Nicole's eyes lit up like Jen just told her the meaning of life. "Can I bring you a list of everything so you can help me figure it out?"

"You don't have any idea what he takes or when?"

Nicole shook her head. "No. He doesn't really bring it up, so other than what's on the bottles, I'm kind of in the dark."

"Why won't he tell you?"

"He doesn't like to talk about it. Seriously, I mean. He'll crack jokes all day long, but when I try asking about the meds, he just makes another joke and changes the subject."

"So you have no idea what he takes on a daily basis." Worry slid around Jen's heart and squeezed.

"No."

"Okay, you need to find out. I can't tell you anything without knowing what he's currently taking. So you're going to have to make him tell you."

Nicole pushed a hard breath through her pursed lips. "I was afraid of that."

"You really think he'll give you grief if you insist on knowing?"

Never in a million years would Jen have thought that Nicole would have a hard time talking to her husband about anything.

"No. I think he'll make a damn joke and dodge the question and I won't be any closer to finding out. Hell, at this rate, I'm lucky I know when his physical therapy appointments are."

"Everyone processes trauma differently. The fact that he's making jokes is pretty normal for him, right?" Nicole nodded. "Maybe it's his way of coping in the short term, and that's okay. But he'll have to deal with it eventually."

Jen had heard almost the exact same words from Laura once. Her friend had practically stripped her bare and forced her to look in the mirror. Jen didn't look at her scar often, but when she did, she still felt the same revulsion she'd experienced that first time. And the second time. And the third.

She hated it, but she'd decided early on that she didn't want to have more surgery to fix it. It was part of who she was now and she couldn't—*wouldn't*—change that. Just because she'd made that decision, though, didn't mean she was completely at peace with it.

"I'll try to figure out what he's taking, and when. Can I call you when I think I've got it?" Nicole asked.

If Shane knew about Nicole's concerns, he'd worry, too. But maybe Carponti had talked to him about all of this. She'd have to figure out how to bring it up without alarming him unnecessarily.

"Thanks so much." Nicole surprised her with a quick, energetic hug. "By the way, Vic asked me to suggest that you bathe Shane more often."

"Will you stop?" Heat flushed down her neck, but Jen couldn't help laughing. "Shane's hygiene is not an issue."

"I'm sure that's exactly what my husband was referring to," Nicole said dryly.

"Are you done?"

"Almost." Nicole stood and offered a hand to pull Jen up. "Look, I'm going to completely butt in where you haven't asked me to so here goes. I think Shane is one of the best men I know." She breathed deeply. "Now I'm done. And I'm leaving before you throw something at me."

Jen took a deep gulp of coffee after Nicole left. The possibility that Shane *might* feel something for her teased at the edge of her memory.

If it *was* something more, she knew that a man like Shane wouldn't be content with what she was comfortable giving. He'd tear down all of her barriers. She wasn't ready for that. Not yet. And she couldn't stand the thought that if he did strip her bare, he might look at her differently when he saw the whole picture.

The idea of his pity curdled in her belly.

"You're sure Osterman's going to be in PT today?" Shane asked, eyeing the wheelchair that sat near the foot of his bed.

"Yes, I'm sure. Now get in the damn chair," Carponti said.

"Give me a hand."

"Nice." Carponti narrowed his eyes and flipped Shane the middle finger. "Real mature." He broke out laughing. "Took you long enough to start giving me shit. 'Bout damn time. Come on."

Carponti moved to the side of the bed and slid his arm beneath Shane's shoulders. It was damned difficult to get him from the bed to the chair without jarring his legs, but somehow they managed.

"Grab me a sheet, will you?" Shane asked. He looked down at the metal pins and frames that lined his flesh. His legs jutted straight out in front of him. He held his breath and turned his head, looking anywhere but at the freak show that were his legs.

For once, Carponti didn't argue. Instead he snapped the sheet over Shane and let it drift down until it hid his legs.

"Let's go find Osterman. Maybe you can knock some sense into him," Carponti said as he pushed the automatic door button.

Shane struggled to maneuver the wheelchair out of the room and the automatic door swung closed before he'd made it three feet. He'd never questioned why every door in the hospital was automatic before, but right now, it irritated the hell out of him.

"Man you suck. How hard can it be to drive one of these things?" Carponti mumbled behind him.

"It's not as easy as it looks, dickhead."

"You've never sucked so bad at something. This is awesome." Carponti palmed the automatic door button a second time and pushed Shane through. Faster than Shane was comfortable going, but he wasn't about to argue. Carponti was liable to push him into a wall just for laughs. "I've got to take pictures and send them to the boys in Iraq. They'll get a kick out of this."

He was damn glad to be out of that bed. It was strange being outside of his hospital room after all these weeks, but the rest of the hospital wasn't all that different. It had the same sterile smell. The same beige walls. The same faces hustling here and there with trays of pills, equipment, and overflowing file folders.

What struck him most about his first trip from his room was how he found himself scanning the faces of the nurses, searching for one person in particular. Despite the embarrassment of the whole catheter fiasco, he wanted nothing more than to see Jen. After the long hours she'd spent caring for him, it felt wrong to take this first trip out of his hospital bed without her.

He didn't see her. He should have been relieved after what had happened between them the other morning, but instead he felt a longing. He missed her. And damn him, he wanted to know when he'd see her next. He couldn't stand not knowing if she was embarrassed or irritated or what.

Despite Carponti rambling on behind him as they wound through the corridors, he kept replaying the scene over and over again in his head. The one where her hand was wrapped around his hard cock, him wishing like hell that it was for any reason other than a medical one.

"You're going to have to do something about that little obsession you've got going on." Carponti's voice intruded on Shane's self-flagellation.

"What obsession?"

"The one with my wife's friend. Since when did you turn into such a pussy when it came to women? I mean, I know your wife took everything in the divorce, but did she take your balls, too?"

"Wow, that is really none of your damn business."

"Sure it is. Your sex life—or lack thereof—is a key component of your mental health. Since you decided to psychoanalyze me, I'm returning the favor. And as your counselor, I'm recommending that you find a way to get her into bed. It'll do you both a world of good."

"Are you high?"

"Not nearly enough," Carponti said with a grin. "But whatever is going on, you need to get on with it or I'm going to think you lost your balls, too."

Any other time, Carponti's smart-ass remarks might have been a welcome distraction from the weight of his thoughts. Today they were too heavy. And the closer they got to physical therapy, the heavier they got. He'd never been at a loss for words with his men, but the thought of seeing Osterman ran every thought from his brain. As they approached the physical therapy room, Shane was scrambling for something to say that wouldn't make him sound like a douche bag.

Guess he'd start with hi and go from there.

"Holy shit, man, I've been in your platoon since I was a private and I've never seen you this indecisive," Carponti said. "Except maybe that time outside Fallujah when I rescued those puppies."

Shane laughed at the memory and some of the anxiety filling his lungs drained out. They'd been in a perimeter defense position for two days and it had been close to a hundred and twenty degrees in the shade. All Shane could smell was balls and friggin' dirt. And then along came Carponti, crawling through the dust along the length of the barrier with three mottled puppies sticking out of his assault pack.

"You're lucky you didn't get rabies."

"Or court-martialed. Remember how pissed LT Randall was over that? I still can't believe he ordered them to be put down."

Shane sobered at the memory. The whole platoon had been ready to mutiny over the order. General Order Number One, though, forbade pets or mascots. Then brand-new lieutenant Randall had insisted that the puppies either be shot or abandoned.

"I wonder if that Iraqi guy kept them as pets or ate them?"

Shane sighed and rubbed his eyes. "I'm gonna continue to believe he kept them as pets. I'm not going to let you ruin that little fantasy."

"Speaking of fantasies . . . "

Shane looked up and saw Jen walking toward them. The moment she saw him, her expression ran the gamut from embarrassed to flushed to surprised. She finally smiled softly and pushed the button for the door to PT, then kept it from closing by standing against it.

"How does it feel to be up and about?" she asked. He caught her looking at Carponti for a little too long, and he felt a tiny spike of jealousy in his blood. He wanted to get her alone. To ask her what, if anything, she'd felt that morning. He flushed. Of course she'd felt something. Shit, he was a mess.

He hadn't seen her since his dick had run her off. He wanted to say something profound, wanted to apologize for his erection and the awkwardness that had followed. Instead, Carponti left him sitting by the check-in counter, completely alone and tongue-tied. The long row of chairs down the narrow hallway blocked the view of the rest of the physical therapy floor. He'd have to get past the gatekeepers before he could see if Osterman was there or not.

"It's good. Different. But good."

"And your pain?"

"Managed. Kind of a low burn and ache." He fiddled with the paper he'd dropped onto his lap before he'd left the room. His workout regime. With weights so light he felt like crying.

"Good. We need to stay ahead of it, so don't get overly ambitious, okay? Mike is going to be your therapist and he's promised to take it easy on you today. He should be here in a few."

He loved the way her throat moved when she swallowed. Damn, he was pathetic. He felt seventeen again, with no idea what to say to the girl who'd just touched his dick for the very first time. He cleared his throat. "Will do. We're looking for one of my guys. Osterman?"

"I think I saw him a while ago. He may or may not still be here. But let me look." She flipped through one of the folders.

"Is there any chance you could give me a copy of his schedule?" Shane asked.

"You're his platoon sergeant, right?" Her eyes sparked. There was an opening, right there. But before he could push through it, Carponti piped up.

"Can you even be in charge if you're in a wheelchair? I mean, isn't there some rule about being able to stand in front of a formation? Hell, at least I can stand at attention, right?"

"Shut up, Carponti." Jen shook her head and disappeared into an office, reappearing a moment later with a sheet of paper and held it out to Shane. He glanced down at the printout of Osterman's appointments.

A slow burn started in his guts, and then it sparked into something that was at once odd and familiar and terrifying. Responsibility.

By taking this single sheet of paper, he was resuming responsibility, no matter how bastardized, for one of his men.

But as soon as the feeling came, so did the realization of all that had changed. He couldn't do this. He couldn't make sure Osterman made it to formation on time or take him for a run when he finally got a prosthetic leg. He couldn't do anything but sit in PT with him. Who was he kidding? Carponti was right about him not being a leader anymore. And this little sheet of paper wasn't going to give that back to him.

He stared down at it. It mocked him for everything he no longer was. He was lying to himself and everyone around him. He had nothing left to give. All he could do now was take.

IT WASN'T her normal habit to leave the hospital on her breaks. Nor was it her habit to seek relationship advice from her friends. But she'd seen the pure terror on Shane's face when she'd handed him Osterman's schedule, and she'd had no idea what to say. The awkwardness from the catheter removal was still hanging between them and now this. She missed the easiness that had once been between them; hell, she'd even take the arguing. Anything was better than this thick silence she couldn't seem to cut through.

She drove across post, hoping that Laura hadn't moved out of her office. She knew Laura had given notice, but she was hoping that she wasn't finished working quite yet. Her friend wasn't answering her phone, and Jen had been desperate enough to drive the mile and a half to her office on the off chance that she was there.

Things were that much of a mess in her brain at the moment.

"Okay, who died?" Laura asked, when Jen burst into her office. She had a bulky box in her arms and was in the process of organizing folders.

"That's certainly a cheerful attitude," Jen said dryly. "Here, I got it."

She lifted the box from Laura's arms, immediately noticing her friend's red-rimmed eyes. "What's wrong?" she asked, as Laura dropped papers in on top of the folders, then set them down on the desk.

"With me? Nothing. What could possibly be wrong in my life right now?" She snatched the box back from Jen and left the office, Jen just steps behind her. "Except that my husband is sexually harassing his soldiers," Laura continued. "He sends single-word replies to my emails and doesn't respond at all when I send him pictures of our kids. What could possibly be wrong?" Reaching her minivan, she dumped the box inside, and then slammed the door shut. She sighed hard and rubbed her face in her hands. "And none of that is your fault."

"Wait, go back to the sexual harassment," Jen said.

Laura swiped her fingers through her hair. "The rear detachment commander was just talking with the brigade's equal opportunity representative. He doesn't know I heard. But yeah, supposedly, my husband—you know, the one whose been ignoring me—has been trying to screw the one female in the battalion."

"While I recognize that things are really crazy in the war right now," Jen said, wishing she had something to do with her hands, "and none of that gives Trent an excuse to ignore you like this, I'm going to go out on a limb and say never in a million years would Trent try to sleep with one of his soldiers."

Laura blinked and looked away, biting her lips together. "I can't *not* hear from him. I'm apparently not important enough to him for him to call. I can't listen to these rumors and not think there's something to them when I add in everything else that's been going on. And while I understand that it makes me a stereotypical bitchy Army wife, I'm tired of being his second choice."

Jen wrapped her arms around Laura's shoulders and squeezed. "He might be at war, but that doesn't mean he gets to do this to you."

"If I knew what was going on with him . . . If he just bothered to explain everything, maybe I could sleep at night. I've got nothing left from him but faith that he still loves me, and honestly, I'm running out of that after five deployments."

"Laura—" A deep disquiet slid through her belly.

"Yes, Jen. That means what you think it means."

"Laura, wait a sec."

"No, he's been gone more than six months. This year. Last year, he was only home for three months. The year before that, five and a half. The year before that, six. Iraq. Afghanistan. It doesn't matter where he is, because the one place he isn't is home. He never did this when he was still enlisted and he damn sure never tried to sleep with one of his soldiers." Laura's eyes filled. "I love him, but I feel like the man I'm married to is a memory. I can't do this anymore."

Her tears came hard then and Jen pulled her friend close. Her own worries slipped by the wayside as her friend wept bitterly.

Abruptly, Laura pulled away. "And we are not doing this here anymore. I cleaned out my office. I'm done with being the family readiness group leader. . . . You know, he used to tell me he'd do anything to stay home with me for more than a few months at a time. Now? Now I know that was all just another lie. I'm done with the stupid Army."

"Why now, Laura? Why not just wait till he gets home to work through this?" Jen didn't know what it was like to be with a man who chose the Army over her. She had never sat and waited for the phone to ring, hoping that just a few words would tide her over until the next brief phone call. Divorce happened. Everyone knew soldiers had higher divorce rates than civilians. But divorce while Trent was deployed?

"He'd rather soldier around than be with me and the kids. Amy Kingston—who is on the short list to be my replacement by the way —just asked me how I was able to stand it that my husband volunteers all the time. He *asked* to go on every single one of these missions. He could have moved to a different job or a different brigade or a different post. Instead, he's been asking to deploy to combat."

Laura's words sent a cold chill down Jen's arms. "Trent's been volunteering? The whole time? You're sure?"

Laura's laugh was bitter. "Unlike her husband, who is a complete asshole, Amy Kingston is the most sweet-natured girl on the planet. I actually have no idea how she's going to survive as the FRG liaison, but that's not my problem. None of this is. Trent volunteered. I quit."

"Laura, at least sleep on this decision about Trent." Jen struggled to keep her voice calm, as if she were speaking to a skittish colt.

Laura shrugged and looked away. It was a long time before her voice broke the awkward silence. "I know there's no forgiveness for leaving a man while he's off to war, but he's been cheating on me with the Army, and maybe with one of his soldiers. I'm just stepping aside."

"As much as I hate him for doing this to you, I feel like I should be talking you out of this right now."

"It's already done." Laura offered a watery smile. "You didn't come here to hear about my drama. What's wrong?"

Jen shook her head. The fiasco with the catheter seemed so unimportant at the moment. What kind of friend would she be to lay her trivial problems on Laura's shoulders right now? "Nothing important. Want to go get coffee?"

"Can we spike it with Irish cream? It's been one of those days."

"Let me call my boss and yes, we can spike it with Irish cream. But I'm driving." Jen laughed and guided Laura gently toward her car. At least for the moment, she could distract her friend.

Shane and his erection would have to wait.

15

———————

Shane didn't know what to expect when he rolled into physical therapy. He supposed he expected something sobering and depressing. He hadn't expected cheering and laughter. The small celebration was for a young soldier—no older than twenty-three—who was standing in her prosthetic leg. The joy was contagious, and it slipped in when Shane wasn't paying attention, buoying his spirits. His heart caught in his throat when the soldier took her first wobbly steps with the prosthetic. The triumph in her face touched him. Deeply. Everywhere he looked, he saw soldiers in motion. Halting, sometimes hesitant, but in motion nonetheless.

Then a soldier who was using a weight machine tucked away in the corner caught his eye. Osterman. He wasn't watching the celebration and his face was expressionless as he worked his body. He bent his leg into the motion of the machine, but didn't seem to be making a real effort—his movements were listless, uninspired.

Once upon a time, Osterman had been hell on the heavy weapons systems, especially the fifty-cal. Now, though? Now he looked like life had beaten him down and had taken part of his soul instead of one of his legs.

"It's just a damn leg. He has another one." Carponti's voice interrupted Shane's thoughts, but for once, Shane didn't mind.

"So missing an arm doesn't bother you?" Shane asked.

"I think we covered the only part that bothers me and using my other hand is more like learning a new position." Carponti scratched his beard. "It's not the end of the world."

"Yeah, well, how the hell do we get him to see that?"

"You could kick his ass . . . never mind. Bad plan."

Shane groaned at the weak joke. "What the hell can I say to him?"

"This is supposed to be your area of expertise. I ran out of ideas after dick jokes."

"Let's leave those as Plan B for now. Wait here, okay?"

He was surprised when Carponti didn't argue. Osterman shot Shane a quick look as he approached and then looked back down at the weights he was using. "Finally got out of bed, huh?"

"Something like that." Shane snorted quietly. "Sorry I haven't been by to see you earlier."

"Don't worry about it. No one else has." Even Osterman's voice was flat. Lifeless. "Except my fiancée, who looks at me like I'm about to blow my head off every day, and Carponti, of course, who won't leave me the hell alone. Not everyone thinks dick jokes are funny."

"You used to laugh at them."

"Yeah, well, I think I left my sense of humor back there in the sand."

Shane tried not to stare at the empty space where the rest of Osterman's leg had once been. He was grasping at straws, desperate for any topic that might span the space between them. "Yeah, well, it'll find its way home at some point. Hang around Carponti a little more."

Finally, Osterman met his eyes. "Feels like we're not part of the unit anymore."

Shane sighed. "I know. Hell, I can't even get Captain Davila on the phone downrange."

"Yeah, well, it's better this way." Osterman shifted the weights in his hands. "I'd cut me loose, too. Dead weight and all that."

"That's a whole lot of self-pity from someone who should be walking by now," Shane said. Irritation surged inside and it was pointed dead center at himself. He felt the exact same way about the unit. Osterman had been the bigger man and had at least admitted it.

Osterman lifted himself from the machine and dragged his crutches beneath his arms. "I'll pass on the ass chewing, thanks. I've had enough of those from you to last a lifetime."

Never in the fourteen years since he'd first pinned on sergeant's stripes had Shane ever been at such a loss for words. Once, he would have blasted the kid with both barrels and had him doing the mountain climber until his arms felt like rubber and he puked his guts up.

Now? Now Shane kept his mouth shut. He didn't open his mouth to remind Osterman that he was still a soldier, that he was still one of Shane's men, and that their boys still downrange expected better from him. He simply sat and let him quit. On him. On the team. On himself.

He had no fucking idea what to do next, except watch as Osterman hobbled away.

"I TAKE IT THAT WENT WELL?" Carponti said, strolling up to where Shane sat in his wheelchair near the free weights. Physical therapy buzzed with noise and activity, but Shane heard none of it. The weights felt like a ton of bricks and he couldn't find the strength to do even a light curl. He'd wanted to leave a half hour ago but he hadn't because he didn't trust himself to navigate in that stupid fucking chair. At least no one had bothered him. His therapist seemed to think he could handle lifting weights by himself and had been in a corner, talking to one of the female patients for the last twenty minutes. Apparently, the staff in PT was used to seeing a guy sitting quietly by himself. Shane didn't want to consider what that meant about how often it happened. A *snap hiss* punctured the noise, then Carponti took a huge swill from a Dr Pepper can as he sat down next to Shane on the bench.

"Swimmingly." Shane scrubbed his hand over his face then looked up to see Randall walking toward them, a black scowl on his face. "Why does he look pissed?" Shane asked.

Carponti took a long drink to buy himself some time. "Oh, maybe something about me ignoring a direct order."

"About what?"

"Osterman."

Before Shane could ask any further questions, Randall planted himself in front of them, blocking any possible exit for Shane unless he felt like using his legs as a battering ram to get past him. Which he didn't. As much as the idea of running over the lieutenant appealed to him, it wouldn't be worth the pain. Course, the moment Randall opened his mouth, Shane reconsidered.

"Explain to me why you released that soldier when I tasked you to hold him, Sergeant Carponti." Randall's voice was like nails on a chalkboard.

Shane was reasonably sure that he was the last person on earth he wanted to see at that particular moment.

"Sorry." Carponti raised the can to his lips again and there was no humor in his eyes. "My bad."

Shane choked back a cough. *Sorry, my ass.* "Carponti, can you go get that file I asked you for?" Carponti opened his mouth to argue, but a dirty look from Shane made him snap it shut. They'd played this game one too many times for Carponti not to know the deal. Shane needed him gone but couldn't come out and say it. His sergeant didn't usually argue, but today, he stood fast.

Shane would digest that little tidbit of information later but right now, he turned his wheelchair so that he was facing his company executive officer. He hated that he had to look up at the lieutenant. "Seems like you need reminding that while Carponti might be a sergeant, he's not back at work, and he damn sure isn't your errand boy."

"Sir. You will still observe military courtesy," Randall said, "and call me fucking sir."

Carponti folded his arms over his chest and grinned. "How's the investigation? It can't be that hard to find a couple of night vision goggles, can it . . . fucking sir?"

Randall turned a deep scarlet purple as Carponti finally sauntered off. "Guess you think that's funny?" he asked Shane.

"They don't respect you."

"They don't have to respect me, they have to respect my rank."

"And it's never occurred to you that if you're constantly telling people to respect your rank, it probably means they *never will* respect you?" Shane asked. "That doesn't bother you?"

"I have an investigation to complete and you, Sergeant Garrison, are interfering with said investigation. You've instructed your men to avoid me and not answer questions, you've been flagrantly disrespect-ful, and you've encouraged the same behavior in your subordinates."

"Are you done?" Shane folded his arms across his lap, elbows propped on the chair. "One, I never told anyone to avoid you. Two, I told them to keep copies of anything they give you from this point forward because I don't trust you not to doctor evidence. Three, they're fucking healing from combat injuries, you self-centered son of a bitch. Worrying about you is the last goddamned thing on their minds."

"Goddamn it, I've had enough of your insubordinate cond—!"

"Excuse me, is there a problem?"

Jen's voice sent a shiver of relief shooting across his skin. He didn't answer her question. He simply raised both eyebrows at Randall, who was fuming.

"I'm going to have to ask that you keep your voice down or leave. Otherwise, I'm going to call hospital security," she said calmly. She braced her hands on her hips and widened her stance like she expected to have to dodge him if he moved suddenly. But instead, Randall turned his attention back to Shane.

"You're not going to continue to interfere with this investigation, Sergeant Garrison." Randall marched off smartly, leaving wounded pride in his wake.

Shane fought the urge to high-five Jen. "Nice timing," he said.

"Thanks. You looked like you needed a hand." She sat on one of the wide, low benches. She'd never looked more beautiful to him. Her smile was warm and sexy.

"Do you always try to piss him off?" she asked, folding her hands in her lap and resting her elbows on her knees.

"I make a special effort for him."

"Can I ask why?"

"He got two of our men killed because he was a coward."

She gasped and sat up abruptly, horror painted on her face. "Why isn't he in jail?"

"There was a line-of-duty investigation and a Fifteen Six." He frowned at the confusion on her face. "A Fifteen Six is like a fact-finding investigation run by the Army and a line of duty determines whether something happened during duty or outside of it. Both investigations found him not at fault."

"But you think he was?"

"I know he was. I was there."

Jen frowned and rubbed her upper arms with her palms. "It doesn't change anything, though, does it?"

"No. But I can do my part to keep him from forgetting. Every time he looks at me, I want him to know that I remember. And he will be judged someday. I just hope I'm around to see it."

Jen shifted and twined her fingers in her lap.

"Does that bother you?" he asked.

"Does it matter what I think?" She lifted her eyes to his face, her expression inscrutable.

Shane cleared his throat. "So thanks for running him off."

"Any time." She smiled faintly and Shane wished for anything to banish the awkwardness between them. "Anyway. I have paperwork for you."

Shane swallowed and glanced down at her hands, missing the quiet ease that had been between them. At least she hadn't brought up the hard-on from hell. He had that going for him, anyway. "What kind of paperwork? It's not another green insurance form, is it?"

She shifted and crossed her legs, wrapping her joined fingers around her knee. "The, ah, catheter was the last thing keeping you in the hospital. You'll need regular pin cleaning and PT, but other than that, the docs looked at your progress and decided there's no real reason to keep you in the hospital." She sighed and folded her hands in her lap. "I know this is sooner than what we'd talked about."

A loud buzzing filled his ears. His mouth went dry as the reality of what she was saying sank in. "So you're saying..."

"Yeah. It's discharge paperwork." She shifted again and he wished he could come up with something to say. Anything other than the truth, that he had no place to go and no way to get there.

Shane closed his eyes and sighed hard. Reality really was a bitch sometimes.

～

JEN COULDN'T NAME the emotion etched in the lines of his face. She'd figured that being released from the hospital would be a bad thing for Shane. His change in status was too new. He wasn't comfortable in the chair yet. But the rules ... she couldn't argue with the rules. And now that his internal injuries no longer required monitoring, now that he was mobile, he was going home, no matter how much she disagreed with the doctors.

She remembered how she'd felt when she'd been sent home after her first chemo treatment. She'd been scared. Afraid of being alone. Afraid of falling down or drowning in her own vomit. Afraid of being too weak to get up the stairs by herself.

"This should be a good thing," she remarked quietly, not believing her own lie.

"Would be if I had a home." The muscles in his jaw jumped. He didn't open his eyes, didn't give her a clue about what was going on inside him. "I need to get Carponti back here."

"Where did he go?" Jen asked.

"I sent him out of here so I could argue with Lieutenant Randall. He might have left."

"Will you be staying with him?"

Shane snorted and dragged his hands over his face. "Not in this lifetime."

"Why are you so pissed about this?" she asked abruptly.

Finally, he looked at her. "Before my divorce was all said and done, I let my ex take everything I had. I didn't think it was worth fighting over. I canceled the lease on my apartment before I left for Iraq."

There was such loathing in his voice. Such contempt. And she couldn't find a reason for it.

Laura had been steadfast and loyal to Trent, and he'd still traded time with his family for time in the war zone. Laura didn't deserve that. How could Jen judge Laura? The fact was, she couldn't. Laura had decided she couldn't hold her marriage together by herself, and it was the hardest decision she'd ever made in her life. Jen wondered if Shane knew what was going on between them, but it wasn't her place to say anything.

"Doesn't it take two to make a marriage fail?"

"Yeah, it does." Shane shrugged and stared down at his hands. "The bottom line is that I wasn't home. I can be angry at her for cheating on me, but when it counted, I wasn't there."

"She cheated?"

"Yeah. I'm trying to be grateful that she just left and wasn't blowing half my platoon."

"That doesn't really happen."

Shane shot her a baleful look. "You'd be surprised."

His mood shifted like lightning, and the storm she'd seen on his face finally tore free. He slammed his fist against the arm of the chair, then dragged his hands over his face. "I hate this shit. I hate being fucking useless. I hate being stuck in a goddamned chair and I fucking hate having to call that miserable son of a bitch Randall sir."

The force of his anger was sudden and unexpected. Several people in physical therapy turned to stare but the fury radiating from him was enough to force most to look away quickly.

"Shane—"

"Don't." He clicked the locks on his chair free. "Don't tell me everything is going to be okay. Just . . . just don't."

It broke her heart to see him hurting. She watched him as he wheeled away from her, toward the automatic door. She wanted to fix this. She wanted to fix him, but he kept everything bottled up inside until it exploded. Except for when he'd first come home, he'd kept all the raw emotion hidden. Until now, when he realized he had nowhere to go and couldn't—no matter how badly he wished it were otherwise —be on his own just yet.

Jen knew that feeling. Her home was the only thing that mattered and the one thing that was her shelter when she'd finally beaten the sickness that had taken her breast. As she watched the double doors close behind Shane, the germ of an idea began to take shape. It was a long shot, but right now, she didn't have any better ideas.

What's the worst that could happen?

16

A Texas-sized thunderstorm rumbled closer as the sun sank lower into the horizon. Shane wasn't sure if the storm would hit, but the stunning demarcation between the dark clouds and the blue sky lifted him briefly out of his bad mood. It did not stop him, however, from taking cover beneath the cement awning in front of the hospital.

Carponti had already left the hospital by the time Shane got ahold of him, but he'd sworn he'd be right back. It was bad enough that he had to sit here, helpless, as he waited for his sergeant to come pick him up. It was another thing entirely to have to face the stares and pitiful glances from the people walking by. He knew the looks, the ones that said *thank God it wasn't me*. Bitterness stuck in his throat and tasted like bile. He should have known better than to trust that Carponti would show up on time. Damn it, he should have come up with a Plan B before now.

Now he was stuck sitting outside the hospital with nowhere to go. The medical hold barracks across the parking lot and down the hill weren't an option. They were just a half-assed effort at providing shelter for wounded soldiers who had nowhere else to go and didn't have the ability or funds to move off post. Shane was pretty sure Osterman was staying there, but he was damn sure he couldn't. They didn't have any more first-floor rooms and the Korean War era buildings didn't have elevators. There were only a few wheelchair accessible trailers so far and Shane would be damned if he'd take a room from a soldier who needed it just so he could have a place to lay his head.

He wondered if the Fisher House had any wheelchair accessible rooms. He sighed and tried to beat back the black thoughts that were damn near drowning him. Fisher House was for families. Again, something he didn't have.

Was it too much to ask for his divorce to have left him with something other than bad memories? She'd maxed out every credit card he'd owned and a few he hadn't even known about. He couldn't even afford a bed, let alone an apartment or food. He should have at least split the debt with her. But at the time, he'd just been grateful for the marriage to be over. Talk about a great decision.

"For a guy in a wheelchair, you're pretty good at hiding." Jen sounded ready for a fight. He wasn't in the mood. At least, not one with her. Now if Tatiana had chosen that moment to show up? Yeah, then he probably would have been in the mood for a fight.

Shane cleared his throat and looked out at the street. Anywhere but at her. He shrugged and didn't answer. It was hard to swallow. It was harder to think around her, looking like she did. She'd changed into casual clothes, and she looked like a woman, not a nurse. A woman with soft skin and gentle curves.

A woman he couldn't touch.

"Where are you going?"

Shane struggled to hide his frustration. The change in her stunned him into silence. Her green eyes glittered in the darkening sky. A soft black skirt swished around her hips and the toned muscles in her thighs managed to look sleek and sexy all at once. He snapped his mouth closed to keep from gaping like a lovesick eighteen-year-old private.

Her scent surrounded him, snapping him back to the present moment. She was just Jen. Amazing, sexy Jen. In a dark corner of his heart, he admitted that the idea of not seeing her every day was part of what was eating at him. Somehow, she'd become part of the fabric of his daily life and, in addition to losing the only place he had to lay his head, he was losing her, too. Somehow he'd started needing her, less for her medical care than for her soft touches, smiles, and companionship. He wanted to pull her close and just hold on to her.

"You need somewhere to stay, don't you?"

"I'm good." And he would be, if Carponti would get his ass over here and pick him up. He had too much pride to call his unit. With the way his luck was holding, that damned Lieutenant Randall would be the one to pick him up. Hell would freeze over before he asked that guy for anything.

The storm rumbled closer, but no rain fell from the slate-colored sky. He kept his eyes closed. She sat near him on one of the concrete benches, close enough that he could hear her breathing.

Her fingers on his jaw surprised him. She turned his face toward her and for once, he didn't have the energy to fight.

He opened his eyes. She lowered her hand.

Would he ever again be able to interact normally with people? He was utterly and completely at a loss, not knowing what to do or say.

Apparently so was she. He saw her lip disappear beneath her teeth and he wondered what she was nervous about, even as he realized he felt the same way.

"Carponti forgot to pick you up, didn't he?"

Seeing how it looked like he'd be sleeping outside in a thunderstorm tonight, he really wanted to kill Carponti. "Yeah."

"Where will you go?"

"You ever see that SNL skit where Chris Farley played the motivational speaker?" Shane released a breath. Nothing like being homeless to drive a woman wild. Homelessness and wheelchairs were so sexy these days. He figured he might as well be honest. It couldn't be any worse than his boner fiasco. He sighed hard and offered a weak smile. "I'm thirty-five years old and yes, I am divorced, and I live in a van down by the river."

Her laugh escaped her, despite her attempt to lock it down. Some of the strain loosened from around his heart. He had to get away from her before his want turned into a need. A need he couldn't act on. And he really didn't want to think about where this conversation could lead.

"Do you actually own a van?" she asked.

"This isn't really all that funny."

"Yes, actually it is. That skit is one of my all-time favorites."

"Carponti should be here soon," he mumbled. An odd mixture of emotions churned in his stomach. She was laughing, and he wished he could find humor in the situation, too. The storm rolled closer, rumbling over the hills. Yeah, this was definitely not funny.

"My house is surprisingly wheelchair friendly."

Shane exhaled hard, unable to break past the blockage in his throat. "Do I want to ask why?"

"Well, if you're going to be a jerk . . . "

He sighed and rubbed his eyes. "Why would you do that?"

"Do what?"

"Open your home to a complete stranger?"

"Seeing as how I've held your penis in my hand, I think that puts you firmly in the not a stranger category."

He coughed and choked and felt his face turn sixteen shades of hot.

"Finally. Jeez, I was starting to think your sense of humor had gone AWOL."

He studied her then. Really looked at her. Her eyes sparkled in the darkening sky.

"Won't you get in trouble? Patient living with his nurse thing?"

Jen smiled. "I won't tell if you won't."

Shane snapped his mouth closed. Her smile spread across her face, loosening the knots around his heart.

"I can't go home with you." He could. That wasn't the issue. Crossing into her home would bring down the last barrier between them. And he needed that barrier because he wanted to give, not take. He wanted her to be his and that was as selfish as he could be, because once he started, he wouldn't stop until he claimed all of her. The urge to protect and cherish this woman was strong, stronger than anything he'd ever felt, and he didn't want to ruin the one good thing he still had in his life. "I can't ask you to do that for me."

"This isn't about you asking me. It's about you getting better. Bad stuff happened. It's not the end of the world. So you have a choice. You can wallow in self-pity or get in my car. But it's about to rain, so can we please go if we're going?"

She marched off, the click of her heels against the concrete fading. He was tempted, so damn tempted, to follow her and bare his soul. To talk about his failure to keep his men safe. His concerns about Carponti. Trent's silence. How he'd always fucked up the good things in his life. He'd gone to Iraq to make a difference, to protect his men. Instead, he'd ended up being dragged across the battlefield himself.

The words wouldn't come, nor would the admission that his life was better with her in it, and as he watched her walk away, he couldn't find the words to call her back. Then she was gone, and it was too late. He swallowed and looked down at the duffel bag in his lap. Carponti was a dead man. Frustration clawed at his soul.

A familiar ancient Neon pulled up and Jen got out, slamming her door a little too hard. Relief popped in his chest. She opened the trunk and snatched his duffel bag from his lap before he could react. Then she opened the rear passenger door and waited, arms crossed over her chest. He just stared.

"Are you coming? I'd like to beat the traffic off post."

"Where?" He felt dense, like his brain was moving in slow motion. It still felt strange to have the use of both of his hands, but he had nothing to do with them now.

"Down by the river. I might as well drop you off, on my way home."

He rolled over to the backseat and looked in skeptically. The backseat was a tin can, tiny and small. "There's no way I'm fitting in here with my legs like this."

Jen's expression suggested otherwise. "Wanna bet?"

17

She wasn't really going to drop him by the river, but as they drove farther down Highway 195, he started to wonder. He watched the subdivisions fade away and tried to occupy his thoughts with all the ways he was going to kill Carponti for leaving him high and dry.

The Texas hill country spread out for miles all around them. Finally, Jen turned right down a long dirt road that led to a large, two-story ranch-style home. It wasn't new, like so many houses in the Fort Hood area. The yard was mowed, well kept, and the bushes were trimmed. There was a bright grey-and-white barn a few dozen feet from the house and an attached garage that looked like it had been added on long after the original house was built.

But it was the wheelchair ramp in front of the house that caught his attention.

He caught her gaze in the rearview before she switched off the ignition. "You have a real wheelchair fetish."

"Are you going to be this pleasant all evening? Because I'll be happy to leave you alone and not give you the grand tour." She helped him out of the car and back into the wheelchair. He swallowed the bitter pill of needing her help and rolled toward the ramp. She paused before slinging his duffel bag over her shoulder. "And just to ease your mind, my grandmother was in a wheelchair. I took care of her before she died."

Her house was spotless, no dust or dirt anywhere. Nothing out of place. It was warm and inviting. It felt like a *home.* Something Shane hadn't really had. Ever. He rolled through the main room into the kitchen, and nearly wept when he smelled the warm and comforting aromas wafting from a bread machine on the counter. Beneath that was a hint of apples and cinnamon.

He was overwhelmed. She'd opened her home to him, a man who had failed everyone he'd ever cared about. But for some reason Jen had decided to help him rebuild the foundations of his life by sharing a little bit of hers. He had no idea what to say. Thank you seemed so small and insignificant.

She kicked her shoes off at the base of the stairs and padded over to him in stocking feet. "Don't freak out, you're staying in Gran's old room."

He followed her through the main room. The entire first floor was perfectly suited for someone in a wheelchair, the furniture spaced widely apart. Not once had he come close to banging into anything.

"How come you never moved stuff around after your grandmother died?" he asked quietly.

"What makes you think I didn't?"

"I haven't bumped into anything."

She flushed and folded her arms over her chest. "I figured I'd at least offer you a place to stay." Jen stunned him with her thoughtfulness—she'd arranged the furniture for him. She smiled at him, her eyes sparkling. "I can put everything back, if you want. Make a real obstacle course. It might improve your reaction time."

"Thank you" was all he could manage. He hoped she understood everything he couldn't say.

"There's no old lady smell or anything." She pushed him through double French doors to a bedroom that left him speechless again.

"This was your grandmother's room?" It was painted a deep burgundy red, with white trim around the doors and the crown molding. The mixture of scents was a welcome change after the sterile hospital smell that had taken up permanent residence in his nostrils. A large bed sat in one corner of the room, leaving plenty of space for maneuvering.

He wheeled into the bathroom connected to the room, and immediately noticed that there were handles all around the room. Something simple that would allow him to take care of life's basic needs without help or any more ill-timed erections. He turned slowly in the oversized bathroom, awed. Even if he lived a hundred years, he could never do enough to thank her for this. He could win the lottery and give it all to her, and it would never be enough to repay her kindness. "Jen . . . "

She leaned against the door frame, her feet crossed at the ankles, hands tucked into the back waistband of her skirt. She didn't let him finish. "Hungry? I've got some steaks."

"Steak? As in real food?" He seized onto the distraction. Whatever he might have managed to say wouldn't have made much sense anyway.

"Yeah, well, even I get tired of hospital food sometimes."

"When do you have time to cook?" He followed her into the kitchen, which was painted a pale, cheery yellow. He wanted to help her, but had no idea how.

The feelings churning inside of him were so different from those that had defined his new normal. Things felt right and normal and good.

Wide, dark granite countertops, spotlessly organized, were topped with shiny light cabinets. She opened one of them, and pulled out a chopping block, setting it down on the counter. Then she went out onto the porch and he heard the snap of the ignition as her grill sparked to life. She came back in, and set bright red tomatoes and a knife on the chopping block.

"What?" she asked, smiling at his incredulous gaze.

"You are the single most amazing woman I've ever met."

"Maybe I'm a sucker for a man in a cast." She shot him a quick look before sliding the chopping block toward him, and then went outside to put the steaks on. She was still smiling when she came back in, smelling like barbecue and heaven. "There's just something missing without it."

Here was a side of Jen he'd never really seen before. That night at Ropers, she'd been edgy. And at the hospital, she'd been confident and competent. Here, though, in her home? Here she relaxed. She was easy and comfortable.

The want burned inside of him. "I can break my arm again to get another one."

She laughed as she pulled a bowl of potato salad out of the fridge, and dumped large scoops onto two plates. She paused, and looked up at him from beneath heavy lids. "Don't do it on my account."

He chopped the tomatoes into chunks and slid them to one side of the chopping block. It felt so incredibly free to have the use of both his arms. The little things in life had never seemed so huge until he couldn't do them for himself.

"If I broke my arm, would you shave me again?" he said, a wicked grin spreading slowly across his lips at the thought.

She cast a sideways glance at him. "I could probably do that for you," she replied.

The thought of having her hands on him again made him ache. He followed her out onto the porch.

The porch encircled the house and was completely screened in. It allowed a little bit of Texas in without letting *all* of it in. They settled around the small patio table, and Jen doled out the food. The silence was comfortable, filled with the sounds of the night.

The sun hung low, casting reds, pinks, and oranges across the horizon that still threatened a storm. He winced as the memory of another red-streaked sky slipped in, the night of the attack that had sent him home. His throat constricted and he drank deeply to break up the knot. His heart beat faster against his chest, as the echo of the machine-gun thunder hammered in his ribs again. He pushed out a hard breath to force the memory back.

Crickets chirped in the encroaching darkness. There were no crickets in Baghdad.

Her hand covered his suddenly, pulling him out of the past. "You okay?"

"Yeah. Just realized I can't remember the last time I heard crickets."

She squeezed his fingers. "When I first moved here, it took a whole summer for me to realize it didn't cool off at night like it did back east."

He turned his hand so that his palm opened beneath hers. "How long ago did your grandmother pass away?"

"Four years. Sometimes I can't believe it's been that long."

"How did she die?"

"In her sleep." Jen pulled her hand back and picked at her potato salad. "It wasn't bad. She was in a lot of pain."

"You don't look like it wasn't bad."

"The fight that followed was the bad part. My family decided that her will wasn't valid and that they wanted to fight over the house and the couple thousand bucks in her checking account."

He studied her in the shadows. They danced over her features and tugged at his heart. He wanted to reach for her and soothe the hurt he saw in her eyes. He hated that anyone would hurt her over something so trivial as money.

She glanced up at him. "My grandmother raised me. My parents divorced when I was three. Dad's out there somewhere, I guess, but Mom was killed by a drunk driver when I was six. It really hurt to lose her." She released a deep breath. "Anyway. Do you need help tonight?"

He swallowed and shook his head. "I should be good. Thank you, though."

She opened her mouth, then closed it. He wanted to know what she'd been about to say but she left the table, clearing the best meal he'd had in he couldn't remember how long.

The truth was that she'd crept into his heart when he hadn't been looking, and now?

Now he had no idea what to do next.

~

Despite trying to get back on normal footing, the space between them was quiet. Not quite to the point of being strained, but close.

She left him, needing some space to sort out everything in her head. He was just as quiet as she'd been at the end of dinner. She hadn't felt like sharing the rest of her family drama, how they'd tainted the memory of her grandmother's life over a checking account. Or how her brother had accused her of faking her illness to keep the house.

She wasn't ready to give voice to the fear that nagged at the back of her skull. She sighed and looked toward the closed door across from the kitchen.

Shane was there, on the other side of that door. Today had been overwhelming. She understood that. The bravado she'd grown accustomed to whenever he was around Carponti was gone, replaced by a deep disquiet.

His inability to get through to Osterman had knocked him back a few paces. She hoped that she had at least lifted some of the burden he carried by offering him a place to stay. But she was worried that he wouldn't bounce back. For all his tough talk, Shane was a man searching for a purpose.

She took a deep breath and stepped back onto the porch. She'd felt the full force of the demons he wrestled with tonight, swirling in the darkness around him.

Shane was out there, too—he'd wheeled himself out through the sliding glass doors of her guest bedroom, and was facing the fading sunset, watching the impossibly huge Texas sky fade into an inky blackness that could only be seen at a distance from city lights. He'd taken his shirt off, and she wasn't about to object to the view. Light from the bedroom painted his pitch-black tattoos in shadows and light.

His legs, though, remained covered by a cream-colored chenille throw from the edge of the bed.

He looked into her eyes when she sat down on the bamboo patio sofa next to him. The wood creaked as she shifted to pull her legs beneath her.

Crickets filled the silence between them.

So much for anything being easy with this man. At the end of the day, she could guess at what was bothering him, but she didn't want to. She hugged her arms to her chest and decided to simply be, rather than hounding him with questions. She would just sit, and be there if he needed her.

The lights from the house backlit his profile and she studied him. Strong. Steady. Troubled.

After a moment, he dropped his head back against the wall behind him. Shane's voice was quiet in the evening darkness when he finally spoke. Like he was testing out his words carefully before he voiced them.

"I had no idea what to say to Osterman today." He scrubbed his hands over his jaw. "I haven't been at such a loss with one of my guys since I was a brand-new sergeant."

Jen tucked her hair behind her ear and waited. The urge to reach for him, to offer comfort, was strong enough to be a compulsion. But he didn't want comfort right now. She wasn't even sure he was seeking absolution. The recrimination in his voice suggested he wanted judgment.

Shane shifted and the wheelchair creaked under his weight. "I don't have any way to relate to what he's going through. Carponti nailed it dead to rights. I've still got ten fingers and ten toes."

"That doesn't mean you're not hurting. That doesn't mean you can't relate to him."

"Yeah, actually, it does."

"No, actually, it doesn't. You don't have to have similar injuries to have similar emotions, Shane." Now she reached for him, threading her fingers with his. "Just because you haven't lost a limb doesn't mean you're not hurting. It's not like you just got a scratch and were returned to duty. You know what it feels like to get sent home before your team. Just like he does."

He flinched and looked away, but he didn't pull his hand free. "It feels like shit."

"I know."

Instantly his gaze returned to her, intense and fierce. In the darkness, her scar throbbed against her bones.

"You don't know that, Jen. You're a nurse, you're not a patient. You're not a platoon sergeant who left his entire platoon in the middle of a firefight."

She shook her head and removed her fingers from his. "You're not just a soldier to your men. Carponti isn't just a squad leader, is he?"

"No, he's a pain in the ass." But there was no vehemence in Shane's voice.

"Don't you think you should give yourself a bit of a break?"

Shane snorted. "I'm divorced, in a wheelchair, and homeless. I can't do a fucking thing to help my guys when they're hurting the most. I don't need a break, I need to get back to my men. Until then, I'm just another statistic."

"What you need to do is take some time to heal. And you're more than just a number." She tipped her head at him, breathing deeply to gather the courage she needed. He was in deep, so far down the hole he'd fallen into he couldn't see any way out. "If you believe that, then maybe you need a different perspective on things."

She reached for the top buttons of her blouse and flicked them open rapidly before she lost her nerve. She kept one side of her clothes pressed to her torso and lowered the other, holding the shell of her bra and the form in one hand. She knew what he saw when he looked at her.

A half-inch-thick scar crossed her chest where her left breast used to be. Red and puckered, it stood out starkly against the white of her skin.

"Being hurt only defines you if you let it. You're more than just a wounded GI, Shane. You need to get over it and start focusing on getting better."

Shane dragged his gaze from that jagged scar to her face. She met his gaze and dared him to pity her. She didn't see the slightest trace of that emotion. What she saw, instead, stunned her. Awe. Yes. Amazement. Yes. But not pity. He sat speechless as she turned her back to him and readjusted her clothing. She didn't know what to expect when she turned back to face him.

"I know a little bit about learning to live again. I know about being so weak and helpless you want to die. I know what it's like to look in the mirror and hear that little voice that whispers you'll never be whole again."

"Then maybe it's time you heard something else." He tugged on her hand until she moved closer. His fingers hovered over her shoulder. The hard planes of his cheeks were shadowed, his eyes hidden in the darkness now. "You are absolutely amazing."

"Thanks, Shane. That's really nice of you to say."

"Screw nice." His voice was a low growl in the darkness as he reached for her. Before she could react, he'd half dragged her across the handles of the chair.

His bare chest was hot and hard beneath her fingers as she gripped on to him for balance. Then nothing else mattered as his mouth claimed hers. He stroked her lips apart with his tongue, demanding. Taking. She knew in the space of a single second that she would never again feel this potent intensity that pulsed into her with a single kiss. Her fingers curled into his flesh, above the black lines swirling around his shoulders, and she lost herself in his taste, his touch.

She shifted and opened for him, taking him inside her mouth. He groaned and heat bloomed inside of her, trailing down her belly and throbbing at her center.

She traced her fingers over the tattoos covering his heart, down his massive arms as desire ached inside her. He went completely still as her fingers trailed over his skin, and then she felt his heartbeat. A subtle vibration beneath her touch. He tightened his fingers in her hair and angled her mouth to take her deeper, filling her. His touch chased away the darkness of her own doubt. In that moment, she felt whole and beautiful and fully alive.

"You don't know how bad I've wanted to do this again," he whispered raggedly against her lips.

SHANE COULD NOT REMEMBER EVER FEELING SO completely aroused in his entire life. She was the sweetest pleasure he'd ever tasted. Her fingers explored his chest and no single touch had aroused him so completely. He slipped one arm around her waist and tried to drag her farther into his lap. God but he wanted her. Just her. Naked. He wanted to bury himself inside of her, to lose himself in her soft warm depths.

Her hips bumped into one of the pins sticking out of his thigh and brilliant pain exploded. He swore before he could stop himself, and Jen froze. She traced small kisses over his jaw, his neck, his ear, and the pain slowly receded. He skimmed his fingers over her face, easing her back.

Her eyes were dark, her lips a swollen shadow against her pale skin. His hands found hers, stopping her explorations.

"Jen, you make me crazy," he whispered against her lips. So damn beautiful she hurt his heart.

Her breath brushed against his cheek as she pressed her lips to his ear. "So why did you stop?"

"Really?"

"No, I was kidding."

He hesitated for a moment before he reached for her again,

angling his mouth to taste all of her before she could change her mind.

He tipped his face up before he cupped hers with his fingertips. He kissed her, wanting so badly to take her inside and make love to her. A distant ring shattered the moment. He closed his eyes and she rested her forehead against his. "I don't suppose you can ignore that?" he murmured.

"Not really."

She extracted herself from his lap and walked into the house, leaving him aching and hard. The moment was gone now, but it left a promise of something more in its wake. Seconds later, Jen slipped back onto the porch. Her movements were quick, controlled, her lips pressed into a thin line. It was her eyes, though, that gave her away. Still, he never imagined her next words would steal the breath from his lungs.

"Carponti's in the hospital."

18

S hane dragged his hand over his face and closed his eyes. He didn't say anything as she drove them to the hospital as fast as her small car could take them. He wasn't allowed in the back where the emergency room team was working on Carponti. Jen could have joined them, but she opted to stay with Shane.

"Too many people just get in the way."

He would have paced if he thought it would do anything to unleash the rage churning inside of him. He would have torn the pictures from the walls. Instead, he sat, the bitter feeling of absolute uselessness churning inside of him.

It might have been hours or minutes before Nicole came out. Shane had never seen her with a hair out of place, without perfectly colored lips or an outfit straight out of *Vanity Fair*. He'd never thought she looked like a CID agent, but that's what made her effective. No one saw her coming.

Tonight the cool, composed special investigator was gone and in her place was a scared-to-death wife, wearing blood- and vomit-stained pajamas. There were dark streaks beneath her puffy eyes. She sucked in a huge deep breath in an effort to gain control of her words before she spoke.

"He overdosed." She wiped her palms on her pants.

There was no mistaking Nicole's sadness and hurt. "I'm going to kill him," she said. "I swear, if he survives this, I'm going to kill him."

She ran her fingers through her hair, pushing it away from her face. She turned and screamed at the ER doors where a medical team was still working to clear the poison from Carponti's system. Jen wrapped her arms around Nicole's shoulders as her friend collapsed against her.

Finally two doctors pushed into the waiting room and walked up to them.

"Mrs. Carponti? Will you come with me?" the shorter one said. "He's okay. But I need to talk with you."

Silently, Nicole left, leaving Shane alone with Jen and the taller doc, a colonel according to the ID badge hanging from the pocket of his lab coat.

"He's okay?" Goose bumps crawled over Shane's skin, and he was grateful when Jen rested her hand on his shoulder.

"He's fine. We were able to pump his stomach and get most of the alcohol and pills out of him. It was close. If his wife hadn't found him when she did, we might have lost him." The doctor wiped his glasses on the fabric of his shirt.

"Can I see him?"

The doctor shook his head and set his glasses on the top of his salt-and-pepper buzz cut. "He's sleeping. The unit's sending in the guards we'll need for the night."

Shane swallowed the bile in his throat. Attempted suicide. Of course. Carponti was going to be under constant supervision to ensure he didn't get belligerent with the medical staff.

And tomorrow, he would face the psych eval.

Goddamn it.

Jen squeezed his shoulder. The wooden arm of the waiting room couch jutted between them. Shane sat perfectly still, unable to move. Relief and reality paralyzed him, like a weighted stone crushing his lungs.

Carponti had taken a Jimi Hendrix tonic of narcotics and alcohol and had almost died on his bathroom floor. And Shane hadn't done a damn thing to prevent it. The guilt crept in as the doctor walked away. He'd seen the warning signs, but he'd let his friend convince him he was fine. He'd been wrong.

So goddamned fucking wrong.

Shane covered his eyes with his hands, pressing hard against them. His throat was tight. He ground his teeth, trying to focus on anything but the pain aching in his chest.

A light touch fluttered across his upper arm. So light he almost missed it. Then Jen's hand came to rest on his upper back. Her touch wasn't nearly enough to stop the violent emotions thrashing inside him like a wild thing trapped in a cage, but it soothed part of the ache in his heart.

"I'll take you home."

~

SHANE HADN'T SPOKEN at all on the ride home. She hadn't expected that he would. He worked so damn hard at hiding every even remotely painful emotion. He didn't get it. He couldn't be all things to all people. Would it kill him just once to be human and let himself feel?

He'd pushed himself into his bedroom as soon as they walked in the door, closing himself in with a quiet click. It felt like a slap when she realized he wanted nothing more than to be alone.

Jen stood in the kitchen, staring at his door. She wasn't going to let him do this. Not now. She couldn't leave him alone. Not tonight.

When she opened the door, she saw that he'd pulled himself onto the bed. Uncovered for once, he simply stared at the metal pins and frames holding the wreckage of his legs together. The muscles in his jaw jumped in a rapid, angry rhythm. He wouldn't look at her. It didn't take a rocket scientist to figure out that he didn't want her there. She ignored his unspoken demand for solitude and approached the bed. His room was dim. A sliver of moonlight slithered in across the floor between the drawn drapes.

One hand covered his mouth and he stared bleakly at some far off point only he could see. She reached for him, pulling his hand away from his mouth.

Still, he didn't speak. Just looked at her with those deep grey eyes, filled with rage and guilt.

"He's going to be okay." He swallowed and looked away. "This isn't your fault, Shane."

The silence wrapped around them in the predawn darkness, then everything exploded all at once.

He slammed the lamp off the nightstand as his rage finally broke free. "Bullshit. I fucking knew and I didn't call him out on it."

She didn't flinch as the bulb shattered, but it was a close thing. "You knew?" She stepped over the mangled lamp and slapped her palms against his chest, forcing him back. It wasn't the lamp she was worried about. It was him.

She hated that he almost instantly retreated into the sullen silence of a moment before. "I suspected."

"And we're right back where we've always been. You. Are. Not. God. You didn't know."

"I should have."

"How, Shane? How should you have known? Your mystical sergeant powers? Did you monitor his meds? Did you go to his house and force-feed him alcohol? Stop blaming yourself for everything bad that happens!"

He looked so lost. Her heart broke for him. She fidgeted with the buttons of her blouse as she leaned against the bed, trying to think of anything to say that would make this better.

"Shane." She cupped his face in her hands. "This isn't your fault."

He was still for an eternity.

And then he reached for her.

SHE WAS close enough that he could smell her shampoo—the familiar scent of strawberries and vanilla.

Shane threaded his fingers through her hair and pulled her to him, clinging to her like she was a lifeline. The cool satin strands of her hair caressed his hands as he simply held her. She wrapped her arms around his shoulders. He sat for a long moment, just breathing her in. Taking her strength and using it to rebuild the foundation beneath him.

Then Shane pulled her down until her lips met his in the darkness. She was soft and warm and wet and her tongue slid against him with a desperation born of mutual pain and need. Jen's fingers curled into his cheeks as she met his need with her own.

Jen. She was beauty and strength and life and everything that was still good in the world. Desire surged inside of him and he dragged her against him, giving in to it.

He traced one hand down her throat, her pulse beating erratically beneath his thumb. His hand ran down her back to cup her backside and with a quick jerk, he dragged her on top of him. She caught her foot against one of the external fixators and white hot pain exploded. He groaned and she froze immediately. "This is an omen," he said when he could speak.

"No, it's not."

She pressed her hips against his still-clothed erection. That simple erotic contact nearly sent him over the edge. The one thing that mattered was Jen. Her taste, her touch. His lips traced down her throat as the pain receded. She arched her neck and he dragged his teeth over her pulse until she gasped.

He slipped his hand beneath her pants and her skin was satin and heat. His need nearly overwhelmed him, and he yanked it back.

This was Jen rocking against him, releasing soft gasps in his ear as his hands played over her body. He would never hurt her. Not in this lifetime would he ever use her for a simple physical release.

He wanted to lay her on her back and thrust inside of her, leaving the pain, the heartache, and the despair behind as he lost himself in her. He needed *her*, not just another warm body.

Slowly, so slowly, he slid his hand over her belly, inching her blouse up.

She gripped his wrists. "Don't."

Reality crashed over him.

"No one has touched you there." It wasn't a question.

She pulled away. Not physically, but she might as well have. The juncture of her hips lifted away from his fading erection, her hands braced against his chest instead of curling into him like they had a moment ago.

She started to move away, but he held her to him gently, his thumbs stroking her lower back.

He couldn't let her go. Not now, when he'd fucked up so badly. He would get this one thing right.

"Don't pull away." His whisper was the only sound above their still ragged breaths. "Please don't."

She stilled above him, and then nuzzled his palm with her cheek. "I didn't mean to freak you out."

He tugged her down so he could nibble on her lips. "You didn't."

She sighed as his tongue flicked over the corner of her lips. "You stopped."

He stroked her lower back and pleasure spiked through him as she began to respond to his touch. "You were surprised."

"You're right." She arched against him. Her breath warmed his neck as her fingers curled into the base of his neck and shoulder. "I . . . I just haven't been touched there . . ." Her words brushed against his skin and he shivered, wanting so badly to fix this.

The silky fabric of her blouse caressed his skin and he loved the fullness of her breasts—breast—against his chest. He wanted to touch her there, to tease that nipple to a hard peak. He wanted to look up into her eyes as he suckled her. But tonight, he would find another way.

He stroked her skin, slowly, his fingers trailing lower.

He'd never felt such arousal, such a need to claim. To give. He'd never felt the desire for this slow build. He wanted to take his time with Jen, to watch her eyes darken, her lips part. Her breath hitched as he drifted lower still, her body frozen in anticipation of his touch. She bit her lip and let him explore. Watching. Waiting.

He slipped his hand under her pants and her underwear and cupped her sweetness, his palm absorbing her heat. Her hips jerked and a low gasp escaped her. He kept his hand still, cupping her heat. So slowly, he parted her and slick, hot moisture covered his finger.

She trembled beneath his touch, and her hips rocked against his hand. She gasped his name into his ear as her orgasm burst through her, an intense explosion riding over both of them in waves.

Her gaze darted between his face and his shorts and realization dawned on him like hot pinpricks racing across his skin.

"We need to get these off of you." She reached for the snaps on the athletic shorts he'd worn since they'd taken the catheter out, the only article of clothing other than a man-dress that he could get on and off easily over the pins.

"Are you sure?"

She kissed him and he prayed that meant yes.

Thank you, Jesus.

She quickly shimmied out of her own pants then flicked off the overhead light before climbing back into the bed. She'd clean the lamp up later. His breath caught at the sight of her kneeling over him, exposing the glorious blond hair between her thighs. He wanted to lift her hips and drive into her until they both exploded. He yanked back the fierce arousal. He wasn't going to screw this up.

He closed his eyes as her fingers slithered down his chest. Over the tattoos and the scars. Her fingers lingered over the tiny scar on the right side of his stomach and the more recent ones that were still healing, including one of the two that had almost kept him home from the war. Then she drifted lower again with aching slowness. She paused at the top of his penis and he waited for her to go just a little lower.

A smile crept over her lips. He scowled. "What's so funny?"

"It's not quite the same without a tube sticking out of it."

"Ha-ha-ha." He gripped her hand and guided her to him, cutting off her laughter. He sucked in a hard breath as her small fingers wrapped around his cock. He damn near came when her thumb stroked over the head, already slick with his own wetness.

If she kept stroking him, he wasn't going to last. It had been months since he'd been with anyone, but nothing had ever felt like this. The emotion churning inside him was anticipation mixed with dark pleasure and something more.

She pressed a foil packet into his hand. His hands shook as he struggled to cover himself. Then she braced her palms against his chest and shifted her hips. And he was there, right at the opening of her tight heat. He groaned when she teased the tip of his cock with a tiny rotation of her hips.

She was so slick. He could glide deep inside her with a single thrust. Instead, he held infinitely still as she slowly, so slowly, sank onto his erection. Her beautiful body tightened and stretched around him.

He couldn't move, couldn't complete their union the way he wanted. He slid his palms down over her hips, and showed her the rhythm he craved.

She closed her eyes and raised herself off of him, rocking in that perfect, primal motion. The pressure built inside of him as she tipped her head back and rode him, small gasps of pleasure bursting free with each smooth rise of her hips. His own need grew more urgent, more demanding. His eyes rolled back in his head as she rode him faster, taking him deeper. Her body clenched and spasmed and then she burst around him, his name a gasp on her lips.

He held her tight against him as he shattered, and her body trembled and exploded as her orgasm crashed over her again and again. He wrapped his arms tight around her when she collapsed against his chest, her breath brushing against his sweat-covered skin.

He felt alive. And for the first time in months, it didn't feel wrong.

JEN MANAGED to nestle into Shane's body without bumping into his pins, her own body humming with electric energy. Her palm was resting against his chest, a puckered scar pushing against her fingertips. She could feel his heart thumping, strong and steady, beneath her cheek.

His thumb absently stroked her shoulder. She shivered from the light caress and then reached down and pulled a blanket over them both. He shifted and tucked her closer to his heart.

She felt filled and sated and so deliciously feminine. She was still awake when his breathing went deep and regular. Then he twitched suddenly, like he was jolting out of a dream.

She pressed her lips to the corner of his mouth. He didn't say anything, but he tightened his arms around her in response.

"Carponti is going to be okay, Shane." She pushed herself up on one elbow, painfully aware that she was wearing nothing but a blouse. She might have shown him her scars, but that didn't mean she was ready to go full frontal. Sex, sure. Naked? Not so much. "This wasn't your fault."

He dragged his hand over his face. "I should have pushed him. I should have made him talk to me. I've been so wrapped up in all my own bullshit, I ignored his."

She planted her palm against his chest, anger sparking in her breast. She didn't understand his need to hold himself responsible at all costs. She tried to remember how she'd felt when she first got sick. How she'd been convinced that no one would ever love a woman like her. How she'd considered having reconstructive surgery just to hide the scars, but had refused because she didn't want to hide who she was. She still wondered what she might have done differently.

"You. Weren't. There," she said again. "You didn't force him to drink all that Cuervo. You didn't make him take too many Vicodin. You didn't do that."

He jerked away from her touch and a sudden coldness radiated from him. She wanted to comfort him, but something about him pushed her away. She suddenly very much wanted to get dressed.

"Shane, this isn't your fault. You need to accept that."

Her words rang hollow in the heavy silence and he scrubbed his hands over his face. She was more than a little surprised when his fingers twined with hers. "I still feel responsible. He's one of my men. I'm supposed to see these things coming."

She squeezed his fist. "You're not Superman, and you're not God. You're human and you're fallible just like the rest of us. What Carponti did isn't your fault."

He stared at her for a long moment, then pulled her down into his embrace. The warm afterglow was gone, though, replaced by a distant chill.

In the silence, he laid his cheek on the top of her head. "I wish I could believe that." He scoffed in the darkness. "When I first pinned on sergeant stripes, one of my squad leaders told me that now I *was* a god, as far as my soldiers were concerned. I was responsible for all they did and all they failed to do."

"Shane, your soldiers are still their own people, and they still make their own choices."

"You don't understand. There's no other job on earth that makes you as responsible as I am for my men. I'm responsible for their training. I'm responsible for the way they live. For the choices they make downrange, including each time they pull the trigger."

Jen pushed up on her elbow again and looked down at him. "What do you think I do at work every day, hand out candy? Do you know what it feels like to lose a patient who you've spent weeks or months trying to save? Or to have someone look you in the eye and tell you they'll be fine when you know they're not expected to live through the night?"

Shane swallowed and looked away. "I—"

"Don't tell me I don't understand. Don't tell me it's not the same.

No one understands life and death like soldiers do. Just like no one understands life and death like doctors do." She couldn't keep the anger from her voice, the edge that chased away any warmth that lingered between them.

"Jen, that's not what I meant."

She wriggled from the bed, careful to avoid the broken lamp. "I think it's exactly what you meant. You've been so wrapped up in everything that you can't do, you've convinced yourself that the only thing you can do is soldier. Now you can't do it anymore, so you're just going to sit around and dwell on what might have been? Well, guess what, Shane? Life doesn't work like that. We all have choices to make, but even if we knew the outcome of every single one, we still wouldn't be able to control everything. I gave up my breast so that I could live—"

"That's right, Jen, you made the choice to give that up. I didn't choose to be here—"

"You chose to deploy. Remember? You begged me to let you go when you were still healing from your surgery. You made the choice to be over there. You can't control how that turned out."

"Don't lecture me about choices! This isn't about my choices."

She dragged on her pants. "No, it's about control. And you don't have any, isn't that right? You couldn't control Carponti's choices. Hell, you couldn't even find the right words to talk to one of your soldiers. You look in the mirror and see a used-to-be soldier." She snatched the rest of her clothes up from the floor. "Try taking another look in the mirror. You might be surprised by what you see if you really bother to look."

She didn't slam the door behind her but it was a close thing. She couldn't get back to sleep after that, couldn't forget the anger that had been etched onto his face. He hadn't asked for a lecture. He'd needed comfort.

She stared at the ceiling and considered the truth that she might have pushed him too far, too fast.

19

———————

He really didn't know what to expect before he rolled into her kitchen. Truth be told, he'd sat behind the closed door of Jen's guest bedroom and contemplated how hard it would be to wheel himself to the base.

Considering it was over fifteen miles away and he'd been in a wheelchair for exactly forty-eight hours, it didn't seem like a likely course of action.

Shane had never been a coward before. At least, not that he remembered. The first time he'd been in a firefight downrange, he'd pissed his pants but kept on going. His sergeant at the time had told him it happened to all of them at one point or another. Pissing himself didn't make him a coward, it only meant that he was combat tested.

But this? This was different. This was worse.

Shane snorted and dragged his hands over his face. He'd screwed up last night. Big time. It didn't help that Jen was wrong. He'd come to that realization somewhere around four-thirty in the morning. She simply didn't understand the responsibility he had toward his men. He was supposed to see stuff like this coming. He was supposed to know his guys and know when something was off. Wasn't that what the Army had drilled into him ever since he'd pinned on his sergeant stripes? And now she was trying to tell him this wasn't his fault? No, it might not have been his fault, but it was still his responsibility.

He'd heard her moving around in the kitchen for the better part of an hour, but he couldn't move past the barrier of his own inaction. So he sat, unable to find even a trace of courage for the coming confrontation. He wasn't good at apologies. His failed marriage was a testament to that. So was his life as a sergeant. He'd been a good one. He hadn't had to apologize often.

Having finally summoned up the resolve to face her, he pushed himself through the French doors. He did it too quickly, though, and they rebounded, banging into his leg. Pain shot through every nerve ending in his body and exploded in his brain.

Breathe. His only thought was to breathe through the pain. In through his nose. Out through his mouth. Deep, hard breaths to keep the pain burning in his throat from tearing free.

Instantly she knelt by his side. Her fingers were cool against his skin. It was the only thing he could feel through the pain and he latched on to it. "I'm sorry," he whispered before she could speak. "Look, last night—"

"Please, don't say it was a mistake." She squeezed his forearm. "Whatever you say, just don't say it was a mistake."

"I wasn't going to," he said quietly.

She sighed, and relief surrounded both of them, permeating the space between them. "Okay. Then how about I stop interrupting."

"That would be great." She offered a mock scowl and he reached for her. Her fingers were smooth beneath his rough ones, reminding him again of the stark differences in their lives. Her fingers healed. Shane's ended lives. How could he hope to make her understand his savage need to get back to his men when their very lives were built on such polar opposite foundations?

He looked at her now and remembered how she'd looked in the bar that first night. Her hair brushed against her cheeks, framing her face. It had always been her eyes that had claimed him, had marked his soul. Those grass-green eyes looked at him and he felt exposed. Like she knew his every sin, every secret.

The words he needed escaped him, leaving him mute. She didn't push through his bullshit today, and it took him a moment to recognize the feeling inside him as regret.

"We need to leave for the base in about a half hour. Do you want coffee?" Her voice was quiet, and it did nothing to conceal her disappointment in him. She wished he'd said more, done more. He could tell in the stiff awkwardness between them now.

"Yeah. That'd be great, thanks."

That awkwardness stood between them like a wall. Shane felt his own inaction clutch at his throat. He wouldn't get a second chance to fix this. He'd screwed up. He'd driven away the one person who could look past his tattoos and bad attitude and get to the man inside. He sat in her kitchen and saw the one thing he hadn't known he'd feared.

Her, walking away.

JEN WATCHED him as he rolled down the hallway toward physical therapy. She watched him and wished he could get past all the baggage that kept him stuck in that chair. She wished he could just be the guy he'd been before he'd gotten hurt.

She suspected he'd never been a great orator, or one for flowery speeches or eloquent letters. If he'd ever gotten the chance to write a response to that care package she'd sent, she'd bet money that the note would have been short, perhaps written into a preprinted Hallmark card.

Just because he didn't have many words didn't mean they weren't the right ones. She had hoped she'd gotten through to him last night. His silence this morning convinced her otherwise. His inability to talk to his men, to be the leader he once was, was driving him quietly to the edge. He worried about everyone but himself.

Jen didn't know what to say to Shane. He worried about others so he wouldn't have to face his own reality. A reality that might not involve a future in the military.

"What are you daydreaming about?" Nicole asked as she slid up to the nurse's station.

"Hey. How's Vic?" Jen asked. She wasn't about to dive into her own problems, when Nicole obviously hadn't even left the hospital last night.

"He's good. His stomach is empty and he's whining like crazy for McDonald's Hotcakes. That's where I'm headed now."

"You sure that's a good idea?" Jen raised both eyebrows. Nicole looked like she was in no condition to drive, let alone fetch Hotcakes. "How are you holding up?"

"I'm great. Vic's okay. What else do I need right now?" Her voice cracked and Jen was instantly around the counter, wrapping her arms around her friend. Nicole sagged against her. "I'm so fucking tired," she whispered.

Jen bit her lips together. It was exhausting caring for someone else, even someone like Vic, who claimed not to need any help. He'd insisted he was fine and they'd all believed him. Now they knew differently, and worry was a constant presence for Nicole and all of those who cared about him.

Jen held her friend, offering the only thing she could. Someone to lean on. "It's okay, Nikki," she whispered. "It's okay to be tired. It's okay to not be okay all the time."

Nicole straightened and dragged her fingers beneath her eyes. "I'm fine." She smiled thinly. "I have to be. Now, I have to get Hotcakes." Her phone chimed and she pulled it from her sweatpants pocket. "And Fritos, apparently."

She was gone before Jen could say another word.

"What is it about these people that make them so determined to be okay?" she mumbled. Nicole was determined to be fine. Shane was determined to be fine. Carponti, despite what had happened last night, seemed determined to be fine. Was she the only one who ever crashed and burned out so badly that she didn't want to get out of bed for a week?

She looked down the hallway toward where Shane had disappeared, and shook her head. There was no reaching him.

Eventually he was going to wake up and realize that no, he was not okay.

The question was, what would happen when that day came?

SHANE'S FINGER hovered above the elevator's buttons. He sighed and pressed the three until it lit up. He sucked in a deep breath as the doors closed.

How would Carponti act? Would he look different?

After damn near fourteen years in the Army, Shane was no

stranger to suicide. Carponti wasn't the first to have tried it. It was so much worse than losing a soldier to enemy contact. At least then there was someone you could blame. What could you say to a guy who'd tried to kill himself barely twelve hours ago? *Hey, pal, you're looking good.*

He knocked softly, the coward in him almost wishing that Carponti didn't answer.

A loud "Yo!" crushed that hope, and he pushed open the door.

Out of every possible scenario Shane imagined, the one that greeted him shocked him the most. Carponti sat up in the bed, an IV taped to his left forearm, munching on a bag of Fritos and watching a football game. He had an open jar of salsa and a twenty-ounce Dr Pepper on the tray in front of him.

"Come on! That was pass interference!" Carponti chucked a chip at the TV, only to have it land on the Dallas Cowboys blanket covering his legs. "Cowboys are down and the refs are totally screwing us."

"Where's your guard?"

"You mean that sorry sack of shit Randall tried to post in here? He left."

"What do you mean 'he left'?"

"Just what I said. It's not like I was going to kill myself or anything." Carponti glanced at Shane and offered the Frito bag. "You look like shit."

Anger exploded in Shane's chest. "Maybe because I was up half the night worrying about you."

Carponti pulled back the bag of chips, chewing slowly. "Nice to see you, too. What the hell's your problem?"

Shane breathed deeply, slowly, trying to get a handle on the urge to smother the smart-ass.

He failed.

"You! You try to fucking kill yourself but now you're sitting here, eating chips like it's any other day. What the hell is wrong with you?"

"I didn't try to kill myself. And fuck you for thinking I did."

"Bullshit. Don't lie to me. The doc said you had enough Cuervo in your system to give you alcohol poisoning, and the Vicodin just about put the nail in your coffin. What, did you forget you took the pills or something?"

Carponti balled up the chips against the bandage on his shortened forearm and threw it at Shane. "Fuck you, man! You think I don't wake up every day and feel so goddamn depressed I can barely get out of bed?" Carponti swung his feet out of the bed and advanced on Shane, stopping when the IV threatened to yank out of his arm. "The fingers I don't even have anymore itch like hell, but I deal with it. Not like you, who sits around oh, poor me I can't be a soldier anymore because I'm in a wheelchair." He mocked Shane's voice, then reached down and scooped up the Fritos. "Get the hell out."

Shane's anger dissipated like a cloud of poison gas disbursing on the breeze. He dragged his hand over his face and sucked in a deep breath. "What happened?"

"Fuck you." Carponti sank back onto the bed and turned the TV up.

Shane slammed his fist into the arm of his chair. "God fucking damn it, Carponti, what happened?"

Carponti clicked the TV off and threw the remote onto the blanket covering his lap. The silence grew uncomfortable in the room's stillness.

"I forgot I took the Vicodin."

"You forgot?"

Carponti's eyes widened and then narrowed. "Yes, Mother, I forgot I took the Vicodin. I don't expect you to believe me. Shit, ever since I've been home, you've been acting like I've had one finger on the goddamned trigger. Oh, wait. My trigger finger isn't there anymore. My bad."

"Carponti—"

"No. You wanted me to talk. How 'bout you shut the hell up and listen?" He dragged his hand through his bushy red hair. "I. Am. Fine. I'm not suicidal. I'm not trying to drink away my sorrows. I have a good wife and a good life that I will get on with one way or another. I lost an arm. So what? You're the one who has a problem with it. Not me."

Carponti reached into the cooler beside the bed and pulled out a fresh Dr Pepper and offered it to Shane. Shane accepted and kept quiet. Barely.

"I screwed up. I thought I'd only taken the meds for the phantom limb pain, but I guess I must have taken Vicodin, too. Then Nicole and I were watching the game and I thought I could handle a few drinks. I can't help it that my tolerance is as weak as a fourteen-year-old girl's after all of this."

Carponti was making jokes about trying to kill himself. Cold waves of relief crashed over Shane and his eyes burned. He blinked hard and fast.

Carponti held his hand to his heart and his expression was mock offense. "I can't believe you thought I tried to wax myself."

Shane dragged his hands over his face. "I'm sorry."

"Damn right you are. Now will you please get over the nub? It wants to be friends and you've offended it."

Shane's laugh nearly choked him. "The nu—your arm doesn't bother me."

"Bullshit. I see you watching it. Wondering if I'm freaking out. I have some bad times. Who doesn't? Get over it. You've still got a life to live, too." Carponti shrugged and snapped open his drink. "Guess I'm really out of the Army now. They tend to frown on suicidal ideations." He leaned over and pulled another snack-sized bag of Fritos from the duffel bag near his bed and stuffed a handful into his mouth. "Oh well, I'll figure something out. Maybe I'll work at McDonald's. They like to hire handicapped people. I'll be good PR for them."

The remaining tension in Shane's chest popped like a balloon. "You have the most twisted sense of humor."

Carponti nodded and held the open bag up to his mouth. Golden crumbs fell down his cheeks and his chest and he brushed them off as he munched on the remains. "Thanks." He swallowed. "You still look like shit though. When are you getting out of that chair?"

"Not soon enough." Shane cleared his throat.

"So guess who I saw yesterday? Our favorite lieutenant," Carponti snorted. "That weaselly little shit said he was stopping my pay. Said I was being found liable for the loss of the equipment. He hasn't told you the same thing?"

A slow burn of rage twisted inside Shane's guts. "No. He can't do that. There's an appeals process."

Carponti shrugged. "I don't know if he can or not but I think he already has. I'm pretty sure you're going to get hit up, too."

"How do you feel about public crucifixion?" Shane asked. Nailing Randall to a wall wouldn't be punishment enough.

Carponti laughed. "That's more like it. Our boys need you back in the fight. Someone has those missing optics and weapons."

Our boys. Shane closed his eyes. Jesus, he needed to get back on his feet, literally and figuratively speaking.

"Randall is crossing too many lines to force this stupid investigation through. Something else is going on."

Carponti snapped open a new Dr Pepper of his own. "Watch your back. Randall gave a senior NCO a letter of reprimand for disrespecting him."

"Should you really be drinking soda and eating chips after last night?" Shane raised his eyebrows, his expression feigning innocence. "What makes you think I'd disrespect our esteemed lieutenant?"

"You? Right, what could you possibly say to piss off our favorite lieutenant?" Carponti nearly snorted his Dr Pepper. "And I almost died, so yes, I'm eating Fritos and whatever the hell else I want."

"Your stomach might have other ideas." Shane maneuvered toward the door, shaking his head. He stopped and glanced back. "I'm glad you're okay."

Carponti sniffed and raised the soda to his lips. "Yeah. Me, too."

20

———

A week later

S hane swore for the seventeenth time that morning. He was lying flat on a wide bench that supported his entire body, his legs stretched out flat in front of him. He was embarrassed and frustrated that he'd broken a sweat trying to bench-press the lousy seventy-five pounds that his trainer had instructed him to try. It was humbling enough to not be able to lift even half of what he could just a few months ago. Add in the fact that Carponti was royally pissing him off, and he was having a real banner day.

"Come on, man, I can bench that with one arm!"

Shane slammed the weights back on the bar and sat up. "Do you mind? It's hard to concentrate with you running your mouth all the time."

Carponti had on a bright yellow tracksuit and he stuck out like a sore thumb in the room full of dull green carpet and tan weight benches. It would be hard to miss him anywhere except next to a flock of baby ducks. Or maybe Big Bird. Carponti was expending more energy harassing his platoon sergeant than doing any physical therapy of his own.

"Man, wait till I tell everyone back on the FOB that you're a total pussy! You can't even lift two hundred pounds. Even Ramirez should be able to beat you now."

Private Bill Ramirez was one hundred and ten pounds soaking wet. How the guy even moved with all his gear on remained a mystery to everyone in the platoon, but he was a tough little bastard, and he always requested to tote the M240B machine gun around on foot patrols. Considering that M240 machine guns weigh over twenty-five pounds *before* you added in the basic load of ammo, Ramirez was able to carry his own weight and then some.

"Carponti, go bug someone else, will you?"

"Can't. Two women have threatened to file sexual harassment complaints if I don't leave them alone, and they're the only ones here other than you. Man, I tell you, the little brown-haired girl, the one missing the foot? She is smoking hot!"

Shane groaned at Carponti's description. "Does Nicole know you talk like that?"

Carponti dismissed his remark with a wave of his bandaged arm and then tucked it close to his body again to resume his reps. "I guarantee Nicole's heard worse locker-room talk around the CID interview rooms. I know for a fact that I saw the little brown-haired one— her name's Kristin, by the way—checking you out."

"Carponti, have you forgotten that a private could get me courtmartialed? I'm. Not. Interested." Shane leaned back and slid under the weights again.

"A private could not get you court-martialed. You're both enlisted. What, did your dick get blown off or something?" Shane's face flamed but Carponti drove on, tactless as always. "Hello! You haven't been laid in how long? I mean, let's see, we were gone for four months and you've been back for." Carponti ticked off the numbers on his fingers. "Why don't you try talking to her? Unless the foot freaks you out. Which would be pretty fucked up, if you ask me."

Shane rubbed his hands over his face before gripping the bar. "Carponti, I swear if you don't shut up, I'm going to rip your other arm off and shove it down your throat," Shane growled.

There was a time and a place for this kind of conversation and the middle of the physical therapy floor at the hospital was not it. Shane couldn't recall the last time he wanted to beat someone up this badly. And a week ago, he'd been worried about the guy.

Carponti started coughing suddenly and Shane uncovered his face. Shane sat up and twisted his upper body, coming face-to-face with what was quite possibly the strictest-looking woman he'd ever seen on a military installation. She'd painted at least two inches of makeup on her face, and the effect was almost certainly not what she'd been going for. She looked like a cross between a drill sergeant and Dee Snyder from Twisted Sister.

Not a good look. At all.

"Gentlemen, while I appreciate that you two have the common bond of being mannerless heathens, I would appreciate it if you could keep the profanity to a minimum. Others have to share the air with you." Her voice had the thick rasp of a heavy smoker.

Shock of shocks, Carponti kept his mouth shut. Barely. Carponti let the silence stand for a few minutes. When he broke the silence, his voice was low. Sober. "Hey, man, did you hear what happened last night in the medical hold barracks?"

Shane grunted and slammed the bar back onto the rack. He sat up, his legs extended in front of him. "Uh-uh."

"A soldier tried to kill herself."

Shane rubbed the crease between his eyes and sighed. Another suicide attempt, the third in a week at Fort Hood. The medical hold barracks were a nightmare—they were poorly managed and seriously wounded soldiers were left to their own devices there, with no one to take accountability for them. They were in the process of setting up a Warrior Transition Unit, but so far the transition process had been chaos and the soldiers were paying the price. It was worse, by any standard, than Shane's own company, Randall and all.

"What happened?" Shane asked, stretching his arms out behind him.

"Husband left her. She ate her entire bottle of Percocets and half a bottle of Ambien. Her roommate found her. They pumped her stomach at the ER. And no, I'm not getting any ideas."

A quiet anger pulsed through Shane's blood but it didn't have a chance to boil over. Carponti was on to the next subject already, one that was infinitely more personal.

"Hey, check it out, here comes Jen. Have you decided to use the fact that you're staying with her to make a play for her yet? Because Nikki says all you have to do is snap your fingers and—"

Shane watched Jen approach, loving the way her scrubs hugged her hips. He wanted to smile in her direction, to see her smile back at him. But the awkwardness was still there, and for the life of him, Shane didn't know how to make it go away. Watching her approach, though, was exactly the wrong thing to do. Carponti took a long, lingering look at Shane and Jen. Jen and Shane.

"Ah, crap." Shane groaned and gave up. He was just going to have to put up with Carponti ragging on him for the next six lifetimes.

"Hey, how's it going?" Jen said as she walked up.

"I'm fine Ms. St. James. I think, ah, Sarn't G here could use a muscle massage. He strained pretty hard under those weights." Carponti paused dramatically, but before he could open his mouth to say more, Jen interrupted.

"Sergeant Carponti, Ms. Dunham at the desk has some paperwork you need to review. Would you mind going to see her before she takes off for lunch?"

Carponti smiled and winked at Shane behind Jen's back as he strolled over to the receptionist's desk. Shane ignored him and looked up at Jen. He needed to get things back to right between them. It was about damn time for him to apologize.

"Any pain?"

"Not pain so much as everything's throbbing."

"That's okay. That's just your body getting used to exertion again. You're not light-headed or dizzy are you?"

He looked across the room at Carponti, who was doing his best to antagonize the Dee Snyder–looking Ms. Dunham. "I'm sure Carponti is already mentally drafting an email telling the platoon what a pathetic weakling I've become." But he laughed when he said it, to ease the concern he saw on Jen's face. "I'm okay. I'm going to finish the routine and then I'll come find you."

"Do you need any help?"

"No, I've got my new best friend, the most annoying man in the world, to help me out. Thanks, though."

"Okay." She paused halfway between sitting and standing, then suddenly walked away.

He swallowed. He desperately wanted a do over. He wanted to erase the past week—to greet her with a kiss the morning after that night they'd spent together. A barrier had gone up between them, and it was so tall, he couldn't see a way over it. Shane couldn't be with Jen. Not until he was free of the restraints of his old life. Until he could hold her properly and not worry about whether he would walk again or be able to afford a place of his own. Until he could be with her, completely and utterly, and not be a goddamned leech.

Across the room, Osterman went through his routine silently. He waved a fuck-off banner to the world by having little white headphones stuffed into his ears, the music so loud that Shane could hear the tinny sound from across the PT room. He frowned. He'd watched Osterman a lot over the past week. He'd made several half-assed attempts at conversation, but Osterman had shot down every one. There was more to it than just Osterman's reluctance to shoot the shit like they used to do on the headsets in the Humvees when they'd been running patrols. His new taciturn nature worried Shane, and the way he treated his fiancée sent off warning signals in his gut.

Osterman's fiancée, Becky, was a cute, girl-next-door type, with brown hair and freckles. She helped Osterman through everything, day in and day out, no matter how silent her other half remained. But Shane saw a storm cloud gathering. Osterman's eyes were dark and distant—he didn't look at all like the fresh, eager kid he'd taken to Iraq just a few months before. And he was polite, freakishly so, with the girl who he'd been over the moon in love with before his injury.

He was pushing her away when he needed support, now more than ever. Becky had stood by Osterman through everything so far. She was pretty damn special to have stuck by his side through multiple burn surgeries and physical therapy. Osterman had no idea what he was doing: running off someone who cared enough to support him when things got rough.

Shane started to roll his wheelchair over to Osterman. Maybe if he kept trying, he'd eventually find a way to get through to him.

"Sorry for the disappearing act. I wanted to show you something," Jen said, returning suddenly and lowering herself to the bench beside him. Shane wished he had something more articulate to say to her other than, "What's this?"

"Your latest images. The doc had to rush down to emergency surgery, so I get to be the bearer of good news for once. Your right leg is healing much faster than anyone expected. In about two more weeks, we can start looking at surgery to remove the external fixators and see how you do."

Two weeks. In two weeks, he could potentially be on crutches instead of in a wheelchair. He'd be able to stand again. He was one small hurdle closer to getting back to his men. Something surged inside him. A feeling so foreign and strange he almost didn't know what to do with it. It fluttered a little against his heart—faint but strong—and he found a name for it.

Hope. And just as quickly, that hope shattered.

"I'm tired of this, Aaron!"

Shane looked up sharply. Becky was glaring at Osterman, who was balancing on his crutches with a scowl.

"I said I'm going to work on it. What else do you want from me?"

Becky shoved him and Osterman rocked back on the crutches. "I want *you* back. I'm tired of this cranky, sullen crap. What about me, Aaron? Did you ever stop to think that this isn't just about you?"

For a moment, Osterman looked like he was going to take a swing at his fiancée. Time hung still and Shane cursed his inability to separate them before one of them said or did something they'd regret. Osterman recoiled and the look on his face was pure anguish.

"Screw you, Becky! You sat back here and watched the war on TV while I was off fighting in some shit-hole country and getting blown half to hell. You think nagging the hell out of me is the best way to help me? I don't need your sympathy, and I damn sure don't need your pity!"

The Dee Snyder look-alike rushed up to intervene, but she was too late. The crack of Becky's palm against Osterman's cheek stunned the rest of the room into silence.

"I don't deserve that, Aaron. But congratulations. You wanted me to leave. I'm gone. You want to kill yourself, do it alone. I'm not going to stand by and watch." She snatched up her purse and left. The automatic doors swung wide, then slowly closed behind her, sealing the room into an awkward silence. Someone coughed after a moment, and then a throat was cleared. Osterman didn't look around as he palmed his iPod and hobbled out of the room, his head hanging low.

"Shane?" Jen said, her voice a whisper.

Cold fear gripped his throat. He watched Osterman go, dead sure if he let the kid leave without saying something, the next time he'd see him would be on a gurney.

"I've got to try and catch him." He maneuvered through the

benches and weight machines and pushed himself down the hallway, hoping to make a difference, just once more.

~

"OSTERMAN!" Shane powered his wheelchair through the hospital parking lot, toward the ancient medical hold barracks. It was a goddamned travesty that the soldiers who had nowhere else to go, some of whom required constant medical care, lived in these condemned buildings.

Right now, Shane had the more immediate concern of catching Osterman before he got into the building and up the stairs—where Shane couldn't follow him. Elevators hadn't been a part of Army life when these buildings were designed half a century ago and guys like Osterman were forced to hobble up dark stairwells to mildew-infested rooms.

He hated the damned bureaucrats who made decisions like this. They focused on the almighty dollar instead of the well-being of the soldiers. They were the same bureaucrats who sent soldiers off to war without adequate ammunition or armor, then sniffed and said they were working on it when the media finally roused themselves enough to care.

"Osterman!"

He stopped. Thank God in heaven, Osterman stopped, right in front of the door to the barracks. Shane let gravity power him down the gentle slope and damn near burned the skin off his palms when he tried to stop suddenly. "Hey. What happened?"

So much for eloquence.

Osterman fiddled with his iPod, one earbud still dangling around his neck. "I'm so fucking tired of her crap. Have you taken your medi-cine? Have you eaten? Have you wiped your ass? I'm sick of being treated like I'm a fucking baby. By her. By Carponti. By *you.*"

"I haven't treated you any different. You're still my best gunner."

"Ha-ha. Nice. I'm not a gunner, and I'm not an armorer. And you keep looking at me like I'm going to blow my fucking head off. So don't try and play the hero, Sarn't G, 'cause I've known you since I was a private, remember? You always sucked at bullshitting us."

Shane bit back a surge of anger. "Who the hell do you think you are? You think you're the only one who's gotten hurt? Shit, I know amputees who run marathons. Hell, they're better with the new legs than with the ones they were born with."

"I'm twenty-three fucking years old! I don't want to be a fucking cyborg. You don't see the looks I get every time I hobble around the hospital. The goddamned pity. You think I want to wave the freak flag of a fucking mechanical leg? I want my life back!"

"This isn't the way to do it. You're running everyone out of your life who gives a shit about you."

"You're going to sit there and lecture me, too? I'm the one missing a fucking leg. You'll be up and walking soon."

"And I'm going to be in fucking rehab for at least a year. Are you really sitting here playing a who-has-it-worse game with me? That's unworthy of you. You're better than that, Osterman."

"Correction. I was better than that. Now? Now I just want all of you to leave me the fuck alone."

Osterman disappeared behind the ancient, rust-colored door of the barracks. Shane closed his eyes and let out a vicious stream of profanity. Goddamn it, he needed to get up to that kid's room and snap him out of it. That wasn't the kid who'd patrolled Sadr City with him. That wasn't the kid who'd taken down an entire house laden with explosives with a fifty cal. He needed to find Carponti and send him up after Osterman.

Shane stared at the door, and at the stairs behind it, and swore as helplessness gnawed at his soul.

21

"How's Vic?" Jen set a bottle of wine on the coffee table in Laura's living room, sidestepping a Tonka truck.

Laura started to pick up, but Jen stopped her. Once upon a time, her living room had looked like a Pottery Barn display. Now? Now it looked like a playroom with a couple of push toys stuffed in the corner near the fireplace. "Sit. Clean later. It's just us."

Nicole smiled sadly and reached for the bottle. "He's fine, now that I've taken all his pills away. He got pissed when I asked him about his prescriptions for the first time. After the accident, though, he practically dropped them into my lap."

"He did?" Jen said.

"Yeah. Said he was sorry he screwed up. He thought he had everything under control and he didn't. He didn't want to accidentally kill himself, so would I please keep him from overdosing again."

Laura frowned and looked up at the ceiling. "Sorry, thought I heard the kids. Is this the same Carponti I know?"

Nicole offered a faint, lopsided shrug. "At least he's okay and he's letting me help. I felt so powerless before. . . . What's this?" she asked, as she reached beneath the coffee table and pulled out a large photo album. "Laura and Trent, circa August 2001."

A younger version of Laura stood smiling on the front of it, her hand pressed to the heart of a much younger looking Trent, who was also smiling.

"I borrowed that wedding dress," Laura said, leaning over. Instead of looking away, she scooted even closer so that she could look over Nicole's shoulder. A hint of a smile played on her lips. "Trent looked so good in his Dress Blues."

"Most men do," Jen said.

"Oh no." Nicole ran the tip of her finger around the rim of her glass. "You obviously have not been to a military ball. Some of the paunches those guys try to squeeze into uniforms they wore when they were privates or lieutenants are downright scary. Should be criminal."

Laura laughed and turned the page. "Most men look sexy in their blues, how about that?"

Jen stopped hearing anything. Trent stood next to Shane on the page in front of them. Younger, his face not quite so worn by the elements or time. His shoulders were just as broad and his blues tapered into narrow hips that were clothed in lighter blue pants. She leaned closer and looked at the awards on his chest and wished she knew what they represented. There were a lot of them. At least, it looked like a lot to her.

"Maybe you'll share your good news with us when you're done undressing Shane with your eyes?" Nicole asked.

"What good news?" Jen blinked and looked up from the photo. There might have been good news had things not gone so badly between them. But they had. So many times over the last few days, she'd almost stepped over the barrier between them. And each time, she'd turned away. *He had to be the one to cross it.*

"Don't lie. You and Shane, you know . . ."

Embarrassed heat crawled over Jen's skin. She tried to find somewhere else to look besides at her friends, but her gaze just landed back on the photo of Shane.

"Spill," Laura said. "I've spent so much time with my vibrator, I've forgotten what a penis looks like. I'm living vicariously through your sex life."

Jen flushed and Nicole pounced. "Laura, look, she's blushing."

"So it was good then?"

Jen closed her eyes and nodded and wished this wasn't such a disaster. The conversation or the sex, for that matter. "Yeah."

"Um, I can't have some sexy hot fantasy involving Eric Bana if you don't give me more details than just a yeah," Laura said. "Where is he tonight, anyway?"

"He's home. He's been quiet lately." Jen lifted a page and peeked on the other side. Shane was dancing with a striking woman with black hair and pale skin. She looked like a goddess.

"That's his ex-wife," Laura said, tapping the page with her middle finger.

"She's beautiful," Jen murmured. She tried not to compare the woman in the picture with the scarred woman she saw every time she looked in the mirror. But she did. Where Tatiana was willow thin and gorgeous, Jen was petite and, well, she supposed she wasn't hideous. At least not until her bra with the silicon mold came off.

"She's a bitch," Nicole said. "I don't care how lonely you are, you don't cheat." Laura flipped the photo album closed. "This whole trip down memory lane is pointless. I don't need to look at my wedding pictures. I was there, remember?"

"Just because something went wrong doesn't mean you can't still love him," Nicole said.

"Loving Trent isn't my problem. He's the father of my kids. I'm always going to love him. I can't be in love with a picture. I'm tired of waiting for him to come home." Laura set her wineglass down with a hard tink and stood. "I love you both, but you have no idea what it's like raising two kids by yourself. I'm not a single parent by choice, I'm a single parent by my husband's choice. He's literally been home for long enough to get me pregnant and that's it." She bit her lips and stared into space. "I can't trust him. Not about being faithful. Not about his reasons for deploying. How can I possibly stay married to him?"

Laura didn't speak for a long moment. When she reached for her glass, her hand shook.

"It doesn't sound like that will make you happy," Nicole said.

"It won't. But I'll stop caring eventually." She poured another glass.

"Maybe he's busy," Nicole said. "I know Trent. I really don't think he would cheat. You should give him the chance to explain."

Laura scoffed and dragged out two large scrapbooks, one pink, one blue. "Want to see what more time gets me? Look. Here's Emma's birth. Just me and my little girl alone in the hospital. And here's Ethan's. Noticing a trend so far?"

"No Trent," Jen murmured.

"And we have a winner. But wait, there's more. If you turn the pages of these albums, you'll see first birthdays, second birthdays, Halloween, and every single Thanksgiving since 2003. You know what you won't see? Any pictures of Trent. Because he wasn't there." Laura dashed her fingers beneath her eyes and attempted a watery smile. "I've tried. I've done five different tours alone now and I would have waited a decade or more for him if things were different. But, cheating rumors aside, he's been *volunteering* to go. I'm done waiting for a man who doesn't want to come home to me."

And Jen couldn't argue with that. No matter how badly she wanted Trent and Laura to fix things, Trent had hurt her friend, and badly. It was going to take a miracle to get through her pain, and Trent wasn't even trying.

He'd given up his family to go to war and Laura had every reason to be furious and hurt and finished.

SHANE LOOKED up from the magazine he'd been pretending to read for the last three hours. The front door open and Jen walked through. He was hit with a potent kick of relief mixed with desire. He was fixing this. Tonight, one thing in his life was going to go right, damn it. Maybe he couldn't be with her, but he could damn well get things back to what they'd been like before he'd screwed up. He could get back to being her friend.

"Hi." Damn, that was brilliant.

"Hi." She dropped her purse by the door and kicked off her shoes. She moved with an almost fluid grace to the love seat across from where he sat on the couch. Jen rubbed her temples.

She looked beautiful. Beautiful but exhausted. "You look tired."

She turned and looked at him, a glint of light from the kitchen spilling onto her face. "It comes with the job."

"I know."

He swallowed as she rubbed her head with her hand again. "You don't have to sit and make small talk, if you don't feel like it," she said after a moment.

"What if that's exactly what I want?"

She looked at him again and Shane wished he could read her thoughts. Her body language was too fatigued to reveal much. "Okay. What do you want to talk about?"

He met her gaze. Steady. Afraid to blink. Afraid to look away and risk breaking the fragile peace between them. "I screwed up, okay? I never meant to hurt you by suggesting you don't know what it feels like to lose someone."

Jen sat up abruptly and leaned forward, her elbows hitting her knees. "I was trying to goad you into looking past your legs all the damn time."

"What you said about control? You were right. I'm used to being in control. I'm used to having my finger on the trigger and knowing the plan and, hell, even writing the plan. I can't plan now. I can barely think half the time. All because these fucking pins take up my entire field of vision and I can't see anything else."

"That's just it, Shane. You're more than your injuries. You're hurt. So what? You're not dead."

"I'm also not going through the same thing Carponti and Osterman are. They've lost limbs."

"I lost a breast and I'm doing just fine. Carponti will get better and he'll be fine. I'm willing to bet he fights to stay in the Army and learns how to shoot again."

He wanted to tell her that Osterman was not going to be fine. That he was going to wake up one day and realize that he'd driven away everyone who'd ever cared about him. That Randall was going to badger each person on Shane's team until they broke and admitted to something they didn't do just to get the damn lieutenant to leave them alone.

"Carponti was one of my best sergeants," Shane said quietly. "Osterman was hell on a fifty cal. So much potential there, and now it's gone."

Jen moved before Shane could even register the movement. The couch bent beneath her weight and the heat from her body began sinking into his skin. "Stop talking about them like they're dead.

They're not. You're not. Tomorrow's another day. You'll get another chance to make a difference."

"It's not that," Shane said.

"Then what is it? Explain it to me so that I understand. Because I don't."

The words got stuck right beneath the hollow in his throat. He cleared it then, and forced them out. "It's that I can't fix this. I can't fix what's wrong with Carponti. I can't fix Osterman's head so that he stops looking like he's about to off himself." He dropped his head back and closed his eyes. "I have never been this useless before in my entire life."

"Shane, you're not supposed to fix everyone else's problems."

"Yes I am!" The force of his words stunned them both. So much for fixing things. He was making this worse, but he couldn't stop now that the dam had broken. "I am. That's what I do. I fix my soldier's problems. I let them lean on me when things in their lives are broken. I take care of them."

Her fingers were cool on his cheeks as she traced her fingertips over his skin. "Then maybe it's time you accept that you need a little help fixing your own things," she murmured.

"I can't. Because I'm not supposed to be the one who needs fixing."

He sat with his hand covering his mouth. So still he might have been a statue. It was a long time before he moved his hand from his mouth. His voice sounded cracked and rough. "The first soldier I ever buried committed suicide."

He rubbed his hand over his face before he continued. "I was too young and too cocky to see it coming. The signs were all there. He started showing up late to work. His performance started falling off. Then one day, he didn't come in. I lied when I reported I had all my men accounted for. I was almost court-martialed for dereliction of duty when they found Dickerson's body." He sucked in a deep breath. "He killed himself on Friday, right after end-of-day formation, and no one knew until Monday." He pressed his mouth into a flat line. "It took two and a half days for me to find out that one of my guys killed himself."

The muscles in his neck were tense, straining against his skin. "And he was just the first soldier I buried. Do you want to know the names of the other ten? Martinez. Neils. Jablowski. Mercado. Davis. Williams."

"Shane. Stop."

"Stupediwictz. We called him Widget. Zublow. Mitchum. Adel. But only one killed himself." He closed his eyes, covering his mouth with his hands again. "Today, I felt like I was sitting at the bottom of a fucking mountain because I couldn't climb the goddamned stairs at the barracks to get to my soldier."

"Shane." She knelt at the edge of the couch, her fingers digging into his forearm. His skin was hot against hers. "This isn't your fault. There's still time to get through to him." Please, God, don't let her be wrong.

Finally he looked at her and the pain in his eyes tore at her soul. "I need these pins out. I need to be able to get places where wheels can't take me."

"I can't do that for you, Shane. Even if I could, getting them out requires a surgical team and you're not fully healed yet."

His mouth opened but no sound came out. Nothing, then he snapped it shut.

"Look, instead of worrying about what you can't do, let's figure out what you can. Osterman comes in for physical therapy—"

"Every time I try to talk to him, he avoids me, and climbs up stairs so I can't follow him. Do you know how fucking pathetic that is? One of my guys went to the hospital for screwing up his pills. Osterman is just a matter of time. I know it in my soul. This is my team. These are my boys, and they're floundering because I can't get my ass out of that chair."

Jen stood abruptly. "You know what? Fine. Sit here and wallow. You're letting a flight of stairs do you in? Really?"

Finally, emotion sparked in his eyes—dark fury roiled there in a massive ball of energy. "This is my fault!" he shouted. "Both of them were hurt on missions that I was running."

"So what? They got hurt. They're alive, damn it. They're still alive." Her words started with a shout but ended with a whisper. Shane's boys were alive but he was dying sitting in that wheelchair. It was as though it was doing more than atrophying his muscles, it was chipping away at his soul.

"Shane." She reached for him, cupping his rough jaw and turning his face toward hers. "This is not your fault. You are a soldier. You cannot save everyone. Good men die in combat and you can't save them. Your boys are alive. Be happy for that."

"Every time I see Osterman, I'm reminded of Dickerson," he whispered.

"Then we'll figure out how to get him to stick around longer so you can talk to him. We'll figure it out. Stop acting like you had the power to change this. You're just a man. You're not supposed to be okay all the time, either."

Silence hung between them for a long moment.

"Jen, I can't do this."

"Do what?"

"Us."

"Well, you know, we already did the 'us' thing. And unless you want to stay in that van down by the river, brushing me off right now is the last thing you want to do." She paused, waiting to see his reaction. "Yes, that means I'm blackmailing you. I need to keep the Great Penis around a little longer."

He choked. "What?" he managed.

"Never mind. Inside joke."

"Seeing how I assume this is my penis we're talking about—"

"Will you shut up and kiss me?"

He pulled her to him and kissed her like a dying man. Like he wasn't going to get another chance at this, whatever this was. Because she'd been wrong. He couldn't count on being able to try again tomorrow.

He only had today. Tomorrow, he had one less day to make a difference. But he didn't tell her that. He slid his tongue against hers and tasted her, Jen, and something so much more.

Something stronger than anything he'd ever felt. Something that felt like pure heaven.

He'd fallen for her and he didn't even know when it had happened. He just knew that today, she'd pushed her way into his personal hell and shoved him out of it. And he was so damn grateful that she was there.

It was what she did, he realized, as he urged her closer. He wanted to feel her weight against his chest, the brush of her hair against his shoulder. He ached for the day he could see her beneath him and touch her the way he craved.

But for tonight, he would take her however he could have her. Her breath sighed into his mouth as she made tiny, sexy gasps. Her fingers curled into his shoulders, her nails dug into his skin in the most delicious pain.

He twined his fingers through her hair and angled her mouth to claim all of her. She shifted and he pulled her to him until she sprawled across his lap. His legs ached in this position, but he was unwilling to move, to lose that intimate contact between them that he needed.

He needed this. He needed it with her. He traced his fingers down her neck and watched as she arched, tipping her head back and giving him access to the soft skin of her throat. His fingers trembled as he traced her jaw, feeling the soft pulse of her heart beneath the pad of his index finger.

Jen pulled away abruptly, unwilling to cede all control. She'd worried that he might never touch her again after how she'd reacted last time. Tonight, when he'd reached for her, she'd gone willingly into his embrace. The strength in his arms amazed her. Even after weeks of limited activity, he was so strong. So solid.

He'd tried to push her away tonight and it had taken everything she'd held within her to push back. To not let him dictate everything in their relationship. Because she was at least done with lying to herself about that. They had a relationship.

Shane and his boys, Carponti and Osterman, had somehow become spheres in her life, always there. Always present. With their presence came worry, but she wouldn't give that worry up.

She cared deeply for this man. She pulled his T-shirt over his head, and reveled in the sight of his powerful chest.

His breath was coming hard and fast. When she lowered her face to press a kiss onto the black lines above his heart, he stilled. There, in the stillness of his body, a deep tremor began. She felt it beneath her lips, beneath her fingertips as she traced them up the inside of his arms and down his ribs, to his navel. His stomach jumped beneath her fingers and a delicious female power circled through her veins like liquid fire.

THERE WAS no way he could sit here and let her explore his body without the most powerful desire beating against his skin. Every inch of his flesh ached as she teased him. Stroked his skin and smiled like she knew exactly what she was doing to him.

He pulled her up abruptly. "I need you naked," he whispered against her mouth.

She kissed him deeply as she somehow shimmied out of her pants and helped him ease his shorts down and off. "Thank God for athletic shorts," she murmured.

He didn't miss the fact that she kept her shirt on again. But then she was kissing him and her heat slid over his erection until he damn near exploded at the contact. He gripped her hip with one hand, urging her to sink down onto him.

Then she did, and he was lost. He was drowning in her, his hands roaming her body, slicking over her belly, her hips. He wanted to touch her everywhere. He slid a hand up her shirt.

He stopped thinking and just felt. Wanted to cup her softness in his hand. Needed to feel her nipple pucker against his palm.

Her sudden stillness struck him like a freight train. Her fingers dug into his wrist and her body was no longer welcoming. "Don't," she whispered, pushing his hand away.

He leaned up, trying to kiss her. "It's just a scar, Jen. It doesn't matter."

"It does to me. Please don't."

Jen couldn't explain the chill in her veins that had doused her arousal as quickly as if she'd been thrown in a Minnesota lake in the dead of winter. He was still buried deep inside of her and part of her ached for him, for his touch. For this union that completed a missing part of her soul.

Still, she didn't release his hand. "Jen, relax."

"It's not that important."

"You're beautiful to me. Scars or not. Let me see you," he said, his voice rough. "Trust me with that."

"I can't."

The shadow fell across her face and she looked away, a new tension in the set of her shoulders as reality sank in. No one had done this to her. The voice she heard in her head telling her she was a freak was her very own.

Shane let her go. He couldn't do this with her. Not like this. Not if she insisted on keeping this barrier between them. As she stood beside the couch, Jen's jaw was set, her eyes shadowed with an old hurt. She didn't leave. Not yet. "Getting help and not feeling sorry for yourself only applies to other people, doesn't it, Jen?"

Her fingers shook as she reached for her pants. "Let it go, Shane," she said quietly as she yanked them on and padded up the stairs.

She could talk all she wanted about getting better and facing his problems.

But she'd never moved past her own. And until she did, they were dead on arrival.

22

———————

I t was quite possibly the worst she'd ever felt. Her lips tingled from his kisses and her belly felt warm and heated. Her blood hummed.

What on earth had she been thinking?

She hadn't been. Jen remembered what it was like to question her value as a woman. As a person. Something in Shane gave her the confidence to feel desirable again. Something she hadn't felt in oh-so-long. Yet it still wasn't enough to overcome how she felt about her scar. Last night, it had crushed something beautiful between them.

She wished she could have taken that final step and opened herself to him. That she'd let herself feel his fingers against her breast and his lips on her nipple.

She'd been weak and afraid to drop that barrier between them, just like she always was when it came to that stupid scar.

"You, my dear, are an idiot," Laura said to her from across the table.

Of course, she was an even bigger idiot for sharing what had happened with Laura. Now she was never going to hear the end of it.

"Wow, that's something I usually say to you when we talk about your divorce," Jen said, cradling her coffee in both hands. It was the only source of warmth she could hold on to. Hence, the emergency coffee trip first thing in the morning. Jen hadn't even bothered to hide any of the details. She'd told her friend everything.

"We're not talking about me today, we're talking about you. And it's your issues that are keeping you from having a real relationship with someone who cares for you," Laura said as she pinned Jen with a hard look over the edge of her coffee cup.

"Well, how do you really feel? 'Cause I'm completely in the mood to be beaten about the head, neck, and shoulders with your opinion."

Laura laughed. "At least your sense of humor isn't dead," she said. "Look. I love you. You're the sister I never had. I've known both you and Shane for years. He doesn't deserve to have your hang-ups thrown at him like this. And you're better than that."

"So much for understanding," Jen muttered.

"I do understand. I get it. You're short a breast. I was there, remember? I held your hair when you were throwing up and I held your hand the first time you looked at the scar. I do understand. You're alive because you made that choice. You keep telling everyone else that it's okay not to be okay every once in awhile. So why don't you take your own advice?"

"Laura, we were having sex and he wanted me to take my top off. It was the biggest buzz kill I've ever felt."

"You already showed it to him. What's the difference? You were turned on. He was turned on. Let him see it and feel it through a sexual haze of lust and desire. What's the real problem here?"

Jen opened her mouth, then snapped it shut. "I can't. Yes, he's seen it, but it's a whole different ball game to get fully naked in front of him. I want to feel sexy around him, not like something is missing. And I wouldn't have been able to relax at all."

"You don't know that. You didn't even try."

Jen ignored her and drove on, letting everything out. "Now he's not talking to me. He called Carponti to come get him today rather than ride into work with me."

"Do you blame him? Jen, hon, you left him with blue balls last night."

Jen's horrified laugh escaped before she could slap her hand over her mouth to stop it. "This really isn't about his balls. Blue or otherwise."

"No, it's not. I guarantee you, he's not pissed about the coitus interruptus. He's hurt about your lack of *trust*."

Jen closed her eyes and took a sip of her coffee, letting the liquid burn down her throat slowly as she absorbed Laura's words. Shane's whispered plea burned in her memory. *Trust me with that.*

"I trust him." But she hadn't. Not when it had really mattered.

"Not enough for him. Shane defines trust as watching his back in a firefight. Keeping your shirt on was like telling him you might not fire if you had to."

Reality of what she'd lost crept in, closing off her throat. "I can't fix this, can I?"

"I don't know. You'll have to talk to Shane about that. I think you're going to have to work on that trust thing. I'm pretty sure it's a deal breaker for him."

Jen sighed, wishing she was dealing with something easier. Like maybe a root canal. Or a Pap smear. But this?

This was hard.

This was not something she was going to be able to just decide to do. It involved changing years' worth of habits. Years' worth of seeing herself a certain way and still pretending everything was fine.

Everything was not fine.

It wasn't fine because she wasn't fine.

She was broken.

Flawed.

Damaged.

She didn't know how to trust someone to look at her and not see that. How could she, when it was all she saw when she looked in the mirror? But the alternative was losing Shane.

Somehow, she had to find a way to walk through the fire and trust him. She needed to fix this.

The question was, how?

"Sarn't G! Got an emergency here." Carponti raced into the PT room, ignoring the protests from the Dee Snyder look-alike.

The minute Shane saw the look on his friend's face, panic curled in his guts.

Carponti jerked his thumb over his shoulder. "Osterman. Dude is barricaded in his room and won't come out. Supposedly he has a gun, or a knife or something. The kid finally just started talking through his door, and he's been asking the MPs what the point of it all is."

They raced out of the hospital, all the while Shane praying that it wasn't too late. As Carponti helped him into the truck, Shane kept on thinking that this was his last chance. If he screwed this up, Osterman died.

Goddamn it, he was not burying another soldier.

The parking lot of the medical hold barracks was blocked off. Carponti pulled his truck up onto the grass and helped Shane out of the cab. Three police cars created a barrier between the building and the small group of people outside. Shane thought he saw Becky, Osterman's fiancée, in the crowd but he wasn't sure and he didn't have time to check because Randall broke away from the military police, his mouth pressed into a tight, humorless line. "You're not authorized to be here."

"And you can pound sand," Shane snarled. He pushed around the lieutenant only to have Randall step in front of him again.

"What part of what I said don't you understand?" Randall asked, holding a manila folder to his chest.

"The pound sand part, obviously," Carponti said from behind Shane. "Oh wait, that was your line."

"Move, Lieutenant. Because I am getting up those stairs."

"You're not on duty, Sergeant. That soldier is attempting suicide to get out of having to accept responsibility for losing night vision goggles."

Shane lunged up from his chair and grabbed the front of Randall's uniform. He kept his voice low. Low enough that even Carponti couldn't hear. "I don't care who your father is or who you've jerked off to remain an officer after you killed two of our boys, but listen to me and listen to me well. I will tear your fucking heart out if you don't get the hell out of my way."

"That's communicating a threat. Violation of Article 134 of the Uniformed Code of Military—"

Randall was ripped from Shane's grip suddenly. Carponti had his fist wrapped tight in the LT's uniform, and he marched him backward until his back collided with one of the squad cars. The little brown-haired soldier from physical therapy—Kristin—came around from the other side, wearing an MP brassard and a concerned smile. If

Shane hadn't seen her every day for weeks on end, he'd never have known that a prosthetic foot filled her left boot. Her partner, a heavyset guy who looked like he might have been Samoan, circled the car, his palm resting near the butt of his weapon.

"Kristin, can you help me out for a sec?" Carponti asked. "I think this lieutenant's got a problem with his driver's license. And you know, it's so hard to get troops to do the right thing when their officers don't do it themselves."

"Sure, Sarn't C. This is the guy you were telling me about? The one who's been fishing without a license, too?"

"That's the one." Carponti smiled at Randall and patted his chest, smoothing the ruffled uniform. "You wouldn't hit a girl with one foot, would you? Now be a good lieutenant and show the young MPs here your license and registration so she can see what she needs to verify."

Randall attempted to bluster his way out of the conversation but the big MP blocked his escape.

"That was easy." Carponti walked back toward Shane, who sat dumbfounded. "What? I took a play from you and made up some bullshit to get him out of the way. Kristin has been listening to me bitch about Randall for a couple weeks now. Glad she played along. That could have been awkward, to say the least."

"Wasn't she one of the females in PT going to file a complaint against you?" Shane asked.

"The Nub talked her out of it. Now, where were we? I've got the master key to the barracks room, by the way." Carponti called over one of the MP sergeants. "Hey, Sarn't Jack, any problem with us going up there?"

Sarn't Jakelov frowned and looked between Shane and Carponti. "Not supposed to. But I'm thinking I might have something else going on that keeps me from stopping you."

"How do you know all of these people?" Shane asked in amazement. He'd known Carponti was good under pressure, but this was unprecedented, even for him.

"Jake lives upstairs from my apartment. He filled me in on the situation before I came and got you."

"Do you know everyone on Fort Hood?"

Carponti didn't smile. "Almost." They stopped at the bottom of the stairs. Shane swore, long and colorful, when he realized how futile their mission was. He'd forgotten about the goddamned stairs. Carponti groaned and rolled his eyes. "Oh great. Guess this means I get to carry your heavy ass up the stairs? You can bet it isn't going to be the princess carry."

In the end, Carponti wrapped his arms around Shane's waist and kept most of the weight on Shane's left leg, the one that Jen had told him was the closest to being healed. Between Shane holding himself up with the rails and Carponti's assistance, they managed to get him up the stairs to the second floor. Carponti went back for the wheelchair, then helped Shane into it.

"This is all on you, man." He handed Shane the master key and waited at the top of the stairs. "But I've got your back if you need me."

Fuck, he wished Carponti had cracked a joke.

Shane rolled down the darkened corridor alone. The smell of mildew and old cigarettes permeated the air in the hallway. The only light flickered from one working overhead fluorescent bulb and the daylight filtering in from the dirty windows at either end. This was worse, way worse, than clearing a building by himself. Shane held his breath and knocked on the door.

"Osterman? Hey, man, it's Shane. Sarn't G? Can I come in?"

No sound acknowledged Shane's words.

"Just want to talk, buddy. I'm going to open the door, okay? Just me." Shane figured that the silence meant agreement. He sucked in a deep breath and slid the master key into the lock, pushing the door open slowly, surprised when there was no resistance.

Osterman's room was immaculate. Shane had half expected to find it trashed, destroyed in some kind of tantrum with mattresses and furniture blocking the door. Nothing was out of place. Not even the soldier's toothbrush, which was stacked neatly in a little black holder by the small sink.

Osterman sat in the bottom of his closet. He just sat there, showing no recognition when Shane rolled into the room. He had no weapon. He was just alone and distraught, an orange bottle of white pills near his hip.

"Want to tell me what's going on?"

Osterman looked up and Shane saw a lost little boy. A kid who'd gone off to war and had seen things that no one should ever see no matter how many years they walked the earth. Shane could lie to himself and pretend he'd dealt with everything he'd seen and done, but sometimes he still couldn't sleep at night.

"He was my best friend and he's just gone," Osterman whispered, his voice flat, dull. Like he'd given up and was just waiting for his turn to check out. Shane glanced at the pills, wishing he knew how many were in there and what they were. "One minute he's there and the next I'm covered in his blood and bone."

"How long did you know him?" Shane asked. He'd known Osterman since he was a private. How was it that his buddy had gotten killed and Shane didn't know about it? Who the hell was he talking about?

"Man, we grew up together. Since kindergarten. Same school, everything. We went through basic training together." Osterman rubbed his hands over his eyes, rimmed red and swollen.

"Who are you talking about?"

"Jimmy Peters. He died when our chow hall got blown up when we first got to Iraq."

"I didn't know you and Peters were close. Why didn't you say anything? Shit, man, you've been carrying this around for months."

"Because we were all busy. I just shoved it away and stayed focused on the mission. I didn't want to let anyone down. But now? Now all I do is think about Jimmy and the rest of the guys we lost." He swiped his forearm across his eyes. "His mom calls me still, all the time, and I— Man, I have no idea what to say to her."

"Do you think she blames you?" Shane asked quietly, his voice steady and strong, barely controlling the chaos inside him.

"Heck, no. She keeps telling me she's so grateful that one of her boys is okay, that she didn't lose both of us. She tells me that I can stay with her, whenever I want."

"Sounds like an awesome lady."

Osterman smiled. "She is. She took me in a lot when I was a kid. I always stopped by Jimmy's on the way home from school. Mrs. Peters always fed me because she knew my mom didn't always remember to keep food in the house."

Shane remembered many nights when he'd gone to bed hungry for that very same reason. In Iraq, he'd listened to Osterman talk about how he and Becky were going to have a different life than the one he'd had growing up. How his kids were never going to go to bed hungry. Now, though, Shane wondered if Osterman remembered any of that or if all he could think about was his friend's death.

"I feel like she calls me because she wants to hold on to Jimmy. Tells me how glad she is that at least I'm okay. It's like she wants me to replace Jimmy, though, and I can't do that."

Shane wanted to chase away the demons that tormented Osterman. He wished he could take all of this kid's pain into himself, so that he could grow up like a normal person would, not some scarred veteran carrying the ghosts of a war with him for the rest of his life.

"What would Jimmy want you to do?" When was he going to get the words right? This small talk was killing him, like taking screws to his soul.

"He'd kill me if I didn't talk to his mom."

Shane sucked in a deep breath, holding it until he felt a shade steadier. "You know, it's hard to hear, but, sometimes, moms know a whole lot more than we give them credit for. Maybe she's telling you she's grateful you're still alive, because she is. Did you think of that?"

Shane rubbed his hands over his face. Was he getting through to Osterman at all? Had he already taken the pills?

"How can she be glad that I'm okay? I'm not her real son. I'm just some stray she picked up off the street. Her real son, he came home in pieces." Osterman dug his palms into his eyes and Shane saw more tears leaking from beneath his hands. "So did I."

"One thing I know for sure is that family is not defined by blood. If she thinks . . ." Shane swallowed and cleared his throat, a lump blocking his words. "If she says you're family, then, son, you're family. Don't run off someone who cares about you. Because most people don't stick when times get hard."

Osterman was quiet. "How do I get that picture of Jimmy out of my head?" he asked, his voice barely a whisper. "How do I talk to her when all I see is him exploding in front of me?"

Shane didn't have any answers and for once, he didn't try. He couldn't offer advice or counseling. Not on this. "I wish I knew. I know she's hurting, too, and talking to you must help her in some way. Maybe that's how you start to heal. You know, helping Jimmy's mom heal."

His voice cracked, and Osterman finally let the sorrow escape in great, racking sobs. "Why did he have to die, Sarn't G? Why couldn't it have been me instead?"

Shane set the brake and heaved himself out of his chair, ignoring the fire that exploded as he jarred his pins when he dropped to the ground. It was so much harder than dragging himself into bed or off the weight bench in physical therapy, but he didn't care. He reached into the closet and dragged Osterman against him. And Osterman let it all go, let his pain and sorrow and the guilt tear free until Shane thought it would destroy them both.

There were no words to make the pain stop. Nothing Shane could do to help him through it. He could only offer the understanding of shared experience. Of loss. Of grief for fallen friends and fellow soldiers. That grief never went away, and only time would make the sharp stabbing pain subside to a dull throbbing ache.

Osterman finally eased away, his eyes red and puffy. "I think I need to call Becky," he said softly.

Some of the tension around Shane's heart eased back. "She's right outside, buddy. She's been here waiting for you this whole time. You just needed to figure that out."

Osterman nodded and helped Shane back into his chair, then pushed him out of the room. The silence around them was filled with the ghosts of the friends and brothers who'd made the ultimate sacrifice so that men like them could make it home.

For once, Carponti had nothing smart to say as he and Osterman managed to get Shane back downstairs. They nearly fell a half dozen times. Shane was damn near certain Carponti had a joke in there somewhere about the three gimps, but he kept it to himself. At least, for now.

The moment they were outside, Becky rushed up and threw her arms around Osterman's neck, and sobbed that she was sorry she'd left him alone. One of the MPs started to break them apart but Shane waved them off. There was nothing else Osterman needed at that moment and it seemed like forever before Osterman eased Becky back, a whispered "I'm sorry" tearing from him.

Later, Carponti helped Shane into his truck, and they watched as Osterman went in the other direction, following Becky into the hospital. He wouldn't be allowed to go home. Not right away. Osterman would spend the night with the hospital psychiatrists, who would make sure he wasn't going to hurt himself.

Shane knew Osterman was going to pull through. Sitting in the driver's seat, Carponti was looking over at him like he'd just moved heaven and earth. Carponti was wrong. He wasn't a hero—he just hadn't screwed up today. The sooner they all accepted that, the better it would be. Osterman had finally trusted him with what had been gnawing on his soul. It was more than Jen was willing to do. He needed to pack up his stuff and find a place of his own, where he could figure his life out.

Alone.

Because that's how it was for him. Even when he'd been married, he'd been alone. Now that his boys were safe, he could finally rest. Alone.

Because he was so damn tired of fighting.

Shane and Carponti didn't talk much on the way to Jen's. His friend's failure to crack his usual jokes had Shane watching him out of the corner of his eye. He could see stress in the lines between Carponti's eyebrows and in the way his knuckles stood out stark white on the steering wheel.

"How'd you know Osterman wasn't going to hurt himself?" Carponti asked quietly.

Shane didn't answer right away. "I didn't," he said, after clearing his throat.

"Yeah, but you just went into his room. The MPs were out there for over an hour before you showed up, and they wouldn't risk going in. I'm shocked I talked Jake into letting you through."

Tension squeezed around Shane's heart again, a vise that prevented him from breathing deeply as he relived that first push through the door. It had felt like being the first man in a stack to enter a room, the first man in a fatal funnel—only worse, because Shane had been forced to slowly enter the door rather than using violence and overwhelming firepower. "The MPs have protocols for dealing with situations like that. I figured, worst-case scenario, I'll get shot. Osterman was just— He was just lost."

Carponti didn't speak as he pulled onto the road leading to Jen's house. He put the truck into park next to her property and his eyes stared forward, over the field toward a distant line of woods.

Shane cleared his throat, wishing the block in there would break up. "You had my back today. Thanks."

"More like I had your ass on my back," Carponti muttered.

Shane cracked a grin as relief pushed back some of the tension.

"Osterman didn't know how to deal with what happened to him. With losing guys on our team let alone someone he grew up with."

Carponti's fingers twisted on the steering wheel. "How do you deal with it? With the guys we've lost?"

Shane rubbed his chest, hoping to ease the ache throbbing there, just above his heart. He was going down a road he'd deliberately avoided until now, but Carponti seemed determined to explore it. "I don't know."

Silence filled the truck again, but neither man made a move to leave. Shane sucked in a deep breath. "Man, when you first came to see me, you messed me up. You weren't feeling sorry for yourself or anything. I still had all my fingers and toes and I couldn't find the energy to get out of bed. Man, you awed me."

Carponti cracked a wry grin, his fingers drumming on the steering wheel. "I could say the same thing. 'Cause the whole time I was in the hospital in Germany, every time I started to get depressed, or feel sorry for myself, I thought about you. Mostly I thought about how heavy you were, when we dragged you across that field. I thought, Sarn't G would tell me to quit being a crybaby." Carponti swiped at his eyes. "You getting hit and getting evac'd out, I think that's why I'm here today."

He pinned Shane with a hard look, with eyes that had seen all the horrors of hell. A hell that was very, very real, and Carponti had walked right through it.

Shane's stomach twisted. Carponti blamed him for losing his arm. Guilt pulled Shane a little further into the hole he'd been sliding into all day, but his friend didn't seem to notice.

"You're the reason I'm alive. I couldn't let you down. When we got hit again, I thought, man Sarn't G is going to be pissed if I fuck this up. If I hadn't crawled onto that vehicle, if my arm hadn't gotten stuck, that secondary explosion would have tore me to shreds. I'm here because of the way you trained me."

Silence, and Shane had no words to fill it. His throat was blocked.

Then Carponti grinned and just like that, the moment was gone. "Hey, I lost my arm, but I got to keep my ass intact." He cracked a wide grin but then, just as quickly, turned serious again. "I guess what I'm trying to say is . . . watching you today with Osterman just proves that you're still in there." He glanced over at Shane. "You're like decrepit and broke, but you still got what it takes to get through to soldiers. So, ah, just don't forget that. You know, when you have trouble sleeping?"

Shane cleared his throat, unable to speak past the lump. "Yeah. Sleeping is overrated."

"Yeah."

Silence stretched between them, and Carponti finally got out of the truck, and moved toward the back.

"Do you ever wonder why you're here and they're not?" Shane asked quietly.

Carponti paused as he hoisted the wheelchair from the bed of the pickup. "Every day, man. Every day."

Shane had no response for that one. Carponti helped him out of the truck, and into his chair, then pulled away, off to meet his wife for lunch. Shane desperately needed a bit of time to pull himself back from the edge. Carponti was coming back in a few hours to pick him up and help him find a place to live. He'd even promised he wouldn't forget this time.

Once he was inside the house, Shane wheeled himself in front of the mirror in Jen's guest bedroom. He looked hard at the man staring back at him. He stared down at his legs, the pieces that were still held together with metal and borrowed flesh. There were chunks of muscle missing, large scars deeply grooved into the skin on his legs.

Pieces of him had come back from war, wasn't that what Osterman had said? He held his two hands out in front of him. His reflection moved, responded to the commands issued by his brain, relayed by his muscles. Living flesh.

He would never be the same again. When he looked at the man in the wheelchair, he saw a stranger. Why had he lived when others had died? Why did he have his legs when others didn't? He would have gladly given his life to save the men he'd lost. His life. His legs. His fucking soul. Anything would be better than sitting here with a second chance when so many of his boys had gone onto the next life far too soon.

The man looking back at him in the mirror covered his face with his hands and wept.

JEN WATCHED him cover his face with his hands. Shane's back was to the door, so he didn't see her, hadn't heard her come in. He dragged his hands across his face, and Jen's heart broke for him.

He jerked when she placed her hand on his shoulder. Wiping his eyes, he looked up at her with such grief that she wondered how many of the men he'd lost he'd blamed himself for. Looking in his eyes now, she came to a painful realization: all of them. She captured his hand in hers and it was damp from his tears. She crouched down next to him, looking up at him, and prayed that what she was about to say was the right thing.

"I'm so sorry for the men you've lost." She swallowed before she spoke, making sure he couldn't mistake what she said for anything other than what she truly meant. "But I'm so glad it wasn't you."

His mouth pressed into a hard line, the red around his eyes darkening as he watched her, a myriad of emotions flashing across his face. He finally pushed out a heavy sigh. "It should have been."

"No, Shane. It shouldn't have."

He shook his head sadly, avoiding her gaze. "I don't have a family. No kids who are going to grow up without me. I've lived a full life. I'd give anything to bring them back."

"Osterman's alive. So's Carponti. So are dozens of other men who you've brought home safe. You told me once you wanted to make a difference. You have, Shane. Why can't you see that? Why isn't that good enough?"

"Osterman . . . he's got to face his whole life with a missing piece."

"So what?" Jen tucked her hair behind her ear and leaned away from him. Her fingers slid free from his as anger wrestled with fear inside her. "So he's missing a part of himself. It doesn't mean he can't live a full life."

"Jen. I didn't mean—"

"Stop." She reached up and cradled his face with her free hand. "This isn't about me. It's about you." She bit her bottom lip and closed her eyes. "Are you going to throw away the life you have left?"

She wanted to touch him, but she was too wound up with worry that he'd slide right back down the pit he'd already fought his way out of so many times before. "I'm not—"

"Yes, you are, Shane. You're sitting here now, beating yourself up because you're here. You made it through. Yes, you've got to heal, but today you made a difference. Isn't that what you wanted to do when you begged me to let you deploy? Isn't that why you needed to go? Maybe this was the way you were supposed to make a difference." She leaned forward and pressed her lips to the corner of his, hoping he wouldn't feel her tremble. He opened his mouth a little, but she pulled back before he could deepen the kiss. "Not to an entire platoon. To one guy."

He dragged her into his lap, his arms holding her tight, his cheek pressed against the top of her head. She felt the deep shudder run through him and she simply sat, her arms wrapped around him.

His words barely made a sound when he finally spoke. "It's so goddamn hard accepting that I got a second chance." His lips pressed against her hair.

"What are you going to do with it?" Her thumb stroked the back of his hand, and she threaded her fingers through his. His fingers were rough and strong. She remembered that first brush of his knuckles against her hand, the strength she'd felt from him even then.

He glanced down at their linked hands and she saw them through his eyes. She saw the black tattoos covering his forearms marked by pink scars and thought about the contrast between the man's appearance and the man. For all his harsh exterior, he was a good, kind man.

She cupped his cheek and forced him to meet her gaze. She swallowed, still afraid to speak the words burning in her throat. Afraid because she was pushing him back toward the life he loved, and she was sure that life wouldn't include her when he was finally whole again.

He tucked her head beneath his chin again and Jen nestled against him, this big, powerful man who'd shown her such tenderness. His eyes shimmered and he pulled her close. "What have I done to deserve you, Jen St. James?"

She simply smiled. "You made me laugh when I badly needed to laugh."

She pressed her lips against his. He stilled and his body went tight, then his mouth opened to her. His tongue traced her bottom lip. She shivered and delicious heat settled between her thighs.

"I missed you," he whispered against her lips.

"Then we may need to get on the bed." She laughed and helped him onto the bed, and then Shane was kissing her and she surrendered to the desire storming through her blood.

She shifted and knelt next to him. He watched her as her fingers drifted up her chest, freeing each button as she went. Slowly, so slowly, her eyes never leaving his, she pushed the blouse off her shoulders. She blinked rapidly, her eyes burning, and she kissed him deeply as her fingers unhooked her bra.

She didn't fight the urge to cross her arms over her chest, and even though she tried not to, she flinched when his gaze drifted over the flat scar peeking out behind her palm.

He noticed. His eyes darkened as his nostrils flared a little. His hands drifted over hers and tugged her arms open. The cool kiss of air against her breast was more than she could stand. This was a mistake. She wasn't ready for this.

His hand blocked her movement. It settled against the curve of her breast and his heat penetrated her skin. Slowly, so slowly, his thumb caressed the swell of her breast, giving her time to move his hand. Her lips parted as she tried to breathe. She wanted him to stop but her body quivered with the anticipation of his touch.

His thumb barely brushed over her nipple, sliding over the sensitive skin. "Oh!" She felt it shrivel into a hard peak and when he touched her again, she arched toward him. Electric energy coursed through her.

"I forgot how good it felt to be touched there," she whispered.

His only response was a satisfied groan against her skin. She closed her eyes as he tugged her other arm down, revealing the flat scar where her left breast should be. She couldn't watch, but she couldn't stop him, either. This. This was incredible. Then, her nipple felt warm and wet, followed by cool goose bumps.

She opened her eyes and saw his lips poised near her breast. Their eyes met as his tongue traced another warm circle over her nipple. He cupped her and pulled her into his mouth and she couldn't stop the moan that escaped.

He suckled her and she couldn't tear her eyes free from the sight of his lips on her.

His next move stunned her into complete stillness. He traced tiny kisses across her chest and pressed his lips to the center of her scar, their eyes locked together. Tears burned to the surface and she blinked rapidly.

"You're perfect the way you are." He traced his thumb over her scar and kissed her there again. "I wouldn't care if you had none." He pulled her mouth down to him, and she felt the purity of that kiss, the force of his emotion. "I love you."

Tears leaked down her cheeks and he pulled her to him. She straddled him and felt his erection through his shorts. He loved her.

She rocked against him and felt him jerk beneath her. She helped him pull his shorts off, then her own quickly followed and her heat covered the length of him. She rubbed herself against him and the sensation nearly sent her over the edge.

"Jen." He breathed her name against her lips and his arms tightened around her.

She rolled a condom down his thick length and then her body stretched as he slid inside of her, slowly, so slowly, as she took her fill of him. His lips locked on her breast and she cried out as pleasure flowed through her. She moved faster, his fingers digging into her hips to guide her.

She wanted this.

Wanted him.

Wanted . . .

"Shane!"

She exploded around him, her body shuddering to a release that went on and on and on with each stroke. He tightened at once and she felt him pulsing inside of her as his release pulled them both under.

For the first time, she felt completely and truly loved, just how she was. Her words, whispered in the darkness, patched the wounded hole between them.

"I love you."

23

"**Y**ou are hereby notified that you are being found liable as the proximate cause of the loss of—"

Randall's voice droned into the vacuum of space. Shane knew there were words coming out, but he heard nothing, saw only the LT's moving lips. He was sitting in his hospital room, waiting to go into pre-op for the first surgery that would get one of his legs back in the game, and Randall was reading him the findings of his investigation. Ten minutes later and Shane would have missed him altogether.

Liable for the loss of equipment that went missing after Shane had already been flown out of the theater. Liable for equipment that by rights, Lieutenant Randall should have been responsible for as the company supply officer.

Judged guilty by a lieutenant who couldn't even figure out how to spell LT. Didn't that just about nail it?

Strange, but there were no emotions circling inside Shane. There was none of the rage he normally felt when he was around Lieutenant Randall. There was simply nothing.

He was picking up the pieces and he was starting a new life with Jen. Randall couldn't take that away from him. Whatever amount he wanted to charge him for the missing weapons was nothing compared to what he'd lose if he lost Jen. Money could be replaced, but something fragile was growing between the two of them. Something fragile that he was going to nourish and cherish.

"I need you to circle here and initial here," Randall said, handing Shane a folder.

"What?"

"Circle. Initial."

Shane raised both eyebrows at the lieutenant's condescending tone. "And if I don't?"

"Nothing changes. You're still going to have to pay Uncle Sam four thousand six hundred and eighty-two dollars and sixty-three cents."

There it was. The loathing he felt for this officer bubbled up and overflowed. "Right and just how did you get me for the full amount? I'm only supposed to be charged one month's base pay."

"Negligence. By failing to inventory your equipment, you failed to perform basic requirements. So I found you negligent and can therefore recommend that the full amount be taken from your pay." There was a certain smugness to Randall that Shane wanted badly to drive from his features.

Oh, but Trent had some serious explaining to do. If he ever got ahold of him.

"How long do I have to appeal?"

"You'll need to talk to legal."

"In the meantime, you've already notified Osterman and Carponti that they're liable, too? You've stopped their pay without due process?"

"Osterman and Carponti? Of course. As the armorer, Osterman was responsible for these. And Carponti? He signed them out from the arms room."

"You sorry bastard. You've found two seriously wounded men liable for equipment that was more than likely destroyed in attacks when they were hurt and you act like there's nothing wrong with that."

"The regulations are clear. You and your men were negligent." Randall straightened a little. Just enough to let Shane know that he'd struck a nerve. The door opened and Shane prayed it was Jen or some other nurse to cart him off to surgery.

Shane looked up, then did a double take as Trent Davila strolled into the room. Trent's black hair was ragged, like he hadn't had a haircut in weeks. His skin was drawn and tight, his mouth set in a hard flat line, but when his eyes met Shane's, it cracked into a wide grin.

"What the hell are you doing here?

"It's a long story," Trent mumbled, pushing his glasses up on the bridge of his nose. He snatched the file from Randall's hand as two MPs, both females, came around the corner, filling the narrow entrance. Nicole Carponti completed the party, her movements stiff and sure as she stalked into the room, her heels clicking against the tiles. "Lieutenant, you are hereby relieved of your duties as the investigation officer for this case. Captain Montoya, please ensure he's read his rights before Agent Carponti questions him."

"With pleasure," the female MP said.

Shane half expected Randall to argue or fight or flee. But instead, he held his chin high and walked stoically down the hall toward the elevators.

"I think you owe me some answers, damn it," Shane growled when he could finally talk.

"And I've got some." Trent looked exhausted. Like he'd been living on MREs and two hours of sleep a night for the last four months. There were deep purple slashes beneath his eyes and the lines around his mouth were worn deep into the grooves of his skin.

"What happened?" Shane couldn't keep the worry from his voice and he didn't really try. This was Trent. It would be like trying to conceal something from Carponti.

Trent nodded and sank onto one of the chairs. He shoved his glasses to the top of his head and leaned forward, planting his elbows on his knees. "First the good news. Randall is being court-martialed. Those night optics you were being investigated for? Turns out Randall had stolen them and falsified the monthly reports."

"Holy shit."

"But wait, there's more." Trent's attempt to lighten the mood fell flat.

"What else could there be?"

"He was pinning it all on you guys because you hadn't done that stupid inventory in Iraq. He almost got away with it." Trent glanced over at him. "Carponti's wife tipped us off that something was going on back here, and that we better start digging. That's why I had to send Randall home. I needed access to his computer, and I couldn't get it if he was hanging around."

Shane was impressed. "You're a sneaky bastard, that's for sure. Remind me never to send any dirty emails to your wife."

Trent snorted and leaned back against the wall. "Yeah, well, that's not a problem. Turns out Laura's leaving me. On top of everything else, I've lost my family."

"Holy shit," Shane mumbled and wished he had something more profound to say than, "I'm sorry, man."

"They didn't want me tipping Randall off so I couldn't call her. They seemed to think that as his commander, I might have been part of the whole weapons selling thing." He sighed and rubbed his eyes beneath his glasses. "I'm being court-martialed."

"Because of that shithead lieutenant?"

"No. That's got nothing to do with it. I'm being charged with some heavy-duty shit."

"Like what?" Shock burned through him at the grenade Trent had lobbed into the middle of their conversation.

"Can't go into the details right now. You'll be called as a witness. Eventually. These things tend to take awhile."

"How did you get to come home, then?" The thought of Trent back in Iraq, pending court-martial was damn near crushing him. But still, he couldn't explain why Trent was home. "What the hell did you do?"

"If I did what they accused me of, I'd want to kill me, too. So they sent me home. For my own protection."

"Trent, what did you do?"

Trent met his gaze then, and Shane had never seen such flat resignation or hopelessness in his longtime friend's eyes. "I can't talk about it. You'll know soon enough. I've got to go. Laura owes me some explanations, starting with a brown envelope I got in the mail a few weeks ago." Trent stood, then sat back down again. Like he was remembering something. "Nicole mentioned you've got some good news?"

After everything Trent had just dropped in Shane's lap, sharing anything good felt like a betrayal of their friendship. "Yeah. Jen and I . . ."

Trent smiled. It was a pale shadow of his former grin, but it was there and it was genuine. "That's good, man. That's real good."

"Yeah." Shane swallowed and turned the subject back to Trent. "What can I do to help?"

Trent shrugged. "Nothing, really. Just. Don't lie for me when you get interviewed and questioned. Tell them the truth, whatever they ask you about."

"I won't make that promise."

"Then we'll be cellmates up at Leavenworth," Trent snapped. "Don't fucking lie for me. Tell them the truth."

Trent strode off, leaving Shane confused, pissed, and hurt. What the hell was going on? The silence didn't last long. Jen walked in and he'd never been so glad to see her as he was at that exact moment. He didn't give her the chance to sit—he snagged her hand and tugged her up against him.

She looked into his eyes even as she shifted to get closer. "Are you ready for this?"

Shane glanced down at his legs. "I have no idea."

Jen threaded her fingers into his. "The surgery will be fast. When you come out, you'll be one step closer to being back on your feet."

"Trent's home." Shane swallowed and looked away. "He's being court-martialed."

"Trent was here?"

"Yeah. I'm surprised you didn't see him. He just left. He's going to find Laura."

"Go back to the part about court-martial. What's he being court-martialed for?"

"He won't say."

Jen tried to sit up. "I have to call Laura."

Shane squeezed her tight. "Don't. Let Trent be the one to tell her."

"I'll be here when you wake up, okay? You better wake up," she said with a watery smile, cupping his hands between hers.

Shane pulled her forward suddenly and kissed her. "I will. I'll see you in a few hours."

She nodded and the last thing he saw as he was wheeled into the operating room was Jen, her hands tucked beneath her arms and a smile that belonged to him alone on her lips.

He carried that smile with him as the drugs pulled him under, and it was the first thing he saw when he woke up.

She'd stood by him. When he'd been an asshole. When he'd been broken. And because of Jen, he'd fit the pieces of his life back together.

They had put their two broken lives together and created something better. Something that was theirs alone.

Something that chased away their fears of being left, wounded and alone.

Something beautiful.

EPILOGUE

J en ran a comb through her still wet hair as Shane approached her in the mirror. "I like your bedroom," he murmured.

She shook her head as she tipped her neck sideways to give him greater access to the sensitive flesh behind her ear. She rested her hands against his on her stomach. A small diamond sparkled on her finger. "Should you be up without your cane?"

He rested his chin on her shoulder. "I'm just trying to get used to walking without it. Plus, I might be able to beat Carponti with it." He paused. "I love my ring on you."

"You shouldn't have spent so much of your back pay on it," Jen said with a warm smile. She'd protested when he'd bought it for her. But once she'd seen how important it was to him that she wear it, she hadn't protested again. "What's Carponti doing now?"

"He's being a pain in the ass with his prosthetic arm. Do you know what he did in the latrine the other day with that thing?"

Jen closed her eyes, enjoying the feel of his arms around her. But she knew her next words would destroy the peace and quiet enveloping them. "I'm thinking about having reconstructive surgery," she said in a small voice.

His arms tightened around her before he turned her to face him. He tugged her to him and walked backward toward the bed—the bed in their room, upstairs. He sat and pulled her between his legs. He rested his hands against her lower back and placed his cheek against her chest where her breast had once been.

"I don't like the idea of you having any surgeries," he whispered. His grey eyes glittered darkly. His words and actions surprised her. He cupped her cheeks and pulled her lips down to his. "And the scar doesn't bother me. It's a reminder of something that made you stronger. Because of you, I'm stronger."

His words wrapped around her and held her close. She closed her eyes and lost herself in their kiss, still stunned that she'd found someone who had drowned out the little voice in her head. Someone who loved her. Just her.

Scars and all.

***

Thank you for reading Shane & Jen's story. I hope you enjoyed their journey to find each other.

Keep reading to find out how a man who is never serious faces the biggest challenge of his life and what the woman he loves will do to stand by his side. Find out what happens in I'LL BE HOME FOR CHRISTMAS.

Carponti is never serious - that's what Nicole loves about him. But some things just aren't funny. Keep reading to find out if Carponti will find a way to make Nicole laugh when everything about this Christmas goes wrong.

One click I'LL BE HOME FOR CHRISTMAS now!

EXCERPT FROM I'LL BE HOME FOR CHRISTMAS

Fort Hood, Texas
Early 2007

Sergeant Vic Carponti paused outside his company operations office, taking a deep breath. It was funny how their corner of Fort Hood felt deserted the night before a deployment. The company colors had already been cased. They would uncase them in a few weeks, once they got settled into their new home across the ocean in the middle of the war.

He didn't know why this deployment was bothering him so much. It wasn't his first time heading off to war, so he knew what to expect when the shit hit the fan in combat. But there was something hanging over his head this time. A fear that maybe this time his luck would run out.

He sighed and rubbed his face with both hands before walking into the company ops. The only thing they'd left up was the plaque that bore the names of their fallen brothers from the last deployment. The commander—Captain Trent Davila, a man Carponti had known for years—was planning on carrying that with him personally so it couldn't ever get lost.

And so no one would ever forget. Carponti reached up and took it gently off the wall, then strolled into his company commander's office with a nonchalance painted on his face that he damn sure didn't feel.

But people expected him to laugh and joke and make them forget the bad shit all around and so that's what he was going to do.

"Don't forget this," he said, placing the plaque on Trent's desk. He plopped down in a chair, then kicked his feet up on Trent's desk. "Are you coming out with us tonight?"

Captain Trent Davila lifted one eyebrow at Carponti's feet and said nothing. Carponti looked at his commander and longtime friend, then at the plaque next to his boots.

"Fine," he said with a sigh, dropping his feet to the floor. "So answer the question."

Trent sighed. "I can't go out with you guys. I'm the company commander. I'm not allowed to have fun," Trent grumbled. "Besides, my boss would have my nuts in a sling if anything happens while I'm there."

"It's the last day before our deployment. You're allowed to have fun. You can just say you're supervising all of us miscreants." Carponti took the last Dr. Pepper out of Trent's fridge. "The deployment hasn't even started and you already look stressed the hell out. You should be working your lieutenant to death instead of trying to do everything yourself."

Trent shook his head and pushed his glasses to the top of his head. "Yeah, well, my new executive officer seems to think he's God's gift to the Army. He's good but he's not as good as he thinks he is."

"Oh, the boys just love him," Carponti said.

"Really?"

"No, not really. He's an arrogant fuck who believes his own press. Personally, I can't stand him, but luckily I don't have to deal with him much. I just sic Sarn't Garrison on him."

Trent grinned and reached for the plaque, sliding his hat on top of it so he wouldn't forget it. "Yeah, Garrison has a way with words."

Garrison was Carponti's platoon sergeant. Garrison and Trent had been squad leaders many moons ago when Trent had still been enlisted. In Carponti's world, it meant a whole lot that Trent had stayed close with his enlisted friends even after he'd crossed over to the dark side and become an officer.

"I'm swinging by his place on my way home. He needs to go out before someone shoots his grumpy old ass. He's been a complete buzz kill since his wife left him."

"Your sympathy is astounding," Trent said dryly. He grinned and shook his head. "Why do we put up with you?"

"Because I'm charming and funny and good in a firefight?" Carponti said with a grin.

"Pretty much. You can make anyone laugh."

"It's an important life skill. Like balancing a checkbook. So seriously, find a babysitter and come out with us. Your wife could use some fun before she has to spend the year dealing with all the spouses in the Family Readiness Group and chasing your kids around while you're off on another fun adventure."

"I wouldn't exactly call going to combat a fun adventure." Trent rubbed his chest. There was a scar there, Carponti knew. A scar that had damn near killed Trent several years ago. Carponti wondered just how much stress his commander was carrying and not telling anyone. Trent's face flushed when he realized Carponti had caught him rubbing his scar and he tapped the pencil hard enough to snap the eraser off. "You know, you're right. Let me see if we can't find a sitter."

"Excellent. We'll be congregating by the bar when you get there. Now I just have to go convince Garrison to come out with us."

"Good luck with that," Trent said, pulling his glasses down. "He's on the verge of becoming a warrior monk."

"Not if I have anything to say about it," Carponti mumbled as he strolled out of his commander's office. He wished he hadn't seen the flicker of worry that flashed in his commander's eyes when he'd mentioned his wife. He'd thought that Laura and Trent were one of the strongest couples he knew. She'd put up with him deploying back to back to back since he'd almost died a few years ago.

But that flicker of worry? Yeah, Carponti hadn't missed it. There were problems there, hopefully small ones that Trent would take time to fix after this rotation into the sandbox.

Carponti looked down at his own wedding ring. It was his last night home and his last night with his wife.

He was glad he'd convinced her to come out with him and the boys. That way he could make sure they had a most excellent party and spend time with Nicole at the same time. He was going to spend part of the night chaperoning his guys to make sure they made the most of it— which meant making sure no one ended up in jail—but then? Then the time he had left was going to be spent making his wife laugh.

Because try though he might, he couldn't shake the quiet dread that settled in the pit of his stomach that tonight was the last night of normalcy he had on this earth.

Nicole Carponti breathed deeply and fanned her eyes, trying to stop the burning of hot tears. She leaned against the wall of the bathroom in *Ropers* and tried to stuff down all the churning emotions chained to the fact that her husband was leaving for war tomorrow. Again.

The first time he'd left she'd been scared, but then the war, the deployment...the waiting...it had all been unknown. She'd worked on finishing her degree and kept herself busy and waited by the phone like all the military wives who had gone before her.

The second time he'd left, she'd known better what to expect. The long waits between phone calls. The silence when he couldn't talk long. The quick e-mails saying "I'm alive" that once upon a time would have been too little, but during the war were more than enough to keep her going.

But this time? This time was different. The Surge was different. They were sending in massive amounts of soldiers to try to quell the Iraqi insurgency. It was bloody and deadly and soldiers were getting attacked at higher rates than at any earlier time during the war.

And Nicole was terrified.

She had to hide it, though. She'd agreed to come out with him tonight just because it gave her a chance to pretend that she was fine. She had to keep everything in check until after he left. She couldn't let him know how much she worried this time.

Fanning her eyes once more, she stepped out of the bathroom and into the rowdy country bar. A place like this was guaranteed trouble on a normal night, but tonight her husband's platoon was rolling deep. Which was either going to be a really good thing or a really bad thing for her future job at the Army's Criminal Investigation Division, depending on how cantankerous tonight got.

She spotted her good friend Laura Davila at the bar with a cute blond woman Nicole had met in the bathroom a little while ago. She had already completely forgotten the other woman's name. She was terrible with names.

She wound her way through the pulsating crowd until she reached them. Laura grinned at her and she exclaimed, "I can't believe you came out tonight."

"You've already said this twice," Laura said. They had to shout to hear each other.

Nicole flagged down the bartender and leaned around Laura to her friend. "I'm a terrible person but I already forgot your name. I'm Nicole Carponti."

The petite blond held out her hand. "Jen St. James."

"Nice to meet you, Jen. I won't forget this time," Nicole said with a smile.

Laura leaned toward Nicole. "I'm trying to get her out of her shell. She had cancer and she's been struggling with her self-esteem ever since."

Nicole frowned, glancing toward Jen, who was now trying to get the attention of the bartender. On the other side of her, though, was Garrison, her husband's platoon sergeant. He was a big man and he was currently leaning down to talk to Jen. "How's that for a self-esteem boost?" Nicole said, gesturing toward the two.

Laura glanced over, then quickly looked away before she was caught. Her eyes lit with a brilliant smile. "Oh, that couldn't be more perfect if I had planned it."

Nicole studied her friend through narrowed eyes. "Did you plan it?"

"I wish. But let's just see how this little situation develops, shall we?"

Nicole raised her beer in mock salute to her friend. "You, m'dear, are a devious and loyal friend."

"I'll drink to that," Laura said. "So how's Carponti taking this deployment?"

Nicole heard the undercurrent in her friend's voice. "You know how he is. Always cracking jokes, which I suppose is a good thing. I'm terrified, though."

"Yeah, I know. I've been talking to some of the spouses. The Surge has everyone terrified. One of the spouses told me it was a death sentence." Laura took a sip from her beer, scanning the bar.

Nicole scoffed quietly. "How's that for melodramatic?" But she didn't voice her own fear that this deployment was going to be worse than the previous ones. "I don't envy you as the Family Readiness Group leader."

"Oh, come on, don't you want to volunteer? You can be responsible for keeping me from going crazy. It's a primary duty position, you know."

Nicole laughed. "Not in this lifetime," she said. "I always feel out of place once the spouses find out I'm pretty much a cop."

Jen leaned over, rejoining their conversation as Garrison wandered off in the direction of Laura's husband. "What's going on over there?" she said, pointing at Laura's husband.

Nicole sighed heavily and took another drink. "Oh joy. Looks like Trent is giving one of his lieutenants some love. Couldn't have the rest of the night without drama, could we?" She glanced back at Laura and Jen. "We should go interrupt before the second round of fireworks go off."

Earlier, Vic had gotten into an argument with Lieutenant Randall and now it looked like Laura's husband was finishing things off with the arrogant prick. The LT made Nicole's skin crawl and she wasn't looking forward to another bar fight. Not two in one night, that was for sure.

But whatever had happened was over now. She watched as LT Randall made a beeline for the door. Out of the corner of her eye, she saw Garrison talking to Jen again. And Laura? Once Randall was gone, she and her husband moved off to a dark corner of the bar and were deep in conversation.

She hoped it was a good one. She didn't like the worry she'd seen in her friend's eyes when she talked about her husband.

She snuck up behind Vic, sliding her hands over his hips and up under his t-shirt and the smooth hard skin of his body, placing a kiss at the indentation between his shoulder blades.

He turned and wrapped his arms around her shoulders. "There you are." He kissed her fiercely, reminding her of how much she loved this man. "I was about to send out a search party for you in the little girls' room."

Nicole wrapped her arms around his waist and lifted her chin to meet his eyes. He was leaner than he'd been when he'd come home last year. His body was more solid from long ruck marches and hard training for this deployment. His eyes, though, were the same bright, mischievous green that they'd always been and she counted herself lucky that whatever he'd gone through in the war, he'd come home okay so far. She just prayed their luck held.

"No search party required," she murmured against his lips. "I was talking to Laura. I'm impressed that you got Garrison and Trent to come out."

"You should be," Vic grumbled, biting her bottom lip gently. "I had to guilt both of them into it. It's like they both turned thirty and amputated their fun genes or something."

Nicole laughed against his mouth. "Dance with me?" she asked.

"What in our history makes you think I know how to dance?" he grumbled even as he allowed her to lead him onto the dance floor.

"You'll figure it out," she said, sliding her arms around his neck. She rubbed her body against his, sensuously moving her hips in time with the music.

He dropped his hands to her hips, guiding her exactly where he wanted her. "Keep that up and we'll have to sneak out to the car," he said, his breath hot on her ear.

She nibbled on his bottom lip, biting it gently. "I think you're trying to seduce me," she whispered. She dug her fingers into his back, her blood humming with latent arousal. God but she loved this man.

"I'm absolutely trying to seduce you," he said. He angled his thigh between hers, pressing close to the juncture of her thighs. The pressure sent vibrations through her body and straight to her core.

"I'm kind of ready to go home." Her words were a gasp as he rubbed his thigh against her swollen center. "Before you get into any more fights with your lieutenant."

"Can we not talk about work when I'm trying to turn you on?" he mumbled. He slipped his hand beneath the hem of her shirt, stroking his thumb down the centerline of her back. A shiver ran through her.

"You don't want to talk about work? That doesn't turn you on?" She undulated against him, grateful for the crush of bodies that swayed around them and enabled them to be lost in the crowd.

"No, trying to get you naked turns me on," he said. "We really need to get out of here." His breath traced over her ear a moment before he bit her earlobe gently, a fierce burst of pleasure in the pain.

"That sounds like a brilliant idea."

He sighed as a commotion cleared a corner of the dance floor. "I hate being one of the responsible adults." He kissed her hard. "Let me get everyone out of here first? That way no one goes to jail on our last night in the States."

She kissed him fiercely. "I'll be waiting over here for you to get done being all caveman."

"I'll show you caveman later," he said with a grin before wading into the crowd and diffusing the situation between Garrison and Trent.

It took the better part of an hour before they'd shuffled everyone off to their respective cabs and vehicles. Nicole talked with Laura and Jen and tried not to notice how Jen kept watching Garrison.

It felt like forever before her husband strolled across the parking lot and scooped her up, carrying her toward their vehicle.

Their car was parked deep in a shadowed corner of the parking lot, and the moment her husband closed the door, Nicole crawled into his lap on the passenger's seat. He pulled her close, kissing her hard and fast. Pouring a thousand unsaid things into that kiss. His hand threaded into her hair and he slanted her mouth until he owned her —all of her—and she was lost in his taste, his touch.

Then he broke off abruptly. "What the hell?"

"What?"

"Who is that with Garrison?"

Nicole twisted around in time to see Garrison, one of Carponti's oldest friends, lean in to kiss Jen.

"Oh, now that's interesting," Carponti whispered.

Nicole spun around. "Don't you say anything to him," she said.

"Why not?"

"Because this is the first time Garrison has done anything for himself since his wife left him. Leave him alone."

Carponti blinked innocently. "What makes you think I would say anything?" he said. His words slurred and Nicole grinned before fishing around in his pockets for his car keys. "A little more to the left."

Nicole laughed then climbed into the driver's seat as Garrison stepped back, letting Jen walk to an ancient sedan. "She's cute. She's friends with Laura."

Laura, who was being carried across the parking lot by her husband. She hoped for Laura's sake the happiness lasted longer than just tonight. The war was taking its toll on everyone, and Nicole had noticed more than once that there was a strain in her friend's voice when she talked about her husband.

Vic just looked at her. "Oh really?"

Nicole drove them away before her husband could interrupt what had looked like something very sweet between Jen and Garrison. She'd known Garrison as long as she'd known her husband and it was long overdue for him to find someone that made him happy outside of the Army.

She glanced at her husband, who had closed his eyes the moment the vehicle started moving, a lazy smile on his lips. Something warm bloomed inside her.

She wished Garrison could find the kind of happy that she had with Vic.

One click I'LL BE HOME FOR CHRISTMAS now!

AUTHOR'S NOTE

There are many old and rickety buildings on Fort Hood, including the setting for my fictitious Warrior Transition Unit barracks. Those buildings exist but haven't had soldiers living in them in decades. There are no barracks near enough to the hospital to house wounded Warriors, so I hope you'll forgive a little creative license in putting an old building just across the parking lot.

The people in this book are all works of fiction.

The cadre of doctors and nurses and NCOs and officers who care for our wounded Warriors bear a burden greater than any other, and I am in awe of their sacrifice every single day.

THANK YOU

Dear Reader,

Thank you so much for reading. If you'd like to make sure you never miss a new release, sign up for my newsletter at http://jessicascott.net/subscribe and please like my Facebook page at https://www.facebook.com/JessicaScottAuthor/. You can also join my reader room, affectionately known as The Pint for exclusive first looks at new releases.

If you enjoyed the story, please consider leaving a review. Word of mouth is incredibly important for helping other readers discover new authors. I appreciate any and all reviews (whether positive or negative or somewhere in between).

Until next time!
Jess

ACKNOWLEDGMENTS

The sheer length of time it took from the first words of this book to now makes it nearly impossible to thank everyone who had a part. Please forgive me if you're not listed here. But in no particular order here goes:

I have to thank Chris Keach for reading the first draft and making me write in complete sentences. Julie Kenner, for talking me down off the ledge more times than I can count and for being there for me during OIF 09-11. The server room gang in OIF 09-11: Rasa, Mayo, Davis, and Vargas: thanks for the laughs. Doc Hepler, thanks for not turning me in to the psych ward when I asked the best way to commit suicide. I told you I was writing a book! Jane Perrine, thank you for writing to me almost every week while I was deployed.

To everyone who wrote, emailed, shipped books or school supplies to me while I was deployed, thank you. Books made the year bearable and in some cases worth it.

Candace Irvin, mentor and most important friend, thank you for seeing something in my writing, waaay back at the beginning and kicking me in the pants when I needed it. I still do. Allison Brennan and Roxanne St. Claire, who both offered amazing publishing advice over the years. Sarah Franz, who edited me on multiple occasions and helped me look like less of a raving lunatic. My mistakes are my own.

Julie Butcher, who helped me get some of the medical stuff right. Elyssa Papa, who told me to submit this book, just one more time. JoAnn Ross, who made my day when she stopped by my blog and who has encouraged me from a distance for years. Cindy Gerard, who was willing to read one of the first versions of this way back when it was still unformed.

My sisters in the Austin RWA and the ROMVETs. Thank you for suffering through my long absences and silence on the loop. I wouldn't be here if not for your supporting me through the good times and the not-so-good times and suffering through all the newbie questions over the years.

I'd be remiss if I missed the entire team at Ballantine Bantam Dell. Gina Wachtel, thank you for seeing something in the first draft you read. Angela Polidoro, thank you for bleeding red all over this manuscript and helping make it better. My agent, Richard Curtis, thank you for believing in me, even when I couldn't sell the book you'd signed me for.

My girls, thank you for letting me write and loving me anyway. And mostly, thank you for letting me sleep in on the weekends. Yes, I will get up and make you French toast.

And last but definitely not least, the hero in my life, my husband, who has supported my writing through four combat deployments. Thank you for loving me, even when I spent more time on the computer than with you some weekends. Yes, you can buy a new bass boat.

"Jessica Scott should be on every reader's list." ~Brenda Novak | New York Times Bestselling Author

Dying has a way of changing a man. Ever since the day Army captain Trent Davila lost his life, he's been fighting the demons that haunt him from that terrible day. Time and again, he's left his wife and their two children behind as he's volunteered to put himself in harm's way until his wife had enough.

Laura gave her husband everything, believing that if she was strong enough, patient enough, that he would eventually come home to her. She believed in him until she learns he betrayed her by volunteering for multiple deployments instead of spending much needed time with her and their two small children.

Sent home facing a court martial on trumped up charges, Trent needs her to stand by him one last time. Being close to him reignites the spark in their troubled marriage that had almost been extinguished.

As the fight for his career and reputation threatens to destroy them both, their marriage will be tested like never before.

THE COMING HOME SERIES
Because of You
I'll Be Home for Christmas: A Coming Home Novella
Anything For You: A Coming Home Short Story

Back to You
Come Home to Me: A Coming Home Novella*
Carry Me Home*
A Place Called Home*
Take Me Home*
Homefront
After The War
Last One Home*

Note – these books are fiction. Any resemblance to real people or events is purely coincidence

Learn More At…
http://www.jessicascott.net
Follow Jessica on Twitter
Like Jessica on Facebook
Sign up for Jessica's Newsletter

Author's Note
The Coming Home series and Homefront series were originally published as separate series. I have rebranded them to get things organized as they were originally intended.

Come Home to Me: A Coming Home Novella* was originally published as part of the Homefront series

Carry Me Home* was originally published as **Until There Was You** as part of the Coming Home series

A Place Called Home* was originally published as **All for You** as part of the Coming Home series

Take Me Home* was originally published as **It's Always Been You** as part of the Coming Home series

Last One Home* was originally published as **Find My Way Home** as part of the Homefront series

To
Fluffy and Hammy
The original escape artists

PROLOGUE

Fort Hood
2007

"I put your checkbook in the front pocket of your ruck sack. Did you find the sleep medication? You'll need to sleep on the plane so that you're rested when you land. And I put your calling card—"

Captain Trent Davila looked up from where he sat on the edge of their bathtub. He held a tiny folded flag in his hands. For a moment, he'd been somewhere else. Sulfur scorched the inside of his nose. The thunder of the fifty cal reverberated off his breastbone.

"What's that?" she asked softly, watching him from the bathroom door.

He held out his palm so she could see the little flag. "Good luck charm. I can't deploy without it."

A thousand questions flickered over her face as her gaze fell onto that tiny flag. She bit her lip and turned away, but not before he saw the naked fear looking back at him.

He moved, stepping in front of his wife and capturing her face in his palms. Her skin was smooth and soft and achingly familiar, and a deep part of his soul missed her already.

But that part of his soul wasn't in control right now. The moment she touched him, his soul recoiled, refusing to let him take even the simplest pleasure in her touch.

He'd cheated death and he knew, *knew* he didn't deserve to be there with his wife when so many of his men had died.

That's why he had to leave. Again. It didn't matter to where. It didn't matter if it was the war in Iraq or a transition team somewhere in the mountains of Afghanistan. He needed to get away. To get back into the fight.

And pray that his wife would understand why he had to go.

"Laura." He whispered her name, capturing her attention.

She tried to look away, to pretend that today was just another day. But Trent knew her too well. He saw the doubt and the fear that she tried to hide. Her eyes, though, her eyes always gave her away. He stroked an errant strand of copper hair away from her forehead, meeting her golden eyes, unable to speak any words of comfort. He knew they'd just be more empty lies.

She offered a watery smile. "I'm terrified of losing you again," she whispered.

"I've deployed since I got hurt. This time is no different."

"You didn't get hurt." She refused to meet his gaze. "You died. Your heart actually stopped beating. And this time is worse. This is the Surge." Her voice broke. "I can't lose you again," she whispered. Her voice cracked as the tears tumbled down her cheeks.

He hated to see her cry. Worse, he knew he could prevent those tears.

He pulled her close and simply held her, wishing he could feel as alive with his wife and family as he did when he was at war. Maybe someday, when the war was over, he could figure out what had broken inside him and how to fix it.

He stroked his thumbs over her cheeks as the kids shrieked in Ethan's bedroom. The sound sent a spike of anxiety through Trent's heart, but he smiled, hoping to cheer her up. "Sounds like someone just lost a Lego."

"Daddy!"

"He's probably going to beg you for a hamster again," she said. Laura swiped at her eyes, blinking rapidly. "Can't let them see me like this."

He slid from her embrace, regret sealing the walls that four deployments had erected around his heart. Trent tried not to notice how intently Laura watched him, her gaze sweeping over the scars on his body as he finished getting dressed. His dog tags banged against his ribs as he dragged his t-shirt over his head and pulled on the rest of his uniform and then his boots.

"Well, you could get one," Trent said, needing the distraction of simple conversation.

"Or," Laura said with a smile that didn't reach her eyes, "you could promise him one when you get home. It'll give him something to look forward to."

Trent frowned at the odd note in Laura's voice and focused on tying his boots and tucking the laces beneath the cuff of his pants. "He won't even notice I'm gone. They're both too little."

Trent straightened as Laura approached, placing her palm over the scar on his heart. It burned where she touched him. It took everything he had not to flinch away from the gentleness in that touch. "Keep telling yourself that," she said with a soft kiss. "They miss you when you're gone. We all do."

He sighed quietly and glanced at her, resting his hands gently on her hips. "Laura, you know I have to go."

He couldn't explain it. Didn't have the words to explain the emptiness inside him that consumed every waking moment when he wasn't over there. And worse, he didn't ever want her to see the emptiness he tried so hard to hide from her.

She believed he'd come home. As long as she continued to believe that, his world would continue to exist.

She brushed her thumb over his bottom lip. She blinked rapidly and the sight of her tears almost penetrated the cold empty space where his heart had been. "I just wish it got a little easier waiting for you, that's all." Her fingers wrapped around his dog tags, her thumb sliding along the chain. "But we'll be here when you get back. We always are."

He ran his fingers lightly over her face. The lie he'd told his wife so often sat like a concrete wall between them. She didn't know that he'd volunteered for this deployment, for so many others, and he had no way of killing the lie without killing their marriage. "Don't go getting a deployment boyfriend while I'm gone."

"I don't think you have to worry about that." Laura wrapped her arms around him, nuzzling his neck. They stood for a long moment before Laura eased away.

Trent swallowed and let her go. Again.

FIVE HOURS LATER, Trent kissed his wife good-bye for the fourth time in six years. His four- year-old son and two-year-old daughter were getting antsy, climbing up and down the bleachers non-stop. As he walked away from the gym where he and the rest of his unit had checked in for the deployment, he glanced up at her in the stands. She was steady. Stoic. Trying valiantly not to join the ranks of the wives and children who were crying as their soldiers left them, assault packs and weapons in hand. God but he wished he didn't have to go. That he was man enough to stay home and fix whatever was broken inside him. Wished that he were man enough to need her more than the heady, uncertain terror of war.

"You ready, sir?"

Trent glanced over at First Sarn't Roy Story, a man who'd taught Trent the right way to kick in doors and the difference between knowing when to wipe a nose or whip an ass. The war was lined into Story's leathery face. Fifteen years as an infantryman that had started in Mogadishu and continued with the long slog through Iraq.

"Are we ever really ready for this?" Trent asked, taking one more long look at his wife and kids. And then he turned away, needing to harden his heart for the battles to come.

Outside, Trent climbed aboard the bus that would take them to the airfield. Spouses filed out from the gym along the sidewalk. In the seat behind him, Sergeant Vic Carponti was harassing one of Trent's platoon sergeants, Sergeant First Class Shane Garrison. He almost smiled. With those two around, things would never be dull.

He scanned the crowd, searching for his wife amongst the blurry faces of other people's spouses lining the sidewalk. There. She held her vigil in front of a light pole, a tiny hand in each of hers. Beside her, Ethan stood bravely, tears streaming down his face. He held a tiny salute, his mouth pressed into a flat line as he tried to be a tough little man. Emma waved brightly at the bus, still too little to fully understand that Daddy was leaving for longer than a trip to the grocery store.

He looked away but it was far, far too late. When he closed his eyes, the image of his small family was seared onto his retinas as the bus pulled out of the parking lot and headed for the airfield.

"Never gets any easier, does it?" Story asked quietly, sucking on the end of an unlit cigar while he fiddled with a light on his helmet. There was little love left between Story and his wife. Story deployed to avoid his wife.

But Trent deployed to avoid his *life*. Because life back in the rear was too complicated, too loud, too chaotic. War was simpler.

The scar on his chest ached and he rubbed it, wishing he could forget the way his family looked as the bus pulled away.

He closed his eyes, trying to put them out of his mind. He didn't want to remember his wife with her cheeks streaked with tears or the raw grief in her eyes. He wanted to remember her face as she slept curled into his side. Or laughing with their kids. He needed to carry those memories into war with him. Because that was all that would steel him against the long hours and bone-crushing fatigue to come.

He had soldiers to command. His family would be there when he came home.

He hoped.

1

───────

Fort Irwin,
California 2008
One year later...

Trent walked out of the ops tent, needing a few minutes to himself. They'd just sent word that the wife of a kid in one of the companies was in the hospital. She was going into labor while her husband was enjoying the fun and sun of the National Training Center.

At least the kid wasn't deployed. He'd be able to get home quickly. Sure, not as quickly as if he was back at Fort Hood, but still. It beat the hell out of trying to get home from Iraq.

The notification was something simple, and yet it had struck Trent that yet another soldier was going to miss the birth of his child because of the Army.

He knew exactly how that felt and right then, a thousand bitter memories rose up, reminding him of everything he'd willingly squandered. The resurrected hurt was so raw, the regret so powerful, he nearly choked on it.

He should be used to the hurt by now, but lately it seemed to be getting worse. It overwhelmed the dead space inside him, forcing him to feel things he didn't want—and wasn't ready to feel.

He didn't know *how* to feel them, how to deal with them. So for the moment, he sat outside the ops tent and let the raging emotions storm inside him. Until he could get them under control. Until he could function again.

It had been happening more and more this year. The things he'd stuffed away had started having a nasty habit of reappearing when he least expected them.

He was starting to get comfortable with the crazy, but at least now he was starting to recognize the warning signs. Which was why he was sitting outside the ops tent.

"So your BFF Marshall is looking for you." Story walked out of the ops tent, a smirk on his face that only meant bad things for Trent. It was so strange calling him "master sergeant" instead of "first sergeant" but Story wasn't a first sergeant anymore. Just like Trent was no longer a commander.

Trent sat on the hood of a Humvee, smoking a cigar and contemplating his sixth cup of coffee since he'd come on shift twelve hours ago. He pushed his glasses up higher on his nose then glanced over as Story hopped up next to him.

Since they'd both been fired more than a year ago, they'd been hanging out on the staff together, responsible for nothing but PowerPoint slides. Funny how getting fired meant giving up the hard jobs in the Army. You still got to stay in the Army, but you just weren't trusted with taking care of soldiers anymore. It was a punishment, being put in the easy jobs. Trent would have given anything to get his old job as a company commander back, but that wasn't going to happen so he and Story and Iaconelli kept each other sane and avoided the new commander. Captain James T. Marshall the Third drove everyone fucking crazy.

"Should I be worried?" Trent asked dryly, adjusting his glasses again. He'd long ago given up getting upset when Marshall attempted to piss in his corn flakes. Marshall had been tapped to take over Trent's company when he'd gotten himself fired and Marshall took great pleasure in reminding everyone that he was fixing all the things that Trent had screwed up. It grated on Trent's last nerve every time the words, "Well, sir, I'm still fixing the mess I was left when I took over" came out of Marshall's mouth at staff meetings, but what could Trent say? He *had* gotten fired. It didn't matter why. He supposed part of his penance for being a shitty commander was having to listen to Marshall without knocking his teeth out. He'd leave that for Story and a few of the captains, like Ben Teague, who were leading the insurgency on the staff. Trent had other things on his mind.

Like his wife. His two kids. The house that was no longer his.

He cleared his throat and tried to listen to Story.

"I don't know," Story said. "Marshall wasn't screaming so I think maybe you should be okay?"

Sergeant First Class Reza Iaconelli, one of Trent's former platoon sergeants, stepped out of the ops tent. "No, you should definitely hide," he said, interrupting the conversation. "He's bitching about having to transport you back to the rear early and he's pretty cranky."

Iaconelli was a big man: broad shoulders and built like an ox. He was steadfast and solid downrange but when they got home? Yeah, that's when things went to shit for Iaconelli. He'd never met a bottle of alcohol that he didn't like. He was lucky he still had a career but the sergeant major liked him. Trent respected his ability in combat enough to overlook any personal failings. Trent was the last one to judge someone's personal failings.

He reined his thoughts back to the present and the feeling that flittered in the dead space around his heart. "I'm getting sent back?"

Iaconelli shrugged. "Maybe they're finally going to court-martial your sorry ass," he said lightly.

Trent flipped him off. "That would be nice, actually. If they'd at least get the damn thing over with. If I never see Lieutenant Jason Randall ever again, it will be too soon."

"He is a special little fuckstick, that is for certain," Iaconelli said, staring at the end of his cigar for a moment.

Iaconelli may or may not have threatened to kill LT Randall downrange. Twice. But all of Randall's interpersonal hostility had been a sideshow, a distraction to keep Trent or anyone else from figuring out that he had been selling sensitive items and funneling the money to bribe the Iraqis to stop blowing their boys up. Randall had finally gotten caught and now was determined to take down Trent and anyone else he could with him. Iaconelli chopped the tip off his cigar and sucked on the end while he tried to light it.

"Too bad I won't be around for his court-martial," Story said.

"Did you get reassigned?" Iaconelli asked Story.

"Yeah. I'm deploying again in about two weeks. As soon as we get back from here," he said.

"Your wife isn't going to be happy," Trent said quietly.

"Actually, she's going to be thrilled. It'll give her a chance to find her some twenty-year- old boy toy to keep her busy while I'm gone." Story spat into the dust.

"So you're still married because...?" Iaconelli sucked on the end of his cigar.

"Because it's too fucking expensive to get divorced," Story said. "I'll take care of it after this next deployment. I'll save up some money first, though."

"Sure you will," Trent said. "You've been saying that since '04."

It was Story's turn to flip Trent off. "At least I'm willing to accept my marriage is over."

Trent rubbed his heart, knowing his first sergeant hadn't meant to score such a direct hit. At least, not with malice. "Yeah well, my divorce is complicated."

"These things always are." Iaconelli leaned against the truck. "Which is why I've never gotten married."

Trent snorted and was going to make a crack but Marshall took that opportunity to step into the darkness outside the ops tent. "Davila, you're going back to Fort Hood."

Trent glanced at his watch. "It's four thirty in the morning."

"And you're going to be on a plane in three hours. Pack your shit." Marshall turned to stalk off, mumbling about pain in the ass captains and not having enough time for this shit.

Iaconelli blew a smoke ring into the darkness. "God but he is such a charmer."

Trent sat there long after Story and Iaconelli went back into the ops tent.

He wanted to go home. But now that it was happening, fear slithered down his spine.

It had started slow. One day, he'd wake up, dreaming about Laura. Other times, he'd be in the mess tent and he'd think he heard her laugh. He'd hear a kid giggling on the TV and he'd look up, expecting to see Ethan or Emma.

Always, though, he was alone. He'd wanted it that way for so long. He'd wanted quiet when they'd been running around his feet, shrieking and bickering like kids did. He'd craved silence at the end of the day when someone would get out of bed for a glass of water.

He'd certainly gotten the silence and the solitude.

And the oppressive emptiness of it all ate away at him. He'd thrown himself into work here in the California desert. He'd pulled eighteen hour days gladly. The longer he spent away from the war, the less he felt its siren call, luring him back. And somehow, work wasn't enough anymore. Nothing he did pushed away the aching need to get to the one place he simply didn't belong: home.

He was back in the States but he couldn't go home. Not with an investigation hanging over his head and the potential for a very long jail sentence standing in front of him. And the worst part about the entire court-martial was that his brigade commander was changing command soon. If Colonel Richter left before the case was resolved, Trent would be at the mercy of the new commander—a new man with no loyalty to the soldiers he'd put in leadership positions.

It was not a comfortable place to be. The power plays between the senior officers never ended well for junior officers, and Trent? Trent was caught right now. He had to trust that Colonel Richter would take care of this before he left.

But a year after Trent had been sent home, Trent was running low on trust and patience.

Patience had never been his strong suit. Every other time he'd been home, he'd been prepping to go back to war. This time, the year had stretched in front of him like an unending slog.

It was the longest time he'd spent in the States since he'd gotten shot. It had taken him almost that long to realize just how badly he'd fucked up everything in his life that was supposed to be important.

His marriage. His kids. His family.

If there was a grade lower than an F at being a husband or a dad, he'd earned it. He'd come home from Iraq nearly a year ago— pending a court-martial and a divorce. And since then, nothing had happened. The case had been stuck in investigation mode forever. And the divorce? He just wasn't able to sign the papers. His life had been frozen in carbonite on all counts.

The investigation had moved slower than molasses in winter. And he was glad.

Because standing out here in the California desert, he'd come to a conclusion. He wanted his family back. He wanted his *wife* back. When she'd slapped him with divorce papers last year, he'd refused to sign them, hoping that the investigation would go away and that he could fix things with her. But that hope had proved futile. The distance between them was too much. The warmth he remembered was gone, but still, he'd been unable to let her go. He couldn't. Sure, they spoke on the phone or when he saw her at the office, but they were a few stolen minutes here, a quick chat about the kids. There was nothing there to give him hope that he could fix things with her.

He'd volunteered to train soldiers anywhere he could so that he didn't have to face the cold emptiness of the reality that he was no longer welcome in his own home. And if he volunteered, someone else wouldn't have to.

Now? Now he sat in the middle of the California desert and thought about the new dad who wouldn't be there for the birth of his child. He looked down at his wedding ring and thought of all the time he'd willingly given up.

He was a goddamned fool. He wanted her back. Damn it, he wanted his *life* back. The life with this woman who had once smiled and laughed with him and wrapped herself around him while she slept. Who was as beautiful changing Emma's diaper as she was dressed up in an evening gown for the Cav ball. This woman who used to ask about his day when he called home at two in the morning, even after she'd been up half the night with one of the kids.

He sobered, his hands trembling at the thought of his children and the tiny family that had grown while he'd been away. The tiny family that overwhelmed him and terrified him and dropped him to his knees with a need so strong, it crushed his lungs until he could not breathe.

He didn't know how to feel good, but he knew he'd never figure it out without them.

He had no clue where to start. He had no idea how to be a father to his kids. Or a husband to a wife who could barely look at him.

Trent hopped off the top of the truck. He had a phone call to make.

Because it looked like he was getting exactly what he wanted.

And it was time to figure out how to be the man his family needed him to be.

~

Fort Hood

"Son of a bi-iscuit!"

"Bad Mommy!"

Laura Davila wrapped her scraped and bleeding knuckles in a paper towel and prayed to the patron saint of Army wives for patience. Her six-year-old dishwasher was currently spread in carefully laid out pieces across the kitchen floor and counters. And now the cavernous white interior was splattered with her blood. Awesome.

Her son Ethan looked up at her with disapproval in his dark brown eyes, and Laura flinched. "Sorry, honey. Mommy just hurt herself."

"You said a bad word." This from her daughter, Emma. "Agent Chaos said you're not allowed to say those words."

Laura glared at the fat brown hamster that was clutched in her daughter's hands. Agent Chaos looked up at her with disapproving beady brown eyes. Sitting there, silently judging her.

She had joked with Trent that he should buy the kids a hamster when he returned from his latest deployment. By the time he came back, things between them had already crumbled but he still remembered the damn hamster. He'd bought not one, but two of the stinking, smelly creatures. The hamster cuteness factor did not override the pain in the ass factor of having to clean their cages every other day to keep the smell from overpowering the entire house.

Maybe if Trent had been around more over the last year, she wouldn't have minded them so much. But instead of sitting at Fort Hood and working in an office like any other officer who was under investigation, he'd volunteered for several rotations at the National Training Center in Fort Irwin. He'd spent more time there than at Fort Hood over the last year. He might as well have just moved there.

She took a deep breath and pressed on her throbbing knuckles, focusing on the pain so that she wouldn't feel the tension that squeezed her heart every time she thought about her husband. She regretted sending him the divorce papers. She could admit that now, but she'd done the only thing she could at the time.

She could still remember that stupid flare of hope when he'd stood in her office that day. Hope that maybe, finally, he had come home to her.

But he hadn't.

And as time had ticked by and he'd refused to sign the papers and let her go, she'd moved beyond regret. Now, she wanted to move on with her life. Maybe someday she'd be able to think of Trent without the hurt and frustration that kept reminding her of everything she'd lost.

"You have to pay us each a quarter," Ethan said, stroking the fat orange hamster in his hands. Laura was seriously thinking about buying a cat—that would solve the hamster problem quickly enough. But it would be just one more thing to clean up after.

And she wasn't really up for the trauma of finding a dead hamster under the bed.

She could only imagine the therapy bills.

She pursed her lips and counted to ten...thousand. "Okay, guys, why don't you go play in the garage or something? Mommy has too many parts in here, and I don't want you to get hurt."

Or move anything. But she didn't say that out loud, because that would only encourage them to run off with some vital component that it would take her three days to identify and two more days to find online and order. A new dishwasher was not in the budget at the moment. Besides, she wanted to see if she could actually fix the thing herself.

She shooed the kids and their accompanying hamsters out of the kitchen and made her way through the master bedroom to the cache of Band-Aids she hid in her bathroom. The kids were all too eager to use every bandage in the house if she let them, which always meant that she couldn't find a Band-Aid when she really needed one. She'd resorted to hiding them like they were some kind of precious commodity. In her house, they were.

Laura pulled down the shoebox that held the first aid kit. She held her breath as she cleaned the cuts on her knuckles with iodine, then wrapped gauze halfway down her fingers, covering the empty space where her wedding and engagement ring had once been.

She paused, staring at her ring finger. Blood pooled on the pale band of skin there, as if her finger refused to forget the rings that had been there since forever.

Her finger might not forget the rings but that didn't mean it was a marriage worth waiting for. No amount of waiting or wishful thinking was going to change that. Trent had seen to that. And broken her heart all over again.

She knew in her heart that they were finished. He had lied to her so many times about his deployments. That alone had destroyed her trust in him. And then there was the rest of it...

She was ready for the pain to stop. Ready for her heart to stop waiting for the phone to ring. Waiting, so desperately, for her heart to stop beating for a man who was never coming home.

A spike of melancholy pressed on her lungs. Damn it, what was wrong with her today? She was past mourning the death of her marriage. At least, she kept telling herself that. So when was it going to stop hurting?

She briefly considered a shot of vodka to numb the pain, but that wasn't really a good idea since she was alone with the kids. She barely ever had a drink these days. She sighed and glanced wistfully at the discreet box on the top shelf in the bathroom closet. Droughts were not limited to alcohol.

She had gotten used to it, this new normal. While the kids were vibrant chaos, full of life and joy, the married part of her life was... well, it simply was. There was nothing there anymore. No joy. No hatred. Just silence and cold detachment overlying a dull aching sadness.

She simply wanted it to be over. And damn Trent to hell for dragging it out when he wasn't even willing to fight for them. And the silence between them? Between her and the man she'd thought she'd love for the rest of her life?

She sat on the edge of their bed, one finger rubbing absently over the bruised knuckles and her empty ring finger. She could hear the kids shrieking in the garage. One of the hamsters had gotten away. She smiled. She really didn't mind them, not when the kids loved the judgmental little beasts so much. It was a gesture of kindness from a man who couldn't be a father. She knew that.

It didn't make it hurt any less. She'd married him knowing what she was getting into, thinking her love for him was strong enough to withstand whatever the Army could throw at them. Knowing that the Army was a demanding job, that he'd be gone a lot. But that first deployment had done something to him, something deeper than just the visible scars on his body.

Once, she never would have thought the silence would grow too loud or that his empty side of the bed would become too heavy to bear. Once, she would have waited forever for him to come home to her.

But forever was a long time.

And her faith in their love had died long ago on some distant battlefield.

2

Eight hours and a flight from hell later, Trent left his duffle bag in the operations office before walking down the halls of the Reaper Brigade headquarters. It was late summer in Fort Hood, Texas and it was mid to high nineties every day.

It had been a hot summer. The heat, Trent could deal with. He'd been in Kuwait when the temperature had hit one hundred and thirty-two. Ninety was a cold front.

But it was the cold from the office at the end of the hall he feared.

He was glad he'd been called back to Fort Hood. He'd let his mind drift the entire flight home. What would happen if he walked into Laura's office? He hadn't gotten through to her before he'd gotten on the plane home. She didn't know he was here.

It gave him a little more time to figure out what to say. How to ask for a chance. Maybe not to be the father of the year but maybe for a chance just to be a dad. If he could figure that out.

He rubbed his thumb over the smooth edge of his wedding band. Laura was an entirely different challenge.

He'd hurt her. Badly. And he had no idea how to fix it.

Maybe he could start with asking her if he could sleep on the couch. Because if he stayed at Fort Hood for more than a few weeks, he was going to have to find a more permanent place to stay than crashing at Shane and Jen's. The thought of asking Laura if he could come home sent a cold sweat prickling over his skin.

The likelihood of her allowing him through the front door for more than a short visit with the kids was snuggled up between slim and none. He had a better chance of hitting an IED and blowing the hell out of his truck in the middle of Highway 190 in Killeen than he had of getting her to agree to that.

Not that he blamed her.

At least she let him see the kids. And even that was a challenge. He didn't know how to be a father to the two small kids who'd morphed from babies to mindless banshees with needs and wants and an uncanny ability to strike all the right nerves and detonate his patience.

No matter how much he wished things were different, when it came to his family, he'd been a failure—and he was determined to fix things. No matter how much he wanted to be a bigger man and let his wife go, he simply could not bring himself to sign the papers that left him cold and empty. He'd tried. And each time, he'd put them away, choosing to wait just one more day.

Hoping that someday, he'd find the right words to explain to Laura why he'd had to go. To put the ragged emptiness into some form she could understand. He'd never wanted her to see that part of him, the dead part that walked and talked but felt nothing. He was alive. He should have been grateful.

Instead, the emptiness had swallowed everything, leaving him hollow. Until the only thing that felt right was the war.

He didn't want her to know that side of it. Never wanted her to see him for what he was—a burned out warrior who was only good at one thing. God but he didn't want her to know what he'd become.

He glanced at his watch. Right on time for the brilliant end to his career. Shoving aside the worries from home, he walked through the headquarters that had been his sanctuary from the tribulations of real life.

The headquarters was largely empty as most of the rear detachment staff had already left for the day. Apparently, the staff were taking the new post commander's directive about being out of the office by five p.m. seriously and since they were the "lucky" ones who'd escaped the National Training Center, they were apparently skipping out of real work, too. That wouldn't last, though. About a week would go by before they all realized they couldn't get anything done when everyone left that early. He turned into a conference room and rapped his knuckles on the doorframe.

Major Patrick MacLean looked up from his laptop screen and nodded at the chair next to him at the conference room table, motioning for Trent to take a seat. Trent sat and waited silently for Patrick to finish writing an e-mail.

Trent had known Patrick for years, since they'd both been lieutenants on another brigade staff a lifetime ago. His friend's dark blue eyes were lined with stress and strain. Patrick often said that being an Army lawyer was slowly but surely sucking the life out of him. He only saw the bad parts of the Army. He never got to see the Soldier of the Year, except when said Soldier of the Year was being charged with something terrible, like aggravated assault or misuse of his government travel card.

Because there was nothing worse than misuse of the government travel card. He'd seen men killed, subordinates abused, but the fastest way to end a career was to get caught defrauding the government. He pushed his glasses up on the top of his head. He wasn't sure what that said about the organization he'd sacrificed everything for, but it didn't leave a good feeling in the pit of his guts.

Trent wished he was being charged with simple misconduct—simple fraud where he could be sent on his way and avoid the lengthy investigation. Instead, the allegations against him seemed like a cruel twist on reality—and a complex, year-long investigation to boot.

"How was your flight?" Patrick asked as he closed the lid of his laptop.

"Terrible. We sat on the jetway for two hours before we took off." Trent sucked in a hard breath through his nose, pushing down the riot of emotions churning inside him. "What's so important that I had to be yanked off the training mission three days early?" Not that Trent was complaining. But it was fear that filled the emptiness inside him now.

Fear that Laura had really gotten over him and let him go when he'd finally gotten his head out of his ass.

Fear that he'd truly lost everything.

Patrick rocked back in his chair. "First off, you should be at home, spending time with your family instead of volunteering for training mission after training mission, but we'll get to that in a minute."

Trent sighed. "I know."

Patrick lifted a single brow and started to say something. Then he snapped his mouth closed, opened a file, and slid the contents toward Trent. "We're getting ready to start the Article 32 hearing."

"That's the one where they decide if there's enough evidence to go to trial, right?"

"Got it in one. The prosecution at division wants a guilty plea, but I didn't accept it." Patrick slid a second manila folder across the desk. "You're in a world of shit, Trent, but we've got a good chance at beating this thing."

Trent snorted and shook his head quietly. "What makes you say that?"

"The witnesses against you are crap, for starters. Your former lieutenant Randall has very limited credibility, no matter who his daddy is, especially since he married his subordinate."

"Speak English?"

"Your lieutenant says you harassed one of your soldiers. That soldier is corroborating his story but since they got married, it looks like they're just backing up each other's stories instead of independently testifying to true events."

Trent frowned. "So the fact that my lieutenant was sleeping with one of his subordinates ruins his credibility?"

"More or less." Patrick sighed. "Ready for the heavy lifting? I need to go over what you're being charged with."

Trent braced himself. Then nodded once.

"I'll read through the specific violations of the Uniform Code of Military Justice first. We can go into the specifics of each charge after that." He flipped over the first sheet. "In that, on or about Fifteen October 2007, you were derelict in your duties to wit—"

Patrick's voice faded as the memory reached up and took hold, sucking him down into a swirling vortex.

"Sir, I don't understand."

"You're under investigation, Trent." Colonel Richter, the brigade commander himself, had broken the news to Trent. He was a man Trent had admired since they'd first rolled into combat together, six years prior. A man he looked up to.

"Am I being relieved, sir?"

"I'm sorry, son."

A man who was relieving him from command. Taking the responsibility, the honor of being a company commander away from him.

"Sir?"

"You're missing sensitive items that no one can account for. Your company funds have come up short on their audit. You've lost control of your officers and your soldiers. And your parts clerk Adorno has made an allegation of inappropriate conduct against you." Colonel Richter shook his head slowly.

"Adorno, sir? I rarely even see her. She works in the motorpool.

"She was recently pulled up to the company ops?" Colonel Richter asked.

"Yes because she was having problems in the motorpool."

"And she worked long hours, alone in the company ops with just you."

Trent closed his eyes, seeing how neatly the trap had been sprung around him. He'd never even looked at that soldier funny and yet, simply because he had been alone with her, the allegations were enough. "Sir—.
"

"I can't leave you in the job. I've lost faith in your ability to command."

"Sir, this is all bullshit. I accept responsibility for the missing items but you can't take me out of command in the middle of the fight. With Garrison and Carponti being wounded, I've lost two key leaders in my company. Give me time to build the new team. Please, sir. Don't do this."

Colonel Richter held up one hand. "I've made my decision. You're restricted from any unsecure communications while the investigation is ongoing. Do not attempt to contact Adorno. Do not attempt to contact Lieutenant Randall. Let the investigation run its course."

Panic. Fear. Humiliation.

All of it rose up again now, circling like vultures over the kill as Patrick finished listing the charges against him. He'd waited months for the investigation to be complete.

He'd done what he was told. He hadn't called anyone—not even his wife. He'd let the investigation run its course. But he'd had no idea that in doing so, he'd nailed the coffin of his marriage shut. The letter had come from Laura a few weeks later, ripping out his soul and smashing it into the dusty, dried up desert earth. He'd lost everything in ninety-seven days.

"Are you listening to me?" Patrick asked.

Trent looked up. "Yeah. Sorry. What?"

"I said the only thing they have that has any legs is the inappropriate conduct allegation. Everything else, I've already got enough to rip their case to shreds."

Trent flipped through the documents Patrick handed him. "If the case against me is so flimsy, why are they going to all of this effort? What's the point?"

"You want my honest opinion?"

Patrick leaned forward and rubbed his hands over his face. His blue eyes were sharp and weary. "You're the sacrificial lamb."

"Meaning what?" Trent pushed his glasses to the top of his head.

"Lieutenant Randall is one very well-connected lieutenant. His father is connected to every powerful four-star general officer in the Army. If you take the fall for this, Randall gets to continue the family name."

The bitterness roared back and this time, it brought its friends, anger and hatred. Oh, but he hated that selfish, lying bastard lieutenant. Trent had been working round the clock to try and keep his boys safe, and Randall? Randall had been getting blowjobs in the motorpool from Adorno instead of doing his fucking job.

And yet, Adorno had accused Trent of inappropriate conduct when nothing, *nothing,* even remotely close to inappropriate had happened. Oh the irony; it galled.

"Lieutenant Randall stole weapons and traded them for cash. That was his crime and his alone. Your crime was your failure as a commander to be aware of your subordinate's actions," Patrick said quietly. "The accusations against you are very serious. And unless we can prove that Randall and his wife are lying—that you didn't know about what he was doing, and weren't a part of it—he's intent on taking you down to lessen his punishment. He pleas down his punishment to testify against you. As the commander, you're a bigger fish."

"So then the inappropriate conduct allegations against me are just icing on the cake?"

"It's an attack on your character. Do you have any proof that Randall and Adorno were already involved during the deployment?"

"Sure. I've got YouTube videos of him and Adorno doing the nasty in a Porta Pottie." He swore viciously and tossed his glasses on the table. "Of course not."

"YouTube videos would probably help. At this point, a grainy cell phone photo might do the trick."

"I don't see how we can fix this," Trent muttered, rubbing his eyes.

"You should have more faith in me than that."

"Yeah, well, my faith is in short supply these days."

Trent scrubbed his hands over his face in frustration. From the moment his commander

had called him into the office and told him he was being investigated for dereliction of duty, maltreatment of subordinates, sexual misconduct, and a litany of other really bad things that Trent would have never dreamed of, let alone done, his faith in the very military he'd devoted his life to at the expense of all others had been shaken to the core.

The endless deployments, the constant strain to be everything a leader was supposed to be to his men, seemed somehow empty. Futile.

Pointless.

Patrick leaned forward, his mouth set in a grim line. He slid a business card across the table. "I have a plan."

Trent pushed his glasses on and read the card. "Captain Emily Lindberg. Licensed Clinical Psychiatrist." He looked up at Patrick. "What the hell is this?"

"Tomorrow, you're going to call Emily and schedule an appointment. She's expecting your call."

Trent tossed the card onto the table. It floated a bit before it settled next to the folder. "For what?" The words stuck in his throat, dry and harsh as the desert against his skin.

"You didn't hear the part about the wronged hero to your stressed-out villain? I need a doc—an Army doc—to give you a clean bill of health before we go to this Article 32 hearing. No unexplained anger. No urge to kick puppies. None of that."

Trent folded his arms across his chest. "So I got a little stressed as a commander. Someone told me once if you're swimming as fast as you can and you're barely keeping your head above water, you're probably contributing to the organization."

Patrick shook his head slowly. "Not in this case. We need to show that you were busy commanding your formation and your lieutenant took advantage of that busyness. Not your poor stress management techniques."

Trent frowned. "What exactly are you getting at?"

"Nothing more than what I've said." Patrick looked away, suddenly fascinated by the folders in front of him. "Call her. This needs to happen sooner rather than later."

Trent said nothing for a long moment. He bounced one leg, wrestling with the hundred thousand questions that burned inside him. "So what about the other allegations?" he finally asked.

Patrick scrubbed both hands over his face before releasing a harsh breath. "Here's how you have to handle this...you're not going to like it, but hear me out." He paused before speaking again. "I'm going to need you to play nice with your wife."

Trent went utterly still. "What do you mean, play nice?" he whispered. The emotions inside him twisted and swirled violently.

"I need you to pretend like you two aren't getting divorced. That you love each other. That you can't live without her."

Trent shoved away from the table and pushed to his feet. He stared at the photos in the glass case behind him of the last deployment. "I can't put Laura in this position," he said after a moment. "I won't." He paused. "It won't work anyway. Everyone knows she's taken off her wedding rings."

"The officers on the board will be from this brigade but that doesn't mean we can't make this a believable lie. It's them we have to convince. No one else."

Trent rubbed the scar over his heart. It ached where he touched it. A dense fire that fucking *hurt*. If he asked her to do this, he would destroy any chance he had of winning her back. But goddamn it, he couldn't win her back if he went to jail.

"Listen to me. When this whole nightmare first reared its head, you told me you didn't want to drag her through a court-martial, right?"

Trent turned back to face him and nodded, unease twisting in his belly.

"The only way to keep this from going to court-martial is to stop it at the Article 32 level—before it gets to court. We don't do that by attacking Randall and Adorno. We do that by showing the officers on the board that you're a good soldier, a good officer, and a good husband and father. That you wouldn't dream of cheating on your wife. *That* is how we beat this."

Trent shook his head slowly, holding his breath until his lungs felt like they'd burst. "Patrick, I've known you a long time, and you've never suggested anything half as fucked up as this."

Patrick scrubbed one hand over his mouth. "I know. And I hate that I'm asking you to do it. But if you don't want to watch someone else raising your kids because you're in jail, you and Laura need to start looking like a happy husband and wife. And every single officer sitting in that Article 32 hearing needs to believe that it's true."

There was no way he could ask Laura to do this. He'd lost her ages ago, when the rumors about the missing weapons and Adorno had spiraled out of control. When she'd lost faith in him—in them. Not that he blamed her. But goddamn it, that didn't make it hurt any less. She'd ripped his soul out with those papers. There was too much distance between them now for him to ask her for something like this.

But that wasn't the real reason. He didn't want to do this to her. It would hurt her all over again and he'd done enough of that. There had to be another way.

"You need to figure out another plan," Trent said, keeping his voice low. "I won't ask her to lie for me. I won't risk her future. She's been through enough."

"Laura's job as the family readiness liaison is not at risk here. Believe me, she's valued here. They pretty much got down on their knees and begged her to stay when she tried to quit last year."

"That's not the issue," Trent said quietly. *Please don't ask me to do this to my wife.*

Patrick looked at him, his blue eyes filled with sympathy at Trent's unspoken plea. "I know what I'm asking you, Trent."

"Then you know why I won't do it." He pushed his glasses down and pinched the bridge of his nose with his thumb and forefinger. "Find another way to keep me out of jail. I won't use Laura like that."

FOR A TRAINING HOLIDAY, the office was ridiculously busy. Normally on training holidays, the only people in the office were her and the commander. Sometimes the sergeant major. There certainly wasn't the constant stream of soldiers and spouses that she'd already seen this morning. They were looking for information on when their family members were due back from NTC. Laura knew that and she was doing the best she could pushing out the information that she had as soon as she had it.

Apparently, that wasn't good enough. If one more eighteen-year-old spouse stomped into her office, Laura was liable to lose her furry little mind. Just because the Internet existed did not mean communication was either instantaneous or flawless. But you couldn't tell some people that.

Laura clenched her pencil in both hands and pasted on a calm smile. Maybe if she held it long enough, it would bleed over into her mood and she wouldn't feel as stabby as she felt right then.

Not damn likely. She loved her job as the brigade's family readiness liaison, but sometimes, it took everything she had. Some spouses were more trying than others but it was her job to keep the family readiness group running smoothly no matter whom the current leadership was. Some days she felt like she made a difference; other days it was absolutely exhausting. But she had a purpose. And she loved it.

Except for moments like this.

When the woman who had accused her husband of inappropriate conduct sat across from her and pretended like it was just another meeting. Like Laura didn't know who the young soldier was.

Laura wanted to break something. To scream and rail at the insanity of the world that would have this young woman sitting across from her. Instead, she smiled. Her expression could have cracked glass.

"PFC Adorno, I can't give you the phone number and I'm not calling the brigade commander over your husband's cat."

"Do you know who my husband works for?"

With that single sentence, Laura's patience inched closer to snapping. She forced her smile wider.

"PFC Adorno, I don't really give a flying leap if your husband is on the brigade commander's personal security detail. A cat having kittens is not a reason to call the brigade commander while they are in the maneuver box at the National Training Center."

One would think that after all this time, years into the war, families and spouses especially would understand how things worked.

PFC Adorno, however, turned a deep shade of pink beneath her too-thick foundation. Laura had half a mind to ask her if her makeup was in accordance with regulation but she managed to keep that comment to herself. Barely. She was supposed to be the mature adult here.

As a soldier, PFC Adorno should know how these things worked. And yet, there she was, sitting in Laura's office, asking about a phone call to her husband because of kittens.

"I'm calling the inspector general. I'll have your job."

Laura didn't even blink. She reached into the stack of cards on her desk and handed it to PFC Adorno. "Here's the number. Please spell my name correctly."

She'd been threatened with the IG one too many times to let this latest addition to the roster upset her too much. Half the time, the threats were empty anyway. And? The IG didn't have any authority over her. She was a civilian.

PFC Adorno looked like her head was about to explode. She sucked in an outraged breath, then stalked out of Laura's office.

The air was instantly clearer and Laura inhaled a deep breath. Did that soldier honestly think Laura didn't know who she was? Or did she not realize that Laura was her former commander's wife? Dear God in heaven, Laura needed to rail and scream at the heavens.

Instead, she released a deep sigh and tossed the pencil on her desk. It wasn't nearly as satisfying as say, stabbing something violently and repeatedly, but then again, the Army as an employer tended to frown on fits of violence. Didn't look good on the performance review.

She rubbed her eyes and wished—not for the first time—that she'd slept better. But she'd gotten used to the fatigue that hunted her, keeping her awake at night and rising with her in the morning.

The stress in her life was not work-related.

She was the family readiness group liaison for Death Dealer battalion, a job she'd taken before her marriage had gone to hell and before she'd gotten run down by life, the war, and everything else.

She covered her face with her palms and just breathed. She was so goddamned tired. The mistakes she'd made haunted her, reminding her that her current predicament was as much her fault as it was her husband's. She should have been stronger. Should have been able to wait for him until he came home.

She shouldn't have let the war break her.

She glanced at the picture on her desk, the picture of the lie she'd lived for far too long. Her husband, holding their daughter, their son between them. A smile on his face, love in her eyes.

Yes, once she'd been part of a happy family. At least, that's what she'd told herself. But the lies and the war had wormed their way into the marriage and destroyed her faith in the man she'd pledged to wait for. She didn't know why she left the picture on her desk when she'd taken her rings off. It wasn't like people didn't know.

But something about that picture made her unable to put it away.

She closed her eyes, wishing she could forget the way he looked. Wishing she could forget the way he'd made her laugh and feel, once upon a time. He was out at NTC now, too, but not as someone who would be deploying. The Army wouldn't let him leave Fort Hood, at least, not until the charges against him were fully investigated.

And since the investigation had been ongoing for the last six months, she was starting to wonder if it was ever going to be finished. Her family—her life—was in limbo.

Her heart? Her heart didn't matter anymore. She'd given up trying to piece it back together. Trent had broken her one too many times.

Running off to war, leaving her alone.

Lying to her about the most important things.

She breathed deeply and focused on three p.m., when she could head out to pick up the kids at Shane and Jen's. She loved Jen, she really did, but especially on days like today when Hayley, Laura's babysitter, called in "sick" when she was clearly anything but, so she could spend stolen time with her new husband. Laura would have preferred that Hayley be honest about it, but she couldn't really blame her. She'd just gotten married and even though Laura's newlywed days were a distant memory, she could still remember all the hope and promise of that first year.

"Whoever pissed you off, it's not the keyboard's fault."

Laura looked up as Patrick walked in and sat down. "Hey. How's Natalie?"

"She's good. Getting bigger and bossier every day." Natalie and Ethan were in school together. Natalie wasn't technically Patrick's daughter but she was in every way that mattered. Patrick and her mom were in an on again-off again disaster of a relationship but Sammy had continued to let Patrick be active in Natalie's life.

Patrick was a good man. Sammy didn't know what she was giving up.

Or maybe she did. Sometimes, being a good man simply wasn't enough to keep a relationship together.

"So, to what do I owe the honor of this visit?" she asked, minimizing her e-mail to be able to focus.

"Don't throw me out of the office," he said, trying to keep his voice light. "But I need to talk to you about Trent's case."

Laura leaned back in her chair, folding her arms over her chest, and started counting to ten. Thousand.

"I know you're having a hard time with him."

Laura sucked on her top lip for a moment before answering. "I wouldn't necessarily call filing for divorce a hard time."

"And that's what I need to talk to you about."

"Patrick..."

"Just hear me out, okay?"

She ground her teeth but after a moment, nodded.

"Listen, there's no case against Trent. It's weak, at best. With the Article 32 about to start, we have a good chance of getting it stopped here before it goes to court-martial. But I need to plant doubt that the allegations against him are true." He met her gaze. "I need you to do that." Laura chewed on her bottom lip, playing his words over and over in her head, not understanding what he was asking of her. "What do you mean, you need to plant doubt?"

"The primary witness against your husband, PFC Adorno—"

"Oh, we've met," Laura said dryly.

Patrick's smile was humorless. "Yes, well, that's part of the prosecution's problem. She's alleging that Trent was inappropriate but the problem is that she and Lieutenant Randall were caught in their shenanigans downrange."

Laura frowned. "So you think this is a ploy to get herself out of trouble?"

"Her and her husband. If they were working together to steal the missing weapons systems, then what better way to get out of trouble than to make this stuff up against Trent? Takes the focus off her and her husband completely." Patrick leaned forward, tapping his index finger on the desk. "If I can cast Trent as a sympathetic family man who would never do anything like what she's alleging, this case is all but dismissed. I'm not attacking her. All I have to do is make Trent look better than the story she's telling and we've got a win."

"And you need me to paint on a happy face and be the loving wife."

Patrick shook his head. "No, I need you to be one half of a loving couple. And I need you to do it publicly where everyone can see it—in the PX, in the chow hall, everywhere. I need the officers on this board to believe exactly what I'll be telling them on the day of the hearing."

She looked down at her empty ring finger, rubbing the bare skin beneath the bandage absently. "Everyone knows that we're having problems, Patrick."

"Then make sure everyone knows you've fixed them." He leaned back. "I wouldn't ask you to do this if I didn't think it was our best shot at getting this whole thing thrown out."

She looked up at him. "Why didn't Trent ask me to do this?"

Patrick swallowed and looked away. "He refused to drag you into this," he said quietly. "For what it's worth, I don't in a million years believe the allegations against Trent. I don't think he would ever, ever be unfaithful to you and I don't think he would ever abuse a subordinate like that."

Laura pressed her lips together in a flat line. "You're wrong, Patrick. He's been cheating on me for years. It was just with the Army instead of another woman."

"Laura—"

"Let me think about it," she said quickly. "I won't say no out of hand but I can't make this decision on a whim."

Patrick leaned across the desk, gripping her hand. "I know this is hard for you, Laura. I know what I'm asking you to do."

She said nothing for a long moment and he gave her a sympathetic but firm smile. "Give it some thought, okay?"

When she was alone, she sat there, staring at the picture of her family. Wondering how she was going to bring him back into the kids' lives and then rip him out again. What Patrick was asking wasn't fair. He had no idea what this was going to do to her family.

She glanced at the photo on her desk as she typed furiously, trying to get ahead of the flood of e-mails in her inbox.

There was a quiet rap on her office door. "I'm not here," she said quickly, looking up.

Her fingers froze on the keyboard. Her heart stopped in her chest.

Trent stood in the doorway. He had a duffle bag slung over his shoulder. His glasses hid the darkness of his eyes. There was a streak of dirt on his cheek. An assault pack hung limply from his left hand.

A thousand emotions ripped through her all at once, rioting for supremacy as she drank in the sight of her husband.

Ex-husband, she reminded herself. Or, at least, he was supposed to be.

She wished that this were a normal homecoming. One where she would rush across the small space and crash into him. His arms would come around her and she would inhale the strong spicy scent of his skin. Feel the heat of his touch. Savor that first, wild kiss.

Instead, she had this. This empty chasm between them, echoing with loneliness.

And she had no idea how to cross it.

3

———

Her husband stood in her doorway and damn it if her heart didn't act like he was a sight for sore eyes. His shoulders were broader than she remembered, weighed down by the heaviness of the war. There were tired lines around his mouth, as though he'd forgotten how to smile. But his face was still the same. Lined more with weariness and too much time in the sun but that did nothing to detract from his looks.

It wasn't his looks that kept her longing for this man. No, it was a deeper, more secret part. The part of her heart that had loved a good man. An honest man. And part of her, the tiny part of her heart that soared when she saw him, still loved him.

She wasn't prepared to deal with this today. She stood as he stepped into her office. She wanted to go to him. To cross that space and feel his arms wrap around her like they had once upon a time. But that would be just another lie. Like when he'd told her that he missed her, that he'd do anything to be home with her and the kids. Like when he'd told her he'd never betray the vows they'd made.

Just like everything between them these days.

She shoved aside the crushing pain that threatened to break her yet again. In a thousand lifetimes, she would never be able to explain what he'd done to her. His quiet abandonment, the empty place in their lives he'd left unfilled.

He looked tired. She wished she didn't notice. Behind the rims of his thin black glasses his eyes—those gorgeous, almost-black eyes—were filled with sadness and regret. There was something more there now. A stark determination she hadn't seen in...she couldn't remember the last time he'd looked like this.

For one moment, the lies and the fear and the sadness were forgotten and she savored the sight of her husband. A man she'd loved for as long as she could remember. But she couldn't do this anymore. Not to herself. Not to their children.

Damn it, she was tired of caring about this man. She'd thought she'd loved him enough for both of them. She'd never been so wrong in her entire life.

"You're home early," she said. Her fingers found the pencil on her desk. It comforted her to have something to do with her hands. He said nothing for a long moment. She could have said hello. Could have been polite. Instead, her voice grated, sounding harsh against her own ears.

"Yeah. I, ah, tried to call you." Trent stuffed his free hand in his pocket She wished she didn't see the fatigue etched into the lines around his mouth. She wished she didn't still care.

"Oh." What could she say to that? What did it mean? "So why did they send you back early?"

"They're ready to start the hearing."

She swallowed the lump in her throat. "Is that good or bad?"

He looked away, the muscle in his jaw pulsing. "I don't know."

Silence stretched between them. Laura didn't know what to say to fill the gap. There was nothing she could say so she focused on the best things to come out of the mess that was their marriage. "The kids will be happy to see you," she said quietly.

A half smile cracked the edge of his mouth. "How are the hamsters?"

"Fluffy escapes once a week, at least." If hamsters were what it took to make conversation, she'd take it. Anything was better than the awkward silence that hung heavy and oppressive in the air between them.

"They don't cause you too much trouble?" he asked.

She shrugged. "Not too much."

He looked at her then, his eyes dark behind those glasses that really, really worked for her. She remembered when he'd gotten them.

He'd been worried she wouldn't like them. Who knew she'd had a thing for men with glasses?

"Thank you. For letting me get them for the kids."

She tipped her head and cupped her chin in her palm. It had been almost a year since he'd bought those hamsters. "You're welcome." A simple response. The only thing she could say.

Another silence. This one less damning. All because of a couple of fat, fuzzy rodents. She swallowed the nerves that tickled the back of her throat. "Where are you staying?" she asked quietly.

She wanted him to ask to come home. Just once she wanted to remember what it felt like to have him in the house. To have another adult to balance out her life. To hear him in the other room or down the hall.

She knew things between them were over but that didn't stop the longing for just one blessed day of normalcy. Just one memory of the way things had been between them. Before the war had torn away everything that he'd meant to her.

"At Shane and Jen's."

Sergeant First Class Shane Garrison had been home from the war for the last year, recovering from injuries that had landed him in the care of Jen St. James, a nurse at Darnall Army Medical Center at Fort Hood.

"I think they're both terrified," she said. A tiny frown drew between her brows. "Aren't you going to be a third wheel? They should be preparing for their wedding, not having a houseguest."

"I know," he said quietly. Trent pushed his glasses higher on his nose. "Shane insisted. Says he needs help with the wedding."

Laura smiled wistfully. "Jen is going to be a beautiful bride."

For a moment, Laura glanced down at her empty ring finger. She'd cried as he slipped the wedding ring onto her finger. His gaze locked with hers. For a brief moment, she was looking at her husband. No fear. No regrets. Just the man she loved looking back at her with the same love in his eyes. She blinked, and then it was gone so fast she wondered if she'd really seen it at all.

Trent looked away, clearing his throat roughly. No, she hadn't been seeing things.

"When is the wedding again?" he asked.

"Four weeks."

"That's going to go by fast," he murmured.

Laura glanced down at her watch. "I need to get the kids," she said quietly, ending the moment before it really began.

Silence filled the gulf between them, a silence that once again felt absolute and unbreakable.

She lowered her gaze and it collided with the ring he still wore on his left finger. She looked away, wishing she hadn't seen it.

But she had. He still wore his ring. He hadn't signed the papers. What was he waiting for? Why couldn't he just let her go?

She looked up then and met his gaze. And what she saw looking back at her shocked her. Ripped away at the bandages that had held her heart together and slashed every protective barrier she'd put in place.

His mouth crooked at the corner. His eyes were dark and hungry, his gaze locked on her, devouring her. Looking at her like she was the most precious thing in the world to him. The man who cherished her, who made her feel loved. Who reminded her of the aching desire she felt for him. For just an instant, the damaged warrior in front of her had slipped away, revealing the man she'd loved. Whole. Determined.

Hers.

But then his expression shuttered closed, leaving the man she'd come to know. The man who was distant and closed off. The speed of it almost gave her whiplash. She'd believed him when he'd told her he had to go, that the Army needed him. That he couldn't argue with the powers that be.

All the while, he'd been volunteering for deployment after deployment. Leaving her and the kids willingly time and time again. Leaving her hoping and praying for the day when he would come home to her.

She knew in her heart of hearts that day would never come. Because no matter how much she might wish it, the man who stood before her, tired and beaten down by the war and the weight of his own sins, was not the man she'd married.

"I'm going to be around for the next few weeks," he said. His voice was soft, his words sharp. "I'd like to see the kids." A hesitant pause. "I'd like to see you, too."

She stopped breathing. She searched his eyes, looking for a glimpse of the old Trent, but he was gone. Maybe he'd never been there. Or maybe he'd simply been wish fulfillment. Maybe her husband was really dead and gone and the man in front of her was a shell; nothing more.

That wasn't true. The man in front of her had been forged in fire and come out steel. He'd been cut from the mold of a warrior, an ancient god of war.

The warrior in front of her had perfected the art of war. He knew his profession. He took pride in it. He'd given it everything he had. She knew that now.

But the warrior had sacrificed for his skill. He'd sacrificed his ability to love, to laugh, to smile. She saw the warrior now for who he was.

Because the man in front of her was not the man she'd married.

He was not the man she loved.

∾

Trent knew fear. In that moment, he knew naked, soul-crushing fear as he waited for his wife's response to his tentative gesture. He refused to think of her as his ex-wife. She wasn't.

Not yet.

He had to fix this.

A better man would walk away. Would release her from the purgatory of their sham of a marriage.

But Trent was not a better man. He loved this woman. He'd always loved this woman.

The overwhelming love that he felt for her was there. Like a sleeping thing waking from a long dormancy. It was fragile. Malnourished.

But there, stretching after a long slumber.

He held his breath, waiting for her response. Held it until his lungs burned and his hands shook. Still, she didn't respond. She toyed with the pencil in her hand. Rolled it along the edge of her desk calendar.

"The kids will be glad to see you," she whispered finally.

It was a dodge. An obvious one.

He could let her go, let her slip away.

But that's not what he wanted. And he'd seen her gaze flicker to his wedding ring. He hadn't made that up.

She didn't want this, either.

But fear was a powerful thing. He recognized the look in her eyes, the stiffness in her posture—it was like looking in a mirror the moment she looked back at him. He deserved that. He'd failed her so many times in so many ways. But right then, gazing at her copper eyes and dark copper hair, what he truly saw was her strength. The strength to love his children, to keep their home together.

To walk away when he hadn't been enough.

Now? Now he needed her strength in a different way. He needed her to be strong enough to stay. To give him one more chance. And if he was going to deserve her, that had to start now.

"I was wondering if I could catch a ride with you?" he said, stepping into the breach and facing the possibility that once more, she would back away.

He didn't know how to just be around her. He wanted to be alone with her. Just to see what it felt like. It had been so long since it had been just her and just him. When he'd come home after getting shot, all he'd wanted, all he'd needed, was time with his wife. But Ethan had been little and needy in the way that toddlers often were.

The kids had needed her more. And after too many late night diaper changes and dirty sheets, he'd stopped vying for her time. He couldn't take any more from her. Not when the kids were taking so much. How could he ask her for more time for himself? But he supposed not wanting to ask for more time was how the distance between them had grown into the impossible chasm that stood between them now.

He had to find a way to get her to need him. To want him. A simple ride alone would be a start. A single step on the journey that would take him a lifetime to manage. If he got that far.

Right now? He was just hoping for a yes. And as the silence grew, so did his dread that what he would hear would be no.

It felt like forever before she said, "Sure. But where's your truck?"

"I let Carponti take it. He needed to go pick something up for Nicole and didn't want her to see it." A version of the truth. Obi Wan would be proud.

Laura's expression softened when he mentioned Carponti. She

had a soft spot for Trent's friend and his wife. Strange jealousy slithered through him. Not of her friendship. No, not that. But of the way her expression softened. She would never look at him that way again, and the loss? That loss hurt, cutting him quick and deep.

He took a tentative step forward.

"Laura?"

She wanted to look away. He could see it in her eyes. But she didn't. She was so close, close enough that he could reach out and stroke an errant strand of hair that had fallen across her cheek.

He looked down at her left hand, clenching the pencil like a lifeline. It was a long moment before she turned off her computer and stood, her face a mask of caution. Her bare ring finger haunted him. It never should have gotten this far.

"I need you to be a happy couple." Patrick's words rang through his head. How could Patrick suggest that Trent ask his wife to lie for him and pretend everything was wonderful in their marriage when he could barely get past an awkward hello?

He wasn't asking her for that. He refused.

He wanted this time with her for its own sake. Nothing more.

There was no way he would ask her to do this for him. He watched as she slipped her wallet into her purse. The elegance of her fingers as they flew over the zipper. Longing punched through him.

Laura stood, shouldering the simple black tote he'd bought for her two Christmases ago. It warmed him to see her using something he'd given her. He'd had this mental image of her throwing away everything even remotely tied to his memory and he held on to the ridiculous pleasure of seeing she still had it.

She shifted the tote to her other shoulder, her hand releasing the strap. She caught him looking at her hand and tried to tuck the injured hand behind her back. He moved quickly, capturing it before she could slip it out of his reach.

It was a mistake, touching her. Heat bolted through him the moment her soft fingers were cradled in his and he hung on to the sensation. Her skin was soft and smooth, a stark comparison to his. He'd dreamed about her hands on his body so many times and touching her sparked a thousand images, some real, some pure fantasy.

With a single finger, he traced the top of her knuckles. He brushed his thumb over her bandaged knuckles and felt her jerk. Chilled by her rejection, he let her go. Never would he have imagined that she'd flinch from his touch.

"What happened?"

"I scraped my knuckles trying to fix the dishwasher." Her voice was thick.

"What's wrong with the dishwasher?"

"It's not cleaning the dishes right. I looked up what was wrong, and there's probably food stuck in the chopper. I was trying to clean it out when the screwdriver slipped and I busted my knuckles."

Trent wanted to be able to smile at his wife's stubborn independence. The first time he'd deployed, she'd filled their small study with bookshelves she'd assembled herself. The second time, she'd landscaped. Each time, she learned some new skill around the house, so that when he came back, he was never faced with the honey-do lists that other soldiers had to wrestle with.

He should have been there to do those things for her. But he hadn't, and she'd made one thing abundantly clear. She didn't need him.

He looked at her then and wanted to beg her to give him another chance. To hell with the court-martial, to hell with the rumors. He wanted her back. Wanted to explain everything that he hadn't been able to say for the last year and the year before that and the year before that.

Lay his sins at her feet and allow her to judge him as harshly as she deemed fit. Anything to keep her from casting him out entirely... *Don't give up on me.* But he kept the plea to himself, the gulf between them too wide for a single plea to cross.

"I'm sure you'll figure it out," he said. He wanted to ask if he could help. But the words lodged in his throat. He couldn't.

He met her gaze, unable to walk away, despite everything that said he'd already lost her. "I'd like to see you," he said again.

She bit her lip and looked away, down at where his index finger rested near the edge of her pinky. "I can't, Trent," she whispered.

"Can't?" She lifted her gaze at his single word. "Or won't?"

"You can't come in here and ask me that," she said. There was steel beneath the sadness in her voice. "You have no right."

"You're my wife."

"I was your wife," she said. "And you chose the Army over your family."

He heard what she didn't say. *You chose the Army over me.*

"I did. You're right." Her mouth opened, then closed again quickly. Surprise flashed in her eyes at his admission. A simple thing. But so very important. He had so many sins to atone for. She bit her lips hard enough that he winced. "I want to try. Just once more, I want to try and make things right."

She swallowed hard, shaking her head. "You can't. You lost that opportunity."

"I screwed up last year."

"This isn't about last year, Trent." She took a step backward. He felt the loss of her warmth in the air around him. "This is about all those years ago. You died. And you never came back to me. You never planned on coming home, not really. Not to me, not to the kids. So why should I believe you now?" she whispered.

He twisted his wedding ring around his finger. Light bounced off white gold. "I can't give you any good reasons." He lifted his gaze to hers. "Other than I screwed up."

Silence stretched between them, harsh and unforgiving and filled with bitterness, sadness and lies. It was forever before she spoke.

"I can't give you what you want anymore, Trent." Her gaze didn't waver from his. "Because I don't have anything left. You broke me," she whispered. "You finally broke me."

4

———————

Laura supposed she should be used to the awkward silence filling the space between them by now. As she turned down Highway 195, heading toward Jen's out of town property, Patrick's words weighed heavily on her soul. She drummed her fingers on the steering wheel, trying to figure out what to do with all the uncertainty twisting inside her.

She thought about turning the radio on then thought against it. The sound would be jarring. Grating. Too harsh.

The silence, at least, was as familiar as it was empty.

Trent kept shifting in the seat, fidgeting with his glasses. There had been a time when they would talk about pointless things. Laugh and share jokes or, better—find a place to pull off on the side of the road because they couldn't keep their hands off each other.

Now the distance between them was silent and cold.

She sighed heavily. Might as well get started on the old familiar routine. God, but she wanted to break free of all this. She wanted this resolved. She was so tired of ripping the bandage off the wounds on her heart every time he reappeared in her life.

"Is there something on your mind?" he asked. His voice jolted her out of her thoughts.

She considered her next words carefully, knowing they were going to cause a fight and knowing she could do nothing to avoid it. "So Patrick came and talked to me today," she said quietly.

The silence turned frigid, like shattered ice frozen and suspended in the air around them. Trent swore loud and long. The force of his reaction momentarily stunned her. He pushed his glasses onto the top of his head and scrubbed his hands over his face. "I'm sorry. I asked him not to."

"I know," she said. He glanced at her. "He told me." She took a deep breath. "Were you even going to give me a choice or just make the decision without talking to me?"

"Laura—"

"You weren't, were you?" She paused, breathing deeply, fighting for control of her temper. "No, you did this just like you do everything. You shut it down, you don't talk to me about it and you don't let me in on the really big fucking decisions that oh, I don't know, impact more than just your life. *Our* life." She gripped the steering wheel so tightly that the leather creased beneath her fingers.

She couldn't do this. Not like this. She needed to move. To get away. To release some of the anger and hurt inside her before she lashed out and did something she could not take back.

Laura slowed the car and steered it to the side of the road, breathing deeply through her nose to keep from losing her temper completely. She needed space, needed to move, to do something with the twisting anger inside her. She knew what most of the charges against him were. Dereliction of duty. Conduct unbecoming an officer and a gentleman. But it was the allegations made by another woman that had nearly crushed her soul.

He leaned forward, keeping his hands over his mouth. "He thinks that everything hinges on their impression of my integrity. That means it's really important to beat the morality charges..."

It was a long moment before he spoke again. "Laura, they're lies."

She swallowed. His denial echoed in her ears. She opened the door, then got out and slammed it shut with extreme violence. He followed her. "Then where did these allegations come from, Trent? Why would your soldier say these things?"

"I don't know. Because of her husband, because she's as guilty as he is? I don't know." He paused and she fought the urge to turn around. Hated that the sound of his voice drew her to him when she should be walking the other way. "Laura, I've done some horrible things in my life. But not this. Never this."

She turned back and looked at her husband and for a brief moment, felt a deep twinge of sympathy. He looked lost. Formal charges of adultery were not something the Army did often, and those charges were usually only filed when the commanders had incontrovertible proof that a violation had occurred. Such charges were almost always tied to other—more serious—charges. She'd seen far too many cases like this in her job as the family readiness liaison for the battalion.

She turned away and started walking down a well-worn path near a small stream. The anger overwhelmed her, clawed at her.

She needed a minute to cool down before she could face the kids. She didn't want them to see her like this. This needy, sad thing who still, despite everything, hoped her husband would love her enough to come home. God, she was pathetic. But the day he'd died, she'd lost everything. The foundation of her world had been ripped from beneath her feet.

She rubbed her upper arms against a sudden chill.

The snap of a twig behind her told her she was no longer alone with her thoughts. A brush of air against her neck told her he was closer than he had any right to be. But he made no move to touch her. At least, none that she could see or feel.

"I remember when you died," she whispered. She wrapped her arms around her waist, a phantom pain rippling through her belly, the memory etched into her very bones. "Ethan was barely two. I was pregnant with Emma."

"I couldn't hear for a day and a half," he murmured.

"For two whole days I thought I'd lost you. I couldn't move, I couldn't get out of bed. I just stared into the darkness, hoping, praying for five more minutes with you. I would have traded anything." She gripped her upper arms tightly, bracing against the cold inside her, fighting the tears that burned behind her eyes. "And when you called, when I heard your voice...I didn't believe it was you." She bit her lips together, fighting to keep everything inside from breaking free. "I was so...I was so happy. You were alive. I got everything I hoped for. But it was all a lie because I never *really* got you back," she whispered, her voice breaking. Finally, she turned to face him. "Why can't you just let me go?" She released a shuddering breath, afraid to look him in the eye. Terrified at what she would see.

"Because I can't," he whispered. "I know I broke us. By not calling, by following that goddamned no-contact order instead of breaking the rules and calling you. I know I did this." He lifted one hand. It trembled near her cheek and she hated herself for yearning for his touch.

She didn't speak until she was confident she could, past the block in her throat. "Trent, you've been closing me off and shutting me out for years. Last year? Last year just solidified the death of our marriage. All the rumors. All the allegations? What was I supposed to believe when I didn't hear anything from you?"

"I will regret following that no-contact order for the rest of my life." His voice cracked. "Then why did you?"

He closed his eyes. His shoulders rose and fell with a deep breath. Finally, he met her gaze again. "Because I still believed the system would work. I still had faith."

"Really?" She searched the deep brown eyes behind the soft reflection of his glasses.

His throat moved as he swallowed and looked away. "Yeah."

"Then why stay? Why not get out of the Army and have a nice, nine-to-five civilian job?" She needed to know what made this man who had sacrificed everything for the Army turn against it.

"Because it's the only thing I've ever known. It's the only thing I'm good at. Hell, I'm not even very good at it anymore." He paused, letting the silence hang between them. Finally, he spoke. "I'm being court-martialed to placate the father of the lieutenant who stole arms from our unit and sold them for cash. They want me to take the fall. There are men who have done far worse than me in the name of God and country but I'm the one who's been chosen for public crucifixion."

The bitterness in his words struck her forcibly, and a renewed anger washed over her. Only this time, her anger was directed at the Army.

"You're serious? After everything you've sacrificed, the Army is just going to throw you away?"

"Not the Army. My esteemed brigade commander." His gaze did not waver from hers.

She hesitated, her mind racing over the implications of her decision.

"If I do this..." Her voice broke and she fought to keep tears from filling her eyes or her words. "If I do this, it changes nothing between us. You'll sign the papers and leave once it's over."

His nostrils flared slightly, the muscles in his neck tense. "Why would you agree to this?" His voice was harsh.

Because I've lost you too many times. I have to walk away. I have to protect myself. But she didn't voice the silent cry. She lifted her chin and refused to look away from the dark gaze that held too many secrets and lies. "I don't want our children to have to visit you in jail."

BECAUSE HE COULDN'T HELP himself, Trent reached for her. Terrified that she would pull away, his fist trembled. The barest brush of his knuckles against her cheek. She shifted, a slight movement away from his touch. A sharp bolt of hurt sliced through him.

"Why would you do this?" he asked again, dreading the answer. He had to know if he had a chance, even the most minute chance, of fixing things with her.

Conflict passed over her features. "Because I want this over and done with. I'm tired of hurting. If this ends the court-martial, then so be it."

He heard what she did not say: *This ends our marriage.* Standing there in the fading sunlight, he looked at his wife. At the hurt written on her face. At the stubborn line of her mouth.

He wanted to see her mouth soften. To see her look at him like she used to. He wanted to be that man again: worthy of her.

His sins were legion. He was not a good man. The war had seen to that. But he felt a faint brush of warmth inside him and knew it for what it was: hope. And he reached into the darkness, cupping the light. It was a long time before he spoke. "Thank you, Laura," he whispered.

"This isn't for you," she said softly. She offered him a flat smile that did not meet her eyes. "This is about moving on. You and I..."

"Laura—"

"Don't." Her eyes flashed and he realized he'd pushed too far. "Don't ask for more than that." She released a deep breath, looking away. "I have to get the kids."

He swallowed and nodded, waiting a full breath before following her back up the hill to the car.

Their children had no idea about the world's dangers. About the pain and suffering he'd seen beaten into younger kids' faces before they could even walk.

His kids were always there in the back of his mind, but he'd needed to lock away his love for them and focus on his mission. Some of the most important years of their lives were memories captured only in photographs and videos. Memories he would never be a part of. Because war and children did not mix. That much he knew from brutal, firsthand experience.

He'd tried so hard to protect them but he'd failed so miserably. He glanced at Laura as he climbed into the passenger's seat. In his head, he nurtured a hesitant, fragile fantasy. A fantasy where he offered a tentative smile and her eyes warmed in return. Where for one aching moment, he saw in her eyes the love that he'd betrayed.

A stronger man could fix this. A better man could capture his wife's love and reclaim her heart. Lay down his weapons and become the husband and father she'd promised to wait for.

The fear was back, tormenting him with doubt and all the ways he'd failed.

It whispered in his ear that he'd already lost her.

He refused to listen to the dark thoughts, the whispered torment. It couldn't be true.

Because if he lost them, he lost everything.

5

———

"Daddy!"

"Daddy?" Emma's tiny, squeaky voice echoed her brother's as both kids barreled toward him as soon as he and Laura walked into the house.

For a brief moment, the noise and chaos of their cries overwhelmed him, and he fought an ingrained reaction to shout for silence. These were his children, not his soldiers, and they were still babies, barely out of diapers.

He knelt and met their full-frontal assault head on.

"Daddy, did Mommy tell you what Fluffy did last night?" Ethan asked, jockeying for position directly in front of him. Emma squawked and elbowed her brother.

"No hitting," Trent said, more sharply than he'd intended.

Emma's tiny black brows furrowed. "Not nice, Daddy," she said, waggling a finger at him. "No shouting."

Trent raised both eyebrows and almost smiled at the serious look on his daughter's face. A look he'd seen on Laura's face once or twice. She was a miniature version of his wife, except her hair was longer and darker, her cheeks rounded with the chubbiness of childhood.

From across the small living room, someone laughed, and Trent looked away, meeting the eyes of his longtime friend, Shane Garrison. "Never thought I'd see the day when a four-year-old would leave you speechless," Shane said.

"Yeah, well, she's her mother's daughter." He glanced down at the kids, unsure of how to extricate himself from their embraces. "Do you guys have any stuff you need to police up?"

Ethan frowned. "Why would we put our toys in jail?"

Behind him, Laura laughed softly. "Daddy means go pick up your toys, guys."

The kids disappeared somewhere, and Laura padded over to the kitchen. Shane leaned against the small couch, bracing his hands behind him, only a hint of stiffness in his movements from the injuries that had taken him out of combat less than a year ago. "Any progress on the court-martial front?"

Trent leaned against the arm of the chair next to him. "Patrick is trying to get the whole court-martial thrown out," he said, answering Shane's unspoken question.

"That's good." He was happy to see Shane up and about. His friend was back to shaving his head and he looked like he'd packed on more than a few extra pounds of solid muscle. "Carponti left your truck here and said thanks."

"How's the wedding planning going?"

"I'd rather not say," Shane said with a grimace, running his hand over his bald head. "We—and by 'we' I mean all of us—are going shopping this weekend. Don't argue. I need your support or I might have to turn in my man card."

Trent grinned, feeling more relaxed than he had all afternoon. "What are we shopping for?"

"Wedding stuff. Apparently, there is a whole lot more that goes into a wedding than a pretty dress and a willing woman." Shane rubbed his hand over the back of his neck, a faint smile teasing his lips. "My first marriage was at the Justice of the Peace on a Saturday afternoon. This is much more complex." He glanced into the kitchen at Jen. Shane was not an overly emotive guy but the smile tugging at the corner of his mouth said more than any words could. "And infinitely more worth it."

Trent had never seen the man more at ease, not once in the more than fifteen years they'd known each other. It showed in the relaxed lines around his mouth, the lack of tension in his shoulders.

He turned slightly to look into the kitchen, where Laura was helping Jen clean up. Watching her talk with her friend, he saw the side of his wife that he loved best. Her quick smile. Her easy laugh. The way her eyes lit up when she was surrounded by people she cared for.

The way she no longer looked at him.

Trent cleared his throat and looked away before she caught him watching her. He glanced at Shane, and realized he'd been caught nonetheless.

"How are things going with Laura?" Shane asked softly.

A shriek from upstairs drifted down to them. *How had the kids even made it up there so quickly?* Trent started for them but a quick glance at Laura told him there was no need to go rushing to the rescue. It was amazing how she knew what was serious and what wasn't.

"About as well as can be expected," Trent said mildly.

"That bad, huh?"

Shane threw a quick glance toward the kitchen then looked back at Trent for an explanation. Trent sighed and jerked his head toward the screened-in porch at the back of Jen's house. When they got outside, he filled Shane in on Patrick's Hail Mary attempt to get the court- martial thrown out. As he spoke, Shane's expression hardened.

"That's a screwed up thing to do," he said quietly.

"I didn't ask her to do it," Trent said.

"But you're not going to stop her." There was judgment in Shane's tone, harsh and unforgiving.

Trent ground his teeth, yanking back his temper. "I don't want to raise my kids from jail."

"But you were fine with attempting to raise them from Iraq and Afghanistan." Shane crossed his arms over his chest, bracing his feet wide like a fighter.

"That's not fair."

"No, what's not fair is letting Laura do this. What's it going to do to the kids? Did you think about them?"

He had, but not how Shane had implied. He'd thought about going home and being in the house with them. About putting them to bed at night. Shane's words hit him like a tank: if he did this — if he granted Laura the divorce, he would be lying to them as well as to the world. And they were too little to understand.

They would hate him.

He shoved his glasses to the top of his head in frustration and scrubbed his hands over his face. "I want my family back. And I don't know how to make that happen."

Shane was quiet for a long moment. He shifted against the support beam then folded his arms over his chest. The massive black tattoos that covered his arms writhed with his movement.

"When I was hurt, Laura came to see me in the hospital." Shane stuffed his hands in his pockets and leaned back against the wall. "It was right after she'd found out you'd been volunteering to go on all these missions. She was wrecked. She asked me why you stayed away. Why you'd volunteered for combat time and time again. Why you told her you loved her and still volunteered to leave your family. I told her I didn't know. I still don't know. You love her. You love your kids. You," and Shane pointed a finger at Trent, "came home. That's a gift. And you're wasting that gift, brother." He sighed hard. "I don't like this idea."

"I don't either. It's another lie," Trent said. Added to the ones he'd already told his wife. To the ones he'd told himself when he fell asleep at his desk instead of double-checking the threat assessment from the knucklehead intelligence officer. Or personally checking on the maintenance of the weapons systems. He hadn't pushed hard enough. He could have done more to stop his boys from dying.

Instead, he'd been laid out on a gurney while his boys continued the fight in Sadr City. He should have been out there when Mack and Pete had gotten blown up, when Story had taken their boys back into the fight because Trent had been on his ass. The docs hadn't believed him when he'd said he was fine; he needed to go.

Because he hadn't been fine. But he'd been determined to get back into the fight.

But Mack and Pete were already gone. And the war had gone on without him.

He cleared his throat, yanking himself out of the bitter memory.

"You're right; it would be. It would be using your wife for a chance to gain your freedom. And that's wrong no matter how bullshit the charges against you are. You should fight this court-martial with everything you have." He cleared his throat. "Except Laura."

"I know that," Trent said quietly.

But damn his soul to hell, he wasn't going to stop her. He wanted to go home where officers weren't trying to stab each other in the back to make sure their report card was the best. Where the roads weren't hiding bombs in dead things and debris. Where he could hear all the noise and chaos that the kids made and not worry that a bomb would go off, destroying innocence and lives. It was a facade, a grasping chance at a dream he could never enjoy. It might be a facade but it was still a chance. A chance to be around his wife and his kids without letting the dirt and the grime and the hatred of war into their lives. He could do this, right? Without polluting them with the evil that war made good men do? Here was a chance to prove to himself that he could do this, that he could be more than just a soldier. That he could be a husband and a father.

It was the only chance he had.

"You don't have to help clean up," Jen said, folding a towel in the handle on the stove.

"Of course I do. You've been babysitting my spawn for the last five hours. And you even fixed them a snack." Laura wiped the center island with a paper towel. "Now show me the dress you want to order."

A hesitant smile crept across Jen's lips as she turned over a magazine she'd dog-eared, pulling it open to the marked page. "This is the one."

"Oh honey, I love it," Laura whispered. The gown was a classic A-line, delicate lace over chiffon. Pearls shimmered over the bust. Laura smiled as she imagined her friend in the beautiful gown. "You'll look amazing in this." She glanced up at Jen and was surprised by her wistful expression. "What?"

Jen shrugged her shoulder. "I had to have them alter it. I can't wear a strapless dress."

Laura's throat closed off at the sadness in her friend's voice. Jen had never expected to have the problem of finding a wedding gown. After the surgery that had removed her breast to save her life, she'd been convinced that no man would want her.

She'd never guessed that buying a wedding dress would be in her future.

Laura covered Jen's hand with her own, refusing to allow her friend to sink into sadness. "Do you honestly think Shane is going to care what you're wearing on the day you marry him?" she asked softly.

Jen's smile brightened. "He told me he'd marry me naked if that's what it took to get me down the aisle."

"Sounds like something Carponti would say, not Shane," Laura said.

"They've spent a lot of time together this past year."

Laura grinned. "Carponti's sense of humor hasn't failed him yet."

"Tell that to Shane," Jen said softly. "And while you're at it, tell Carponti there is nothing wrong with red velvet cake."

"Red velvet cake? Seriously? Do you even like red velvet cake?"

Jen smiled. "Shane does, apparently. Carponti insists it was made by the devil."

"Shane does not strike me as the kind of man who has a preference for any kind of cake," Laura said dryly. She glanced over her shoulder at Trent and Shane, who were standing in the screened-in back porch, talking in low voices. She and Trent had had yellow cake with buttercream frosting at their wedding. It had been small but perfect. Just close friends and family. Trent had worn his Dress Green uniform and she remembered how handsome he'd looked. She'd never in a million years have thought that day would lead to this one: the day she'd made a bargain to end her marriage.

"Where'd you go just then?" Jen asked quietly.

"Thinking about the day I married Trent." Laura sighed and leaned on the center island, cupping her chin in her palm. "Trent has a chance to beat the charges against him."

"Oh?"

Laura explained what Patrick had asked her to do. She avoided Jen's eyes while she spoke, unable to face the judgment she was sure to find there.

"Are you going to do it?" Something in Jen's voice made her look up.

Laura nodded slowly. "Yeah, I am."

Jen said nothing and turned to put dishes away. "Can I ask why?" she said after a long moment.

"Because Trent may have done a lot of things wrong, but I don't think I believe..." She stopped and sucked in a deep breath. The rumors might have been something she couldn't ignore but in her heart, she'd never wanted to believe them. And if Patrick thought they were bullshit— maybe—well, maybe they were. "I don't want to take the kids to visit Daddy in prison on the weekends." A convenient lie. Maybe if she repeated it often enough, she would start to believe it.

"A valid reason but this isn't about the kids. At least, not entirely," Jen said quietly. "What about you? This isn't going to be easy."

"I know." Laura looked down at her hands, twisting her fingers together in the towel to keep them from trembling. The empty space on her finger felt heavy. "But it's not about me anymore. Trent and I are over. We're going to put on a happy face for the trial, and whether he beats it or not, he's promised to grant me a divorce."

She looked up to find Jen studying her.

"That's a far cry from the woman who wept the last time he deployed." Jen's voice was a whisper. Laura was sure she hadn't meant the words as judgment; Jen didn't have a mean bone in her body, but Laura felt judged and found lacking anyway.

"Yeah, it is. But I just don't know how to do it anymore. I don't know how to be the dutiful wife to a husband who is never really coming home." Her voice cracked and she blinked rapidly, refusing to cry over him again.

Jen leaned across the island, squeezing Laura's hands. "If he hadn't lied, if he hadn't been volunteering for all those tours, would you still have waited for him?"

Laura's throat closed off and she blinked rapidly. "I don't know," she whispered.

Jen shifted then and pulled her into a hug. "Then do this cautiously, because I don't want to see you hurt any more than you already have been." She paused. "And I'd hate to have to have Shane kick his ass. It might do some damage to their friendship."

Laura gave a strangled laugh and she broke their embrace, swiping at the moisture in her eyes that had nearly leaked out. "Not funny."

"Who's joking?" Jen's smile was wicked. She squeezed Laura's shoulders. "I'm here, okay? Vent, scream, whatever. I'm here for you."

Laura hugged her again. "Thank you." She knew Jen would be there for her but it was still nice to hear. "So let's change the subject to something less depressing. Are we still doing lunch with Nicole tomorrow to figure out the colors and stuff?"

"Oh, yes. You cannot plan a wedding without the queen of makeup in this little club. Nicole is the only reason I will have any cosmetics whatsoever for this little event."

"Oh, come on. Makeup shopping will be fun. And she will ensure you look fabulous for your special day. Add in the bonus of getting to see your dress this weekend." Nicole knew every tip and trick to hide a blemish or make you look like you'd had a full eight hours of sleep after being up all night with a sick child. And she made it all look so effortless. Which was why she was in charge of cosmetics for this wedding.

Jen smiled but Laura didn't miss her nervousness. She'd healed so much from being with Shane but she would always be a little self-conscious when it came to makeup. "We're going to drag the menfolk along this weekend, too. They need to try on their tuxes, and Nicole wants to get Carponti to look at some new furniture at some ridiculously expensive store in Austin."

"That ought to be a blast," Laura said dryly. Any time Carponti was involved there was no telling what would happen, but he would go a long way to filling the awkwardness of Trent and Laura's difficulties. "Explain to me again why the guys aren't just wearing their dress blues?"

Jen smiled. "Because Shane has some strange notions about doing this wedding 'right'."

"O-kay," Laura said.

She glanced outside where Trent and Shane continued their conversation in the fading Texas light. She was bringing her husband back to the house she'd made into a home without him. Back to the family she'd raised without him. She was terrified about being alone with him. Terrified of the memories that he stroked to life.

She wanted their marriage to be over. She wanted to move on with her life.

Somehow, that goal seemed further out of reach than it had ever been.

And that scared the hell out of her.

~

THE KIDS WERE RACING around upstairs, their feet pounding across the floor like a herd of baby elephants. He could hear them clearly even though he stood on the porch outside. He rubbed the scar over his chest, fighting the urge to go upstairs and tell them to just sit still. For just a minute. That's all he needed. Just a minute of quiet to pull everything back inside.

But that wasn't happening. Laura seemed immune to the noise. She was talking quietly with Jen, leaning over a magazine. He stopped near the door, still on the patio and hidden in the shadows. Her hair spilled over one cheek, her expression soft and smiling. God but he wanted to see that smile turned toward him. Just once.

The tightness in his chest squeezed tighter and tighter until he couldn't breathe. He turned away, facing out over the field behind Jen's house. Watching the stars twinkle in the black carpet of the night sky. It was safe. There would be no red flares filling the sky tonight. No explosions to jerk him out of sleep. No big voice on the loud-speaker warning about an incoming rocket attack.

He heard the stampede overhead and he just needed it to *stop*. He didn't trust himself. Laura was letting them run so it had to be okay, right?

"Hey, are you okay?"

Laura had slipped onto the back porch and he had been so consumed by the panic clutching at his chest, the pounding need for silence, that he hadn't heard her. He looked down at her, her face cast in shadows. There was worry in her eyes, concern in that simple, loaded question.

"I can't come home tonight."

He couldn't. There was too much twisted and raw inside him, too much that he was afraid to let Laura see. He could go home tomorrow night.

He'd have a better handle on things then.

"Were you going to talk to me about that or just make the decision all by yourself?" Just like that, the softness was gone, leaving the familiar disappointment in her eyes.

Would he always let her down?

"I...I just figured you could prepare the kids for it tonight and tomorrow would be better. Less crazy?"

When he was ready to face his home and his family and was

better prepared. Because everything was rioting inside him and he felt his temper snapping at the leash. He'd done better at keeping it under control but not enough. He couldn't let her see.

So he said none of those things.

"You're doing it again," she whispered. "Making all these decisions on your own. You think you know what's best but you've forgotten one key point, Trent." She paused, looking away out over the field toward the distant tire swing. "You don't know what's best for me or for the kids. You don't know us anymore."

She walked away, her head down, her shoulders slumped. Her words stabbed him violently in the heart even as the anxiety tightened in his throat and threatened to choke him.

He lowered his head to the beam in front of him. He was never going to figure this out. He was losing her all over again. But how could he explain to her what he was? The men he'd lost, the choices he'd made? The war was an ugly, evil thing and it had left his mark on him.

She wanted him to talk to her, to open up, but she was right. He didn't know how. And worse? He didn't want to. He didn't want her to know about the little kids running through the piss and the shit with no shoes on. He didn't want her to know about the people so fucking poor they'd fight over a candy bar or plant a bomb for ten dollars.

She was safe here in the States. Their kids would never know what the war was really like.

And damn it, Trent wasn't going to be the one to bring the fucking war home to them. He couldn't let them see the nightmares and the fear that haunted his sleep. That woke him, angry and scared and shaking in the night or worse, sobbing for a lost friend. He didn't want her to see what he'd become.

And tonight, he was having a hard time hiding it. So he would stay away. Just once more.

Tomorrow. He could go home tomorrow.

He'd figure out another way. There had to be another way. Because the alternative? The alternative was not an option.

6

Trent sat at his desk, dreading the ticking of the clock on the wall. Fifteen more minutes and he'd have to leave for his appointment. And wasn't he in a right old jolly mood to sit down and discuss his feelings with the shrink?

He hadn't slept last night. He'd lain awake in Shane and Jen's guest bedroom, the silence sending him crawling up the walls. He'd considered getting up and getting a beer or six and letting the alcohol coax him to sleep but he didn't think that would have helped.

"Don't you look like you're in a chipper mood?" Iaconelli swung around the corner of the cubicle that made Trent's "office" and straddled the chair in front of him. "Rough night?"

Trent frowned, pretty certain that Iaconelli had either just woken up or had never gone to bed. "Not as rough as yours, apparently," Trent said.

"Yeah, well, I at least have no idea what happened last night. You look like you remember every single minute."

"Just about," Trent said. He shifted, pushing his glasses higher on his nose. "What are you up to?"

"Back from NTC early because Captain Marshall can't plan shit and now I'm running a range with Captain Montoya. We're going out to do a site recon this morning."

Trent frowned. "I thought we had a burn ban going on and they were limiting ranges." There had been flooding the previous year when they'd all been deployed. This year? Dry.

Really dry. The kind of dry where a cigarette could set off a range fire that would burn for days.

"So far, range control has cleared us so we're good to go. Why do you look like someone pissed in your Wheaties?"

Trent pushed his glasses up on top of his head and scrubbed his hand over his face. "I've got to go see a shrink in a little bit."

Iaconelli looked like he'd told him he was going to a proctology exam. "You can keep that shit. Shrinks don't do a damn bit of good. They give the kids with no backbones excuses and they don't help the kids who really need it."

"Strong feelings, much?" Trent said.

Iaconelli scowled. "One in a long list of failures that have jaded my opinion of the Army's mental health system. And why are you going to a shrink? Isn't that verboten for an officer?"

Trent shrugged. "My lawyer wants me to have a clean bill of mental health."

"Oh, for your court-martial. Good times. Enjoy yourself," he said with an evil grin.

Trent flipped him off but grinned despite himself. "I'm sure I'll have so much fun discussing how not enough hugs in my childhood scarred me for life."

"Yeah, well, watch what you tell them. It goes into a permanent record so if you tell them the war made you crazy, that shit's going to follow you around."

Trent wanted to ask what had happened to Iaconelli to make him distrust the mental health system but the big man was already gone. And it was time for Trent to face the judge, jury, and executioner: his new shrink.

The drive across post was too short. He even had no trouble finding a parking space, something that *never* happened on Fort Hood. So he had no excuse for being late or stalling or any other way of avoiding the doctor's office.

A physical dread uncurled in his stomach as he walked into the R&R Center. His palms were slicked with sweat and his heart pounded in his ears. He checked in at the front desk, rubbing his hands on his uniform, and waited for the admin assistant to lead him back to Captain Lindberg's office.

It was strange walking through the waiting room. The highest-ranking person was a rugged-looking sergeant who looked battle worn and broken down. There were First Cav combat patches on his right and left shoulders but it was the haunted look in his eyes, the strain that Trent recognized all too well.

He felt a rush of sympathy even as he felt all eyes on him from the myriad of soldiers sitting in the waiting room. It was unusual for an officer to be walking through that waiting room. Mental health was something sought by junior soldiers. Officially, anyone could seek mental health without fear of losing their careers. The reality was that officers simply did not go to the R&R Center. Not for themselves, anyway.

Officers didn't break under the stress of war. If they did, they ended their careers. Maybe not immediately, but their inability to cope with the stress and the pressure was there, hanging over their heads.

Trent was leery about using this as a tool for the court-martial. But Patrick had insisted and Trent had known him too long to question his judgment. If he needed to see the shrink and have her tell them he was fine, well then, Trent would play along. He could tell her what she needed to hear then move out and draw fire.

Still, it was a hard thing to walk through the maze of hallways knowing that this was where the Army sent its broken and breaking soldiers. With one more wipe of his palms on his pants, Trent pushed his glasses up on the bridge of his nose and knocked on the door.

"Captain Lindberg?" he said.

The captain behind the desk stood and Trent was struck by how prim she looked. Most women looked the same in uniform as most men: just like another soldier. But there was something about this woman's movements that reminded Trent of Jacqueline Onassis.

Something about East Coast old money. Something desperately out of place in the Army.

But she stood and stuck out her hand, clearly comfortable in her own office.

"Please, call me Emily," she said, sticking out her hand. The handshake was firm, though, shattering his expectations with a single gesture. Guess that's what he got for stereotyping.

"Have a seat. Trent, right?"

"Yes, ma'am."

"We're the same rank," she said quietly. "I may not know a whole lot about the Army but I do know that captains do not call each other 'sir' or 'ma'am'."

"Why don't you know a lot about the Army?" he asked.

"I've only been in a little over a year. So I've got a lot to learn." She glanced down at the captain's bars on her chest. "A special program brought me in as a captain."

"Just add water and stir and poof, insta-captain," Trent said.

"Something like that." She smiled easily. He liked this woman. There was something about her that made him feel...comfortable. Some of the tightness in his chest from walking through the waiting room faded.

"So, how does this go?" he asked.

"Well, you're here for me to evaluate you for the defense. My job is to get a feel for your current state of medical readiness."

"Can you state that in English?" He shifted against the chair, his back protesting the too- soft seat and back. It made him want to relax further. "I was a company commander and I don't understand what you just said."

She smiled quietly, folding her hands in front of her. "We're going to do a mental health eval. It won't hurt a bit, I promise."

Just like that, the strain was back. The pressure built above his heart and the scar throbbed over his breastbone. He breathed in slow and deep and tried to keep the panic at bay.

"It's not nearly as scary as it sounds," she said. She was watching him closely. He felt the walls closing in, like he was under a microscope. All his plans about playing it fast and loose slipped right out of his grasp.

"Sounds terrifying." He tried to make his voice light. He failed.

"Trent." She waited until he met her gaze. "Relax. Nothing I write is going to go in your official file. We're just going to talk, okay?"

He swallowed but his throat was closed off, thick. Finally, he nodded.

"Do you want to talk about what's going on with you right now?"

He focused on breathing. In. Out. In. Held it until his lungs burned.

Emily came around the desk and sat in the chair next to him. "Look at me, Trent. Are you listening?"

"Yeah."

"I'm not a betting woman but it looks like you're having a little bit of a problem with anxiety."

"Is that what this is? It feels like a fucking heart attack." The words forced their way past the block in his throat.

"That's actually a very common misunderstanding," she said. "Does this happen a lot?"

Trent leaned forward, pushing his glasses up to the top of his head. He covered his mouth with his hands. "Yeah."

"And how long has it been going on?"

He swallowed, staring into the distance, unable to meet her eyes. "Since I got shot."

"Do certain things set it off? Just happens whenever?"

"When things get too...out of control. When things are going smooth and easy, I'm fine. But the minute I tense up, I have trouble breathing." He finally looked at her. "Tell me I'm not crazy. I really don't want to be crazy."

She smiled. "Crazy isn't really a clinical term," she said. "Anxiety isn't on the spectrum of crazy, at any rate. It's more of an adjustment issue."

He frowned. "What does that even mean?"

"You said you were shot? What happened?"

Trent breathed deeply as the memories rose up out of the dark, one by one, replaying in front of his eyes in vivid Technicolor. "We were in the middle of a bad fight in Sadr City. A round got between my body armor and my heart. The impact stopped my heart. They thought I died."

"If your heart stopped, technically you were dead," she said. "When did the anxiety first happen?"

He rubbed his hands over his mouth. "The first time I was getting ready to go back out in sector with our boys."

"What did you do?"

"What could I do? I stuffed it down and went out in sector." His skin was slick with sweat. His face felt clammy beneath his hands.

"You've been stuffing things down for a long time, huh?"

"Maybe." He felt a little peevish. It was just one round and he hadn't even gotten evac'd out of theater like Garrison. Garrison was fucking fine after getting the shit blown out of him. Trent had gotten one little bullet wound and his world went to hell. What was wrong with him?

"You don't sleep well, either, I bet."

"Jesus, what are you, a psychic?" He tried to make a joke. Failed badly.

"Not really. But your body language is pretty defensive right now and you're presenting some pretty strong indicators of distress."

"English? Did you just tell me I look crazy?"

"No, Trent, I did not just tell you you're crazy. But, if you're willing to work on things, I think we can make things better."

He glanced over at her sharply. "You can't fix this. You can't make the memories go away or put feeling back in the dead spot inside of me."

"Maybe we can't fix everything but I think we could do better than you're doing right now."

Better than he was doing now? Better so that he could listen to his kids play and not feel the pressure creeping up on him? Better so that he could maybe, just maybe, find a way to fix things with his wife?

Maybe he could go home and just be still for a moment. Maybe there was a chance he could sit on the couch with Laura and watch a movie. He would never complain about Shane and Jen's hospitality but there was something to be said for sleeping in his own bed, with his wife's body curled next to him. A pulse of longing beat through his veins.

Something so simple. Something so important.

He sucked in a deep breath. Each step into this room had made his chest tighter, his lungs more strained, but each question was...it was lightening the load. Just a little bit, but the pressure around his lungs lessened. Just a little. "Is this going into my official medical record?"

Her expression softened. "I'll make sure there is nothing put in there that will negatively impact your future military career, should you choose to continue."

He rubbed his hands over his mouth again. What good was a

worn down infantryman in the civilian world? There wasn't a lot of use for men with his skill set. And how would he support his family? His kids would need money for college and clothes and God knew what else kids required these days.

He needed to take care of his family. What else could he do beyond the military? He'd given it everything he had. Including, apparently, his sanity.

"Okay," he said after a while. "So how does this work?"

"So let's talk about this not sleeping thing," she said. "Not sleeping well is the number one cause of some of these issues. I think if we can address that, everything else, especially the anxiety, will be a lot easier to deal with."

Trent took a deep breath and held it. He'd never thought about avoiding the R&R Center because of how other people would judge him. It was because he'd had work to do. He was a good infantryman, a good soldier. He had tactical skills. He'd needed to be in the fight. It had been the most important thing in the world to him to prove that he hadn't been slacking, that he'd been doing everything he was supposed to be doing.

Because the day he'd gotten shot, his soldiers had died. And while intellectually he knew that wasn't his fault, if he'd been there, if he'd been a little bit faster, a little more prepared...maybe they'd still be alive.

He closed his eyes. But they weren't. And nothing he'd done for the last four deployments had made a damn bit of difference to the Army. To the individuals he'd served with? Yeah, that mattered. But to the Army?

He'd been ready to sacrifice his entire life to that institution and this is where it left him: sitting in a shrink's office, talking about not sleeping.

He'd lost his marriage because of his choices—because the Army had needed him. Or at least, that's what he told himself.

And he'd let Laura slip further and further away.

He glanced over at the doctor, sitting patiently while he waged his own private war. "I have to go home," he whispered. "And it absolutely terrifies me."

~

LAURA OPENED her e-mail and stared at the words scrawled across the screen, her mind foggy from lack of sleep and too many things at home.

Her phone vibrated on her desk. Laura flipped it over. She didn't feel like talking to Jen. It was nothing against her closest friend, but Jen's love for Shane was still so new and shiny that Laura needed sunglasses to protect herself from the brilliance of it. She would never say that to Jen, though, because it would make her feel bitchy and small.

Two days had passed since Patrick had asked her to put on a happy married face. Two days and Trent had found excuses to not come home.

And each day had reaffirmed her belief that whatever demons he was facing, he was going to face them alone. The way he always had.

Just then, as if her thoughts had somehow summoned him, Trent appeared in the doorway, his shoulders filling the narrow entrance. He gripped his beret tightly in both hands, twisting it like he wanted to strip the color from the black wool.

"Hey."

She stopped typing and looked up, wishing she didn't see the worry, the lack of sleep in his eyes. "Hey."

"Can I talk to you?" he asked. His voice was hoarse, deeper than she remembered. It grated over her skin like a callous and she wondered how often he'd had to shout over smoke and gunfire for it to get this gravelly.

Bracing herself, she swallowed the lump that rose in her throat, squeezing out the air along with her ability to speak. She cleared her throat. "Sure." Wariness in that single word.

He glanced at her desk, then his black gaze met hers. He cleared his throat roughly. "I just wanted to see if you could get away. To be alone for a few minutes? It's early. We can go get coffee..."

She heard what he didn't say. He was asking for her. Just her. A chance to be alone with him. To try and talk to him without a thousand things going on around them at once.

It was a risk. But she could do this. She could have coffee with the man and still stick to her guns about ending things. Couldn't she? She picked up her purse and cell phone. An unfamiliar ache pounded through her and for a moment, she couldn't place it.

She stopped short as she recognized the feeling. A latent desire swirled through her belly. Funny how her body recognized him when her heart refused.

He didn't move as she approached. She stopped, stood close enough to see the corded scar running along his jaw. It ended just beneath his left ear, a hard slash through the shadow of his nearly black stubble.

That had happened almost two years ago. He'd called home to tell her about the injury. If she really thought about it, she realized she hadn't ever seen it up close. He was always in motion whenever he'd been home, before she'd sent him the papers. The few times they'd had sex, the lights had been off. She hadn't seen him close up like this for a long, long time.

Curiosity tugged at her.

She lifted her fingers to trace the line on his jaw, her anger fading with the evidence of his pain. God, how it must have hurt. He stayed absolutely still as she traced the smooth, white skin, the edge of his stubble scraping the sides of her finger. He might as well have been made of polished granite. He loomed over her, larger than she remembered. He was leaner, his body hard, the lines on his face deeper.

Alone with her husband in the solitude of her office, the urge to touch him drove her closer to him than she should be. But she didn't fight it.

"This didn't heal well," she murmured.

"I thought women liked scars." His lips quirked at the edges.

"I don't like how much this must have hurt you," she said, lowering her hand.

He slipped his hands into his pockets. "It was a long way from my heart."

It was the wrong thing to say. Her gaze dropped to his chest, covered now by the grey of his Army uniform. She opened her mouth to speak but no words formed in her throat. She withdrew her touch, retreating away from her fragile hopes. What she wouldn't give for a single space of normalcy, a single moment where she could forget the war, forget all that it had done to her husband, to her family. To her marriage.

They could have all the coffee in the world but until he came home, well and truly came home, not this facade they were putting up to convince the world that their marriage was fine, she could never give him her heart again. She knew that. More than half a decade at war had taught her that. And no amount of wishing in the world could change that essential truth.

TRENT WATCHED his wife walk in front of him into the coffee shop in Copperas Cove. He'd deliberately driven them away from Fort Hood and Killeen, away from the Starbucks and the McDonalds to a place where they could get away from the uniforms and the crowds and the prying glances.

He wanted time with her away from the office. Away from the constant demands on her attention. He had only just found the words he needed and they were stuck in his throat. And she was already wary around him, already tense whenever he managed to be near her.

He didn't blame her. He was struggling to find his bearings, struggling to find the strength to walk into their front door for that first time. He wanted so badly to be a good dad, but it seemed like everything he did with his family came out twisted and wrong. So he kept avoiding it. Until he no longer could.

He didn't talk until they had ordered their drinks and were seated in a quiet corner, him on an overstuffed chair, her on an old couch that once upon a time had probably been fuzzy faux brown suede. Laura traced one finger around the lip of her mug, avoiding his gaze. The steel resolve he saw in the set of her jaw was nothing compared to the intense emotion he'd glimpsed in her deep golden eyes.

There was a reason for her reticence. He didn't deserve to be here with her right now. But he wanted so badly to fix things between them.

Trent cleared his throat. "So, um, Patrick has me talking to one of the counselors," he said quietly. "He's trying to build an 'I'm not one step away from a psychotic break' case." He swirled his coffee, unable to look at her. "And I was, ah, talking to her about stuff. About how I feel out of control around the kids." He rubbed his hand over his mouth, taking her silence as a cue to continue. He pushed his glasses to the top of his head, rubbing the bridge of his nose, avoiding her gaze. And after his session with Emily, he felt a cautious optimism that he might actually be able to pull it off. He wasn't happy about walking out of there with a prescription for Ambien and a low-dose anti-anxiety medication but Emily had given him her cell phone number and he was supposed to call if he had any questions or concerns.

It was probably the best medical care he'd ever gotten from the Army.

But right then, all the doctors in the world didn't have the answers he needed.

"She said it's normal." He looked at her then, seeking any hint of compassion in her eyes. He didn't deserve it but still, he dared to hope that maybe, just maybe she could forgive him. "But it doesn't feel normal, Laura. Everything feels wrong."

Her lips parted just a hint. Her expression softened and he thought for a brief moment that he'd broken through the barriers between them. Then she looked down into her coffee.

"I can't fix your normal, Trent." She lifted her gaze to meet his. "And I won't let you keep doing this to the kids. They don't understand what's going on, why you're back in Killeen but won't come home."

Cold crawled across his skin like spiders with icepicks for feet. He leaned back, grinding his teeth. "I understand," he said roughly.

"I don't think you do." There was no acrimony in her soft words. "I don't think you realize what you're doing to them. Emma cried herself to sleep last night because she doesn't think you love her."

"That's horse shit. Of course I love her."

"Yes, I can hear the devotion in your voice," she said dryly. "Emma is barely four years old. It hurts her when you ignore her. She misses you. They both miss you."

"I know that." He gripped his coffee cup tightly. "I just don't know what to do about it."

"And I don't know how to help you," she said, her words hard and filled with hurt. "Because you won't let me."

Tension wound tight around his heart, squeezing the air from his lungs. "You don't understand," he whispered.

"You're right. I don't. Because every time I try to get close to you, you run off to another war. Another training exercise, another deployment. I don't understand what you've been through because you won't talk to me about it. You never have."

"Maybe I don't like talking about it," he spat. "Talking about it doesn't fix anything."

She looked at him with patience and understanding and unbreakable resolve. He'd meant to try and talk to her about things, to try and open up, and even that was turning into an epic clusterfuck.

"And maybe not talking about it is what's causing half the damn problems between us," she said quietly.

"No, the divorce is what's causing the problems between us." His words lashed out at her and she flinched.

"That's not fair and you know it."

"You're right, it's not." Trent set his mug down, scrubbing both hands over his face. "I'm sorry," he whispered.

Silence greeted his admission and it was a long moment before he moved his hands to peer at his wife. Tears had filled her eyes and she blinked rapidly, turning her face toward the door, away from him. "Shit, Laura, don't cry," he whispered.

"I'm so tired of crying over you," she said and her voice broke.

Trent didn't think before he moved. A piece of the tight knot around his heart loosened. He didn't consider whether or not his wife would pull away. He simply moved, sliding onto the small couch to pull her against him. He didn't know what he expected her to do but what she did shocked the hell out of him.

She stiffened the moment his arm slid around her shoulder. But he simply held her. One moment. Then another. And then he felt something he'd been longing for since forever.

She relaxed against him.

For a moment, nothing more, until something, some fleeting sensation unfurled in the dead space inside him. She trembled, then, a violent shudder and he realized she was crying. Deep, silent sobs that threatened to break them both.

He sat there and held her, hating himself for hurting her so badly. Hating the war and the illusions that he'd told himself to justify being gone. Hated the fear that made him hide from his family instead of being there for them.

He held her. Because it was the only thing he could do.

HIS UNIFORM SCRAPED the edge of her cheek. His body was a solid wall beneath her skin and for a brief moment, she simply let him hold her. His strength wrapped around her, his scent pulled her close, reminding her that somewhere inside this man was the man she'd married. The man she'd loved.

She hadn't meant to cry in front of him. Not again. But the truth had simply slipped free of the chains she'd attempted to bind it with, breaking her resolve until it emptied out of her, tearing free and leaving her drained.

It was a long time until the tears stopped. Her eyes felt swollen.

Now, she rested against Trent and closed her eyes. She simply stopped. Stopped fighting. Stopped arguing. Stopped resisting her stubborn heart that still loved this man no matter how many times he hurt her or lashed out.

His leaving, his anger: he wasn't in control of those things. Not like she'd convinced herself he was in those dark days when the rumors and innuendos had been breeding like a live thing in the silence between them. But there was more at work here than her husband simply walking out on her.

He'd made a huge step by talking to the counselor. And he hadn't needed to tell her about their conversation, but he had. Laura leaned back, refusing to believe the insidious voice in her head that said he was just telling her this out of sheer selfishness.

She lifted her gaze, looking deep into his eyes. She started to shift and pull away but Trent moved first, cradling her face with his palms. Gently, his thumbs caressed her cheeks, wiping away the tears.

"I'm so tired of screwing everything up, Laura," he whispered. "I want to fix this. Not for the trial. For us."

"It's not that simple."

"Yes, it is." His voice was urgent and harsh. "I can't fix what I've done. And I damn sure don't deserve your forgiveness." He lowered his forehead to hers, his palms warm and solid against her skin. "But I'm asking you to help me. Help me reset my normal. Help me learn how to be a dad again. A husband." He blinked rapidly.

She pressed her lips together, biting back fresh tears. "And what happens when you leave again?" she whispered. "What do I do then?" She sniffed quietly. "You keep breaking my heart." Her voice cracked.

His fingers crooked around her jaw. "I want to stop."

They were tucked away in a quiet corner of the coffee shop. The couch was blocked by a high booth. No one could see them. Laura kept her eyes locked on his. Finally, he'd laid his fears, his hopes, his dreams in her lap.

She could crush him so easily. A stronger woman might have walked away, doing to him what he'd done so many times to her. But she was not that woman. She wanted to end the pain between them, not prolong it.

She'd thought divorce was the right answer. Ending the sham their marriage had become, protecting their children from more pain. The kids were her life now and she would not apologize for that. For all intents and purposes, she'd been a single parent for years and that was okay because she knew how to do that. Now fear latched on to her heart. Fear that he would leave her again. That he would once again shatter her into a thousand pieces.

But he was here. At this moment, it was all she had. Without giving herself time to think about the consequences, she leaned closer and brushed her lips gently against his.

She pulled away before he could deepen the kiss. Fear and awareness and arousal skittered through her veins, making her off balance, like a needful, sensual thing. She'd grown accustomed to the hugs of her children, their wet kisses and enthusiastic embraces.

What she craved now was something darker. The faintest brush of lips against lips had sparked something primitive inside her. Something deeper and richer. A long-forgotten need to be touched by a man. But not just any man—by this man. His hands, roughened by combat, sliding up her thighs. The coarse pads of his fingertips caressing her skin.

Memories bombarded her as she attempted to lean away and salvage the remnants of her pride.

But Trent was not operating under the get-some-space battle plan. He reached for her, his eyes rich with dark emotion. His palms scraped against her cheeks, his fingers strong as his lips claimed hers.

His breath was a gasp against her tongue and for a moment, Laura was stunned into stillness, unable to move beneath the assault on her senses. But then her body remembered his taste, her tongue remembered his touch, and a warmth awakened inside her. She opened for him, stroking his tongue with hers, her body folding into his like it was meant for him.

Her every nerve came alive. A cascade of long-denied arousal mixed with bittersweet memories of other homecomings, other farewells. It crashed into them both, driving them under a torrent of emotion.

This was the man she had married. A man who could make her body purr just thinking about him inside her. A man who knew exactly how to kiss her to drive her wild.

This was the man she'd been waiting for. She wanted nothing more than to crawl into his lap and have that urgent, passion-filled sex of first homecoming. It was a long moment before the arousal faded and she became aware of the tender, sucking kisses he placed on her lips.

Another moment before he rested his forehead against hers.

An eternity passed before the words she'd never thought she'd ever say again slid past her lips. "I miss you," she whispered.

And for once, he did not pull away.

7

Trent looked out the window of the backseat as Shane and Carponti bickered about the radio station. He grinned and felt a little piece of normal that he hadn't known he'd been missing slip back into place. Funny how being around the guys at work always felt...right. He wanted that rightness with Laura. With the kids.

"We're meeting the womenfolk for lunch, huh?" Carponti drove them off post toward the restaurant later that day. It was no longer strange seeing Carponti driving. Funny how the missing piece of his arm was a side note rather than a major descriptor. He was just Carponti, Trent thought. Not his amputee friend.

Just his friend.

Sometimes it was the little things that struck him. He remembered clearly sitting in his office the night Carponti had been evac'd out of theater. He and First Sarn't Story had simply sat, smoking cigars and remembering all the stupid shit Garrison and Carponti—mostly Carponti—had done. Goddamn but he'd almost broken after those two had gotten hurt.

He'd gone through the motions for weeks and the situation with LT Randall had devolved further and further until Trent had been called into his battalion commander's office and told he was being sent home.

Stripped of command. Disgraced. A failure.

"You okay back there?" Shane asked.

"Yeah," Trent said. "Just thinking."

"About what?" Carponti asked.

"Just glad you guys made it home, that's all."

Silence hung in the truck for a long moment. Finally, Carponti sniffed and swiped his finger beneath his eye. "Damn it, you made me all misty-eyed."

Trent grinned. "Cute."

"So changing the subject to something less depressing, have you been keeping up with the drama back in the company?" Carponti asked.

"No. It's bad form for a commander to go back after he leaves," Trent said. "Or in my case, got fired."

"Yeah, well, screw bad form. Marshall is a raging asshole. I thought guys like him were a myth but apparently, Assholicus Officerus is alive and well and has been sighted in the wild."

Trent laughed quietly. "Really? Assholicus Officerus?"

"What?"

Shane shook his head. "Nah, Marshall is just being an asshole to anyone on a medical profile. He gave me a massive ration of shit about being on restricted duty after I got my vasectomy."

"So how's that working out for you?" Carponti grinned. "You firing blanks yet?"

"None of your business," Shane growled.

"Is Jen still upset with you about that?" Trent asked. A few months ago, Shane had gone and gotten all of the information about the vasectomy before he'd found the courage to talk to Jen about it. She'd found the paperwork and they'd had a huge fight.

Somehow, when he'd explained that he was afraid of having to choose between her and a baby if her cancer came back, it had convinced her to agree to his decision. He closed his eyes, remembering the first time Laura had gotten pregnant. They hadn't been planning on it. He remembered walking into the bathroom. She'd been sitting on the toilet seat, holding one of those little stick thingies.

She'd looked up at him with pure terror in her eyes. "Um, I'm a little bit pregnant."

"How are you a little bit pregnant? Either you are or you aren't."

She'd pressed her lips together and he'd seen tears fill her eyes. He'd knelt down in front of her. "Hey. It's going to be okay."

"I'm going to get fat and you're going to leave me."

He'd cupped her face. "You're going to get big boobs and I'm going to love you regardless of how big your butt gets."

She'd laughed and kissed him and when they'd made love, he'd marveled that there was a little life growing inside her. Neither of them had expected the miscarriage that had come three weeks later. Somehow, he'd said exactly the right thing at a time when she'd been scared half to death. Why couldn't he manage that anymore?

Why couldn't he tell her the things that scared him?

Carponti patted Shane's shoulder as they pulled into the restaurant parking lot. "You must be in love if you were willing to get your balls rewired on a whim."

"It wasn't a whim," Shane said.

Trent rubbed the scar over his heart. Listening to Shane talk about his future wife was...it was good. It was something simple. Something...yeah, something good.

He wanted that goodness back with his wife. If the fucking pills in his pocket and therapy were a way to get back there, then he was going all in. Because he had a long way to go if he ever wanted a hint of the normal that Shane and Carponti had with Jen and Nicole.

And Laura was worth it. Whatever it took, he was willing to do.

"BEER FOR LUNCH is always an indicator that things have gone to shit," Nicole Carponti said as she sank into the booth next to Laura. "You should look happy and instead you both look like you're attending a funeral."

Giving her friend a weak smile, Laura sipped her Heineken. "Yeah, well, it's been somewhat of a banner week, all things considered. We saved you some fries."

Nicole swiped a fry through a pile of ketchup and mayonnaise then sighed dramatically. "Who do I need to arrest?"

Across from them, Jen quirked her eyebrows, raising her beer in a salute. "No one. For now. You missed all the wedding planning fun."

"I know, I tried to break away but work...Here, this ought to cheer you both up," Nicole said, tossing a brightly colored catalogue on the table in front of them.

A brilliant pink penis with a smiling face literally waved up at them from the cover of the magazine.

Jen choked and tossed a napkin over the picture before Laura fully registered that it was a penis wearing a jaunty little pair of Easter bunny ears. "You can't have that in here!" Jen hissed, her voice somewhere between laughter and pure horror.

Nicole pulled the napkin off. "We're in a sports bar for lunch. It's not like there are any children around."

Laura peeked inside and saw something that looked anatomically impossible. "Now where on earth would you put all of…never mind. I really don't want to know." She sighed then sipped her drink.

Nicole tapped her finger on the page. "That one looks damn near lifelike." She tipped her head. "It looks real."

"That is creepy in so many ways," Jen said, flushing.

Laura cracked a wry grin. "There is a shortage of real penis in my life." She covered her mouth at Jen's horrified expression. "What? It's true."

"Speaking of real penises, how is having Trent home?" Nicole asked, swiping another fry.

"He still hasn't come home so there was no penis involved in this homecoming," Laura said. The humor in the random penis comment dissipated in the thick mayo. Damn Trent for ruining a good joke and he wasn't even there.

"Are you ready for this?" Jen asked. "You looked pretty upset the other night when you left."

"I have to be, don't I?" Laura said. She rolled the tip of a fry in the mayonnaise. "I'm scared," she said after a moment. She looked up at her friends. "What if I can't do this? What if I can't pretend to love him because…"

"Because you still do?" Nicole finished.

Laura swallowed the lump in her throat. "Yeah."

"Then you do the very best you can and you hope that it's enough," Jen said.

"And then we'll have him killed," Nicole said. "Instead of 'Good-bye Earl' it'll be Good-bye Trent."

Laura covered her mouth and laughed. "You're both terrible."

"I still think this whole happy family for the court-martial thing is a bad idea," Jen said quietly.

"I know," she said. "But this is something I need to do."

"Why?" Nicole asked, her voice harsh.

Laura hesitated. "Because Trent told me he would finally sign the papers when it's all over."

"It doesn't sound like that's what you still want," Jen said, twirling a fry in the ketchup.

"I've been waiting for him to let me go for almost a year." Laura shrugged and stared into the green glass of the beer bottle. "It might not be easy, but yes, it's what I want." At least, that's what she thought she wanted. Seeing Trent, knowing he was around, in the building at work...He was right there and yet he might as well have been across the ocean.

She didn't know how to tell them about the kiss that had rocked the foundation of her world all over again.

Despite everything, he was still so far out of reach. "I just wish everything wasn't so difficult."

"Maybe ending your marriage isn't supposed to be easy."

"Ouch." Laura winced as Nicole's words scored a direct hit. "Thanks a lot."

"That's not how I meant it," Nicole said quickly. She closed her hand over Laura's and squeezed gently. "I meant that maybe what you're going through isn't anything other than normal divorce guilt."

"I think it's more than that," Laura said. The words she needed lodged in her throat. She didn't want to admit the thing that kept her awake, worrying about a man she was trying not to love anymore. "There's something wrong," she said after a moment. "He gets really tense around the kids."

"I noticed that the other night," Jen said softly. "And it's actually really common. A lot of soldiers have trouble unwinding after deployments and Trent has been gone a lot."

"Does Shane?"

"Sometimes," Jen said. "Sometimes he just sits and listens to music. And I just sit with him. I don't talk or anything. I'm just there."

"I'd like to be there for Trent," Laura said. "But he's done nothing but shut me out since his first deployment. The distance...the coldness...it's too much."

Nicole took a sip from her beer. "Vic was taking an anti-anxiety med when he first got wounded. It made a big difference in helping him reset." She frowned, absentmindedly tearing at the label on her own beer bottle. "He told me once that things were more complex back home. That sometimes everything here is just overwhelming. The anxiety meds helped quiet some of the noise so that he didn't spend all his time pissed off and snapping at people." She blinked and lifted her gaze to Laura's. "And it worked for him. After a while, after he got used to missing an arm and his new normal, he stopped taking them."

"So maybe it's not that Trent can't be around you guys, maybe it's just that he needs time. Time that he hasn't taken for himself yet." Jen was a nurse. She knew what she was talking about, right?

"That could be true," she said quietly. The truth was, she'd suspected this all along but Trent had never given her a chance to do something as simple as sit with him. Just let him lean on her a little bit. He never gave her the chance to be there for him. She wasn't some fragile snowflake that was going to melt at the first sign of trouble. She wanted to feel...needed.

"Did you ever think that maybe he finally gets it?" Jen said. "That maybe he knows he needs to figure out a way to be home? To be a good husband and a father."

"Sure," Laura scoffed quietly. "And maybe we'll have miraculous, earth-shaking sex, the sky will open, there will be white doves and singing, and my life will suddenly be perfect."

"Actually, that's not a bad idea," Nicole said.

"What, the doves or the singing?"

"The sex. Maybe you guys should have sex to see if you can work through this." Nicole smirked. "You know, start with a blow job and work your way into couples therapy."

Laura laughed and some of the pain squeezing her heart loosened. Across the table, Jen snorted and barely managed not to spray liquid all over them.

"If only things were that simple," Laura said when she stopped laughing.

"I think we're supposed to try and convince you to give him another chance." Nicole swiped a French fry. "But I'm not going to push you toward a man who doesn't make you happy. You deserve better than that." Nicole waved at someone over Laura's shoulder and she turned in time to see Trent and Carponti and Shane walking toward them.

Jen quickly flipped the magazine over as the men approached but Carponti caught the movement and leaned over, swiping it without missing a beat as he bent to kiss his wife. "This is what you people do during lunch?" he said, flipping through the catalog. "Seriously?" He held up a centerfold of something called the White Rabbit. "Does this get you horny, baby?"

"You weren't supposed to be here for another forty-five minutes," Nicole said, snatching the magazine away.

Carponti reached for it again, and Nicole burst into laughter. He succeeded in grabbing the magazine and started to flip through it. "Oh, now that's interesting."

"And that's my cue to leave," Jen said with a soft smile up at Shane as she slid out of the

booth.

"What, you don't want to try—" Carponti laughed but Nicole elbowed him in the ribs, silencing whatever he'd been about to say. "Ow!"

"I'll call you later," Nicole said.

After Jen left with Shane, Nicole and Carponti stepped over to the bar, and Laura found herself alone with her husband. If she hadn't known better, she would have sworn it was a conspiracy.

Knowing Nicole and Jen, it probably was.

Laura glanced at her watch, trying to ignore the heat creeping up her neck. There was something both awkward and darkly arousing about being caught with a sex toy magazine by her husband. She bit her bottom lip and reached for her purse. "Day job beckons. I'm going to walk over to Home Depot before I go back to work."

She stood, avoiding Trent's gaze, and made to leave. He stopped her with a simple hand on her arm. She stiffened but didn't pull away —they'd agreed to put on a happy face in public but she didn't know how to do that or what that meant. Too bad it was forced enough that she needed to keep reminding herself of that.

"Need help?" he asked softly.

She lifted her eyes and met his gaze. Behind the glare of his glasses, his eyes were dark and serious. It was such a simple thing he was asking but there were layers of meaning in his words.

She could have said no. She could have brushed past him and kept walking away from him like he'd done to her so many times in the past. Instead, she swallowed the nervous lump in her throat.

And took a chance.

~

THINGS WERE all twisted up inside him and for once, the feelings weren't related to anxiety and stress. It was something new, something he'd forgotten: arousal and fear mixed into a potent, explosive cocktail swirling in his blood.

His wife had been looking at sex toys.

He didn't know what to say to that knowledge. It was something they'd joked about back when they'd still joked. It was something they hadn't talked about or done, in a very, very long time, and thinking of his wife, touching herself, pleasuring herself...the image was powerful and erotic.

He supposed he should be grateful she was looking at magazines instead of hitting up one of the local meat markets that passed for bars and nightclubs in Killeen. Far too many of his soldiers had come home to find that their wives had let a man—sometimes more than one—take their place at home. And Texas law being what it was, if their wives had let someone move in, they had no legal right to force them to move out.

It could be worse. Somehow, that was small consolation as the dark and erotic images took hold of his imagination.

Laura walked a few feet in front of him, her eyes glued to an image on her phone. They'd crossed the parking lot from the sports bar to the home improvement store in a companionable silence that had felt like it was laced with something more profound. Now her head was bowed, her brow knit in concentration as she scanned the shelves looking for some mystery part for the dishwasher.

She still didn't have on her rings. He wouldn't bring it up. He could wait. He needed patience if he was going to do this—convincing his wife that he could do this, that he was serious about coming home and staying home.

About being there for her when he hadn't been before.

This was the most important thing he'd ever do.

"What are you looking for?" he asked. He stuffed his hands in his pockets. He couldn't stand feeling so useless.

"I'm not sure," she said absently. "I'm looking for a clamp that looks like this but I don't see it." She shifted until he could look over her shoulder at the small image of a white—or maybe it was grey—clamp. He couldn't really tell. He was utterly distracted by the soft golden curl brushing against the gentle slope of her neck.

She stilled then, and silence washed over them like a thick blanket, as if she could feel his gaze on her. She lifted her eyes from the phone and looked at him. For a moment, the world fell away and they were alone, the kind of alone that made him want to reach out and touch her. The kind of alone that a man craved with his wife.

Her lips parted for a moment and he felt the tiny huff of her breath against his cheek. He swallowed, his mouth dry. "I don't see that part," he said softly, after glancing at the shelves around him. "Maybe we should ask someone?"

She raised both eyebrows, her expression softening. "Sure." Her throat moved as she pressed her lips together and took a step away.

"So how was lunch?" he asked as he followed her to the end of the aisle. "Other than the vibrator shopping and all that."

A slow flush crept up her neck and Trent fought the urge to smile. On one of his first deployments, she had e-mailed him a video of herself. There had been nothing more erotic than watching her fingers slide down her stomach to the sweet juncture of her thighs on that grainy video. Just that once, he'd managed to coax her into doing it.

The memory had stayed with him forever.

"It was fine."

He swallowed, his mouth dry, wondering if the video was still saved in an e-mail file somewhere.

Her cheeks pink, she turned down another aisle, tracking the errant part like a homing missile. He smiled at her back, a feeling of triumph fluttering against his heart. She could pretend all she wanted, but there had been a time when things were simpler between them. A time when they might have joked about vibrators just like Nicole and Carponti did.

A time when he might have spent hours on the phone with her, content just to hear her voice.

"I heard from Rebecca Story the other day," she said as he walked up behind her. He recognized her attempt to change the subject. It did nothing to alleviate the small victory he'd just won. "You didn't mention Story was back in Iraq."

"Yeah, he just left." Trent pushed his glasses higher, feeling that awkward distance spreading between them.

"He went straight from the National Training Center back to Iraq? Trent, he hasn't been home in months. Rebecca is worried."

"She's probably filling her time with shopping and eating out all the time. She's just pissed that he put her on a budget."

"They fight all the time." Laura looked away. "Why don't they just get divorced?"

"I don't know. Maybe he blames himself for being gone so much." He heard the unspoken accusation in her words. But for once, he opted not to fight. "He's fine, Laura. He needs to be with his boys." The old argument between them stood like stagnant pond water, reeking and stale.

"His wife doesn't count? Maybe they'd get along better if he wasn't gone so much."

Trent breathed in deeply, searching for a way out of this familiar territory. He studied her then, her hair neatly pinned out of her face for work, drifting at the base of her neck. Her eyes were guarded and wary.

He'd hurt her every single time he'd left. Even now he was hurting her by defending Story, another man who'd chosen his "boys" over his family.

He could not make it up to her. He had no way of taking away the hurt he'd inflicted.

But maybe, for once, he could try something different.

He took a single step closer and lifted his hands slowly, afraid that she would step away. But she just cocked her chin, pressing her lips tightly together as he cupped her shoulders in his palms.

He tried to think of a way to put it into words, the compulsion— no, the need—that had sent him back into combat again and again. That burning desire to make a difference, to bring just one more kid home.

He'd yielded to it too often as the war had dragged on with no end in sight. It was only now that he'd fully confronted the reality of what he'd done to his wife, to his family.

Gaining that trust started with a single, whispered truth.

"I can't explain why he needs to go," he whispered, praying she would hear what he could not say. Not because he did not want to but because it was true: he could not explain.

Laura looked up into her husband's eyes as her own filled with unshed tears. No matter how many times she swore she would never cry over this man again, somehow there were always more tears.

With that quiet admission, she knew they were no longer talking about Story and his wife. "It's not right, what he's doing to his family."

She saw the regret ripple across Trent's face, a physical pain, and she knew her comment had struck home. There was no victory in landing that blow. She was tired of all the hurt they kept causing each other.

Trent cleared his throat roughly, lowering his hands. "That's between Rebecca and Story, Laura. You can't interfere."

"Maybe the Army should interfere. Stop these guys from running themselves into the ground with exhaustion."

"Maybe the Army is too deep in the fight to care," Trent said softly.

They stood for a moment at that unrelenting impasse: an immovable object up against an unstoppable force. She didn't know what to say. The Army was supposed to care about the soldiers that fought the war. Wasn't that why she had her job? To help the Army reach out to families.

Maybe Trent spoke the truth but that only meant she'd bought into the convenient lie. Wasn't she the family readiness liaison so she could make a difference to one spouse? One soldier downrange who didn't have to worry about his wife back home. Wasn't that why she did her job? Or had she simply bought into the convenient lie, too?

She glanced over Trent's shoulder and spotted the part she was looking for. Snagging it, she compared it with the picture on her cell phone. "Found it."

When she glanced up, she found him watching her, his dark eyes intense behind those glasses that she loved so much. When he returned from basic training, he'd been wearing what he'd fondly dubbed birth control glasses or BCGs. Thick, black rims and even thicker lenses. On their first day back together, they'd picked him up a pair similar to the ones he was wearing now. Wire rimmed and dead sexy.

Why did she have to remember the good times? It was so much easier to hold on to the hurt and the bitterness. But standing in the middle of Home Depot, for a brief moment, the hurt and the anger were gone and it was just him and just her.

It would be so easy to pretend that today was just another day. That they were on a normal lunch break and things hadn't gone to hell between them.

"What?" she whispered.

His expression softened. His lips parted and his throat moved as he swallowed. "Nothing. Just watching you go through Home Depot on a mission." One side of his mouth twisted upward. "You've done really well while I've been gone."

It was a bitter pill to swallow, hearing him compliment her on an independence that had become necessary because of his own actions. A sharp bite of resentment took the place of the pleasure she'd felt a moment ago. "I've had to," was all she said.

He opened his mouth to say something, then closed it. He dragged his hand through his hair roughly. "I know." He pushed his glasses higher. "I should have been here for you a lot more than I was."

The words were an admission, not quite of guilt, but of something else. A tentative step in a new direction.

Either way, it felt like they were on the same side for the first time in a long, long time.

She didn't quite know what to say. He'd ruined more than their marriage. He'd shattered her trust. And trust, like porcelain, was not easily repaired. Even when it was pieced back together, the cracks still showed. She was so used to fighting.

Instead, she chose the middle ground.

"Thank you for saying that," she said, for once opting to keep the fragile peace between them.

Some dark emotion danced behind his glasses and for a brief moment, she was tempted, so tempted to reach for them and drag them off. To look into the eyes of the man standing in front of her with no barrier between them—to find the man she had married.

For a moment, she saw him. Dark, stoic, and sexy. The man who aroused the deepest love in her. It terrified her how the intensity of that love could be so easily resurrected.

"I'm sorry it took me so long to say it." He swallowed and rubbed the back of his neck. There was so much more they needed to say. But Laura couldn't go down that road with him right now. She took a single step backward, retreating now to save her heart from breaking again.

They walked in silence toward the front of the store. For once, the silence was not filled with acrimony and bitter memories.

He walked her to her car.

"Do you think you'll have to work late?"

"Depends. I usually don't. Why?"

"Just wondering." Heat sparked deep inside her, her blood warming at the first interaction between them that wasn't laced with anger and sadness and hurt. It unsettled her. "I'll see you tonight."

This was not steady footing. This was not a place she knew. "Sure."

She watched him walk into the sports bar, where Carponti had promised to wait for him. There was something aching and familiar about watching him go, but for once it was not filled with pain.

This was something new dawning between them.

And it terrified her. Because she had once loved this man more than anything else and she'd lost him.

She couldn't go down this road again with him.

Because she didn't think she could survive losing him again.

8

T rent sat. Outside the house he and Laura had bought years before, he sat and stared at the tiny orange bottle of pills in his hand. Emily had said take as needed. He was afraid a pill would zone him out but he was more terrified of his own reactions without it.

He was going home for the first time in forever. He couldn't screw this up. But the pressure was back on his lungs and he sat there until the door closed and Laura turned on the outside light. The scar over his heart ached.

He looked up as Laura ushered the kids into the house. There was curiosity in her eyes but no judgment.

Damn it, he was not going to live like this. He took a deep breath, then killed the truck and headed into the house they'd bought before the war had broken him and he'd broken his marriage.

They'd closed on the house the day after Laura had found out she was pregnant with Ethan. She'd miscarried a few months before and the new pregnancy terrified them both. It had made both of them see the house in a new light. That night, on an air mattress in their new living room, he'd simply held her, knowing her fear was as real as his.

The house today was so different from the house they'd bought all those years ago. It was the same four walls but it was the little things that Laura had done that made it a home. A wall was decorated with pictures of the kids, some black and white, some snapshots. He listened to the noise of them in the kitchen as he looked at the new pictures. Ethan's first day of kindergarten. Emma in front of the giraffe at the Waco Zoo.

He stopped, though, in front of one picture that made his heart hurt. It was a black and white snapshot of him. He hadn't known she'd taken it. He was sitting on the swing in the backyard, with Emma on his lap, her cheek resting against his chest.

She'd snapped him in a moment when he'd rested his head against his little girl's cheek. He'd forgotten about that day until this moment. Seeing it now was proof that he hadn't always been closed off and distant. That at some point, he'd been a good, present father.

If he'd done it before, he could do it again. Right?

"Daddy!" Emma rushed him and he unconsciously stiffened for the impact before she skidded to a halt a foot away. "Fluffy is glad you're home."

Emma held up the fat brown hamster, straining her little arms until he crouched down to her level. The hamster's fluff spilled over the edge of Emma's hand. "Hi, Fluffy. You haven't escaped recently?"

"Last week was the last time she got out. She can open the cage," Emma said seriously.

"Hamsters can't open their cages," Trent said.

Laura leaned out of the kitchen. "She's either figured out how to open the cage or someone forgets to close it."

"I do not. Mommy!" Emma said fiercely.

Trent laughed and stroked his index finger along the hamster's back. It flinched and if he didn't know better, he could have sworn it was trying to bite him. "Cute. Antisocial hamster."

Emma took off, streaking toward her brother's room.

He watched her go, still crouched down. He rubbed his hand over his mouth. He'd laughed. For the first time in as long as he remembered, he'd laughed with one of his kids. Dear God, how screwed up was his life that something as simple as a laugh was a monumental event?

He straightened and tried to latch on to the fleeting, unfamiliar sensation.

Trent padded toward the kitchen, soaking in the details that had changed. He hadn't noticed that she'd painted the walls a pale golden yellow. It was a nice subdued color that made the house feel warm and inviting. For whatever reason, being here tonight felt fresh and good, even if he did feel like a piece out of place. It was less than it might have been, though.

He didn't know what he should be doing right now. He didn't know what Laura did, what she needed help with. He didn't even know what questions to ask.

He was a stranger in his own home. It was his own fault, but still. He didn't know how to fit and he was afraid to ask her. Afraid to ruin the tentative truce between them and bring the harsh reality of the court-martial, their divorce and everything else, between them.

He stopped just out of sight. He could see her in the kitchen. She had two lunch boxes open on the counter, baggies next to them. Steam rose out of a pot of water on the stove. She was in constant motion but it was motion with a purpose. She had a system.

Watching her then, the scar over his heart ached. He didn't know when the thing inside him had broken, just that it had. And that break had pushed him away, back toward the war. He'd thought she'd be okay without him.

He'd thought he was protecting her from what the war had done to him.

War wasn't some glorified camping trip. It was violent. It was dirty.

And Trent had lived and breathed in that violence and that dirt for so long, he didn't know how to enjoy the feeling of simply standing in his house. He rubbed the scar absently. He remembered the first time she'd seen it.

She'd cried. He remembered he'd stripped off his shirt and stood there, her fingers dancing up his ribs. She'd tried to touch it but he'd stopped her.

He'd never let her. He never realized that until right then. He'd always turned her hands elsewhere when they'd made love.

He wondered what that said about him. He turned away, taking his bag into the master bathroom. He had no illusions that he would sleep in Laura's bed tonight but short of sharing a bathroom with the kids, he wasn't really loaded with other options for personal hygiene. He figured she wouldn't mind sharing the bathroom even if she wouldn't invite him into their bed.

He had no right to ask her for that, no matter how much he

missed her. It went beyond sex into something more. Something that might break through the emptiness inside him.

He dropped his bag inside the closet then stripped off his uniform jacket before heading to the kitchen to see if he could make himself useful.

LAURA KNEW what she risked tonight but that didn't make walking through that front door any easier with him at her back. She'd agreed to put on the happy face for the hearing. She'd agreed to let him come home, to pretend that everything between them was wonderful and fine. But she hadn't been prepared for the strength of her own emotions when he stepped across the threshold of their home.

Suddenly, the disarray she'd grown used to stood out in stark relief. Did Trent notice the socks and shoes scattered by the door? Or the *Star Wars* toys lined up in mock combat on the fireplace? Was he thinking about how she'd let the place go because there were tire marks on the baseboards?

The kids' clutter had naturally overtaken their modest home, creeping into the corners, on top of the couch and between the cushions. The carpet was worn in places where Ethan rode his bike through the house. The wide-open living room was used daily as a staging area for *Star Wars* battles and pillow fights. The old couch was long past needing to be replaced but Laura refused to buy new furniture until the kids were old enough not to spill food and drinks on it every other weekend.

Plus, she kind of loved that couch. It was one of the first things she and Trent had bought together as a couple. It was older than both kids and they'd spent many a night cuddling on it together.

She glanced at him as he disappeared into their bedroom, wondering how this was impacting him. He hadn't noticed her scrutiny, nor did he seem to care about the mess. He was more focused on studying the kids like they were two little aliens. Strangers who belonged to someone else.

She stopped suddenly. They *were* strangers. She'd been home with them when they learned how to walk, when they said their first words. She'd lived through all of it. He'd only heard about it. The things she knew about them on an instinctive level he simply didn't, and that knowledge could not be gained in a few minutes or days or even weeks.

She needed to be patient with him.

But he was here. The least she could do was allow his children to welcome him home, no matter how awkward it might be. The kids, at least, would not have to pretend they were happy to have him here. Still, that welcome came with a cost. She knew what she was risking. So why did it feel so overwhelming, like she was teetering on the edge of out of control?

She focused on the things she *could* control. She had to cook dinner, get the kids bathed and in bed, pack their lunches, and then get ready for the next day. There was never enough time to get it all done, but she was used to doing it on her own.

She moved through the kitchen as though today was any other day, doing everything in her power to shut down the maelstrom of emotions that threatened to break her. Trent was really home, really walking toward her from their bedroom.

And they both were trying to pretend that the word "divorce" wasn't standing in the room with them as he searched for and found a beer in the fridge and twisted off the cap.

Trent stood uselessly by as the kids attempted to steal cheese sticks from the refrigerator. "No more snacks. It's almost dinner," Laura said, shooing them out of the kitchen.

A few minutes later, Ethan tore through the living room on his skates and nearly crashed into the TV. Emma squealed as she chased him, demanding a turn. The fight faded as they raced into the garage.

"You let him skate in the house?" Trent asked.

Laura tipped her chin at him. She sucked in a deep breath, biting back the harsh retort that was on the tip of her tongue. He was only asking a question, not criticizing her. "It lets him burn off some energy. He doesn't sleep well if he doesn't play. A lot."

"Mom-my! Ethan's climbing the bookshelves again." Emma's singsong voice rang out from the living room.

"That was fast," Trent mumbled. "He must have gotten those skates off in record time."

Laura raised her voice so it would carry through the house. "Ethan! If I tell you one more time to get down…"

Frustration started to twine its way around her. Trent was home. He could be the bad guy for once. It would do him some good, too. Maybe help him fit back into their lives rather than just standing there looking lost and out of place and ripping her heart apart.

"Will you go make sure Ethan isn't climbing?"

Trent stared at her for a long moment. Silence hung between them as he simply watched her, his eyes partially hidden behind the glare of his glasses. It felt like an eternity before he turned and walked into the living room.

"Holy crap, Ethan, get down!"

He sounded so startled that she set down the cutting board she'd just pulled out and rushed to see him pluck Ethan from about midway up the bookshelves.

"Put him in timeout," she said simply.

"What's that involve?" Trent asked as Ethan howled in protest.

"Fireplace. Five minutes. Timer starts when he stops crying."

Ethan, apparently, decided that tonight would be the night he would break the sound barrier. On any other night, Ethan would have stopped with a sniffle and been done with it. He threw himself off the fireplace onto the floor, screaming at the top of his lungs.

Normally, she would let him go until he wore himself down. She glanced over at Trent. The muscles in his neck were bunched, his fists tight by his sides. He was breathing hard and looking at Ethan like he was a monster.

"Is this normal?" he asked harshly.

"No," she said gently, "not usually."

He looked over at her like she'd grown two heads. "What's the special occasion?"

"This isn't normal—you're home," she said warily and saw him flinch. She reached out, placing her hand on his upper arm. "I'm not saying it to be mean. But it's true. Their entire routine is being thrown off by having their daddy home."

"Lovely."

Laura took a deep breath, then scooped Ethan up off the floor. "You don't get to stop listening just because Daddy's home," she said to her son as she carried the screaming banshee to his bedroom. "When you decide you want to act like a big boy, you can come out."

That set him off on a whole new tantrum, dialed all the way up to eleven. She closed the door behind her as he kicked and screamed on his bed.

The kitchen was a disaster, too. The water for the spaghetti had boiled over, steaming off the hot stove. Trent yanked his hand away. "Here," she said, handing him a dish towel. "Don't burn yourself."

He shot her an inscrutable look, then lifted the pot so she could wipe the stove before turning down the heat. He moved out of her way as she stirred the pasta and heated the sauce. She wondered if he was going to like it. It was a recipe she'd found from Food Network and she usually made a massive pot once every few months then froze it.

She tried not to see Trent studying the pieces of the dishwasher and felt a creeping sense of failure that she hadn't managed to fix it as easily as she'd hoped. Embarrassment crept up her neck that she had to keep moving parts around to make room for dinner. "Hopefully, I'll have it fixed soon," she mumbled.

She drained the pasta and tore open the cheese packet, trying not to be self-conscious. Trent said nothing. He stood near the sink, nursing a beer, looking out of place and uncomfortable.

She wished she hadn't noticed. Wished she hadn't seen the strain in the hard set of his back when Ethan had kicked off into his tantrum. Tantrums were part of life with kids.

But he wouldn't know that because he hadn't been there. A wave of sadness washed over her. There was nothing she could say to make this easier. Nothing to do to turn the screaming in the other room off.

She simply prepared dinner with a stranger in her kitchen and tried to pretend everything was normal when it felt like nothing would be normal again.

～

"Hey?"

Laura's voice interrupted the violent introspection thrashing around in his brain. He looked up at her from where he'd been studying the beer in his hand. Some tendrils of hair clung to her temples now from the steam. Her cheeks were flushed.

God, but he wanted to see her cheeks flush from his touch instead of something as mundane as cooking dinner. Would he ever have a chance to touch her again? To feel her body move with his?

He cleared his throat, redirecting his thoughts away from the bedroom. "Yeah?"

"Can you go tell the kids dinner is ready?"

He frowned slightly. "Think Ethan will talk to me?"

"I heard Emma go into his room a little bit ago. They're remarkably good at not holding grudges."

Trent glanced toward Ethan's bedroom, a deep unease twisting in his guts. He wasn't sure he could handle another tantrum. The last one had crawled up his spine and attempted to stab him in the brain. "Really?"

She walked over to him and patted him on the shoulder. Funny, how she never tried to touch his chest. He'd done that to her. He'd made a part of himself off limits to her touch. He was such an idiot. He thought he was protecting her from the ugliness of the war. Instead, he'd only managed to cut one more piece of her out of his life.

"He's six. He doesn't bite. Go. Get your children."

A few minutes later, Trent found himself in the middle of an argument over who got to sit on Daddy's lap.

"I want to!" Emma said, standing with her fists on her hips and glaring up at her brother.

"I called it first!" Ethan said.

Trent had no idea how to mediate this one. Who did he pick? How did he stop this fight?

Laura stepped in to save him. "Neither of you will sit on Daddy's lap because Daddy needs to eat, too. Each of you pick a side and eat."

Trent glanced over at Laura, who was focused almost entirely on getting dinner on the table. How had she managed to diffuse that one so easily? Everything felt strange, unfamiliar. He didn't have a battle rhythm for the kids, not like Laura obviously did. But the night was young. Maybe if he kept trying he could get through this. And maybe tomorrow, it would be a little bit easier.

～

EXCEPT FOR THE tense set of his jaw, Trent was doing his best to make them laugh and let them be the center of his world.

He was trying. She had to give him credit for that. But that didn't stop her heart from aching as she watched him carefully divide his attention between the kids. He laughed and talked with them and she had to keep reminding herself that he wasn't going to stay. That this was just a temporary fix until the court-martial was over and he could run off happily back to the war.

Part of her was so angry with him for leaving her to raise them on her own and not giving her a choice. She knew Army spouses would argue all day long that she needed to suck it up because they were at war and this was what she'd agreed to when she said "I do" to a military man.

And the sad part was, there was another piece of her that was so incredibly, stupidly happy to have him home. When Laura looked at him, she wished she saw the man she'd loved enough to have two children with. The man she would have waited for as the years came and went, until the war was over.

In that man's place sat a father who did not know his children. A husband who was a stranger to his wife.

Sadness ached behind her eyes at everything they'd lost. She got up and walked to the sink, needing something to do with her hands. They weren't going to stay a family, so longing for the past wasn't going to do her a damn bit of good.

If he beat the charges against him, he would leave again. She harbored no illusions that this brief interlude spent at home would end his relentless need for deployments. She knew without a doubt that Trent would deploy again, and she would have to deal with Ethan crying his eyes out because he wanted his daddy. Or with Emma crying just because Ethan was.

She was doing this for them. Maybe, just maybe, Ethan and Emma would remember this one moment of happiness before Trent left again.

A chair scraped against the floor and then he was there behind her. He leaned against her to place his plate in the sink, his body hard and lean against hers.

Months of eating crappy chow at the National Training Center had eliminated any shred of softness he had ever had. Months of lonely nights sliced away at any hint of rational thought.

She froze at the first brush of his body against hers. It was a simple embrace. Nothing the kids would have noticed. Before, the space between them had been filled with awkward silence. Now it snapped and hissed like a live wire.

His breath stirred her hair and sent a chill down her spine.

Laura couldn't have moved if she'd tried. A long-ignored need settled between her thighs and tingled over her skin. In all the years she'd spent alone, she'd never once thought of another man. Never looked at anyone else the way she looked at her husband. Never felt the desire to assuage the deep, abiding longing she carried inside her for him with someone else.

Sex between them had always been good. He'd always made her feel like the most beautiful woman in the world. And damn him, he had no right to do this to her now.

She shifted and pulled free from the embrace a moment before Emma shrieked. The mood disintegrated like a puff of baby powder.

She paused, avoiding his gaze.

"Laura—"

"Don't, Trent." She held up her hand, forcing space between them. "Don't try to make me feel something that isn't there." She swallowed the hard lump of emotion in her throat. "We're going to get through this hearing and then you're going to walk away." *Just like always.* "We're over, Trent. We're just playing the happy family. We'll never be one again."

The sooner he accepted that, the better off they would be.

He gripped the edge of the sink and hung his head like he was in pain. She was sorry for that, really she was.

But all the sex in the world couldn't fix what ailed them.

TRENT'S BODY was so tight it hurt. He held his head under the steaming water, willing his cock to soften. Every time he closed his eyes, he felt the heat of her body against his. Frustration clawed at his insides.

He didn't know what had made him lean close enough to feel the warmth of her skin. The soft flesh of her neck had been within reach. A faint wisp of her skin had wrapped around him, urging him closer, and he'd surrendered to the impulse to touch her. Just feeling her body against his had nearly undone him. She'd been soft and warm against him. He'd almost wrapped his arms around her and pulled her close, just so he could feel her breathing.

But she'd moved before his lips could touch the gentle swell of her ear. And he was paying for it now.

Could a man die from a constant erection? It was one thing to dream about his wife while he was deployed and thousands of miles away from her. But being near her and not being able to touch her? It was hell.

Screw Viagra. Back-to-back deployments were enough to fix erectile dysfunction.

He was so hard he thought he'd tear out of his skin. He could solve that problem easily but he wanted it to be Laura's hand stroking him, not his own. He grasped the nozzle and turned the water from hot to ice.

His flesh puckered, and his dick finally cooperated, a little too well. His balls retreated and tried to climb back inside him. Good. Maybe he could think about something other than laying his wife down on their bed and sinking between her thighs.

He was home. For however long it took the Army to finally decide whether or not he would face charges, he was home. Really home, beneath the roof he and Laura had bought together years ago. He just needed to figure out how to make this something more than just a roof over his head.

Toweling off, he walked into the bedroom and pulled out a pair of sweatpants from his duffel bag. He wasn't sure how much of his clothing she'd left out, if any. He wasn't really willing to dive in and ask, either—he was afraid of the answer. He didn't like the idea of her boxing his things up.

He closed his eyes and instantly, the weight was there, pressing against his lungs, refusing to let him get enough air. He pinched the bridge of his nose and focused on breathing. Slowly, the disquiet in his soul eased back as his breathing evened out and he padded over to his duffel bag, pulling out the small orange bottle.

He didn't feel a damn thing as he tossed back the tiny round pill, chasing it with water from the bathroom sink. The anxiety medication would be a little stronger tonight since he was mixing it with alcohol. But maybe it would help him get through the evening relaxed. Maybe he could read a story to his kids without feeling like he couldn't breathe.

He closed his eyes and reminded himself that he was home. He was safe. He was going to wake up tomorrow and have a nice, normal breakfast with his family. And do it all again the next day. And the day after that.

If he kept repeating it, it would be true.

"Hey?"

He turned suddenly, feeling like he'd been caught with his pants down.

"Are you okay?" She nodded toward the bottle in his hand.

Trent swallowed and looked around for his glasses, buying some time while he searched for the right words. She looked at him with cautious expectation in her eyes. No judgment, just curiosity.

He cleared his throat. He watched her, searching for any sign that she was freaked out. There was no movement on her face beyond a single glance at the orange pill bottle. "I don't have PTSD or anything," he said when he could speak. "They're just...Doc said my normal is a little jacked up."

"You've been back in the States for more than a year since your last deployment," Laura said quietly.

"I know." He looked down at his hands, shame twisting inside of him. "I can function okay enough at work and all. I'm used to that stress and everything. I just, ah, have a hard time with anything else."*Like being a husband. Or a father.*

She looked away, biting her lip and pushing her hair off her forehead. But she didn't speak and her silence hung around them like a heavy, wet blanket. "Oh," she said finally.

"Laura." He felt vulnerable, exposed. Embarrassed that she'd discovered what he hadn't even realized that he'd hidden out of shame. He didn't want her to think he couldn't be around his family without medicating himself into a false state of calm, no matter how close to the truth it skirted. "I just need time to get used to everything back here."

"Okay." He wished he didn't see disappointment shimmer in her eyes a moment before she turned away. "I'm glad you're talking to someone, Trent."

He heard what she did not say. That he wasn't talking to her. That once more, he was

cutting her out of some vital part of his life, pushing her to the periphery.

For a brief moment, she'd looked at him with expectation in her eyes, like she'd been waiting for him to open up and start pouring out his fears and nightmares. But it didn't work that way. He didn't want her to see the man who woke in the cold sweat on the off times that he did sleep. Didn't want her to know about the fear that he hadn't done enough, that he could always be doing more.

That no matter what he did, nothing would ever be enough to bring his boys back.

He didn't want her to see that.

But she had.

And he didn't know what to do next.

9

—————

"Good night, sweetheart." Laura leaned down and kissed her daughter on the forehead. Her hair was already starting to poof out all over her head but she smelled clean and warm. Laura paused for a moment and just rested there, her cheek against Emma's head, soaking in the feel of her breath on her neck. Her little girl was growing up so fast.

"Mommy?"

She leaned up as Emma yawned. "Yeah, baby?"

"Is Daddy going to be here in the morning?"

Laura swallowed the sudden lump in her throat. "Yeah, baby, Daddy will be here in the morning."

A pleased smile spread across Emma's face as she snuggled down in her blankets, clutching her stuffed bunny close to her chest. She made a happy little sound as Laura stood and left the room.

Laura closed Emma's bedroom door quietly, relieved that there had been no more major tantrums from either child. She heard movement in the kitchen and found Trent washing the dishes by hand because she still hadn't managed to fix the dishwasher. Maybe she'd get to it that weekend.

She paused in the archway of the kitchen and watched him move. She'd always joked with her married friends that the sexiest thing their husbands could do was take out the trash. He wore a pair of sweatpants and an old grey college t-shirt that stretched tight across his shoulders.

She did not miss how it hugged the muscles in his back or how he moved with ease and grace. She supposed it must be different, being home and not wearing his body armor all the time. Still, it did something to her insides to watch him—a man who had been the center of her fantasies for all of her adult life—do something as sexy as doing the dishes.

He reached up to put away a plate and caught her standing there. He'd taken his glasses off. His eyes crinkled at the corners as he offered a hesitant smile. "What?" he asked.

She curled her lips in response. "Nothing." She didn't want to admit she'd been caught staring.

"Kids asleep?" he asked, drying the plate in his hand.

"Yeah. They were whipped," she said.

"Do they sleep through the night and everything?" he asked.

The attempt at small talk was awkward at best but he was making the effort. It was something small but something she appreciated. Maybe they needed the small talk.

It was better than the silence that had stretched between them for far too long.

She walked over to the sink, taking over drying duties while he finished washing. They fell into the rhythm easily. He washed then handed her the clean dish. She rinsed.

And they both tried to pretend that this was something normal that they did every night as opposed to an act performed by people who felt like strangers.

"Yeah, they sleep through the night. They're not babies anymore," she said.

He handed her the last plate. His fingers brushed hers. A gentle, not accidental, caress. A sweep of soapy fingers across her knuckles.

A simple touch. Nothing more than his fingers capturing hers and lingering over the empty space on her ring finger. One of his fingers slipped down the length of hers, a warm, soapy caress that made her insides twist.

She watched their hands for a moment, mesmerized by the movement of soap and skin. Her blood warmed as he tightened his grip, giving her ideas about impossible things. Things she shouldn't want anymore. Not with him.

But she did. And that wouldn't help anyone.

She slipped her fingers from his, rinsing the soap from her hands. She wished she didn't miss the fluid strength in his arms as he moved, or the patchwork of scars that crisscrossed his hands from too much time at war.

He turned back and she wasn't quick enough to avoid being caught again. He moved, just a little, and he was in her space. His hands were still wet. The water dribbled down her neck as he reached up to cup her cheeks. His thumb was slick as he stroked her skin gently. "I miss you," he whispered.

He hesitated, giving her a chance to pull away. Giving her a chance to break this contact before it happened. But everything was twisting and alive inside him, feelings rushing in where none had tread in far too long.

He wanted to kiss her. Wanted to feel her mouth move beneath his. Wanted to close his eyes and taste her so that just for one moment, he could remember that once, things had been good between them.

Her breath was a huff against his mouth. A gentle puff of air that brushed against his lips. Her hands rose, colliding with his chest, her palm resting over the scar on his heart. But for once, he didn't care.

He kissed her. That first gentle nudge of lips, that whisper of shared breath. His tongue slid against hers, learning the taste of her all over again. And when her fingers curled into the scar over his heart, he was lost.

This was a mistake. Her brain knew it but her body shut down any protests and leaned in closer to the feel of this man. Her hands tightened, trying to hold on to this fleeting taste of him. It would end, all too soon; it would end and she wanted to savor the feel and touch and taste of him. Her blood hummed through her veins, pounding in her ears until the only thing she could hear was the sound of their breathing over the beating of her heart.

If it was a mistake, it was a good one. One that felt more right than anything she'd done recently. She slid her hands over his powerful chest, threading her fingers through the short hair on the back of his head, and leaned into him. Telling him with her mouth, her lips, her body everything that she could not say.

It was Trent who eased away, nibbling gently on her lips with light, teasing nips. She looked up at him, lost in his beautiful dark eyes, filled tonight with desire, not torment. It would be so easy to take him into the bedroom. To close and lock the door and strip away the hurt and the pain and the loneliness until they were all that was left.

But it would be a mistake. A mistake that would break her heart once more.

His thumb brushed over her cheek. "Do you watch TV or anything?" he asked after an impossible silence.

"Not normally," she said. Her voice sounded off to her own ears. Husky and filled with want.

"Would you tonight?" he asked. She wished she didn't hear the odd note of hope in his words.

Standing there with him this close and, for the first time in recent memory, well within reach, she decided to take a chance. Because her heart was going to break anyway, why not take a few moments of pleasure before it did?

"What did you have in mind?"

If Trent was hoping for a second miracle that night, he didn't get one. He'd wanted her to sit close like they used to, hoped she would lean against him and just be. It didn't happen but he couldn't shake the sense of victory that wound through his insides.

She sat at the other end of the couch, her feet buried in the pillows near his hip. Not quite touching but not eagerly seeking distance between them, either. A tentative gesture. One that he would gladly accept.

He was conscious of her warmth, her presence. He wanted to lean closer, to pull her across that space and devour her mouth, kissing her for hours until they both forgot the barriers between them. Instead, he flipped through the channels, trying to find something for them to watch. He didn't want to admit that he had no clue what was currently popular or worse, what Laura would want to see.

He paused on Animal Planet as her phone vibrated on the coffee table. He frowned.

"Who on earth is calling at this hour?" he asked quietly.

Before he'd deployed, he'd been in command and his phone rang at all hours of the night from soldiers getting arrested and in trouble. He was no longer a commander but apparently his wife's phone was now filling the role of Annoying Electronic.

She offered an apologetic shrug but her eyes were wary. "Work, most likely." She flipped the phone open. "This is Laura."

Her expression shuttered closed. She pushed away from the couch and rushed into the kitchen, writing furiously on the back of an envelope. "Got it. I'll—" she glanced at Trent. "I'll be right in."

She flipped the phone closed. "We have a casualty. I have to go to work."

He opened his mouth then snapped it closed. They weren't deployed. What the hell had happened that they'd lost a soldier during their time at home station? Soldiers weren't supposed to die in the States. They were supposed be safe here. A thousand questions raced through his mind, but instead he simply leaned on the archway leading into the kitchen. "What happened?"

"Fatality at NTC. Kid got hurt on the railhead from someone doing something stupid.

And now his nineteen-year-old wife is a widow."

"Hey." The bitterness in her voice surprised him, so much so that he reached for her, unable to leave the distance between them. "Are you okay?"

She looked away, tense beneath his touch. But she didn't retrieve her hand from beneath his, a tacit acknowledgement of this temporary truce between them.

She breathed out quietly. "It's just hard when we lose a soldier to something stupid." She paused. "This whole war is stupid. What's the damn point?"

She pulled her hand away, her back rigid, her movements stiff. He wanted to comfort her. To pull her against him and tell her that he agreed with her. That the war wasn't worth it.

But admitting what he'd taken too long to realize would mean he'd ruined their marriage for nothing. And he treasured this peace between them far too much to ruin it all over again tonight.

He didn't want to argue with her. And he wasn't ready yet to face the harsh reality of everything he'd done to drive her away.

So instead, he stood with her and watched her write down more information—notes about what she had to do. She rested her head in one hand, her fingers threaded through her hair.

"What do you do with the kids when this happens?" he asked.

Her pen froze in her hand. She turned slowly, her expression telling him that she'd just now realized that for once, she might not have to drag the kids out of bed and to the sitter's house in the middle of the night. But then her eyes flickered with uncertainty. Her doubt in him cut him, harsh and ragged across the already raised scar over his heart, but he said nothing. He deserved her doubt. He'd done nothing to earn her trust.

Maybe that could change. Starting now.

"They can stay with me tonight. You won't be all night, right?"

She tipped her head and studied him quietly. The uncertainty in her eyes shamed him. "Are you up for that?"

"Tonight wasn't too bad." He shrugged and wished he could figure out what to do with his hands. "I mean, I didn't run screaming from the house like a Muppet on acid or anything, so we can take that as a win, right?"

She laughed quietly and the sound of her laugh did something warm and fuzzy to his insides. "I shouldn't be gone all night. Couple of hours, tops."

She took a step toward him, until he could see the concern written in her eyes, the worry in the lines around her mouth. Lines he badly wanted to smooth away.

"I can handle it, Laura," he said softly. "They're asleep, right? Easy."

Her lips twitched from that strange smile to something warmer.

Because he couldn't help himself, because the urge was too strong, he reached up and stroked a stray stand of hair from her eyes. "Go. We'll be here when you get home. And I promise I won't catch the house on fire, either."

"Okay," she whispered. Then she did something completely unexpected. She leaned up and kissed him. A soft, gentle kiss, her lips moist against his. "Thank you."

Her phone started buzzing again and then she was gone, leaving him alone and unafraid in their quiet house.

THERE WAS a strange silence around him without her in the house. The kids were asleep and the silence surrounded him. He could feel the house sleeping, which was weird because in Iraq, there was never real silence. There was always a hum of a generator or an air conditioner or worse, incoming rounds exploding too close for comfort.

This silence was strange. Not oppressive and heavy. Just...there. Something he noticed. He wondered if he would ever get to the point where the quiet didn't bother him anymore.

He wandered through the house, unable to sit on the couch now that Laura wasn't there with him, and looked at the pictures in the dim light. He'd missed so much. His choice.

His fault.

He rubbed his eyes beneath his glasses then looked up. He was standing in the hall between the kids' rooms. He hesitated; then, because it would have been cowardice to turn away, he quietly opened Ethan's door.

His room was filled with the chaos of six-year-old boy. Toys were scattered across every available space and he was pretty sure that was a pair of blue undies sticking out from beneath the bed. But it was his son that drew his gaze.

Ethan was sprawled out across the bed. One leg dangled over the edge, his toes brushing the carpet. His son's hair was sticking out everywhere and Trent had the sudden uncomfortable urge to never see his son with a military regulation haircut.

He leaned down, brushing his hair from his face. Ethan's eyes fluttered open.

"Hi, Daddy," he whispered. He rolled over and Trent pulled the blanket over his tiny shoulders, his throat tight.

He managed to make it out of the room without tripping over any toys, a fact that was actually quite amazing. He stood outside his son's room for a moment and just... stood. He let the stillness wash over him. Fought the tightness in his chest that for the first time wasn't from anxiety or stress, but simply from too much emotion too fast.

It was like everything inside him had been locked at the bottom of a well and was now geysering through him. So much emotion. So raw. So potent.

It was addictive. Actually feeling again, feeling like he was going to really be able to stay home and be a dad. Yeah, this he could get used to.

He pushed open the door to Emma's room, curious to see how his little girl slept. He smiled when he saw her. She wasn't some neat little princess. She was sprawled across the bed like her brother had been, only flat on her back, her arms cast out wildly. A stuffed bunny lay near the edge of her bed, hanging on for dear life by an ear tucked beneath her shoulder. Her mouth was open and she was breathing in slow, quiet huffs. He stood there for a minute, taking her in. Absorbing the clean, warm smell in her room.

He tried to cover her up but the blanket was stuck beneath her butt. So he pulled an extra one from the foot of her bed and tucked it around her. She made a sleepy sound and rolled toward the bunny, grabbing it and pulling it close.

He took a deep breath and closed the door, then settled on the couch. He set his glasses on the table and closed his eyes, wondering if maybe he'd be able to get some sleep tonight without resorting to the little white pills that Emily had prescribed.

For the first time in as long as he could remember, he felt sleep pulling at him—and for once, he didn't fight it.

10

—————

"Daddy."

Trent heard a little voice from very far away. Then he felt something sharp poke him in the chest, right over the scar on his heart. He frowned and tried to ignore it.

"Daddy!"

He blinked and opened his eyes. Emma stood near his shoulder, her little face bunched up in the shadows, her bottom lip quivering. "Daddy, I peed."

He frowned. If there was a significance to this, he was missing it. "Okay, so wash your hands and go back to bed."

"I can't, Daddy. I peed in my bed." Her voice broke. "I'm sorry, Daddy."

He sat up, reaching for his glasses. "You peed the bed?" he asked.

"Yeah, Daddy." She sounded so sad.

"Okay, so what does Mommy usually do when this happens?" he asked.

"You have to change the sheets. And I have to take a bath."

He glanced at his watch. Just what he wanted to do at four thirty in the morning: bathe a

child.

But okay, he could do this.

It dawned on him that if Emma was coming to get him, Laura must not be home. He wanted to know if she was okay but decided not to bother her at work. He could do something simple like this, right?

"Okay, honey, let's get you in the tub while I take care of the bed. Deal?"

She looked up at him, her eyes wide. "Deal."

She padded toward the bathroom and Trent made a mental note to check on her in a few minutes. She was big enough to wash herself up but he didn't want her unsupervised for long in the bathroom by herself.

He walked into her bedroom, hit immediately by the strong scent of pee. Holding his breath, he stripped off the sheets, balling them up and carrying them directly to the laundry room and dumping them on the floor next to the washer. He managed to find clean sheets, then went back into Emma's bedroom to discover that his wife was a genius. There was a thin sheet of plastic on top of the mattress. It looked like a shower curtain liner but whatever it was, it had saved the mattress that night.

He sprayed it down with bleach cleaner then let it air dry before he went to check on Emma.

She was standing in the middle of the tub, both the shower and the bath water running. Soap coursed down her back and over her cute little butt as she attempted to wash her own hair.

"Want some help?" he asked.

She'd scrunched up her eyes to keep from getting soap in them so all she did was nod vigorously. He eased her backward under the shower water and rinsed the soap from her hair then pulled her out of the tub. He wrapped her little body in a massive light blue fuzzy towel then wiped her face gently. She beamed up at him. "Thanks, Daddy."

In that moment, he knew how a superhero felt. He brushed the towel over the tip of her nose then urged her toward her bedroom. "Get some clothes on."

It might be a small victory, something Laura might do on any random night, but hey, it was still a victory. Child bathed? Check. Back to bed?

Yeah, not so much. Because Ethan woke up just as he was tucking Emma back to bed and that's when all hell broke loose.

Two hours later, Trent's patience snapped at the end of its leash.

"Mommy doesn't let us have cereal on school days."

Trent looked down at his daughter, the tiny reflection of his wife down to the disapproving glint in her dark eyes, and counted to ten. Then twenty, while grinding his teeth and trying to keep his emotions from spiraling out of control.

But nothing eased the tension in his chest.

He slapped the cereal box on the counter hard enough that a spray of Kix burst out of the top. He gripped the edge of the counter and tried to keep his voice neutral. "Mommy isn't here, honey. It's okay to have cereal."

Ethan's eyes got wide and he covered his mouth. Trent wasn't sure if his son was laughing at him or upset that he'd spilled the cereal.

Trent wasn't actually sure he cared either way.

Fresh panic gripped his lungs, tearing at his insides, keeping him from taking a proper breath.

Keeping him from thinking clearly. His thoughts raced as he tried to figure out how to get them dressed and ready to go without having the slightest idea what ready actually looked like.

He could handle things blowing up around him. He could handle soldiers completely losing their shit.

But he apparently could not handle two small children.

"Ethan! I thought I asked you to get dressed."

His son lifted his chin and stomped his foot. "I want to wear my Spiderman t-shirt."

"I don't know where it is. You'll wear the green frog t-shirt that Mommy laid out for you."

"I don't wanna!"

Trent's temper snapped its lead. He slammed his palm down on the countertop, hard enough that the shock reverberated up his arm and into his shoulder. "Ethan!"

But that was nothing compared to the shock on his children's faces.

It was past seven a.m. and Laura had been up all night. She was dead on her feet and she had never seen a casualty notification go more wrong. The soldier who had died had been living with a girlfriend and trying to get divorced from his wife. The girlfriend was listed on the official paperwork but the platoon sergeant had contact information for the wife. They'd tried to figure out who to contact and what to do and then the parents got into the mix around midnight.

She felt terrible for all of them but at about two a.m., she'd gotten pissed at the company commander for not having his paperwork together and screwing this up in an epic and unforgettable way.

She opened the front door in time to hear Trent shout from somewhere near Ethan's bedroom. It was already seven o'clock and the kids were well on their way to being late for school.

She rushed into the kitchen, expecting to see the kids finishing their breakfast. Instead, Emma was crawling on the countertop, reaching for a cup in the cabinet and Ethan streaked through the living room like he'd just injected a gallon of fruit punch.

She heard Trent shouting for Ethan from the bedroom.

Then everything exploded in slow motion.

The door to the bedroom slammed violently against the wall. Ethan's red backpack flew across the living room, knocking a picture of Laura and Trent from its nail. Glass shattered across the living room floor.

Ethan dove to the fireplace, picking up the pieces of a now broken dinosaur. Tears ran down his face as he held the shattered remains of his favorite dinosaur from his backpack. His cry rose through the entire house, a slow wail.

Silence crashed over the house. Laura's heart slammed against her ribs. Emma crouched on the counter, her hands over her ears.

Trent stormed into the living room. "Ethan!"

She stepped in front of Trent, pulling his attention away from their crying son. Hands up, fear clutched at her throat. "Whoa! That is enough!"

But she'd be damned if whatever started this was going to continue.

Her husband stood in front of her, his fists bunched at his sides, his chest heaving. His eyes were dark and filled with a thousand angry emotions. Behind her, Ethan's wails dragged down her frayed nerves. "Ethan. Go to your room. Now."

"But, Mommy—"

"Now, Ethan." She didn't raise her voice, didn't take her eyes off her husband. Ethan threw the ruined dinosaur on the floor and stormed out of the living room, his bedroom door slamming behind him like a gunshot.

Laura took a deep, shaking breath, her mind racing over how to calm everything down. "Trent," she whispered. Took a tentative step toward him. Placed her hands on his chest and forced him to meet her gaze. He opened his mouth. Snapped it closed. And then a deep shame filled his eyes as the anger rolled back beneath an onslaught of remorse.

He took a single step backward. And disappeared into their bedroom.

She sucked in a trembling breath and looked into the kitchen, where Emma sat at the table now, focused intently on her cereal. Torn between her husband and her son, Laura turned toward Ethan's bedroom.

He was face down on the bed. She pushed the door open a little farther and moved to sit on his bed. She stroked his back gently and felt his little body shake beneath her touch. "I want Daddy to leave," he said into the pillow.

"Don't say that, honey."

"Why not? It's true."

"No it's not. You're just mad because he threw your backpack."

"Parents aren't supposed to yell," he said, rolling over and sitting up. He crossed his arms angrily over his chest with a huff, a sulk furrowing in his brow.

Laura brushed his hair out of his face, glad to see the anger retreating from his eyes. "Since when?"

He shot her a wry look that looked so much like Trent. Then his expression fell and his bottom lip quivered. "Mommy, he scared me," he whispered.

Laura pulled him into her arms and felt his tears, hot and wet on her blouse. Frustrated tears fell down her cheeks but she didn't care. She simply held on to her son and wished she knew how to hold on to his father. She held him until his little body stopped shaking. But he didn't pull away. He just needed to hold on for a little bit. She knew the feeling.

Too bad there was no one there to hold her right then. She was ragged and raw from the all-nighter and now as the adrenaline washed away, it took with it the strength that was keeping her upright.

So Laura sat there and held him. Because that's what mommies did when the world went to shit around them. Guilt clawed at her. She never should have left him with the kids. Not so soon. Not when he was still unfamiliar with the things that they did to work her nerves and push her buttons. She knew how to navigate around them. He didn't. She'd known leaving Trent with the kids was a bad idea. They weren't bad kids but they were kids, which by definition meant a lot to handle.

And as much as it pained her to realize it, they were a handful he had not been prepared to handle.

But Ethan didn't need to hear any of that. She smoothed his hair down as he leaned back, his eyes already clearing up. "I'm sorry I made Daddy yell, Mommy," he said in a small voice.

Laura kissed the top of his head, then smoothed his hair out of his face once more. "Tell you what, kiddo. Finish getting dressed and go eat your breakfast with your sister. I'm going to go check on Daddy."

"Is he okay?" In that instant, her son was no longer angry with his father. Concern filled his voice, making him sound older than he was.

She wished she knew. She brushed her palm over his damp cheek, wishing she had more reassurances. But the look she'd seen on his face had terrified her. She honestly didn't know the answer to her son's question. But he didn't need to know that. "I'm going to go find out, okay? Go eat?"

SHE FOUND Trent in their closet. Leaning against the wall, his glasses thrown on the floor, he'd drawn his knees up to his chest and sat with his head bent onto his folded arms. Her heart broke for him all over again.

She could leave him there. She could rail at him for yelling at their kids. For not being there and then acting like some stereotype out of a bad movie.

But she wasn't going to do either of those things. In the last few days, she'd seen more vulnerability in this man than she'd ever realized existed. He'd been running from their family, from her for so long he honestly didn't know how to be there anymore.

He wanted to be. No matter what she'd thought before—that he was home because of the court-martial, that he would leave again as soon as he got the chance—the fact was, she was no longer certain. He was hurting. Badly.

So she did the only thing she could.

Fear, not unlike the fear of approaching a wild animal, slithered through her veins but she forced it down. Forced herself to face the wicked realization that her husband had completely lost his shit and terrified the living hell out of her children and her, as well.

She never thought she'd fear this man but for one brief moment, she had.

But she loved him more and she couldn't leave him. Not like this, shattered and broken on their closet floor.

It took everything she had to kneel next to him, careful to move his glasses. His breathing, ragged and harsh, was the only sound over the beating of her heart. She bumped into the pile of uniforms on the floor near his hip. One of the orange bottles poked out from beneath a sleeve.

She took a deep breath and swallowed. Then she reached for him.

"Hey?" She slid her palm over his forearm. Felt the crisp hair on his arm against her skin. Felt the heat. The strength. The power that had terrified their son.

Here was a man who'd given the Army everything, and the fear in a child's eyes had reduced him to this. It was a hard thing she did, simply sitting there with him. There was no excuse for violence; she knew that. But even as his temper had snapped, he hadn't hurt the kids. A little plastic dinosaur hadn't been so lucky. But she could fix that.

She didn't know how to reach him through the tangled guilt and shame radiating off him in palpable waves.

She couldn't leave him there. Not like this. He'd never let her in, never lowered his guard enough to let her fix whatever was eating at him. Maybe, she could see him through this.

Maybe.

He tensed beneath her touch, pulling away to rub his hands over his face, leaving them there. She didn't miss the taint of moisture beneath his eyes. Her heart ached for the pain she saw there. She slid closer, until she could lean against his bent knees. She rested her chin on one, pressing against him.

"Did I ever tell you about the time I broke the window in the kitchen?" she said, breaking the silence the only way she knew how. She shifted again, sitting so that her shoulder rested against his knee. The contact bolstered her flagging courage. "Ethan had just exploded out of his diaper and used it as paint in the hall." The memory raced back, bringing with it the long forgotten anger and frustration. "I'd been up all night with Emma." She released a hard breath. "I just lost it. Something snapped and I threw the entire diaper pail."

He lowered his hands, banging his head back against the wall. She flinched, knowing that had been hard enough for him to see stars.

"Did you see his face, Laura?" His voice was scratchy and raw. "He was terrified of me." She slid her hand up to rest on his knees. He opened his eyes. "I fucking terrified my son."

"Trent, we all have bad days." She squeezed, waiting until he met her gaze, needing him to hear her. "All parents lose their shit sometimes. It's part of raising kids."

He looked away, disgust carved into his face. "I should be better than that."

She scoffed quietly, then reached for him, brushing her fingers over the stubble on his cheek. "Says who? Who says you're supposed to be a perfect father? Trent, none of us is perfect."

He opened his eyes then and she was stunned by the depth of the recrimination and bleak guilt she saw looking back at her. She shifted up to her knees, leaning forward and cupping his face in her hands. His skin was cold, clammy. His nostrils flared slightly at her touch, his body tense.

"I need you to hear me on this." She lifted his chin until his eyes met hers. "You didn't hurt him."

His throat tensed as he swallowed. "I broke a dinosaur." A ragged guilt for something far worse than breaking a child's toy.

"That we can replace for three ninety-nine at Target," she said. "He's fine." She stroked one thumb over his cheek, finding it damp. "Trent, you didn't hurt him."

He didn't look away from her but she saw the doubt, the shame fill his eyes. "All I could think about was getting him to stop yelling and listen," he whispered.

"I know. Believe me, I know." She gentled her fingers, keeping the contact, afraid to let him go lest he shatter there in her arms.

He lifted one hand, covered hers where she held him. "I'm sorry." He pressed his lips together, his throat moving as he swallowed. "I'm so goddamned sorry. I'm a mess. I should be better than this."

She smiled gently. "Yes, you are a mess." His cheeks were stiff with stubble beneath her touch. "But you're home for the first time in a long time. Rough spots are normal." She swiped both thumbs over his cheeks before she let him go. His hand lingered over hers for a moment too long.

"How can you forgive me so easily?"

"Because I've been there, too." Her fingers were hot beneath his touch. "But I know when they're getting to be too much. I can walk away before I let my temper get the best of me. You have to learn those things," she said quietly.

"What if I can't?"

"You can." She leaned down and brushed her lips with his.

He closed his eyes, shifting until he could rest his forehead against hers. "I'm afraid. I'm afraid of how I feel around the kids."

"You've been gone a long time. You have to give yourself time to adjust," she said.

"You're not worried?"

What could she say to that? She had been. She was. But there was something between them now that was more powerful than worry. "I am." A slide of her fingers over his cheek, a soothing caress. "But I have faith in you." Faith she'd lost but faith she'd started to find again. One piece at a time, but it was more than it had been.

And it was enough to keep her there with him as the time ticked past and the kids were late to school. Until the fear and loathing in his eyes faded. Until he looked at her and she saw the man she was coming to know. Not the man she'd married. Someone different.

But someone that she could no longer walk away from.

She slid her hand from his and retrieved his glasses, handing them to him before she stood and offered her outstretched hand. He looked up at her from where he still sat. A thousand emotions flickered across his face. Fear. Uncertainty. Guilt.

But he slipped his hand in hers and pushed to his feet. They stood there for another moment, until he reached for her, cupping her face in his hands and kissing her oh so gently on the mouth. It was meant as an apology, nothing more, but it twisted into something else. Something filled with passion and need and a thousand unsaid things.

It was Laura who eased back this time. "I have to get the kids to school," she whispered. He rubbed his thumb gently over her bottom lip. "I'd like to apologize to him first."

She smiled up at him, her heart swelling in her chest. Knowing it was stupid and savoring the feeling anyway. "I think that's a good idea."

A spark of understanding passed between them, a hint of common ground. She squeezed his fingers then let him go, knowing he was no longer at risk of breaking in her arms.

For now.

11

———

Trent was late. He hated being late but that's how it went sometimes when one was dealing with Fort Hood traffic. Some jackass had just rear-ended some other jackass at the Clear Creek gate and he'd sat on the bridge over Highway 190 and seethed for forty minutes.

He was supposed to be meeting Shane and Carponti at the Community Events Center to make sure things were on track for the wedding reception. It was going to be a small affair but Shane wanted somewhere small that they could have to themselves.

Carponti had suggested Hooters. Shane had not been impressed.

Trent parked in front of the Events Center next to Carponti's bright red truck at the edge of the parking lot and headed toward the front door. The parking lot was crowded from a bunch of conferences being held in the Events Center all this week. They'd be lucky to see the room at all if the sheer amount of rank walking through the parking lot was any indication as to the madness inside.

Trent stuffed his cell phone in his pocket and reached for the door at the same time as another soldier.

He stopped. His skin went cold.

Lieutenant Jason Randall. The weasley little bastard who'd been a pain in Trent's ass since the day he first arrived in Trent's formation. The hackles on the back of his neck rose and he took a single step forward before he remembered that Randall was with a general officer and one simply did not assault one's former lieutenants in front of general officers.

Trent badly wanted to know what ass Randall had kissed to get an assignment escorting a general around when he was pending many of the same charges as Trent.

Trent stiffened as General Ledbetter looked at him. He felt like a hamster being watched by a feral cat. "So you're Davila."

"Sir?" Trent kept his tone neutral, his body at the position of attention.

"I'm sure you two have lots to talk about." He opened the door and Trent spotted a sign for a Warfighter Commanders' Update Brief.

"Roger, sir." Randall looked like he'd rather eat glass.

Trent waited for the door to close completely before he spoke.

"Nice to see your ass-kissing skills haven't atrophied, LT," Trent said, his voice lighter than it had any business being.

"Fuck you. Sir." Randall's face flushed deep scarlet.

"No, you've already done that," Trent said dryly.

"You deserve whatever happens to you. You gave me nothing but shit from the moment I started working for you." Randall lifted his chin.

"So sue me for expecting more from my officers than skating by on their daddy's name. Your father earned that reputation. You did not," Trent said. He clenched his fists, badly wanting to lay his ass out flat. Just once and he'd get it out of his system.

"Maybe if you were a better commander, you wouldn't be under investigation. The Army can't find things if there's nothing to be found."

Trent smiled coldly. "And how exactly are you planning on beating the charges against you? Because, as you said, the Army can't find things if there's nothing to be found."

Randall flushed and clenched his fists by his sides. "I'll never get why the troopers followed you so blindly."

Trent took a single step closer. "See, that's the problem with you, LT. You never figured

it out."

"Figured what out?"

"That no matter how highly ranked you become, the boys will always see through you." Trent rubbed the tip of his finger over the black thread that made up the lieutenant rank on Randall's chest. "They'll respect your rank because they have to. But they'll never respect *you*," he whispered. "No matter who your father is."

They stood toe to toe for an eternity. Trent wanted so badly to hurt him that it felt like battery acid burned through his veins.

"Fuck you. You knew what I was doing."

"No, I didn't. And I never would have allowed you to put our boys at risk so you could make some extra money selling weapons parts." Trent stroked his hands over Randall's collar. "But you're still under investigation, too. Tell me, does Daddy know you married one of your subordinates?"

Everything happened all at once. Randall hauled off and swung at Trent just as the doors to the Events Center burst open. Carponti and Shane dragged Randall and Trent apart before the blow could land.

Randall yanked away from Carponti, straightening his uniform. "Still the same undisciplined bunch of roughnecks you've always been," he spat.

"God, it's so nice to see you, LT." Carponti reached forward to flatten the collar of Randall's uniform. Randall slapped his hand away. "Tell me, has your sense of smell changed from having your nose buried up General Ledbetter's ass?"

"Fuck you, Carponti. Shove your fake arm where the sun doesn't shine."

Carponti lifted his prosthetic and studied it for a moment, a wicked gleam in his eyes. "How about I shove it up your ass instead?"

"Carponti!" Shane's sharp reprimand was a long familiar refrain with them, and Trent almost grinned. "LT, get back inside before you get hurt."

Randall turned to head inside then paused. His fingers clenched by his sides for a moment and then he turned back to face them, his eyes zeroing in on Trent. "You're not going to win this one."

Trent rubbed his finger down the side of his nose then adjusted his glasses. "We'll see about that."

"Ta ta for now," Carponti said from behind him, waving his prosthetic. Trent shot his friend a look as the LT disappeared into the Events Center.

"Why the hell was Randall allowed to be that guy's escort? He's still under investigation." There was real anger in Carponti's voice, a rarity for him.

"Randall's father called in a few more favors, I guess," Trent said. He glanced at Shane. "Let's go make sure this wedding of yours still has a place to party. I need something good to replace the slime that fucker left on my skin."

"So how are things going with the kids?" Emily sat in one of the comfortable chairs perpendicular to Trent.

The office door was closed. His back was to the wall. Still, he felt a level of vulnerability he hadn't felt since his first deployment, when incoming rounds had kept him from sleeping— and when he did, they'd exploded so frequently and so often, he'd only slept bits and pieces at a time.

This was his second session with Emily and already he was unearthing things he didn't want to feel. Things he didn't know how to process. Things he'd run from since he'd gotten hurt.

"They're...tough," he finally admitted. He told her about the other morning and his explosion with Ethan.

"So you're still feeling a lot of anxiety around them?" Emily's voice was calm and quiet. Smooth. She made him want to relax.

"Yeah. And when I get anxious, my temper gets short." He twirled his glasses in his hand, avoiding her gaze. "I feel like I'm failing at everything. Being a husband. Being a father. I can't get ahead back here. The only thing I'm good at is being a soldier."

"I don't think that's true," Emily said. "If it were true, you wouldn't be here, now would you?"

He glanced up sharply. "I guess not," he said. "When is it going to get easier?" he asked. "When is it going to feel normal and not like I'm one egg short of a dozen?"

"It takes time, Trent. You've only been home, really allowed your-self to be home, for a really short period. You can't expect miracles." She tipped her head at him. "This isn't the same thing as preparing for a deployment," she said.

"I know that."

"Do you? This isn't a paint by numbers event, Trent. It's going to take years for you to get your normal back. It's a slow decompression. You've had ten years to wind yourself up, to get used to a certain kind of stress. This is the same thing. New stress. Different stress. Not life-threatening but stressful all the same." She shifted, crossing one leg over the other. "Was there ever a deployment when you came home and things felt more normal than they do now?"

He frowned, staring down at his hands in his lap. He'd deployed so many times. Each time he'd thought he couldn't wait to get home. Each time, he'd rushed back out the door as soon as he could. "Nothing has ever felt right since I got shot," he whispered after a silence that stretched until forever.

"Do you want to tell me about that?" she asked gently.

The memories rose up, sharp and poignant. He could smell the stinking sulfur, hear the screams of his men. The fire that ripped through his skin as the round that had damn near killed him tore him apart.

"I should have died that day," he whispered.

"You did die, Trent." He looked up at her. She tapped his file on her lap. "Your medical records show your heart stopped. You were medically dead." He looked back down at his hands. There was a weight pressing down on him. Like an elephant sitting on his chest. Too much, too many memories. A thousand faces stared back at him, swirling around him, taunting him that he should have been better, faster, smarter. Should have seen the bomb that had taken out their truck.

"Trent?" Her voice penetrated the racing thoughts. He looked up at her. "You came home. But you don't feel like you deserve it, do you?"

Her words settled on his shoulders like a heavy, wet blanket. Thick with recrimination that seeped into his bones. And though he tried, there was simply no way for him to wriggle out of this conversation since she'd laid it so plainly in his lap.

"Maybe I wonder what's the point. Good men go to war. They don't come home." He looked up at her. "I didn't deserve to come home. I'm a shitty husband. A shitty father. There are good men, good fathers, who didn't come home. Why the fuck did I?" Harsh words, ripped from his soul.

"Good men do come home," Emily corrected. "They just don't

come back the same as when they went. And you have to accept that war asks good men to do bad things, that death in war isn't something you can control and that punishing yourself isn't doing anyone any good."

"What am I supposed to do?" He stood abruptly, pacing the small office, unable to sit with the disquiet in his thoughts. "How do I wake up in the morning and not see everything that's screwed up around me? Things that I screwed up by leaving. By running. My wife doesn't deserve this. My kids don't."

The strain was back, squeezing around his heart.

"Start with something small," she said quietly.

He looked down at her where he stood. The woman was unflappable. Calm in the face of his frustration. How did she manage that? "Like what?"

"Take the kids. By yourself. Do something with them, just them. Show them you're still their daddy but more importantly, show yourself that you can do this."

"I'm not sure Laura would be comfortable with that." A very real fear. "What if I lose my shit again?" he whispered.

"Then don't freak out. Then walk away for a second. Go into the bathroom, close the door and give yourself a minute. And if that doesn't work? Then you stay in that bathroom until it does."

Trent sucked in a deep breath, the shame from the other morning crashing over him.

"You have to give yourself permission to take things slowly, Trent. You can't come back from being at war for most of the last decade and expect to just miraculously turn things off."

He smiled bitterly. "When you put it like that, it sounds a little silly."

"This isn't silly," she said quietly. "This is the hardest thing you will ever do."

12

I'll pick the kids up.

Laura looked down at her phone, ashamed that her hand trembled as she set it down. That single text message sent a thousand emotions racing through her, but mostly she hoped that the kids wouldn't try to break him again. Kids were funny that way, always pushing to see what they could get away with.

A little piece of her heart soared when he'd told her he wanted to pick them up. He was still in the fight. Still trying. And it made her heart hurt how happy that little effort on his part made her.

So when she walked in the door to hear the kids shrieking with laughter, she was thrown off balance so much so that she stopped and simply stood there for a moment, taking in the sounds of their joy. This? This sounded like a normal she'd only dreamed about.

"Ethan, get the hamster out of the dishwasher."

"Daddy, she needs a bath."

"The dishwasher is not the place for Fluffy to conduct hamster shower operations."

Laura smiled where she stood just out of sight, listening to the debate between her husband and her son. Trent sounded disgruntled but not on edge.

Emma giggled. "Hamsters don't take showers, Daddy!"

Trent grunted and she heard the scrape of metal on metal. Peering into the kitchen, she saw both kids sitting on the floor next to the open dishwasher, two small rodents crawling around on the space in front of them. Periodically, a set of small hands would scoop up one of the hamsters and move it farther away from its planned route to freedom.

The hamsters did not seem to mind. Stinking little buggers. Probably teaming up to plot their next escape.

"You can't wash hamsters," Emma said wisely. "If you do, they'll catch a cold."

She thought she heard Trent mumble something to the effect of "That's why they smell so bad" but she couldn't be sure. She smiled. He was a man after her heart after all.

"All right, guys. Ready to check it out?"

"Did you really fix the dishwasher, Daddy?" Emma asked.

"Well." He stood and wiped his hands on a towel. "It's either going to turn on or catch on fire. Either way is better than it just sitting here broken, right?"

Ethan frowned. "Why would it be better for it to catch fire than for it to just sit here?"

"Because at least it will be doing something. Action is almost always better than inaction."

Laura stepped into the kitchen and five pairs of eyes settled on her. Well, actually four because one of the hamsters had snuck off around the trash can. The escape was short-lived. "How did you fix it?"

"Home Depot left a message that the part came in. Me and Lieutenant Google got down to business." He straightened, brushing his hands on his thighs. Sweat ringed the neck of his t- shirt, causing the fabric to cling to his torso. Laura swallowed, her mouth suddenly dry, her gaze drawn to his powerful shoulders.

"Should we test it?"

He shoved his glasses to the top of his head and grinned. "I put a few dirty dishes in it, and I was going to run a test cycle. Hopefully it'll clean the dishes." He crouched down to Emma's level. "Want to push the button?"

Emma nodded. Trent slid his hand over hers and pressed the button with her. The dishwasher churned to life with a familiar swish.

Laura met his smile tentatively as the kids cheered around them. Ethan high-fived his father, clutching his hamster to his chest. Trent stood near the dishwasher and braced his hands on the counter, looking easy and relaxed for the first time since he'd come home.

"All right, guys, it's time for the hamsters to go in their balls for a little while. Fluffy is looking a little...fluffy. She needs exercise," Trent said.

Emma rolled her eyes at her dad. "She's a hamster, Daddy. She's supposed to be fluffy." As though it was the most obvious association in the world.

"Scoot," he said.

The kids ran out of the room to go find the hamster balls, leaving Trent and Laura alone without a buffer—separated only by the kitchen island. Trent leaned down, his shoulders flexing as he moved. He brushed his thumb over her healing knuckles.

His expression tightened as he stroked at the pink flesh. "Why didn't you just call someone to do it?" he asked softly.

The ghost of their kisses twisted around them as Trent slipped his index finger over her hand. She shivered, needing more than this hesitant touch.

"Because I like fixing things," she said simply. She glanced over her shoulder at the clock on the microwave. "We've got to get dinner started."

She started to straighten but he caught her fingers gently between his. His palm surrounded hers. "Can I help?"

She frowned then, wanting badly to ask how he had become so calm. Whether this mood had come out of a little orange bottle of pills. But the comfort between them was so new, so fresh, she did not dare broach the subject.

And honestly? She didn't care if the calm was from the bottle or not. It was working. If it had helped Trent have a normal afternoon with his children, then damn it, she refused to judge. He'd been through something extraordinary. "I'd like that," she said quietly.

A distant buzzing interrupted them, refusing to be ignored. "I don't suppose you're going to let that go?" she whispered. Too many nights during his time as a commander, his cell phone had pulled him from bed, only to keep him up for hours afterward. But those days were long gone.

She didn't want that same stress coming back into his life now. Not even for an instant. He was working too hard at being here, at being normal. She closed her eyes and wished she could shut out the war, shut out the world, and just keep him there until he knew what normal felt like. Until he was ready for the world again.

But he was already gone, pulling the phone out of his pocket and stepping onto the back porch. Not before she heard him say Story's name.

And just like that, the war slipped back between them.

"Hey, Top, how's it going?" An odd thing to say to a man in a war zone but then again, Trent had always hated the questions about how often he was getting blown up or shot at. Trent sat on the back porch of their home, listening to the static on the cell phone line, waiting for the call to come back in.

"You there?" Story's voice sounded gritty and far away.

"Yeah, I'm here." Trent leaned forward, cupping his forehead in his palm. "How are things?"

"Bad." Story paused, no doubt to spit into the dirt. The man had an expensive chewing tobacco habit. It was a wonder it didn't break the bank every month. "This is the worst I've seen it."

Fear curled in Trent's guts, twisting with fresh guilt that he wasn't there with Story. That he'd let him go downrange without him. He glanced toward the house, where Laura and his children were waiting for him. The fear remained but the guilt flittered away. He was where he needed to be. The war would get him again if he stayed in. He'd spent too much time chasing the adrenaline and not enough time being a dad. Still, he wished Story wasn't there without him. "What can I do?"

"Can you send me about seventeen boxes of Copenhagen? The PX is out of my flavor and this generic shit they've got tastes like balls."

Trent grinned, glad it was something simple. Something he could handle. There was silence on the line and Trent thought for a moment that he'd lost his old friend. "Yeah, I can do that for you. Is that why you're calling? Not to tell me you love me?"

Story scoffed. Trent could hear the derision in his tone. "Not likely. Nah, I was just...had a shit day. I need a goddamned cigar. Where's Carponti when I need someone to yell at to unwind?"

Trent stilled. "We can do that when you get home. You're only on a ninety-day stint this time, right?"

"Hope so. I've never seen things this fucked up. They have platoons holding sectors that used to be run by full companies."

That meant the troops were stretched thin. That was never a good thing. "Story..."

"Look, just...promise me that if something happens, you'll look out for Rebecca. Don't let some scumbag take advantage of her when she gets all the money from me dying. She's going to run off and get a boob job before she buries me. Just, don't let someone fuck her over, okay?"

"That's a fucked up thing to say, man," Trent said, wishing he could make some kind of smart-ass joke like Carponti would to ease the soul-crushing fear that rose up to squeeze his heart tightly. It pushed away the happiness from earlier.

Left the too familiar cold and emptiness once again.

"So look, there's maybe a different reason I'm calling." Story's voice took on that tone that Trent knew too well. He was about to give him some really bad news. Trent hoped it didn't ruin the rest of his night, not when things were this close to going really right with Laura.

Story cleared his throat on the line. "Maybe Randall had the right idea. Maybe paying the bastards off wasn't such a bad call."

Trent stilled, his mind screaming in denial at what Story's words meant. "What are you getting at, Top?" he finally asked.

He heard the sigh over the static. "Look, we had our damn hands full. We were getting blown up every goddamned time we ran outside the wire, we were losing guys left and right. I was willing to try anything." Another pause. "I'm sorry you got caught up in all this. I knew Randall was a shit, but not this bad."

Trent was speechless. He searched the darkness for something, anything to say. "Top..."

"Look, I've sent a sworn statement to Major MacLean. I knew about this. Randall somehow kept me off the list of witnesses but I've fixed that now."

Anger, cold and violent, surged through Trent's veins. "You knew? Top, you fucking knew he was selling sensitive items and you didn't fucking tell me?"

"I thought it was best if you didn't know," Story said quietly.

"Jesus." He fought to find anything to say but the words were locked in his throat. Anger. Betrayal. A man he'd trusted had stabbed him in the back.

For what?

For fucking what?

The line went dead, leaving Trent alone with the bitter anger of his thoughts. Story, a man he trusted, a man whose advice he'd taken, whose counsel he'd sought, had known what Randall was doing. He'd known and he'd said nothing to Trent.

He'd lied.

And that single admission knocked Trent's whole world off its axis.

The back door opened and Laura stepped into the shadows. He wasn't ready to face her yet, hadn't put all the wrong emotions back in the box and pulled the right ones out again.

He tossed the cell phone on the bench next to him and scrubbed his hands through his hair.

And fought for control. He looked up at his wife—his beautiful, patient wife—who was looking at him with expectation and something else that was a little too close to fear. It settled in his stomach like something fetid and vile.

"Are you okay?" she asked quietly, leaning against the door.

"No." He scoffed harshly, then looked up. He shouldn't have. The sharp worry in her eyes had crossed the line, snuggling up to full-blown fear.

"I'm not crazy, Laura. I don't have PTSD and you can stop looking at me like I do." His words were sharp, meant to wound, and he instantly regretted them.

But he could not take them back. Goddamn it. He buried his face in his hands. He just needed a few minutes to pull all the violent emotions back inside him. But he couldn't push her away right now.

What he did right now, in these next few minutes, mattered. More than anything else. He fought the pain, fought the anger. And did everything he knew how to put it away to avoid lashing out at her.

Because she didn't deserve that.

"I didn't say that you did."

He leaned back, resting his head on the brick. Keep talking. Keep letting things out, one thing at a time. It was better than bottling it up, stuffing it down. "I feel like you keep waiting for me to snap."

"I'm worried about you," she whispered. "I don't think that's unreasonable."

He opened his eyes, looking up at her. Willed himself to stay calm. He was pissed at Story, not her. Then she did something unexpected and changed everything. She took a single step toward him. Crossed the tiny distance and sat next to him on the bench. "You said something the first night you were home. You said your normal was screwed up."

Her palm came to rest over the scar on his heart, his pulse pounding against her hand. She seared him with that gentle touch. His body tightened; the scar ached beneath her touch.

"I think you never gave yourself the chance to reset. And I'm sorry if that's hard for me to deal with." The admission was crushing in its simplicity. The fingers of her free hand danced against his neck. "I'm afraid," she whispered, refusing to meet his gaze.

He lifted one hand, stroking her cheek until she met his eyes. "Of me." It wasn't a question.

She nodded, her eyes filling.

He lowered his forehead to hers, their noses brushing together. For a long moment, Trent simply sat with her. The world was not as chaotic here with her. Everything was calm. Everything was quiet.

Real.

Even her admission, as painful as it was to hear, was real. And that was something he held on to as he lifted his other hand to trace the line of her cheek. "I'm not going to hurt you again, Laura."

"I'm trying to believe that," she whispered.

Something snapped and broke inside him. All restraints ripped from their tethers.

"Believe this," he growled. He held nothing back in this kiss. The kisses they'd shared in the coffee shop had been a tender question. This was violence and pain, hurt and hell all wrapped into one intense embrace. It was an outlet, a release valve that he'd never allowed because he *had* been afraid of hurting her. He kissed her then, pouring everything he had into that single moment, telling her without words how badly everything inside him was hurting.

This kiss was a branding. A violation of the boundaries she'd set between them. He tore

them down and marked her soul, refused to let her breathe or think or protest.

He threaded his fingers through her hair, his other hand on her back, holding her tightly to him. He nibbled on her bottom lip. "I want you so much," he murmured.

She gasped against his mouth, the sweetest pleasure in that sound. He kissed her gently then, his tongue playing over her lips, teasing her, loving her.

He cupped her cheek with his hand, stroking her hair out of her eyes.

"Trent—"

"I miss you, Laura," he whispered right before he kissed her again, drowning out thoughts of anything but him. There was pure heat in his touch. "I miss us."

He sucked on her bottom lip, loving the feel of her mouth beneath his. Everything about her was soft and sensual, this woman who filled the dead space inside him. The stone where his heart used to be was a little softer, a little less solid.

"I don't know how to be home, Laura," he whispered, resting his forehead against hers. "But I'm trying."

Her only response was the slight shift of her nose against his. Her lips, swollen from his brutal kiss, curled slightly. His fingers just skimmed over her cheek, teasing her with the promise of more. "I know." The words scraped past a dry throat. He leaned closer, and their mouths were just a hint apart.

She opened her mouth like she wanted to speak. And part of him wanted to hear her out. But the other part of him was so tired of fighting. All he wanted to do was hold her, take her mouth in sweet nibbling kisses.

He couldn't remember the last time he'd made love to his wife but his campaign to win her back called for patience. He had no doubt he could get her into bed right now, but the moment the sexual haze faded, she'd regret what they'd done.

Instead, he pressed his lips to hers, hesitant, questioning, letting her control the pace, letting the trust and the love that still lived inside of her bloom. She tipped her head and opened her mouth beneath his. His tongue stroked hers and with that simple touch, brilliant heat exploded inside him. Still, he yanked it back. This had to be under her control, on her terms.

HIS FINGERS PRESSED into her hair and angled her head so that their mouths could join completely. She gasped as his jaw scraped against hers and liquid need slid between them. Every touch reminded her of why she loved him, of why she'd waited so long for him to come back to her. And every touch brought with it a renewed intensity that refused to be ignored.

This was Trent. Trent who kissed her. Trent who brought this heat to life inside her and reminded her of all the reasons she loved him. Trent who'd held her as she cried the last time he told her he was leaving.

Trent who was holding her now, making her crazy, one slow, sipping kiss at a time. She did the only thing a woman who loved a man could do when there were children running around in the house.

She leaned back, brushing his bottom lip with her thumb. "Tonight?"

She didn't want to wait. But she also didn't want the first time she touched her husband in almost two years to be interrupted by a child or two beating on the bedroom door. "We have to wait until the kids go to bed," she said against his mouth.

"Can't we tie them up in the bathroom or something?" His words were light. Teasing. Pained and heavy with arousal.

She laughed, then buried her face in his neck.

13

Laura set the bowl of broccoli on the table. "Ethan, I thought I told you no hamsters at the dinner table."

Ethan puffed out his bottom lip, a sure sign that he was about to cry. She was getting ready to intervene when Trent crouched down to look his son in the eye. "Fluffy needs to get put away for dinner, tiny man. She needs her own dinner."

"But, Daddy, Fluffy hasn't been acting right all day. See!" Trent flinched as the hamster was thrust into his face.

He grabbed Ethan's wrist and gently pushed the animal back to where he could see it. Picking the rodent up, he turned her around in a circle like he was doing a detailed inspection. The hamster just hung there, her fuzzy belly exposed, looking at him as if to say, *are you done yet?* "Fluffy is fine. Go put her away, okay? And wash your hands."

Ethan sighed dramatically and walked out of the room, his footsteps just barely shy of a stomp. Trent straightened and walked to the sink to wash his own hands. "Does that thing always smell so bad?"

"Hamsters go into heat every four days."

"Dear lord, that's terrible."

Laura grinned as she finished slicing the top off of a loaf of bread before sliding it into the oven. "You're the one who bought them."

"I had no clue they smelled that bad."

"They're not usually this bad. We keep the cages pretty clean." She turned to find that he'd snuck up behind her.

"I kind of left you in the lurch with them, didn't I?"

"Hello, captain obvious. You bought two rodents, then left the next day for a training exercise." She smiled to take the sting out of her words. "But the kids love them so I'll tolerate them." She turned back to stir the potatoes she had boiling on the stove. "Has Patrick said anything else about the case?"

A long silence stretched between them. She glanced over her shoulder at Trent, whose strain was showing in his eyes. Laura breathed out deeply. She wanted to ask him to talk to her. Wanted to help carry the burden of his war, but she was terrified he would turn away again, leaving her with more unanswered questions.

"Funny you should mention that," he said, and there was bitterness in his voice. "Turns out, Story knew what was going on."

"What?"

"Yeah. Turns out, my lieutenant wasn't the only one I shouldn't have trusted." She glanced over her shoulder to see him rub his hand over his mouth. "But he's apparently sent a statement home to Patrick admitting to what he knew and testifying against Randall."

"I still don't see how Randall is going to beat this by dragging you into it," Laura said. She knew enough about the case to know it was a disaster. Patrick had mentioned there was a flow chart somewhere outlining who they thought knew what and when they'd known it.

"Randall is going to testify that I knew he was selling weapons. I signed off on his reports without verifying them, so he's going to use that against me," he said quietly. Out of the corner of her eye, she watched him pull a beer from the fridge.

She set the spoon down on the counter. "How are you going to fight him on it?"

"My brigade commander taught me back in OIF 2 that commanders must only focus on the command. All else must be delegated. So Patrick and I are going to turn it back on Randall. He was my executive officer. He was supposed to be running the company so I could command it. I shouldn't have needed to double-check his work. It will shred his argument." He took a pull from his beer. "At least, I hope it will."

"It sounds good to me," she said, offering a faint smile. A long moment passed before she sighed softly. "I know you're pissed at him right now but I think Rebecca is cheating on him again."

Silence greeted her. She wasn't sure what kind of response she expected from him, especially not now after Story's call. "I'm not surprised," he admitted.

She frowned, watching him closely, well aware that this conversation danced a little too close to their personal situation. "Why not?"

"Story has been gone even more than I have. And Rebecca isn't the kind of woman who does well on her own."

Laura turned back to dinner. "What's that mean?"

"It means some women need a man in their lives. Any man will do."

"Just like there are some guys who need a woman in their bed," she whispered, hating herself for dragging the rumors into their kitchen. But they could no more deny them than ignore them. It was better to lance the wound, draining the poison so that it had a chance to heal rather than fester.

He stepped into her space, cupping her face and stopping her need to be in motion. "Laura, I meant it when I said that I've never cheated on you. I've never even thought about it."

"I know," she whispered. She turned away before he could see everything that she could not hide. The agony of those rumors had burrowed deep, whispering a horrible explanation in her ear for every moment of silence on the other end of the phone.

"Laura."

She closed her eyes, steeling her heart against the agony in his voice. She sucked in a deep breath and plunged ahead.

"The first time Rebecca hinted around that something was going on downrange, I didn't believe her." Her voice was raw, the emotion ragged. "But the rumors kept getting worse and worse. And you barely talked to me for months."

She was ashamed of her lack of trust. She wasn't, by nature, an untrusting person. But she'd failed. Failed at trusting her husband, failed at standing strong for him when he needed her most. His actions, his silence, had destroyed her faith not only in him but in herself, too. She'd walked away when things had gotten too tough and that single action had decimated the person she'd thought she was. "It chipped away at my faith in you."

She saw it now, everything she'd done to help break up their marriage. She'd been cold on the phone when he'd needed her support. She hadn't looked beyond the rumors. She'd focused on her own hurt, her own sadness, letting the silence on the phone widen the fractures between them. She closed her eyes, unable to let him see the depth of her shame.

His hands on her shoulders were gentle as he urged her to turn toward him. The heat from the stove warmed her back as his hands stroked her. His eyes were dark, rimmed with sadness. "I'm so sorry I wasn't man enough for you to believe in," he whispered.

Of all the things he could have said, an apology was the most unexpected.

There it was again. The quiet admission of everything that was wrong between them. The world tilted beneath her feet as her husband's hands caressed her, bringing to life all of the emotions she'd locked away.

She leaned into him then, letting go of a little piece of the hurt, another weight that bore down on her. He was home. He was working on things, a little bit at a time.

It was enough.

THE KIDS WERE ASLEEP. Tucked away in their beds, all hamsters accounted for; evening quiet settled over their home as Laura padded into their bedroom. Trent been quiet since his phone call with Story, quiet but not unreachable. He did not pull away this time like he would have in the past.

She stood in front of her dresser in their bedroom and pulled her rings from the small jewelry box. Her fingers hesitated now over the cold golden rings, which stood for everything they'd once meant to each other. Everything about this evening had been so achingly normal. So beautiful and twisted.

She toyed with the rings, stopping just short of putting them on.

The significance of something so simple terrified her. She held them in the palm of her hand, remembering the first time Trent had slid them on her finger. She'd been terrified and excited and a thousand other emotions. She remembered looking into his eyes and seeing love looking back.

She'd believed then that they could make it through anything.

The bathroom door opened. Trent stood there in the doorway, watching her. His gaze flicked down to her hand. The muscle in his jaw jumped.

Then he walked toward her. Slowly, until he stood behind her in the mirror, their reflections close, their bodies closer. The scar over his heart stood out in stark relief against the crisp dark hair that dusted his chest. A starburst of damaged skin and blood-red memories.

She closed her eyes, remembering that horrible day.

On behalf of a grateful nation...

His chest radiated warmth and she shifted, leaning back into him. Just a little but it was enough. His arms came around her, his hands sliding down her forearms to cup her hands. His eyes darkened and warmed, but he said nothing. Instead, he traced his index finger over her knuckles, their gazes locked in the mirror. He ran the tip of his finger roughly against her, circling the rings she held there.

Her breath jammed in her throat as he lifted the rings, then turned her hand over. His body surrounded her, his heat penetrating her skin.

He slid her wedding band over her finger. A slight pop over her knuckle and then it was in its place. He lifted her hand until he could press his lips to her palm, then slid her engagement ring, a single solitary diamond, back where it belonged.

He held her then, his arms wrapped around hers, his eyes holding hers in the mirror. Slowly, he started to sway. His hips moved against hers, reminding her of an old familiar rhythm that had once been a normal part of their lives. He traced his hands over her skin. Her arms. Her collarbone. The pulse in her throat. All the while, she watched him in the mirror. Watched her body as though it belonged to someone else.

He dragged his thumb over her bottom lip, nudging her lips to part. She stood there, unable to move, wanting so badly to surrender to the racing need inside her, knowing that if she did, she'd be sacrificing everything she'd fought so hard to retain.

Instead, she simply stood and basked in the warmth from his bare skin so close to her own. He scraped his teeth over the sensitive skin of her earlobe. She felt him, thick and hard against her. She arched into him, needing the intimate pressure.

Trent could not believe his wife was in his arms. Wearing her rings. He simply stood and held her, unwilling to do anything to break the spell that floated around them. An easy, erotic haze built between them as he watched her beautiful body sway with his in the mirror.

This woman awed him. Every day she stood with him, she taught him something beautiful about the world.

He slid his hands down her arms, threading his fingers with hers, loving the feel of her body arching into his. Slowly, so slowly, he lifted her arms, wrapping them around his neck until she was arched in front of him. Her breasts were heavy and full against the thin tank she'd put on after her shower. He slipped his fingers down her ribs, marveling at the shudder that ran through her body.

With one index finger, he traced the exposed strip of skin on her belly. A tiny expanse but one begging to be explored. Hooking his finger, he dragged the soft cotton higher, higher until the soft scoop of her breasts were barely exposed. "You're so beautiful," he whispered, tracing his tongue over her ear. She trembled in his arms but didn't lower her own. Her fingers tensed on the back of his neck.

He skimmed his fingers over the exposed underside of her breasts. Watched her nipples pearl beneath the thin cotton. Ached to taste her.

He slid the tank a little higher, flicking it over one nipple until the pink bud was puckered and exposed. Her breath tumbled from her lungs as he traced his thumb over the sensitive skin.

"I could do this for hours," he whispered. "Just watching your body respond to my touch. I've missed you so much."

She closed her eyes as he pushed her pants off her hips, then lifted her arms enough to slip the tank over her head. "Laura." His voice a whisper. An erotic command. She opened her eyes.

She was naked. Exposed in his arms. He nudged her arms back around his neck, his hands skimming her waist to cradle her hips. He traced his thumb over her hipbone, his touch dancing closer and closer to where she ached for him.

"I want to touch you," he whispered. She couldn't look away from the intensity of his gaze. His hands were sure, familiar and strange all at once. "Can I touch you there?" he asked. He skimmed a single finger over the seam over her sex. Moisture spread beneath his touch. "Please, Laura. Let me touch you." He scraped his teeth along her jaw. "Open for me," he urged. "Just a little."

He knew how to make her body sing. She knew it. He knew it. This was more than just sex. This was about power. About desire.

About healing.

She parted her thighs, just a little bit. Moisture glistened on the soft hair. She watched, entranced, as his fingers slipped over her body, caressing. Urging. Stroking her lightly until her thighs spread farther. She was completely open and completely lost to his touch. Desire spiraled wide inside her as his fingers danced over her swollen sex, tracing the lines of her body until she thought she'd snap if he didn't give her what she needed. She arched mindlessly against him, begging with her body what she could not speak. She needed this man. Wanted him inside her, filling her. Completing the erotic dance with her.

Reminding her of all the reasons she loved him.

He slipped a finger inside her and she exploded. Her entire world shook as he stroked her, drawing out her pleasure until her body hummed and she felt boneless.

He laid her gently on the bed, amazed by the power of her release. She lifted her thighs, wrapping them around his hips as he found the place he'd missed more than anything: the loving sanctuary of her arms. He threaded his fingers in hers and dragged her arms over her head once more.

Waited until she met his gaze. Needing her to know, to be sure that this was what she wanted. "No regrets, Laura?"

He paused then, his blood pounding in his veins, needing to slide into the warm welcome she offered. But he wouldn't. Not like this. Not until he knew she was sure.

She freed one of her hands, tracing it around his neck. "I need you," she whispered, arching her hips to slide her body over the tip of his erection.

Trent was lost. That simple sensation, that slightest touch and he buried himself inside her. Her gasp was beautiful against his mouth, her taste the sweetest pleasure. He lifted her hips as she matched his rhythm, their bodies immediately seeking the synchronicity that came with loving the same person for so long.

Her heart might have forgotten what it was like to love this man but her body had not.

And when he shattered inside her, everything in her world was right for a brief, blinding

moment.

14

———————

"Where are the kids today?" Shane asked as Trent climbed into his truck.

"With our neighbors." He slammed the door shut. "Laura figured it would be easier to pay for a babysitter than drag the kids around Austin all day."

"Probably a good plan," Carponti said from the backseat, where he was fiddling with his iPod. "If Nicole has her way with me, I'm going to end up in a furniture store for half the afternoon." He glanced up, plugging an ear bud into his ear. "Though I suppose it's better than picking out flowers and decorations after we go to the dress shop. Man, I never thought I'd see you emasculated like this. Did you forget to get your balls out of Jen's purse? Oh wait, I forgot, you had them rewired. Never mind."

Shane didn't respond to Carponti's taunt. Instead, he turned the radio to the heavy metal station out of Austin. "First Sarn't Story e-mailed me yesterday," he said to Trent.

"Yeah, I talked to him," Trent said. Just like that, the anger and the betrayal were back. He didn't know how to tell Carponti and Garrison what Story had done, so he kept it to himself. They'd find out soon enough.

"He's at Camp Cooke in Taji," Shane said. "He didn't sound too happy. Man, some bad shit is happening there."

Trent looked out the window, memories from the Triangle of Death rising up to torment him.

"Laura told me she thinks Rebecca is cheating on him," Trent said quietly. "Do you think

he knows?"

"Probably."

"Why did he e-mail you?"

"To say he was sorry he can't be here for the wedding." Shane glanced over at him. "Did he get in touch to ask you about the hearing?"

"Yeah. I told him about Randall being here." Trent frowned, rubbing the bridge of his nose with his index finger and smothering the anger. "I hate that all of you are being dragged through this."

Since Story had been Trent's first sergeant when he was in command, he'd worked hand in hand with Trent to ensure that their troops were prepared each and every time they went out in sector. In theory, he'd also worked closely with Lieutenant Randall. If Randall testified that Trent knew about the missing weapons, Story's counter-testimony would hold a lot of weight.

As the hearing to determine whether or not Trent's case would go to court-martial drew closer, a feeling of deep unease took up more and more space in his belly. It wrestled with his nightmares and the general anxiety he felt about being at home, pushing away the goodness from last night with Laura.

The fear he still struggled with had blossomed inside of him the day he woke up in the hospital bay, unable to hear, unable to move because of the wicked wound that had ripped his flesh from his bones. He'd fought to get back out with his boys, refusing to leave them in the thick of the battle without him. Maybe if he hadn't been so stupid, the wound would have healed better. The scar over his heart had long since healed but the relentless fear had woven itself into his skin as it knitted back together.

That fear was a permanent companion now. He didn't believe Emily when she said it would fade, but he wondered if he would ever live another day without the constant terror that he would lose those who mattered most to him. And while he was pissed and hurt that Story had known about Randall, he still wanted his old friend to be out of combat.

He understood what drove Story. The same urges had driven him to combat again and again. And now that Story was back downrange and Trent was not, a new, unfamiliar feeling twisted in his guts. Guilt sliced at him for letting his friend go back to war without him.

Shane cleared his throat. "So listen, this ah, wedding is kind of a big deal to Jen."

Carponti leaned between the front seats of the car, his iPod cradled in his prosthetic hand. "And it's not to you?"

"Don't be an ass. Of course it is. But this is...I need to do this right for her."

"And you need us because...?" Carponti said.

"Because I have no idea how to be married. Not in a normal marriage where I actually love my wife."

"You loved Tatiana once," Trent pointed out.

"I loved the idea of Tatiana more than I loved her. I know that's a callous thing to say but it's true." He swallowed and dragged one hand over his face. "I haven't told Jen about the deployment. I don't know how to tell her."

"You're assuming you're going," Trent said.

"You're still gimped up from getting blown up last year." Carponti shifted and sat back in his seat. "I qualified expert last week on my M4. The commander was amazed."

Trent grinned. "How hard was it to learn to shoot left-handed?"

"Pretty fucking tough. It's really weird but I figured it out. I spent a week with a shooting coach from the Ranger Regiment out at Benning. Helped a ton."

"That's awesome. Guess the commander is going to let you deploy?"

"Hell yeah. Plus, I threatened to call the division sergeant major if he didn't. And we all know that Sergeant Major Giles is part of my fan club. He'd put in a good word for me."

Trent choked back a laugh. "He is no such thing. He hates you."

"He just acts that way. He told me he was going to shove my prosthetic up my ass if I didn't get it out of his face two weeks ago. But he said it in the most loving way."

Trent laughed and shook his head, turning to look at Shane. "When are you going to tell Jen that you might be on this deployment?"

"I have to tell her soon. Like, before we get married. I need to give her that out."

"Wait, what the hell?" Carponti leaned over the seats again. "You think she won't marry you if she knows you're deploying?"

"I have no right to ask her to wait for me like this. We're already six years into this war and eight into Afghanistan and we don't know how long the war will be. I asked her to marry me when I was still hurt. There was a good chance I was getting out of the military. If I get to stay in... She deserves to make that choice. Before I marry her." His voice grated rough with emotion.

"She's not going to walk away over this," Trent said. He sucked in a deep breath. Once, he'd thought the same thing about Laura and he'd damn near lost her. He wasn't going to feed into Shane's fears about Jen but he wouldn't disagree that he needed to be honest with her.

But Jen knew what she was getting into by marrying the big sergeant. She was marrying a man who would leave and go back to war. When Laura had married Trent, the war hadn't started yet. They hadn't yet known what half a decade at war would feel like, what it would do to them.

He rubbed the scar over his heart. He'd gotten a second chance with her. He didn't know how but he had. And no matter what he did, he refused to screw it up.

Because having her back filled the dead space inside of him with something good, something he would do anything to hold on to.

"I'm not coming out."

Laura leaned against the wall of the changing room as Nicole and Jen laughed hysterically outside the curtain.

"Jen, this isn't funny. This dress makes me look like a fat cupcake with sprinkles. Why would you do this to someone you call a friend?"

The dress was worse than horrid. Bright silver with sparkling red jewels draped over her breasts. The bust was the only redeeming part. Right below her ribs, the fabric exploded into a ruffle of fabric and fluff that made her look like an overdone...cupcake.

"Oh come on, you have to let us see."

"No. Pick a different dress. I love you like a sister but I'm not wearing this."

Nicole finally stopped laughing for long enough to make a threat. "Either come out or we're coming in."

Laura took another look in the mirror and decided that she even hated the bust. "How come you're not wearing this monstrosity?" she asked Nicole.

"Because I wanted to see how it looked on you first."

"Not funny."

Jen giggled and the sound of her friends' laughter bloomed in Laura's heart. Once upon a time, she'd worried Jen would never laugh or smile again. The cancer had taken its toll on her but she'd fought back, refusing to let it beat her. "Yes it is. Come on, let us see it."

"Laura, do you have the car keys?" Laura closed her eyes as Trent's voice broke through the hysterical laughter outside the curtain. She could not let him see her in this. "What's wrong?"

"Laura won't come out and show us one of the bridesmaid's dresses that Jen asked us to model," Nicole said. "Go in and get her."

"No!" She hadn't been able to get the dress done up in the back. It was gaping open, a giant flapping maw of material.

But the curtain was already moving as her husband stepped into the tiny changing room, filling the space.

He still had on the tuxedo pants and crisp white shirt that he'd tried on in another part of the store. The shirt was open at the neck, revealing a sprinkling of dark hair at the edge of his collar. She lifted her gaze from the hard lines of his chest to his face. His lips curled with a teasing smile that flattened when his eyes flicked down her body and back up again.

A quiet look passed between them and the world faded away for a moment. It was just him and just her. Like they used to be. When she'd still loved him unconditionally.

Loving him was not the problem, she thought as his gaze swept down her body encased in the horrid dress. It never had been. The sleeves of his shirt were rolled, exposing the corded muscles of his forearms. Veins stood out against his skin. She lifted her gaze to his face, his expression unreadable.

"What did you need the car keys for?" she asked softly.

"I needed to get the cell phone charger out of the car." His eyes darkened as he watched her.

She offered a faint smile, trying to ignore the heat that ached in her belly. "Tell them this dress is horrendous."

He glanced down, his nostrils flaring slightly as he studied her. Her blood warmed beneath his scrutiny and then he lifted his eyes to hers. He flicked his tongue over his bottom lip before scraping his teeth over it. Memories from loving him last night blossomed inside her, like a flower reaching toward the sunlight.

"It is pretty bad." His throat moved as he swallowed. He didn't smile.

"You look hungry." His expression was tense. "Maybe looking like a cupcake wasn't such a bad thing," she whispered.

"I can help you out of it if you want."

She suddenly became aware of the silence from the other side of the curtain. "I think I've seen this movie," she whispered, her voice sounding husky even to her own ears. "Is this the part where we have hot make-up sex in the changing room?"

"We haven't fought lately," he murmured, stepping as close as the dress would allow.

"No, not lately." She kept her voice low as she ran her finger along the cool fabric of his shirt. The collar was sharp against the tip of her finger, warmed by his skin. "You look nice."

She tipped her chin to study the man of her dreams. The man she'd loved since the ninth grade. And she felt like the luckiest woman alive.

He smiled warmly. "I'd say the same but..."

Laura laughed. She couldn't help it. "I know. I look like a red velvet cupcake."

It was all so achingly normal. He brushed a strand of hair from her eyes.

"What would you say if I admitted to thinking inappropriate thoughts right now?" he whispered, his breath hot on her ear.

"What kind of inappropriate?" It felt good, teasing him. This play of words dancing between them, twining their bodies together like velvet ropes.

He licked his bottom lip, drawing her gaze to his mouth. "The kind of inappropriate that involves you wearing a lot less than this dress."

She lifted her hand, her palm resting over the scars that covered his still beating heart.

Her mouth was dry, her blood heated. Arousal, that's what this was. Arousal caused not by her own hand but by the proximity of her husband.

"Hey, no getting naked in the bridal shop!" Carponti's voice was close to the curtain— too close.

"Go away, Carponti," Trent growled. He moved, shifting his body so that she'd be blocked from view if Carponti ripped back the curtain, which wasn't outside the realm of possibility.

Yards of fabric separated them, but he was so close that the heat from his body radiated off him and into her. She lifted her face to his.

"I'm kind of stuck in this dress," she admitted, lifting her gaze to meet his, the question laced with suggestion. "Can you get the rest of the zipper for me?"

He knew it for what it was. A simple, loaded request. A lesser man would have walked away, avoiding the torment of seeing his wife's naked back without being able to do anything about it. But after the other night, after feeling the pleasure of her body beneath his, he was like a dying man gasping for air. He couldn't turn away from her. Not now. Not ever. How had he ever run from this? From her?

From them?

But Trent was not a lesser man. Trent was hungry. Starving for his wife's body beneath his lips. He breathed in deeply, unable to speak as she turned, offering him the sensitive skin of her back.

He met her gaze in the full-length mirror. He wanted her now. His blood pounded in his ears as he lifted his hand to her shoulders, unable to resist the temptation of her bare skin. The ruffles of the dress kept him from stepping closer.

She lifted her arms, tucking her golden hair beneath her palms and raising them up, exposing the soft curve of her neck. The swell of her breasts was barely contained in the bodice.

Almost afraid to touch her, he finally traced the pad of his finger down her neck, down the centerline of her back.

She shivered visibly, arching beneath his touch. Her lips parted and the only sound he heard was the quiet gasp of her breath.

He shifted his erection away from the painful zipper of the tuxedo pants, then focused his erotic attention on the delicate curve of her spine beneath the black of her strapless bra. Slowly, so slowly, he met her gaze as he traced his thumb down her spine. Her mouth was beautiful, her lips parted and flushed. But her eyes, heavy with arousal, were what held him captive as he pushed the offending zipper lower, lower as he sought to free her from this monstrosity of a dress.

She moved to pull the dress off, but he cupped her upper arms to stop her. "Let me?" he whispered. He nuzzled her ear, her skin hot beneath his touch. "I can't get enough of touching you, Laura."

Touching her now, her response was a gasp, a silent huff of breath against his cheek as she turned her face to his, her mouth asking for his taste.

Slowly, he traced his fingers up her arms, and over her shoulders. They skimmed the swell of her breasts in that sexy strapless bra and the dress fell in a pool at their feet, forgotten.

He watched her reaction in the mirror. Watched as her eyes closed to the barest slits, and she arched her hips against his. While he was fully clothed behind her, she wore nothing but the strapless bra and panties. He loved how small she looked in his embrace, felt a thrill of power spike through him as she surrendered to his touch.

He could take her then. Right there in the dressing room. If he slipped his hand into her panties, he knew he would find her wet and supple and swollen, so ready for his touch. It would be fast and intense.

It would barely scratch the surface of what he wanted to do with her. He urged her back against him, felt the heat of her skin penetrate the clothing he wore. Felt the soft curve of her ass against his erection, the sweetest friction of softness and fabric. It was torture touching her, loving her and not feeling her body wrapped around his.

He skimmed his hands down her belly, skirting closer to the heat that drew him. He wanted so badly to touch her. To feel her arousal coat his fingers. He could watch her face contort as he stroked her, the risk of getting caught adding to the erotic thrill of having his nearly naked wife in his arms.

"God you're beautiful," he whispered against her ear. He cradled her hips, framing them in the mirror, loving the gentle swell of her belly and the curves that she'd always hated. But she was a woman, a woman who'd given him two beautiful children. Her body was no longer flawless but watching her skin flush beneath his touch, he knew he would never find greater perfection. Even if he went to the ends of the earth, his wife would still be the only woman who did it for him.

He traced the edge of her panties with his index finger, loving the thrill of pleasure that shivered over her skin.

This. This was what he'd missed. The beauty of his wife's arousal. The soft cries she made when she was coming apart in his arms. This was the memory he had carried with him into battle.

The fear came from out of nowhere, stealing up from a dark place in his soul, raw and primal, ripping through him like a beast. Promising the loss of the thing he loved more than anything else in the world.

He wrapped her tight in his arms, pulling her flush against him, burying his face in her throat. Inhaling her scent, the warmth from her skin. Feeling her body shudder in response as she wrapped her arms over his and simply stood. Letting him lean on her.

Letting him hold her. A simple embrace laced with unspoken things, twining them together.

15

———————

"So I was called in yesterday by the prosecution's team of lawyers," Shane said as he flipped through a book of candles and flowers. It was a strange sight to behold: big bald man with black tattoos threaded down both arms and yet, there he was, flipping through a book of pink and white and delicate.

Trent would have smiled if not for his comment. "And?"

"Well, she asked me about the paperwork and routine crap. Then things got a little interesting," Shane said. He looked up. "She asked me if I'd ever seen you lose your temper." Shane shrugged. "Said nothing came to mind."

Carponti smiled. "Yeah, it was funny how nothing came to mind when I was asked, either." He paused. "But why is that relevant at all, anyway? I mean, we all argue and fight. So what?"

Trent looked down at his hands. "I don't know. But Patrick has me seeing a counselor, working to build a clean bill of mental health for this case."

Shane swore quietly. "This isn't about you deploying too much. It can't be."

"Maybe it can be," Trent said. "Maybe they're going to paint me as stressed out, et cetera and use it to show my judgment was question-able. Makes it easier to believe I would forge paperwork to sell parts to buy off Iraqis and keep them from blowing us up, doesn't it?"

"Not really," Carponti said. "I mean, that's a pretty convoluted fucking theory. Why isn't it easier to believe that Randall just did some illegal shit for money?"

Trent smiled. "That's the point, actually. The simple answer to the problem is the easiest. This case they're trying to build against me is complex and difficult. Makes it harder." He looked at Shane. Trent shook his head as they headed out of the bridal shop and he wound his way back through the racks and hangers of a thousand different wedding dresses.

Jen had staunchly refused to show her wedding gown to the men in the room but that hadn't stopped Laura and Nicole from modeling dresses. After Laura's disastrous cupcake dress, they'd summoned all of the men over to look at what seemed to be dozens of other dresses, each worse than the last. All of them looked like they had been made by mad wolverines. On acid.

Carponti had declared that he loved his wife but if he had to sit through one more dress, he was going to kill himself, a comment that had earned him a slap on the back of the head from Shane and an elbow in the ribs from his wife. The physical abuse had done nothing to keep him from laughing, and he had still been cracking up as the three men started for the coffee shop next door. Trent had peeled off from the others not only because he needed his phone, but also because he wanted one last look at Laura.

He was eager to get his wife alone. The memory of her nearly naked, encased in his arms in the dressing room earlier, was driving him out of his mind as the afternoon had progressed with mind-numbingly painful slowness. All the things that had gone wrong between them no longer seemed important.

He walked back toward the fitting rooms, hoping to catch her before she tried on the next monstrosity.

"Jen, I think this might be the one," Laura called from behind the curtain.

He paused near the opening to the fitting rooms, unwilling to interrupt them. He held his breath as the curtain moved aside. Nicole stepped out first, followed closely by Laura.

He didn't even see Nicole.

In that moment, everything in his world centered on his wife, her body draped in shimmering silver that hugged her curves and made his palms ache to touch her. The gown pooled at her feet, a cascade of fabric that looked like it had been made just for her.

He shifted then, his skin feeling too tight. The movement caught Laura's eye and she met his gaze. He swallowed and lifted his hand to push his glasses back up.

She offered a hesitant smile, the barest turn of her lips.

Hope soared inside him again. Maybe, just maybe, they'd find their way through the darkness. Together.

"So are you going to spill or are we going to have to pry it out of you?" Nicole asked.

She handed the delicate silver dress to the clerk, who had just rung up Laura's purchase.

"Spill about what?" Laura asked.

"We'd have to be blind to miss the sparks between you and Trent," Jen said. Her wedding gown was already sealed in a black fabric zippered bag, protected from the elements and prying eyes. "You two are getting along."

Laura smiled, more to herself than to either of her friends. "Yeah."

She looked up to find Jen studying her. "This is a good thing, right?"

Laura lifted her shoulder. "It's not a bad thing, if that's what you mean."

"But?" Nicole prompted.

"But nothing." She paused. Her body tightened as she remembered the feel of his hands on her skin, his breath on her ear. "Things are good."

"That's really great, hon." Jen squeezed her hand. "Are you okay with everything?"

"Yeah. I am. I'm just...things haven't been this good in a long time." She bit her lips. "I'm afraid I'm going to wake up tomorrow and it's all going to be over."

Nicole accepted her receipt from the cashier and lifted the dress encased in a sleek black garment bag over the counter. "Look, I love you and I love your husband. You can't live like the rug is going to get yanked out from under you tomorrow."

"But it could," Laura said. "All of this could end tomorrow."

"Then you'll have had today. No one knows what tomorrow is going to bring," Nicole said. "But enjoy today while you have it. Hold on to these good memories because there will be plenty of dark times when you'll need them."

Laura smiled, lifting her own dress. "I know."

"It takes a strong person to do what you've done," Jen said. "Trent's a fool if he throws this away."

She walked outside, her thoughts drifting back to the feel of her husband's hands on her body. The feel of him inside her. The drape of his arm over her waist as they'd fallen into sleep.

She looked up as the men stepped out of the coffee shop. Her gaze landed on her husband's broad shoulders. His hands.

"Hey," she said as he approached.

"Hey." He slipped the dress from her hands and fell into step with her. Nicole and Carponti and Shane and Jen paired off and headed to their respective vehicles. "You're being awful quiet," he said.

She smiled over at him, unwilling or maybe unable to give voice to the needs swirling inside her. She didn't know how to ask him for what she wanted, what she needed.

"We've still got a couple of hours before we have to pick up the kids," she said. Her lips were dry. She traced her tongue over her bottom lip, entranced by his gaze dropping down to her mouth. "We should take the long way home."

"Are you okay?"

She offered him a smile. And let an idea take hold. "Yeah. I think I am."

LAURA WAS BEING QUIET. She hadn't said a thing since they had turned toward home. Every so often, he would catch her watching him.

"You looked beautiful today," he said after the silence grew too heavy.

"Hmmm." She shifted, a lithe tension running through her. He didn't dare hope that he was reading her body language right. There was no way she was getting ready to explore a dark erotic fantasy.

But that couldn't be. Right? His blood hummed as he watched her out of the corner of his eye. The subtle part of her thighs. The slight arch of her back. The barest parting of her lips.

Everything about her made his body ache with sexual awareness. He'd wanted this woman for so long and touching her earlier, watching his hands move over her body today, he ached. Wanted things fixed between them. Back to a normal that would have involved him pulling the car over and taking her fast and hard in the backseat.

"Is something wrong?" he finally asked.

Laura looked at him for a long moment, her golden eyes dark with promise.

Then she unbuckled her seatbelt as Trent attempted to hold on to the fragile remnants of his sanity, as all the blood rushed out of his brain to somewhere decidedly more primitive. He had to be dreaming. Had to be.

Trent stilled, his blood hammering through his veins at the sight of the heat in his wife's eyes. He swallowed, his lips curling into a faint smile as he tried to focus on watching the road. "What are you doing?" His voice was thick. Tense.

"Communicating?" Laura leaned close, pressing her lips to the edge of his jaw. Her thumb traced the line of the scar there, scorching the sensitive flesh.

"Ah..." There were no words for the force of the arousal that slammed into him at the brush of her lips against his skin.

She didn't kiss him. Her lips curled like a cat drinking fresh cream as she urged his free hand onto her thigh, then higher to where she was..."Holy shit."

He yanked the car into the wooded turnoff of an unsold plot of land. Away from the country road and anyone who might happen by.

He cleared his throat, his fingers sliding into naked, hot, wet heat. "When did you take your panties off?"

"Do you like it?"

He glanced at her, his mouth dry.

Before things had gone terribly wrong between them, they had always been passionate lovers, but this was new and exciting. The risk of getting caught thrummed through his veins, wrestling with his arousal, sharp and deep and primitive. He didn't know when she'd gotten the idea for this, but he wasn't about to argue. The way she was looking at him was driving him wild.

"Ah, yes. Yes, I do." His voice was rough.

"Then don't ask questions. Just touch me." She pushed her skirt higher up her thighs, giving him access to her intimate flesh. His hands fisted in the material and she shifted, opening for his touch. There was no hesitation as his fingers stroked her slick heat. She moaned deep in her throat, igniting a brilliant, liquid fire that coursed through his veins.

Trent savored the moment, simply touching his wife. Freely. With no restrictions. She made beautiful sounds as she writhed against his fingers, driving him slightly insane with the tiny movements of her hips. Her sweetness slipped over his fingers and he wanted so badly to be inside her. He drank in this intense rush, this violent passion here and now. He would not question the severity of her response or the force of his own arousal.

He reached across her, tipping her seat back as far as it would go. He leaned over, pressing his lips to her thigh, grateful that the design of the car didn't impede his access to her secret swollen flesh. He slipped his hand beneath her hips, urging her to lift, just a little.

And then she was there, her swollen sex exposed and open, glistening with arousal. He looked up to find her watching him, her eyes heavy-lidded, her lips parted. Her breath a quiet gasp as she waited for his touch.

He slipped his tongue over her and savored the sound of her ragged gasp. In the back of his mind, he wondered what would happen if they were caught. If a policeman happened by. The risk added a sinful urgency to his touch. He stroked his tongue over her sweet center until she arched her back, coating his fingers with slick wet heat. He slid a single finger inside her as he suckled her and she was lost, twisting and vibrating as the orgasm ripped through her and tore her to shreds.

Trent was lost in her pleasure. He could never feel better than now, at this moment. He could spend a lifetime feeling her coming beneath his fingers, his tongue. He had so much to atone for. She made sexy, mewling sounds deep in her throat as he slipped his fingers from her body, kissing her fiercely, needing her more than he'd ever needed her.

Laura gave everything she was to him in that kiss. She wanted her confidence with him back. Wanted to feel the power of his arousal under her touch.

She leaned over, sliding her hand down to stroke the hard ridge of his erection through his pants. Trent went absolutely still, his body tight. "Laura."

"Hmm. Shhh. Watch for cars?"

"Laura..." His voice held a plea.

"Not another word," she whispered, squeezing him gently.

He held his breath as her fingers found his zipper, freeing him from the confines of his pants. Watched her eyes darken as she stroked him, slowly, slowly, until his breath was nothing more than a harsh gasp and he had to fight the urge to close his eyes.

Trent could die a happy man. He glanced down to see his wife's beautiful fingers wrapped around him, bringing to life every fantasy he'd carried with him over the long dark nights he'd spent without her. When she leaned over close enough that her breath floated across his erection, his cock went impossibly hard.

"Laura—" He slid his hand through her hair, wanting what he dared not ask for.

Her fingers were soft and cool on his skin. She squeezed him, her breath flitting over the swollen head, a vicious tease. He was hard as stone, and it felt like every ounce of blood in his body throbbed in his cock. The blood pounding in his ears guaranteed he wouldn't hear a damn thing until it was too late.

"Hmmm. I dreamed about doing this," she murmured.

"Right now?" He could barely speak.

"Yeah." She rubbed her lips softly against the tip and he flinched at the gentle torment. "I've had a long time alone to dream things up."

Trent barked out a laugh, but the sound strangled in his throat when her soft mouth closed over the tip of him. She slowly slid her mouth down the hard length of his cock, caressing him like he'd dreamed about a thousand times before. He threw his head back and fought the urge to fist his fingers in her hair. Her hand stroked him while she used her mouth on him and damn him, he wasn't going to last. Pleasure built deep in his belly and he went infinitely still, praying he'd hold off.

And then he glanced down at his beautiful wife with her mouth on him and his entire world exploded.

16

———

Laura wasn't sure what she'd expected to happen when they got home, but a quick tumble in the bedroom had been high on her list of priorities.

Instead, they paid the babysitter, checked on the sleeping kids, and made sure the rodents hadn't escaped again. Then she went to the bathroom to get washed up. When she came back to the living room, he was sitting in a chair, his eyes glued to the TV screen as he rubbed the scar on his chest.

He didn't see her. He couldn't.

Trent was watching the news. Images of a battle that had been raging for three days north of Baghdad flashed through their living room. Explosions punctuated the silence of their home.

Sweat broke out on his forehead, and stress was visible in the rigid set of his jaw and the harsh dark line of his mouth. She stepped into his view, the movement catching his attention, breaking the spell. Trent's eyes focused on her face even as an acute sadness creased his lips.

He closed his eyes and forced himself to take a long inhale. He winced and she wondered if it physically hurt when he expanded his lungs. His jaw and his shoulders tensed, and his hand flexed as though he were cradling the barrel of his weapon.

Fear licked at her soul. He'd said it himself—he didn't really know why he felt compelled to leave home again and again. But he couldn't help it. And the next time he left, everything they'd rebuilt together would be destroyed.

She did not speak, did not dare to voice the unspoken question jammed in her throat. Instead, she walked over to the arm of the chair where he sat, and leaned down until she was spread across his lap. "Are you okay?" she whispered.

He clicked the television off. Silence wrapped around them once more.

It was a long moment before his arms came around her shoulders.

And when he spoke, he opened part of his soul to her.

"I was just remembering the feel of the fifty-cal machine gun when my gunner laid down covering fire."

"Would you deploy again?" she whispered, terrified of the answer.

Laura's fingers twined with his and she looked up just as he opened his eyes. The emotion she saw there was ragged and raw, the fear a relentless, writhing thing. "I don't know," he said.

His honesty hurt but she shut it down, needing more to talk to him, to hear what he was saying instead of only hearing what she wanted to.

"I used to think it was where I belonged," he said. He leaned forward, slipping his glasses off and setting them on the coffee table. "But I look at everything I've given up, everything I've lost..." He looked over at her, his eyes tortured. "It wasn't worth it. It wasn't worth nearly losing you, it wasn't worth missing all the time with the kids." He scrubbed his hand over his mouth. "I gave the Army everything I had and now I'm being court-martialed."

"Was that so hard?" she whispered, hating the hope that blossomed inside her, knowing that it could be crushed so easily. He had never shared with her before. Tonight? It was simply enough that he hadn't pushed her away.

He squeezed her hand, threading his fingers with hers. He couldn't meet her gaze. "You have no idea."

A lump blocked her throat, and it felt like a weight had lifted, just a little, from around her heart. His hands slid up her arms, stopping to stroke her neck. His palms were hot against her skin, his thumbs tender where he stroked beneath her ear.

"This isn't easy for me, Laura. Talking about it doesn't make it any better." His voice was harsh. Ragged. She wondered if there would ever come a time when he wouldn't get angry when he talked about the war.

"Avoiding it—avoiding your family—doesn't make it any better, either." She pressed a gentle kiss to his shoulder. "I can't help you if you're not here."

She met his gaze and the legion of dark emotions churning in his midnight black eyes. "Maybe I don't want to poison your life with the war."

"It's too late for that." Heat from his skin pulsed against her palm. "I'm not saying that to make you feel guilty," she added quickly. "I'm just saying that the war has been in our lives since the day you died. Not being here has only made it harder on all of us."

"For what it's worth, I'm sorry." He licked his bottom lip a moment before he swallowed.

"I know," she whispered.

A sliver of heat drifted through her blood as she remembered how much she loved him. Oh God, but she remembered. Being with him made her feel so good—like a flower reaching for the sunlight after a long, dark winter. The knowledge hit her again with increased certainty.

She still loved this man.

The war had done nothing to change that.

His kiss was hesitant as he touched his tongue to her lips, a feather light caress. A burst of pleasure rushed through her as he touched her.

His fingers threaded through her hair and angled her mouth to open for him. Desire seared through her veins like a fire banked too long and suddenly exposed to fuel. She felt his breath, warm and soft against her skin. She closed her eyes and felt the ragged vibration of his breathing as he lifted her easily, carrying her to their bedroom.

"I can't do this right now, Laura," he whispered as he nestled against her body. His chest moved against her back, his breathing slow and easy, belying the thick emotion in his voice.

Tears blocked her throat as she lay with him. His quiet words didn't surprise her but they still hurt.

He shifted her until she was beneath him, then he kissed her so fiercely that her body begged for his touch. Instead, he merely framed her face with his hands, his body rough against hers. "I want to." One thumb stroked at her temple. "But I can't do it right if I still hear the war in my head." He nuzzled her nose with his.

She smiled then because she couldn't stop herself. "Your noble notions of sacrifice were strangely missing in the car earlier."

He laughed and she felt it rumble deep in her belly before he lowered his forehead to hers. She cupped his face, needing to chase away the shadows she saw creeping back into his eyes. "It's okay." She waited until he met her gaze once more.

"Really?"

"No." She kissed him then, to show him what she could not say. She understood his racing thoughts. Understood that there were times when he couldn't turn the war off in his head. She wanted to push him onto his back and make him forget everything about Iraq.

Instead, she simply curled into his body, her soul at ease for the moment, content that they were together—that her husband was back in her bed.

~

"Incoming!"

Laura opened her eyes abruptly, her body shaking. The darkness around her echoed with the sounds of a scuffle.

Laura flicked on the bedside lamp, sending pale light casting into the darkness. Trent had tossed one arm over his head, his fists bunched around an invisible weapon. His brow was drawn into a tense frown, his features twisted with hate and violence.

Common sense held her back when instinct urged her to wrap her arms around him and pull him from the nightmare that hunted him. He shouted again and rolled to his side, his arms rising up like he was holding a weapon only he could see.

"Trent?" She jostled his shoulder gently. "Wake up. It's just a dream."

He didn't stop or stiffen. He showed no signs of hearing her. The nightmare pressed on and he grunted like he'd been shoved against a wall. She pushed harder against his shoulder, a clawing, writhing terror ripping at her heart.

She never saw him move.

She landed with a thud on the floor before she knew what had happened, and she had a brief moment to be grateful for the thick carpet. He'd pulled her down to the floor and covered her body with his. "Stay down."

His hands swept down her body in a decidedly nonsexual way. His voice was different. Raw. Ragged. Like he'd been shouting over the thunder of machine guns.

Laura shoved at his shoulder, all two hundred pounds of him crushing the air from her lungs. She fought the panic that he wasn't really there with her in their bedroom. He was somewhere far away, someplace she could not reach him. "Trent, wake up!"

He twitched and buried his face in her neck. "Story! Come on, buddy, don't do this."

Laura froze. Story was deployed. He wasn't dead.

"Goddamn it, Top, get up!"

His elbows were on either side of her head and the heat from his body pressed into hers. He scanned the darkness, searching for an enemy that only he could see. She felt trapped, pinned beneath a man who could not see her. She shoved desperately at his shoulder, the heel of her palm pushing against the scar over his heart. Fear danced down her spine, twisting in her belly. "Trent!"

He grunted and looked down at her. He wasn't seeing her. He wasn't there. His eyes were empty, unseeing. But it was the pain, the pain and the horror in his eyes that made her soul cry out. She had no idea what this man had gone through. All this time, she'd just wanted him home and he was facing things she'd never see and could never hope to understand.

How had she hoped he would share this with her?

He looked lost. And more than that. Afraid. Of things she could not see and would never understand. She panicked, tears streaking down her cheeks as she shoved and shoved and shoved. "Wake up. Trent, wake up!"

He jerked once, his breath sucking into his body with a massive gasp. He blinked, looking around, finally seeing her in the dim bedroom light.

"Jesus, Laura." He scrambled off her, pulling her upright. "Oh fuck, did I hurt you?"

She shook her head and rubbed the back of her neck and sat up. Her body protested the too fast movement after impacting the floor but otherwise, everything seemed okay. "No." She turned her face and looked into his dark eyes. "Are you okay?"

"I think I should probably ask you the same question." His eyes scanned her body, new panic warring with the old nightmares. "Are you sure you're not hurt?"

"I'm fine." She reached for him, threading her fingers with his. She rested their hands on her thigh. "You said Story's name," she said quietly, watching him.

He sat next to her, his back propped against the frame of the bed. She was amazed he didn't pull away. "It was just a bad dream. I have them all the time."

Disappointment clutched at her heart. No matter how many times she tried to walk through the darkness with him, it was one thing he never shared with her. He'd never let her stand with him against the abyss of the war—what he'd seen, what he'd lived through.

She had no idea the things he'd done, the friends he'd lost. She didn't know and God knew she wasn't strong enough to go through what he'd gone through. But she wanted to be there with him. Wanted to be there to help him when the darkness got too heavy.

Their thighs touched where they sat on the floor. Laura fidgeted with the drawstring on the waist of her pajama pants, trying to keep the tears from spilling down her cheeks. She was so tired of crying for him. Each moment that passed took with it the fragile hope that tonight would be different. That he would let her stand with him even when she couldn't know the pain he'd lived through. The silence spread between, a gulf that was more than physical. A gulf that shattered everything they'd done to try and rebuild the fragile trust between them.

Every so often, she'd catch bits of the conversations between him and the men who'd been there with him. A joke about a dud grenade. A comment about the heat or the night vision goggles freezing in the extreme cold. But he always clammed up and stopped talking when he realized she was listening.

Whatever hell he'd gone through, he'd kept it—and himself—from her. Whenever the war reared its ugly head, brutal silence always filled the room.

She sniffed and swiped at her cheeks, hoping he wouldn't notice. The disappointment lodged in her throat. She wondered if he would sleep on the couch tonight, further cementing the chasm that had reappeared between them. How long would it be before he was gone again, leaving her for the war he could never leave behind?

She bit her lips, refusing to cry again. She'd known better than to do this, to trust him with her heart one more time. She'd known better and she'd been a goddamned fool.

He was going to leave her again. He was going to walk out that front door with his duffle bag and his assault pack and head back to the war.

Leaving her alone, just like always.

He broke her. And she was a goddamned fool for letting him.

The silence stretched between them. Laura couldn't move beneath the weight of the devastation.

Then he shifted, the sound of cotton sliding against cotton in the dark. His arm slipped around her shoulders and urged her close, until her cheek was rested in the pocket of his shoulder. She tensed, not wanting the hollow gesture, but he refused to relent, forcing her to either walk away or relax against him. He pressed his cheek against her hair and they sat in silence, Laura's need to tend his unseen wounds unmet and unanswered.

He tensed a moment before he spoke, his whisper barely penetrating the silence. "I don't mean to shut you out." A ragged admission.

He shifted and she felt his lips press to her forehead. She slid her hand onto his lap, resting her palm against his thigh. The silence hung between them, thick and heavy and filled with hurt. And in the hushed darkness, she waited, unable to speak past the block in her throat.

When he spoke, his words shattered more than the silence.

"Story and I were leading a clearing mission. A buddy of mine was inside the village, searching these houses that were little more than mud huts." His chest rose as he took a deep breath.

Laura didn't dare move, afraid she would break the fragile moment into a hundred thousand pieces. She had no idea what this was costing him, could not imagine what he'd gone through.

"There were a few buildings with tunnels beneath them. Story took a couple guys into them after two fighters who'd attacked our patrol with an RPG."

She closed her eyes, imagining a building made of mud and dirt, a tunnel pulling all the light from the room. "The tunnel was narrow and cramped. I tried to get Story to listen to me but he was determined to get the fuckers."

He shifted, rubbing his eyes. His voice sounded far away, like the memory came from a place deep inside him. The ragged pain cut at her, tearing her heart to shreds. "I should have maintained our position when the fighting started." His breath shuddered through him. "I could hear Story screaming on the radio." A pause. "I gave the order to collapse in, to try to get to our boys."

His breath trembled when he blew it out. She shifted, resting her hand on the scar over his heart. He reached up, cupping her face. "I know it was just a fucking nightmare but Story died because of me."

A sob broke free before she could stop it. What had he lived through that he dreamed about his friends dying? "It was just a bad dream."

He didn't notice. His body was tense, restraining violence and motion. He was hurting. Goddamn it, he was hurting. She wanted to help but nothing she'd ever done had prepared her to deal with this ragged grief and blame and all the fucked-up memories from the war.

"But it wasn't. That was a real mission. Except it wasn't Story who died. My guys collapsed in instead of maintaining security. Two of our boys would probably still be alive if they'd been airlifted out in time. But we had to secure a hot landing zone for the MEDEVAC flight three clicks away."

She twisted until she sat facing him on the soft carpet of their bedroom floor. She cupped his face, waited for him to lift his gaze to hers. This was just one twisted memory, just one bad thing that had happened during the war that had driven him away from his home. To try to atone for sins, real and imagined, that he'd committed during war.

Her heart broke for him. But damn it, she was not going to sit there and cry while her husband's heart bled out. "Story isn't dead," she whispered. "And you didn't kill your men."

He tried to look away. "Trent." He met her gaze again. "You made a mistake. You can't fix it. Running away, leaving us, doesn't fix this." His cheeks were wet beneath her fingers. "It doesn't fix you."

"Story told me that once." He looked at her. "When I got the papers from you downrange. He sat with me that whole first night. Smoking a cigar while I tried to figure out how to unfuck our marriage." He paused, remembering that far off night. "Said that if I didn't get my sorry ass home to you, I was going to end up like him, bitter and alone."

He reached for her then, threading his hands in her hair and pulling her close, until her face was buried in his neck. She wrapped her arms tight around him and simply sat, breathing in the warm, real scent of her husband. For the first time since he'd left all those years ago, she'd been given a glimpse at the life he'd lived without her. The life he'd tried to protect her from.

There were no words she could speak that weren't empty platitudes, spoken by a wife who had not lived through the war and the chaos and the hell. Anything she said would only make it worse, expanding the differences between them.

She couldn't tell him she understood because it was infinitely different to comfort the grieving spouse of a fallen soldier than it was to hold one of your boys as he died.

Her heart ached and her soul bled for the man next to her. And she wished more than anything she had some way to take the hurt away.

He shifted then, a rustle of fabric against skin. She reached for him, finding his hand in the near darkness, and threaded her fingers with his.

It was the only thing she could think to do.

"Please don't leave me." He rested his cheek against the top of her head again, hugging her body against his. "I can't do this alone."

17

———

"You're very quiet today," Emily said. He could feel her gaze on him, studying him. He felt like she was waiting for him to go screaming from the room or to put on a tin foil hat and start rocking in the corner.

He released a hard breath. "I had a pretty bad nightmare last night." He swallowed. "It was a mix of one of my buddies dying and a real mission." He looked up at her. "How fucked up is it that I'm dreaming about my friends—who are not dead, by the way—dying at war?"

He shifted and pushed his glasses up onto the top of his head.

It was a long time before Emily spoke. "I think it's reasonable for you to expect more nightmares in the coming months," she said gently.

He looked over sharply. "I can't do that. I think I threw my wife out of bed because of incoming rounds last night."

"Was she hurt?"

He closed his eyes, hearing again Laura's quiet sniffle in the darkness. "Maybe not physically, but yeah, I hurt her."

"I'm sorry. Was she okay?"

"I think so." He remembered falling asleep with her in his arms. It was not a gentle sleep, not a restful one. But he'd woken with her body twined with his, her hand resting over the scars on his heart.

"Has anyone ever talked to you about your emotional rucksack?" Emily asked, interrupting his thoughts.

"No?"

"It means that we all have the capacity to deal with bad news. And when the first piece of bad news hits, we can stuff it down and keep going. But eventually, our bags get too heavy and there's no more room to stuff things down anymore." She looked at him, her expression filled with compassion. "And sometimes we keep stuffing anyway because we don't think we have time to deal with things. What happens to a bag you stuffed too full when you open the top?"

"The laundry pops out of the top."

"Trent, you've been stuffing things for so long, your body and your mind are probably in shock at the fact that you're starting to unpack things. The nightmare felt real because it was real, at least, part of it."

Trent looked at the young doctor. "What if I hurt my wife?" he asked. His voice was thick, filled with things he couldn't say. What if he hit her? Or threw her out of bed. Or hurt one of the kids? Thank God they didn't have any guns in the house.

He flinched from the nightmare thought that could too easily come true.

"I can't promise that you won't have more nightmares. But there are things you can do to avoid them. Avoiding certain foods at bedtime. Turning the TV off."

"That stuff really works?"

"We think it helps. Will it work completely? Probably not. But if you lessen the likelihood, as you continue to unpack and start to heal some of the hurt you've done to yourself, maybe you'll start to see them taper off." She scribbled a note in her file. "How are things with Laura? Any more troubles with the kids?"

Trent leaned back, uncrossing his legs. "Things are good, actually. Better than I thought they'd be in a couple short weeks."

Emily's smile lit up her face. "That's wonderful to hear. How's the medication working?"

"It's okay. I don't take it that often but knowing it's there helps, if that makes sense."

"It makes perfect sense," she said. "We've known for a long time that the placebo effect is a statistically significant result. Sometimes, just having the medication makes a difference."

He sat for a moment, listening to her as she described some new therapy she wanted him to try.

He'd come here because of the court-martial, because Patrick had told him to get a clean bill of health. "Can I ask you something?" he said abruptly.

"Sure."

"Have you already written the report for the court-martial?"

"Of course. I wrote that after your first visit."

Trent ran his tongue over his teeth. "So why am I still here?"

Emily's expression was carefully blank. "Why don't you tell me that?"

He was still there because he loved his family. Because this had helped to at least start him on the road to somewhere approaching normal. He smiled, realizing that if Patrick had planned this, it had worked out.

"Did Patrick put you up to keeping me in therapy?"

"No. But I did get a note from your old first sergeant, telling me that if I could help you be less crazy, he'd buy me a beer when he got home from Iraq." Emily shrugged. "I don't drink and I normally don't try to keep clients here under false pretenses. But Story told me about your kids and your wife and how much you love her. I figured if I could get a couple visits out of you, maybe I could make a difference." She crossed her legs. "I hope you're not upset?"

Trent's smile started slowly then spread beyond his mouth to the empty space in his heart that was not so empty anymore. "No. In fact, I think I owe my first sergeant that beer when he gets home."

"Yeah, you probably do. You have a lot of people in your life looking out for you. You need to take care of yourself so you can take care of them." She paused. "Will I see you next Thursday?"

He looked down at his hands. At the wedding band around his left ring finger. He never thought he'd be the guy that would go and let someone crawl around inside his head.

He looked up at her. "Yeah. You will."

~

Trent walked through the chapel, unable to concentrate on anything to do with Shane's wedding. His thoughts were distracted and raw, a hangover from the ragged memories that had risen up and tormented him. The war was doing it again. Demanding he leave, that he go back to doing what he was good at. Fighting.

But somehow, the war felt very far away. The whispers were there but their seductive promise of adrenaline and power were...diminished. His mind drifted from memory to memory, focusing on home, on ignoring the siren's call of the war. On his family that still loved him.

Emma giggling as he blew a raspberry on her tummy.

Ethan squealing with laughter as Trent dangled him upside down.

Laura's eyes filling with tears as she watched him walk from that crowded gym one more time.

Emotions twisted around inside him, filling the dead space. He wasn't afraid of feeling anymore. There was a time when being around the guys, around Shane and Carponti and Story, would have been the only slice of normal in his life. That being around the guys would have fit better than being around his family.

But the pieces were fitting back together now, better than they had before.

"You're thinking way too hard," Carponti said, leaning on the altar. "We're supposed to be plotting a way to get Mr. Cranky Pants to the church on time and you look like you just stepped in a pile of dog shit."

"Hamster shit, more likely," Trent mumbled.

Carponti laughed. "Yeah, well, you were the one who bought them. I'm still shocked Laura let the kids keep them."

Shane walked up and joined them. He'd been off looking for the chaplain's assistant. "Where did everyone go?"

"Bride's room."

"What are they doing in there, anyway?" Carponti asked, glancing down the hallway.

"Painting each other's toenails. How the hell should I know?" Trent asked.

"Quit bickering like an old married couple and help me. I still need to find the chaplain's assistant to confirm that everything's in order for the ceremony. The little shit's nowhere to be found."

Trent stuffed his hands in his pockets and raised both eyebrows. "Did you really just refer to a chaplain's assistant as a little shit?"

"Isn't that like a speed pass straight to hell?" Carponti said.

Shane shot them both a deadpan look. "I have met some really great chaplain's assistants over the years. This kid? Not even close to the same quality. My calibrated NCO Spidey senses tell me he's using drugs."

Trent sobered. "What makes you say that?"

"Just a hunch. You've been an officer for too long. You're not as finely in tune with the stupid shit our boys are still doing."

"I'll go see if he's in the back office." Carponti wandered off, leaving Trent and Shane alone in the chapel. The silence of the worship center was sterile. Clean. It felt light, somehow untouched by the darkness of the people who walked through it.

"You doing okay?" Shane asked after a moment.

"Yeah. Actually, I am." Last night had been hard, so goddamned hard. But this morning, Laura had lain in bed with him for a few minutes between waking up and having to get the kids going for school and he'd felt something strange—a sense of peace.

It was something he'd never thought he'd ever feel again.

"Do you worry about screwing things up with Jen?" Trent asked.

Shane shifted and folded his arms over his chest. He cleared his throat. "It took me a long time to realize I was a large part of the reason why my first marriage failed. And I am determined not to repeat those same mistakes with Jen."

"Are you going to deploy again?"

Shane sighed. "Probably. I've only got a few more years to go before I can retire. I'll stay in, do this last rotation, then go try to find a desk job somewhere."

"You? At a desk?" Trent shook his head.

"You need to do the same damn thing," Shane said.

"I'm working on it," Trent said. "I honestly didn't think I had a second chance."

"Laura loves you. She's always loved you. You were just too stupid to see that she was right here, waiting for you to get your head out of your ass and come home to her."

Regret twisted against Trent's heart. He'd given up so much, chasing an elusive master that would never let him go. The Army didn't need his sacrifice. It didn't need his blood.

He was one of the lucky ones. He had a beautiful family, a family he'd avoided because he couldn't confront the magnitude of changes the war had wrought in him.

It was time to face the life he had.

Something warm swelled and burst inside him, shocking him with the overwhelming simplicity of being...home. He rounded the corner to find Laura reading a pamphlet. She smiled as he approached.

"Where are the kids?" Trent asked her.

She motioned over her shoulder, then slipped the pamphlet back into its slot. "Ethan took Emma to the bathroom."

"You let them go alone?"

She smiled. Obviously, he hadn't hidden the shock in his voice very well. "Yes. It's good for him to learn to watch over his little sister."

"That means that either she's going in the men's room or he's going in the women's room." Trent sounded horrified and Laura couldn't suppress her smile.

"He's six. He's fine in the women's restroom for a little while longer." She shrugged, a smile teasing her lips. "Besides, it's Thursday afternoon during family time. No one is here right now anyway."

"Oh."

Shane stalked around the corner, fury radiating off him in palpable waves. "We don't have a church."

Just like that, everyone appeared in the little hallway.

"What do you mean, we don't have a church?" Jen said. "What happened?"

"The little shithead stoner chaplain's assistant didn't schedule it," Shane snapped. "The chaplain's free to marry us, but some officers' wives' club meeting is going to be here in the chapel that day."

Carponti scowled. "They should just move the meeting. Why do they get priority?"

"Because it's the post commander's wife's pet project," Shane said. He sighed heavily, covering Jen's hand with his. "We'll figure something out," he said softly.

"Why don't you just get married at your place?" Trent asked. "You've got enough space
   for it."

"Sure," Shane snorted. "We can get married on the back porch."

"We could build a gazebo. Or one of those pergola thingies that have the slating over the top?" This from Carponti, who suddenly looked serious. As if a light bulb had been turned on inside her head, Nicole instantly whipped out her smartphone and started typing.

"We could set it up this weekend. There's an unfinished furniture place in Temple. We could check there," Laura said, brightening at the idea. "And I could get some sheer drapes. It would be beautiful."

Jen didn't look convinced. "That's a lot of work to get done in a weekend," she said. "We could just go to the Justice of the Peace." She lifted her chin, looking up at Shane. "I don't really care where we get married."

"It matters." Shane cupped her cheek and stroked his thumb over it before he looked over at them. "Let's do this."

"I think building the pergola is a perfect idea," Trent said, after they had shut the door.

"I've already found one," Nicole said, holding up her smartphone. "We can pick up the materials today and start building."

"We'll need gravel to level the ground out," Laura said.

Trent looked over at her. "How do you know all this?"

She smiled up at him. "I've kept myself amused with home improvement projects while you've been gone," she said. "How much money are we talking about?"

"We're looking at about $500." Nicole held the phone out so Laura could see. "Trent, we'll need your truck."

"Done. We can go pick up the material now if they like the looks of it." He glanced at Laura.

"We'll need to feed the kids on the way, but yeah." Laura grinned. "This is awesome."

Carponti looked down at his prosthetic. "I wonder if they make a hammer attachment for the Nub."

Laura choked back a laugh as Trent groaned and shook his head. The kids came running toward them from down the hall, and Emma collided with Laura's leg.

"Hey, kiddos, we need to take a little trip."

"Aww! Mommy, I wanted to go to the lake today," Ethan said, stomping his foot. Laura narrowed her eyes, wondering if it was possible for her son to have PMS. Most of the time he was such a great kid. But sometimes? She wanted to volunteer for a deployment.

Trent knelt down to Ethan's level. "We've got to do something really important for Shane's wedding. I'm going to need your help, though, okay? Because I'm out of practice with building stuff."

"Mommy's really good at building stuff," Emma said.

Ethan's eyes went wide. "What are we building?"

"A place for Shane and Jen to get married," Trent said.

"Do I get to nail anything with my hammer?" Ethan asked.

"Can I help, too?" Emma asked.

He glanced up at Laura, unsure about what the age limits were for hammers. She stood there, watching him, her hand over her mouth, her eyes shimmering. He held his breath thinking he'd gone too far, that he'd undermined her somehow. But then she nodded, a hesitant smile on her lips. He was sure she already had a plan to keep them entertained while the adults worked.

"Sure you can. But you've got to be really careful with the hammers and stuff. We've got to head out now to get the supplies we need. Can you and your sister be good for us?"

Ethan nodded solemnly. "Sure, Daddy."

"Promise, Daddy," Emma said.

Laura watched the interchange between her son and her husband. It was such a simple exchange, yet so significant. He'd come so far. She knew there were still long days and nights ahead of them, but watching him with their kids, watching him smile and feel at ease, she knew they had a chance. A small chance, one that could easily be destroyed by a careless gesture or thoughtless word, but a chance nonetheless.

The little things were what mattered most to two people building a life together. Not the big grand gestures. It was Shane telling Jen he wanted their wedding day to be perfect—not because Jen demanded it but because he wanted it to be special for her.

It was Nicole, staying strong while her husband recovered from his injuries.

It was Trent, kneeling in front of their son and daughter and talking them into helping him build something for their friends.

In that moment, she looked at her husband and her son and her daughter and her heart was open and vulnerable. Her soul was stripped bare.

There was no protecting her heart from her love for this man. He could very well leave her again but at that moment, she loved him with everything she had.

18

———————

Laura wasn't planning on staying at work long today. The entire unit was back from NTC and Laura had planned on taking a day off to finish some of the prep work for the building project this weekend. She was trying to get a few e-mails sent that absolutely had to be sent and then she was going to make herself scarce, because the longer she stayed at the office, the more she risked getting pulled into something she didn't have the time to deal with today.

So of course, Patrick knocked on her door right as she was finishing her last e-mail. Because karma hated her.

"You have a sec?" he asked.

She hadn't honestly expected to be left alone to actually get some work done. "Sure, what's up?"

"So this is going to sound like a really jacked-up request but do you have LT Randall's wife's address?"

Laura rocked back in her chair, folding her arms over her chest. "Seriously?"

"Yes, seriously. The company doesn't have her address and her husband isn't answering his phone and we need to find her."

"Why isn't she at work?"

"That's what we need to find out. Apparently, she's been unaccounted for for three

days."

Laura leaned forward. "Are you kidding me?"

"No." Patrick leaned on her door. "So can you help me out?"

"Sure. Give me a sec." It actually took her less than a minute to pull the soldier's address. "Now what?"

"Now I'm going to her house." There was bitterness in Patrick's voice.

"I'm not exactly sure that's a good idea," Laura said. "Why are you going? And don't we usually go in pairs to soldiers' houses?"

"I'm going because most of the unit isn't here today because of the training holiday. It's a long drawn-out story that starts with Colonel Richter telling me to get my ass out there and get her here no matter what before close of business today." He paused. "So are you volunteering? I mean, I know she's a soldier and all but technically, she is a spouse."

Laura sighed and resigned herself to not getting out of there early because Patrick was right. It was part of her job description to do home visits. They were by far her least favorite part of the job because you never knew what you'd find. "Sure," she said and grabbed her purse, along with a log form, so that she could keep detailed notes of everything that happened today.

Adorno lived less than a mile away but a few minutes later, when she opened the door, Laura was reminded of exactly why she hated home visits.

Randall's wife was a walking disaster. Her eyes were red and swollen. Her hair hadn't been washed in at least three days and Laura could see what looked like two boxes of half-eaten pizza on the kitchen counter behind her. There was evidence of a crime against Ben & Jerry's on the kitchen table behind her. "What?" Adorno said.

Patrick released a deep breath. "I need you to get dressed. The brigade commander wants to see you."

"I'm on quarters." She thrust a piece of paper at him. Laura frowned as Patrick's face flushed deep scarlet as he read the sick call slip. Laura looked at him and waited for an explanation. What the hell was on that slip to make him blush?

He handed it to her and Laura read it once, then again, then looked back at the soldier, a deep sympathy twisting beneath her heart. She should hate the girl but what was on that slip was enough to make her feel nothing but compassion for the young woman.

Her husband had given her an STD. It didn't get much worse than that.

"The brigade commander wants to see you," Patrick said again. "This isn't really optional."

Her bottom lip quivered. "But what about...?" She motioned to the paper in Laura's

hand.

"The colonel will clear it up with the docs, I'm sure."

Laura looked at the young woman. "For what it's worth, I'm sorry."

Adorno's eyes flashed angrily. "Thank you but don't be sorry for me. I want to cut my cheating, lying husband's balls off. I'll be much better then."

Beside her, Patrick cleared his throat. "Yes, well, please don't do any of that around me. I'd rather not be involved in any assault cases."

Adorno laughed but it was a harsh, strangled sound. "Can I meet you at brigade?"

Patrick shook his head. "Sorry. You need to ride with myself and Mrs. Davila. No one has seen you for three days."

Her lip quivered again. "My asshole husband won't be there, will he?"

"Not that I'm aware of," Patrick said.

Adorno sighed and it reminded Laura of one of Ethan's sulks. She almost smiled but figured the young soldier wouldn't do well with that. She'd think Laura was laughing at her when she was doing no such thing.

Adorno stepped back and invited them into the house. "Fine," she said. "I have to take a shower."

As she retreated to her bedroom, Patrick and Laura stood in the foyer. Laura briefly noticed that there was no cat and no kittens, either. Looked like she'd been lying about the cat the other day at the office. Nice.

Neither of them was willing to cross any farther into the house. It wasn't dirty. It was messy and had clearly not been cleaned in a few days. But Laura wasn't in any place to judge.

There was a crash from the bedroom and Laura and Patrick rushed back.

Adorno knelt on the floor, her small body wracked by great, heaving sobs as she tried to pick up ragged pieces of broken glass.

"Here, stop. You're going to cut yourself." Laura eased her away from the glass but she was practically incoherent.

"I...can't...believe...he cheated on me."

Laura had seen far too many young wives devastated by one of the ugly truths of the Army life: men often strayed. It could be because of the war, the strain or simply too much distance between them and their spouse.

Adorno had learned this lesson early in life. Still, it came with a price tag because her husband's cheating had come with an STD. One that could be cured, but still. It sucked, and no matter how much Laura had hated this soldier at one time, she felt nothing but sympathy for her right then.

"Want me to call Trent and tell him you'll be late?" Patrick said, picking up the last of the broken glass.

Laura glanced at her watch. She was supposed to meet everyone in half an hour. There was no way she'd make it. "Yes, please."

Adorno looked at her like she'd grown three heads. "Trent? Trent Davila is your husband?"

Laura leaned back. "You didn't put that together with my name and his being the same?" she asked.

Adorno shook her head slowly. "Oh, ma'am, you must hate me." Her voice was the barest whisper.

Laura said nothing. What could she possibly say that wasn't a lie? She did hate this soldier at one point. Maybe not at that exact moment, but there was bitter resentment toward a soldier who would lie to save her own skin and ruin her husband's life.

"You do hate me," Adorno said when Laura didn't respond.

"I think you've made some poor choices," Laura said finally, seeking the only pragmatic thing she could say.

Adorno's eyes filled once more and she covered her face with her hands. "I hate him," she whispered. "He ruined my life." She swiped angrily at her cheeks. "I believed him when he said he was working late." She looked at Laura. "I feel so stupid."

"We all make stupid choices when it comes to love," Laura said. "Did you ever love

him?"

"I thought I did," she said sadly. "Now? Now I'm not sure." She paused. "I am so sorry for what he's done to Captain Davila."

Laura swallowed the lump in her throat. "It's not just what he did to my husband," she said gently. "What he's done has affected our entire family." She could have said what *you've* done, but she didn't. If anything, this young woman needed her support right now. She'd been married, involved in a big news Army scandal, cheated on and now, it looked like, left. Laura didn't need to add anything else to the baggage this young woman was going to carry around with her. But she looked at the young soldier quizzically. "How did you not put two and two together and not know he was my husband? I've been to the FRG meetings."

Adorno flushed. "Davila is a really common name. And I thought you were just there because it was your job," she said. Her cheeks flamed red. "I ruined your life and you're still being kind to me. You knew all along who I was?"

Laura nodded.

"How could you be nice to me?"

"Well, I did want to choke you when you demanded I call the brigade commander over kittens." Adorno flushed and covered her mouth with her hand and Laura wasn't sure if she was smothering a laugh or a sob. "But we were all young once. We all did stupid things in the name of love." She waved one hand. "I generally try to limit my stupid things to ruining my own life and not other people's, but you get the idea."

"How can you sit here and make jokes? Why don't you hate me?" Such a tragic insecurity in her voice.

"Part of me did for a little while." Laura sighed gently. "You've made some mistakes but you can't change those. All you can do is try to learn from them."

Adorno nodded, her eyes filling again. "Thanks for sitting with me," she said.

"You're welcome," Laura said. "Now, we really need to get going. The brigade commander is waiting on you and last I checked, soldiers didn't keep colonels waiting."

"What's he want to talk to me about?"

"Probably what's going on with your husband."

Anger clouded Adorno's eyes once more as she pushed to her feet. Her smile was bitter cold. "Oh, I can't wait."

"Pass me the level?" Trent said from up on the ladder.

Laura handed it up, still bracing the pole in case it needed more adjustments. "Is it good?"

Trent paused, watching as the bubble sought equilibrium in the liquid. After a moment, it settled exactly where it needed to be. "Perfect."

He handed her the level and climbed down, tugging off his gloves. He surveyed the construction site. "Not bad for six hours of work," he said, stuffing the gloves in his back pocket.

Laura grabbed a broom and swept over the fine sand coating the paving stones. He watched her work, awed by her abilities with a hammer for most of the afternoon.

"So the plan is to meet up at first light tomorrow?" Carponti asked.

One side of Jen's porch was now covered with a stack of lumber, and just below the porch four poles were curing in quick-drying concrete. A ten-by-ten space was covered with paving stones, interlocked and held into place by special sand.

"I'll have breakfast and coffee ready to go," Jen said, still looking shocked that they had managed to get the foundation set and the poles in the ground before complete darkness had fallen.

Shane grinned and wrapped one arm around her shoulders. "Stop looking so surprised. This is what we do."

"You guys kick in doors, last time I checked," Laura said. "Masonry and basic carpentry aren't part of that duty description."

Trent glanced over at Ethan, who was busy still pounding away on a plank with a toy hammer. Emma looked far too serious with her little blue plastic saw. Her hair was sticking out over her head in a fuzzy black halo.

"The kids are going to sleep well tonight," Laura said, stepping closer to him as Nicole and Carponti finished stacking the tools on the back porch.

"They will?" He looked down at his wife in the waning daylight. Her face was covered in dust, her skin damp with sweat.

"Oh, they're going to be little monsters right before bedtime, but once they're in bed, they'll be out cold. They might even sleep in tomorrow morning."

"I doubt that."

Laura laughed and the sound did something to his insides. "Yeah, me too."

"They had fun today."

Laura lifted one shoulder and tucked her hands into her pockets. The motion stretched the old blue t-shirt over her breasts. Sweat ringed the collar of her shirt.

She looked beautiful. Sweaty and sexy all rolled into one.

"I liked working with you today," she said softly. "I miss how well we work together on stuff."

He swallowed and shifted, angling his body toward her. "Yeah, we've always done stuff like this well."

She did not pull away or increase the space between them. Her gaze slipped down his body, to the dusty t-shirt that clung to his chest.

He reached for her then, brushing a spot of dust from her cheek. "I think we need to get the kids home," he murmured.

"Yeah." Her tongue flicked out, wetting her bottom lip. The light from the back porch glistened on the moisture.

There was commotion and activity all around them but it felt like a blanket of silence shielded them from the rest of the world. Her scent wrapped around him, sending arousal swelling through his veins.

He gave in to the temptation and leaned closer, intent on brushing his lips against hers.

Time hung suspended as their lips touched, a hesitant kiss. The sweetest pleasure gasped from her mouth, filling a void in his heart.

His hand threaded in her hair almost before he knew what he was doing and he shifted until her chest bumped against his. Her lips parted beneath his and the kiss abruptly turned sensual.

Her tongue slipped between his lips and gently touched his. His wife was kissing him. This was the taste of love he'd been missing. The simplest, most potent pleasure.

He drank from her like he was a dying man. Her arms slid around his back, her nails digging into his flesh through the thin fabric of his shirt. Her body was soft and supple beneath his and he wished with all his heart that they were alone.

"You two should get a room!" Of course, it was Carponti.

Trent broke the kiss but he refused to act like it was something he should be ashamed of. He stroked his thumb over Laura's bottom lip. No words passed between them.

There was nothing that needed to be said that hadn't already been acknowledged in the wicked heat of that single kiss.

~

"I CANNOT BELIEVE Emma spent a whole hour screaming," Trent said, closing the bathroom door behind him and clicking the lock into place.

Laura sighed and stripped off her dirty pants, intensely aware that her husband was in the small bathroom with her.

"I can. I expected worse from both of them," she said, reaching into the shower to turn it to full blast.

"Worse than that?"

"Oh, when they go supernova, it's a nightmare." She turned her back to him, unfastening her bra beneath her t-shirt.

"How do you cope with that?" Trent dragged his sweat-stained shirt over his head and Laura took in the lean strength of his chest as he leaned down to take off his socks. Another moment and he stood in their bathroom wearing nothing but dirty jeans and a smile.

Laura's insides melted a little as her gaze dropped to the trail of dark hair that disappeared beneath the waistband of his jeans.

She turned away, testing the water temperature and wondering if he was going to follow her into the shower.

"On the really bad days, I sometimes sneak a glass of wine after they go to bed."

He slipped his glasses off and set them on the counter. His dog tags bounced against his ribs.

It was far too tempting to pretend that everything in their lives was normal. Instead, she reached inside the shower and tested the temperature again. "It's been a long day," she murmured.

He didn't say anything as she ducked into the walk-in closet to strip off her clothing. When she was undressed, she quickly stepped into the shower, closing her eyes as the steaming water sluiced over her head—the pressure of it pounding at the tension in her shoulders. She'd always enjoyed home improvement projects, but that didn't mean her body didn't protest at the end of a long day.

"Ah, Laura? What the hell is this?"

She wiped the water from her face and stuck her head out from behind the shower curtain.

And wanted to die of embarrassment.

Trent stood in the middle of their bathroom, holding a red plastic penis in one hand. He flicked a switch and a low buzzing filled the whole room, audible even over the sound of the shower. Laura cleared her throat, positive her face was redder than the vibrator Trent was holding.

"Well, ah." She blew out a breath, searching for some words to explain. Heat crawled across her cheeks that had nothing to do with the hot water. "You've been gone a lot."

His eyes widened dramatically. "Yes, but it still hurts to meet my replacement in person. What's this model called, the Drill Sergeant?"

She stifled a horrified laugh. She couldn't help it. "Would you please turn that thing off and put it away?" She pulled the shower curtain shut again, praying that the next time she stuck her head out, the offending vibrator would be back in its box where it belonged. Damn it, she should have hidden it better. But the top shelf of the closet was the perfect place to keep the kids from finding it. Her husband?

Apparently not.

She turned off the shower and wrapped her body in a fluffy towel. Her husband was no longer standing in the middle of the bathroom but his silence made her suspicious. She was afraid to go looking for him because he might have more embarrassing questions about her, ah, deployment boyfriend.

She shook her head and reached for her toothbrush just as he emerged from the closet. She glanced down and choked. He'd stuffed the vibrator between the buttons of his jeans. The plastic penis hung out of his pants, and she burst out laughing. "That's not funny! Put it away!"

"Hey, baby, why don't we..."

"Trent! Give me that!"

She couldn't remember the last time they'd laughed like this but damn it felt good. She whirled and lunged for it, not missing the fact that she was reaching for his groin and had her vibrator not been there, she might have gotten a handful of something else. She pulled the vibrator from his pants and stuffed it behind her back as he made a grab for it.

Her breath caught in her throat as her awareness of this man struck her, reminding her of how much she'd once loved him.

She still did.

He bunched his fists at his sides like he was fighting the urge to reach out to her. Then suddenly, he moved, skimming his fingertips across her forehead, brushing her hair behind her ears. Her breath caught in her lungs as she dropped the vibrator in the sink behind her. Trent took advantage of her position and backed her up against the counter. They breathed in quiet gasps, the only sound over the rapid-fire beating of her heart. His fingers splayed across her hips and she shifted beneath him, spreading her thighs to hook them around his hips. But he held himself back, sliding his palm up her thigh and cupping her slick heat.

"It's a shame," he murmured.

She stilled. "What is?"

His thumb slid over her exposed hipbone—a light, teasing caress. "That you never sent me another video."

"Video of what?" Her breath hitched as he leaned in, nibbling on the edge of her jaw. His fingers danced over her belly, sliding closer to where she was wet and aching for him.

Her fingers clenched on his shoulders, spasming as he traced her collarbone with the tip of his tongue. His breath was hot on her skin, cooling the moisture from her shower.

He nuzzled her ear while he slid the tip on one finger over the seam of her slick heat. "Another one of you touching yourself," he whispered.

In some dim part of her brain not lost to the intense pleasure of his touch, she recognized that she was completely naked beneath her towel while he was still wearing his jeans. "You're wearing too many clothes," she murmured, nipping at his earlobe.

He tensed as she dragged her hands down the crisp dark hair of his chest and reached for his pants. Her fingers trembled over the zipper momentarily before she quickly pulled it down and tugged his boxers and his jeans to the floor, freeing his erection.

He turned her so that she was facing the mirror. Then he stood behind her, his lean, strong body molded against hers as his hands drifted down her sides and over the towel that was the last barrier between them. She dropped her head back against his shoulder, closing her eyes as intense sensations overwhelmed her. He scraped his teeth over her neck, then something cool and soft dragged up her thigh.

She glanced down to see him sliding her vibrator against her skin, tracing it beneath the edge of her towel. She held her breath even as her face flushed.

He nipped at her ear, his breath warm against her damp skin. "So how often did you, ah, use this?"

She gasped as he traced it over her damp skin. "Why? Jealous?"

He tugged at her earlobe with his teeth. "You have no idea."

"Trent—"

He slid one hand up her throat, turning her mouth until he claimed her lips. The tip of the vibrator teased the edge of her intimate flesh. The idea of him doing this to her...

She didn't want it. Not right now. At this moment, she wanted her husband's hands on her body, her husband's flesh filling her. Tonight, she wanted this man—the only one she had ever dreamed of.

She turned in his arms, tugged the vibrator out of his hand and dropped it back into the sink.

Then she dragged her fingers through his hair and pulled him closer to her. He tugged her towel out of the way and leaned against her body until the counter dug into her lower back, a delicious swipe of pain mixing with the thrill of his hands on her.

Slowly, slowly, he pushed his hands over her thighs, urging her to part for him. She arched and tried to shift, but he stopped her, holding her between his strong hands, his eyes darkening as he leaned back and simply took her in.

Her arms were braced against the counter, her breasts heavy and full. Her back arched, her intimate flesh exposed. She was more than beautiful.

She was the center of his world. She balanced him, kept him grounded. And he'd been running from the one person he needed more than anyone else.

He kissed her lips, her collarbone, the gentle swell of her breast. He kissed a trail down her neck, moving ever lower until he reached the apex of her thighs, giving a gentle press of his lips to the warm, wet sanctuary he craved.

He sank to his knees in front of her and nuzzled the inside of her thigh. Her sex was the deepest swollen pink, liquid glistening on her skin, her soft curls. Arousal shot, hard and fast, through his blood at the scent of her, warm and musky and inviting.

He kissed her then, gently, tracing his lips and tongue down her soft skin, licking at the moisture that still dripped over her flesh from her shower.

Her gasp was the sweetest pleasure. And then he parted her with his tongue and her response was beautiful and it shoved aside the darkness in his soul. She arched gently beneath his mouth, her hips hesitantly rocking as he slid his tongue through her soft sex.

When he suckled her, she cried out, his name on her lips, her hips jerking from his grip. Trent went absolutely still except for the movement of his mouth over her body as he savored the taste and feel of her beneath his tongue. He angled his head until she opened completely for him, surrendering in body as well as spirit. She was here. She was his. And by God, he was going to remind her of everything good between them.

Laura didn't dare open her eyes. She knew what she would see. Her husband's mouth where only her own fingers had been for so long. His tongue traced over her swollen sex and an urgency built inside of her. Finally, she looked down at him.

The sight of his mouth on her was more powerful than she could have imagined. His hands spanned her hips, holding her in place on the edge of the counter. One of her calves was draped over one of his strong, wide shoulders. And his mouth moved, sliding through her heat and drawing out her pleasure.

She threaded a hand through his hair.

He looked up, their eyes meeting as he pressed his lips again to her most swollen heat. His gaze locked on hers, he traced his tongue over the swollen core of her body. A hot, possessive pleasure swept over her as he slipped one finger inside her, teasing her with the lightest friction while his tongue drove her wild. She fisted her hand in his hair, rocking against his mouth, her release there, just there. She closed her eyes, dropping her head back, and let the pleasure come, hard and fast through everything that she was until she thought she'd come apart in his arms.

Pleasure still shuddered through him when he carried her to the bed. His skin was slick with sweat. He laid her down on the bed, needing just to feel her with him, but she smiled and urged him onto his back.

Everything felt right and good and *real* between them. As though their separation had been nothing more than a nightmare, still lingering, still trying to crawl into the bed with them.

Feeling mischievous, she crawled into his lap. Bracing her hands against him, he smiled up at her in the dim light, his eyes dark and serious in the shadows. She arched against him, the apex of her heat brushing against the hair on his thighs. The sharp scrape of pleasure at her core made her body melt with new arousal.

He made a sound deep in his throat and it rumbled through his chest. His palms skimmed her thighs, coming to rest on her hips. They were twined together, already naked. A slight shift of her hips and he would be inside her warm, slick heat.

He tried to lift her hips but she arched away from him. He scowled. "Games, Laura?"

"Now it's my turn."

His throat moved as he swallowed, his body tense and oh so ready. "So what do I have to do?"

Her laugh was husky and sensual. Throaty and filled with feminine power. He'd always loved that about his wife. He loved how they'd grown together, learning to pleasure each other's bodies. He could still remember the first time they'd made love. It was a hot, sultry night. He'd brought sleeping bags for the back of his truck. Somehow, he'd made her come that night and he'd gotten hooked on watching her. He loved seeing her lips part, her breath come in quick, harsh gasps.

He'd loved watching her come earlier. She'd been spread open and gorgeous and when her orgasm had spilled across his lips, his fingers, he'd damn near exploded without a single touch to his cock.

Now? Now she rose naked above his body and Trent was lost in a sea of memories that mixed potently with the reality of her touch.

Her hips filled his palms but he didn't try to guide her to his cock. He wanted to let her take the lead.

They'd played this game before. So many times. He loved letting her have her way with him. There was something so beautiful in the way her body rose over his, the way her sweet sex slid down onto his erection.

This was everything that was right between them. Everything that had not been twisted and ruined by the war. She dipped her hips lower and he held his breath in anticipation. Waiting for that first caress of her sex against his cock.

There. Smooth, warm silk spread over his erection, embracing him gently as she slid against his length, not yet taking him in. Her lips parted, her eyes closed. Her gasp was pure pleasure.

She was still his. Her heart knew it. Her body knew it.

She shifted again, slipping her slick, wet heat against his erection, caressing him, teasing him. His eyes shot open the moment she nudged him closer, until his cock was poised at the opening of her sex.

He clung desperately to the ability to think as she twisted her hips on the tip of his cock.

His breath lodged in his throat as she slid the barest fraction of a movement, sucking the tip inside her, teasing him with the warmest, wettest heat. He clenched his fingers into her hips and her answering gasp rocked his world.

Another movement and she slid slowly, fully onto him, taking everything deep, deep inside her.

This was more than just sex. This was more than arousal or a quick screw.

This was coming home. This was coming back to the place where he belonged. His wife's loving embrace. His wife's beautiful pleasure as she lifted her hips from his before sliding down his length once more.

He let her control the pace. Let her take her own pleasure from him. Because watching desire paint her features and slick over her skin was its own reward. Her nails dug into his chest as she rode him, her gasps coming quick and fast and matching her pace.

He gripped her hips as she rocked against him, drawing out the sweetest pleasure, the harshest pain. He opened his mouth to speak but no words could break past the powerful lump lodged in his throat.

He rode the wave of loving her as long as he could, until she trembled and exploded and vibrated in his arms once more.

He rolled them over, lifting her legs around his hips and sinking so, so deep inside her. Her hair spread out on the pillow, framing her in a soft, golden halo. Her body vibrated beneath his, the wave of her orgasm riding over his cock as he surrendered to the darkest need and drove home.

Afterward, he rested his forehead against hers and the damp sting of tears coated his cheek. He would never know if they'd been his or hers.

19

———————

"**S**omebody got lucky last night." Nicole looked up from where she was cracking open eggs.

Laura's face heated as she herded the kids into Jen's living room, armed with snacks, games, and crayons. Somehow, she doubted they were going to be satisfied with anything less than power tools but she was still hoping they'd opt for a safer distraction.

Ethan was convinced he was helping Daddy build the deck, as he called it.

The kids raced to the back porch where Trent was already powwowing with Carponti. Nicole busied herself near the stove, flipping pancakes to add to the already massive stack on the center island.

"None of your business," Laura said with a smile.

Jen walked into the kitchen and Laura knew instantly that something was wrong. "Whoa. What's wrong?"

"Nothing. I just didn't sleep well last night," she said, more sharply than usual.

Laura glanced at Nicole, who shrugged. Walking over to stand next to Jen, Laura put a hand on her shoulder. "You okay?"

Jen's movements were jerky as she flipped the next pancake on the griddle. There were dark circles under her eyes, and they were so prominent that concealer wasn't doing much to hide them.

Silence fell over the kitchen like a shroud. And Laura felt a tiny curdle of panic take hold in her belly.

"Jen?" She dared to reach for her friend, her hand gentle on her shoulder. Fear clutched at her, twisting in her belly like a toxic, living thing. "Are...are you sick again?"

The last pancake came off the griddle and Jen set the spatula down, her eyes fixed on the black cooktop of the stove.

Her bottom lip trembled and the dam broke.

"Where the hell is the gimp?" Carponti asked, standing on the back porch, holding a stainless steel coffee mug.

"Haven't seen him yet," Trent said, eyeing the cup of coffee enviously.

"You look like you had a hell of a night," Carponti said. "Your wife finally take your dick off the no-contact order?"

Trent laughed. "Something like that." He cleared his throat. "Things are going good."

Too good. A goodness that he feared would slip through his fingers no matter how tightly he held on to it.

Nicole stepped onto the back porch, her expression somber. "Shane's upstairs. Go talk to him."

"What's wrong?" Carponti asked.

"Just go. He needs you both right now. And no smart-ass remarks."

Trent was up the stairs in an instant, Carponti right behind him.

They found Shane sitting on the edge of his bed. He was bent forward, his elbows on his knees.

Never in all the years he'd known the man had Trent seen him look so bleak, so drained of hope. His mouth was pressed flat, his eyes damp.

"Oh shit," Carponti whispered, for once serious.

Fear slithered in, dragging the c-word back with it. Jen was a survivor. She was young.

She'd sacrificed one breast to beat the cancer that had ravaged her body. It couldn't be back. Not now. Not so soon after she and Shane had found each other.

They stood in simple, heavy silence. It was a long moment before Shane shifted, dragging his hand over his mouth. The words, when he spoke, came from a voice ravaged and raw.

"Jen's pregnant."

The air shifted around them. The news wasn't so dark after all. But based on Shane's reaction, it was clearly still terrifying.

Trent searched for anything to say that would ease the ragged grief in his friend's voice.

"So," Carponti said slowly, "your sperm are experts at escape and evasion, huh?"

Shane's expression broke, and he gave a sharp laugh that sounded suspiciously like a sob. Trent shook his head and elbowed Carponti in the ribs.

"Ow!" He rubbed his side. "What the hell was that for? It's true, isn't it? How the hell else do you explain how they made it past the vasectomy?"

Shane scrubbed his hands over his face. "I don't know." His voice was pained.

But the tension had snapped, broken a little beneath the irreverence of Carponti's joke. Trent stepped into the room, leaning on the high dresser.

"This is not a good thing, is it?" He had no idea if getting pregnant after breast cancer was advisable. Judging by Shane's expression and obvious distress, it was not.

"No, it's not a fucking good thing," Shane snapped, rubbing his hand roughly over the back of his neck. "I'm freaked the hell out about her cancer coming back and she's busy flipping through baby books." Shane scrubbed his hands over his face.

"Wait. She wanted this?" Carponti said, stepping in and leaning against the open doorway.

"Yeah. She was really upset with me about the vasectomy. I thought we'd taken care of everything. I—fuck."

"Guess your dick overruled you, huh?" Carponti said.

"Not funny."

"It's a little funny. You can picture your sperm in full body armor, trying to batter their little way through the gap to capture the flag— er, egg." Carponti frowned. "I am going to have to go look up exactly how a vasectomy fails now. Call it my morbid curiosity." He turned his attention back to Shane, his expression suddenly sober. "Jen's a nurse. She wouldn't do this if she thought it would make her sick, would she?"

Shane's expression darkened again. "I love that woman so much it terrifies me. And I refuse to risk her life to have a baby. Pregnancy could kill her. The cancer could come back and she wouldn't be able to have chemo or anything." His voice thickened and he cleared his throat roughly.

His voice broke and he covered his face in his hands, scrubbing roughly.

Trent had never faced a burden like this one. Laura's pregnancies had been healthy and normal, except for the first one. The first time she had gotten pregnant, she miscarried. He still remembered finding her sobbing on the bathroom floor after they'd come home from the doctor's office.

He'd picked her up and carried her to their bed, then he'd held her until the pain medicine kicked in and she fell asleep. He'd held her until the pain had stopped. Until she'd accepted that this baby wasn't meant to be. That they could try again. Soon after, she had wanted to try again, even though she knew he was leaving for war and she would need to go through the pregnancy alone.

He'd loved her strength. He'd loved her determination to shove the grief of that first pregnancy behind her. He remembered lying there that first night in their new home, her fingers dancing over his where he'd rested his palm on her belly.

But never had he worried that one of his wife's pregnancies might kill her. It had never crossed his mind.

"Shane?"

Everyone turned at Jen's quiet voice. She'd snuck upstairs, padding quietly up the steps without anyone hearing her.

Shane said nothing. He simply straightened and opened his arms. Jen walked into his embrace, and he wrapped his arms tight around her waist, resting his head against her belly.

"I'm afraid," he whispered as Carponti and Trent left the room.

"Me, too."

Trent walked downstairs, followed by an unusually silent Carponti. Laura looked up from where she stood near the island. He said nothing, merely went to her, wrapping his arms around her and holding her close. He'd come so damn close to losing her. He had her back. For this moment and hopefully a hundred thousand more, he had her back. He kissed her forehead and pulled her close, unable to think of ever letting her go.

~

"THIS IS DEFINITELY NOT A DEATH SENTENCE," Nicole said after a while.

Laura was serving the kids breakfast on the back porch while the adults ate in the kitchen, where they could talk privately while keeping an eye on Ethan and Emma through the sliding glass door. Shane and Jen had not come downstairs yet. Almost an hour had passed and the house was eerily silent. Even the kids had picked up on the fact that something was wrong.

"I take it you've been asking Dr. Google," Carponti said, munching on a piece of scorched bacon.

"Of course. Look." Nicole held her phone out. "There have been huge advances in this field. And a recent clinical trial showed that there was no greater risk of cancer for pregnant women who have had it and those who haven't."

"Then what is Shane afraid of?" Carponti asked.

"The risk," Trent said quietly. "The risk that he's going to lose her." He glanced at his wife out on the back porch, scooping yogurt onto the kids' plates. "It's nothing he can control."

Carponti smiled but it was a distant and unfocused expression. Finally, he glanced at his wife, his expression suddenly serious. "You're not allowed to get cancer, okay? And no dying, either."

Nicole offered a strangled laugh and kissed the top of his head in a quiet, intimate gesture. Nicole and Carponti were both so gruff and sarcastic, but they were deeply committed to each other. After everything Carponti had gone through, after surviving the war and his injuries, their bond remained strong.

Strangely, he wasn't jealous. Laura stepped back through the sliding glass door and put the yogurt back in the fridge.

"They still haven't come down?"

Trent shook his head. "You don't think they're going to cancel the wedding?"

Laura smiled sadly. "No. They'll figure this out. Maybe we should go out there and get started before it warms up?"

"That's a good idea. Shane's probably going to need therapy to get through this one. Maybe we should call the chaplain?" Carponti asked.

"He'll be fine," Trent said. "Think you can wield a hammer today without hitting yourself?"

"Ha ha fuck you ha ha." Nicole elbowed her husband in the ribs. "What? The kids can't hear me."

Shaking her head, she pulled him to his feet and led him onto the back porch and out to the building project. Trent turned to look at Laura, who was struggling to keep herself busy.

"You okay?" he asked softly.

She turned away, busying herself with the breakfast dishes. "Yeah."

"Hey?" He stepped in front of her, gently grasping her shoulders. She seemed so small and fragile. Damaged and wary. "Talk to me?"

The weight of that single question bore down on him. He was asking her for something he'd been unable to give her. But he hoped that maybe, maybe she would trust him enough to lay her burdens on his shoulders for once. She'd been carrying all of his for so long.

She looked up at him, her gaze filled with anxiety. She smiled tremulously and lifted one hand, sliding one finger over the edge of his glasses. "You were gone when she was sick," she whispered. Her voice was thick. Heavy. "Ethan was just a baby and I was pregnant with Emma." She blinked rapidly and he reached out, cradling her neck, offering his silent support. "I spent a lot of nights on her couch. Helping her to the bathroom when she was too sick to walk." Her voice cracked a little beneath the memory. "She was not a good patient."

Trent urged her closer and she stepped into his embrace, resting her cheek against the scars on his. He cradled her face, felt the wetness on her cheeks and wished he could take the fear from her. Of all the things in life he feared, cancer had never been one of them. He had no idea what Laura had gone through with Jen.

"I don't want to lose her," she whispered.

Trent pressed his lips to the top of her head. "You won't." But his promise felt empty and hollow and beyond the scope of things he could control.

IT WAS a long time before Jen stepped onto the back porch, followed closely by Shane.

All work came to an abrupt, anxious halt. Shane stood behind his fiancée, his hands framing her shoulders, his expression tight. No, they hadn't figured this out yet. Her eyes were no longer rimmed with red, her face was no longer swollen from crying, but she watched him worriedly as he moved toward Trent and Carponti.

Laura hung the hammer she'd been using in her tool belt and waited as Jen descended the steps. Her friend put on a brave smile. "I'm not sick," she said. "I'm pregnant."

Laura laughed and pulled her into a hug. "I hope you don't have morning sickness as bad as I did with Emma. It was awful."

Nicole wrapped her arms around them both, joining the group hug. "Guess this means the next shower we do is a baby shower."

Jen laughed with her friends as Shane joined Trent and Carponti, who were standing with a plank propped between them.

"At least we don't have to get you a different dress," Laura said. "Your boobs won't

swell that much in two weeks."

"Boob. Singular."

Nicole laughed. "Guess we're going to have to get you a pregnancy prosthetic. Do they make ones for that?"

Jen offered a horrified laugh. "I'm sure we can figure something out."

"When do you go to the doctor's?"

"I have to see someone who specializes in cancer in pregnant women."

"But you're in remission," Nicole said.

"And I have been given a direct order to stay that way," she said, glancing at Shane. A warm smile played over her lips. "But we're going to take it cautious and slow."

"Is the big guy ready to start drinking?"

Jen smiled softly at Laura's question. "He's thought about it."

Laura pulled her gloves back on. "Okay then, we have a construction project to finish because I need to go to the store to find draperies for this thing. I swear, if I end up having to sew curtains…"

20

———

"Ethan, put the hamster away."

"Dad-dy!"

"Ethan, your mother told you to get in the tub."

"But, Daddy, we haven't gotten to play with the hamsters all day!"

Trent crouched down to his son's level, fully aware that he was being glared at by both a six-year-old human and a hamster that was surely one of the four horsemen of the Apocalypse. "Ethan, I'm not even going to argue about this," he said, fighting the urge to threaten to donate the hamster to Goodwill. "Put the hamster away and get in the tub."

Trent was tired and every bone in his body ached from the day's work. It hadn't been nearly as backbreaking as patrolling on foot in full body armor in the middle of Baghdad in August, but his body was used to those things. It wasn't so used to climbing and hammering.

Ethan sighed dramatically and stomped off. Trent stretched and walked into the kitchen, scanning the fridge and trying to decide what to prepare for an evening snack.

They'd barbecued at Shane and Jen's house, so the kids wouldn't need to eat again before they were tucked into bed. Judging from the sounds coming from the bathroom, that might be a while. His son seemed to be trying to set a new record for tantrums.

He gathered a few stray dishes and then started up the dishwasher, listening to the distant sounds of his wife preparing to bathe his children. He pulled out lunch meat for sandwiches, figuring they would be an easy dinner before everyone collapsed from exhaustion. It was a good exhaustion.

Suddenly, a naked little boy streaked out of the bathroom and ran down the hallway, ducking into one of the bedrooms.

"Ethan?" Laura called out to him. "Trent, can you grab him for me? He still needs to take his bath!" Her voice was tired but not stressed.

Following Ethan's giggles, Trent went off in search of his son.

His son.

His heart tightened. There were other sons whose daddies weren't coming home. And some of them weren't coming home because of decisions Trent had made. He'd made his choice when he'd pledged to become a soldier. He'd never imagined the weight of the ghosts that would one day haunt him.

He walked into Ethan's room and the stone in his chest softened a little more. He loved how Laura had made it into a classic little boy's room—midnight blue with red furniture. She'd given their son his own space. Room to be a little boy, instead of being taken over by his baby sister.

"Ethan?"

The giggling came from under the bed and Trent knelt down to peer beneath it. Ethan was wedged into the far corner, as far away as he could get from Trent's reach. Suddenly, he was struck with the vision of another child, tucked beneath a bed like this one, but cringing instead of laughing.

The flashback punched him in the gut, catching him off guard as he was suddenly transported to another room in a dirty, bombed-out house.

"I escaped, Daddy. You can't reach me!"

Trent sucked in a hard breath and shook himself mentally. He was home. His kids were safe.

He smiled and reached beneath the bed. He snagged a little foot and gave it a tug. Ethan giggled and kicked but Trent managed to drag the naked boy out from under the bed.

Ethan squealed as Trent carried him from the bedroom by his foot. He rounded the corner to the bathroom, his son hanging upside down in front of him, laughing hysterically.

Laura was washing Emma's face when Trent walked into the bathroom. She flashed him a grateful smile as their son continued to squeal and squirm.

Her smile touched his soul. "I caught this for you. I think it's a rare breed of naked fish."

"I'm not a fish, Daddy!"

Ethan hung over Trent's forearm, giggling like mad and looking at his father with absolute adoration in his eyes. Like Trent wasn't a complete stranger. Trent stopped suddenly, overcome with the realization that his son actually loved him, the father who'd been absent for almost his entire life. He clutched Ethan to him and inhaled his clean, warm scent.

Ethan wrapped his arms around Trent's neck and his little hand patted his father's shoulder. "Don't be sad, Daddy. Mommy will make everything all right."

Trent swallowed and blinked rapidly. What could he say? He set Ethan down and knelt down to the boy's level. "Yeah. Mommy always makes things all right."

Ethan's little black-haired head nodded and he wrapped his hand around Trent's index finger, looking at Trent like he was some kind of hero. It struck Trent how small and innocent his son—his children— was. Trent wasn't a hero. He rubbed his eyes beneath his glasses and swallowed. Again. He sucked in a hard breath, trying to keep the weight that settled on his chest from crushing his lungs. He needed to step back, needed to get outside.

A little hand pushed on his shoulder. "Daddy?" It was his daughter's voice.

He opened his eyes, only now realizing that he'd squeezed them shut. He stared into little Emma's golden eyes. He marveled again about how much she looked like a miniature version of Laura. "I love you, Daddy."

His vision blurred, and he pulled his daughter and son close. Their tiny arms came around him, their little hands so small on his back. They were so fragile. Vulnerable. But they were safe. There were no bombs for his children. No men with guns to steal their dreams or send them down a dirt-strewn alley as human shields.

He stayed absolutely still and drank in their innocence, so

completely grateful that they'd had Laura to raise them well. She had done that and so much more.

Alone.

The floor creaked and Trent looked up to see Laura step into the hallway. Her eyes were dark and filled with worry as she looked down at him holding their kids.

"Mommy, Daddy's sad. Will you make him feel better?"

Trent smiled as his gaze met his wife's. He couldn't help it. His son's innocent question had sent his mind to a less than innocent place. Laura blushed and Trent saw that he wasn't the only one with a wandering mind.

"Daddy will be fine. Come on. Ethan, it's time to wash up."

"Daddy will you read to me?" Emma asked. She thrust a book with a disgruntled cat on the cover.

He tipped the book back so he could read the cover. "Bad Kitty Gets a Bath?"

Emma nodded. "Bad Kitty is a bad, bad kitty," she said solemnly. "She hates taking baths."

He glanced at Laura, who stood watching from the door. There was a look of easy contentment on her face, as though tonight were just another normal night. As though this wasn't the first time he had sat and done something so blessedly normal as read his children a bedtime story.

"Sure."

Ethan washed in record time, joining them on Emma's bed. Laura moved a blanket and sat on the opposite side of Emma. Ethan was pressed to Trent's other side and Emma nestled between her mother and father. For once, there was no fighting. Only quiet snuggles at the end of a long day.

He paused for a moment, savoring the intensity of the love bursting inside him. This. This was what he'd missed out on.

He released a quiet breath. Then opened the book.

"This is how Kitty cleans herself," he read. A smile spread across his face as he continued reading about how Kitty licked and licked and licked herself clean. Emma giggled when he got to the suit of armor needed for the bath.

The sound warmed something inside of him. He glanced over at Laura, his throat suddenly thick. She met his gaze as she stroked one hand over Emma's head. "I think it's time for bed, guys," she said gently.

For once, they didn't argue. Emma snuggled down in her blankets and Trent leaned down, kissing the top of her head. "Night night, Daddy," she whispered sleepily.

"Night night, baby girl."

He followed Laura into Ethan's room. Their son lay on his back, and his arms went tight around his mother's neck. "Night, Mommy."

"Night, sweetheart." Laura kissed him on his forehead, then stepped back to give Trent some room.

Ethan's arms came around his neck and squeezed tight. "I love you, Daddy."

"I love you, too." He leaned back, brushing Ethan's hair out of his face. He clicked off the light and closed the door.

And stood in the hallway for a long moment with his wife, unsettled by the power of his own emotions.

He loved this woman. This woman who gasped his name when his fingers slid through her hair. This woman whose fingers traced down his ribs to dig into the small of his back as he walked her backward toward their bedroom.

Trent traced her body with his hands until she arched against him. He cradled her face in his palms, stroking his thumbs over her cheeks. Slowly, he lowered his lips to hers, teasing, tasting. He traced his tongue over her bottom lip and savored the shiver that ran through her and into him.

He wanted to hear his name on her lips when he teased her nipples between his teeth, when he kissed her swollen flesh and made her squirm with his tongue. He wanted to look in her eyes as she came apart in his arms.

She met his gaze and an urgency burned between them, all golden fire and brilliant desire.

"Laura." Her name was a whisper on his lips, a hesitant question.

She surprised him. She didn't look away. She didn't tremble or hesitate. Her hands slipped up his chest, twining with his arms until her fingers framed his cheeks. "I want this." She swallowed, then met his gaze once more. "I want you. I've always wanted you."

Triumph soared within him and he kissed her, drowning in the taste and touch and feel of his wife. He breathed her in, devoured her, claiming her with every ounce of passion and pain he carried inside him.

The lifetime he'd lived before the war seemed like it had happened to someone else. There were two chapters of his existence: before the war and after. But there was one constant, one person who had always helped him. One person who kept the light in his soul from snuffing out beneath the darkness of war and pain and death.

As long as his wife was in the world, waiting for him, loving him, he had the strength, the will to go on. To come home, back to her.

Now, he guided her into their room and lowered her to their bed. He slid her top off her shoulders, revealing her soft skin, then moved her pants down, down, over her hips, dragging her panties with them until she was bare and exposed and swollen, then tugged until she straddled his lap, her entire body exposed for his every whim. He looked up into her eyes while he slipped his fingers over her sensitive skin. Her nipples pearled beneath his thumbs and he pinched her lightly, reveling in her quick gasp.

He looked up at her as she straddled him, loving the feel of her body against his. Slowly, she dragged her nails from the twisting sinew of his forearms down, lower down his sides. He shuddered beneath her touch and a thrill of desire shot straight through him.

"God but I love your chest." She leaned forward and pressed a tender kiss on the scar over his heart. He flinched as she dragged her tongue over the jagged red starburst that should have killed him. She paused, and kissed the center of the scar. "All of you," she whispered.

His body tightened beneath hers and she shifted, sliding against his erection. He gasped and arched, and she wiggled in his lap until he was poised at the very center of her, her most intimate flesh just out of his reach.

"Not fair." His voice was a grunt. But when he tried to thrust deep, she lifted her hips.

He swallowed and his eyes narrowed in the dim bedroom light. She traced her thumb back and forth over the scar on his chest. "It's just a scar, Laura."

She shook her head. "It almost took you from me," she whispered.

"But it didn't."

She leaned down, tracing her tongue over the scar. Cold fire trailed over his skin as she blew on it and he shivered with barely restrained need.

In a single moment, dug his hands into her hips, rolling her over until she was beneath him, and he pushed fully, deeply inside her. She shivered and wrapped her legs tightly around his hips even as she tugged him down, claiming his mouth.

She pressed her lips to his heart once more. "I'm glad you came home," she whispered.

Slowly, he began to move, sinking deep inside her warm, welcoming embrace, his breath a groan as their pleasure built. A riot built inside her as she buried her face in his neck and bit back the fury that threatened to overwhelm her.

And when her release came, it was so intense, so full of pleasure and passion and hope, it stunned her. But it was the feel of her husband's cheek pressed against hers in the aftermath of their loving that touched her soul.

In the hazy aftermath, they lay together, wrapped in the comforter on their bed. She shifted to study him in the dusky light. She leaned toward him and traced her index finger over the pale scar that lined his jaw.

"What?" he whispered.

"Tell me more about how you got this one."

He tensed at her question and a quick bolt of fear shot through her that he would walk away, shutting her out like he had done before. Her hand rested on his shoulder, her fingertips pressed to his pulse. She felt his breath catch, his body tighten.

It was a long time before he spoke.

"Our Bradley got hit by a deeply buried IED outside Basra." He sucked in a deep breath. His palm on her back tensed, his fingers digging into her back with the memory. "I got bounced out of the commander's seat and knocked into my driver." He closed his eyes and Laura's heart broke for the pain in his voice. "I cut my jaw on the manual turret control."

His brow knit together. He looked like he'd cracked the seal on a thousand bad memories and might never be able to banish them. She slid her fingers up to cup his jaw, tracing the scar once more. What could she say to that? What were the right words to say when he'd lived through something she could not even imagine. She pressed her lips to his heart. "I'm glad you were okay."

He turned his face and kissed her forehead quickly. His breathing slowed but his words remained tight. "My gunner died that day."

His Adam's apple bobbed beneath her fingers where they'd drifted down to rest on his throat. "I'm sorry, Trent."

He scrubbed his hand over his mouth. But he didn't pull away. Laura didn't dare move, afraid to break the moment and leave him alone and vulnerable. "Garanji was a good kid. His parents immigrated to the U.S. from Iran. He had a little sister, and he was always worried she was going to date an American boy instead of an Iranian." He grinned. "One of my platoon sergeants used to give him so much shit."

"Iaconelli?"

"Yeah. Reza's Iranian, too. Part, anyway." Trent's eyes shimmered and reflected the glow from the fading sun. "He was pretty busted up when Garanji died." He cleared his throat. "We all were."

She didn't say anything. What could she say? She'd been crying about being alone while Trent had been burying young soldiers in far off corners of the globe.

She suddenly felt selfish and petty, ashamed that she hadn't understood—hadn't known—the full story behind a simple scar on her husband's body.

She closed her eyes. He'd chosen this, she reminded herself. He'd chosen not to share the roughest facts of his deployed life with her. What he'd gone through was hard but he hadn't needed to walk that road alone.

She could never do what he did. His life was so different from hers, and her daily stresses and worries suddenly seemed so trivial.

They lay together in silence. Neither of them moved for a long time.

He shifted then, a rustle of fabric in the quiet evening. He pulled his arms around her and drew her closer. "Thank you," he whispered.

"What are you thanking me for?" She found the words, but they barely slid past her lips.

He leaned closer, and their mouths were just a hint apart. His breath brushed against her lips. "For giving us a second chance."

She wanted to speak. Wanted to tell him about everything she was feeling—her love, her fear, her uncertainty—but his lips pressed against hers, hesitant and questioning. She tipped her head and opened her mouth beneath his. His tongue stroked hers and with that simple touch, brilliant heat unfurled inside her.

His fingers pressed into her hair and angled her head so that their mouths could join more completely. She gasped as his jaw scraped against hers and need sparked between her thighs.

This was Trent. Trent who kissed her. Trent who made her feel this languid heat inside her. Trent who was holding her now, making love to her with his mouth, making her crazy—one slow, agonizing kiss at a time. She did the only thing a woman who loved a man could do.

She surrendered to the need and the heat and the joy and kissed him back.

21

———

Laura walked into the headquarters on Monday sore and stiff and achingly happy for the first time in a long time. She was almost able to believe that they would make it, that things between them would continue to get better. That they were somehow stronger now than they'd been a few weeks before.

But the weight of the court-martial hung around her shoulders, a sobering reminder that just as things were starting to turn around in her marriage, they might be ripped apart once more.

She swallowed hard, trying to ignore the resurgent fear that squeezed around her heart.

She could lose him again. Just when she'd finally gotten him back.

Trent was supposed to meet her there in a few minutes. They were supposed to sit down with Patrick and go over the last bit of her testimony before the hearing in a few days. She was nervous. So much depended on the officers in that hearing having more faith in her husband than she'd had in him.

She walked down the hall toward her office, lost in thought. She rounded the corner and stopped short, nearly colliding with Lieutenant Randall.

Instantly, she took a step backward, needing space between herself and a thick-necked man who radiated violence. "What the hell did you say to my wife," he spat.

"Good morning, lieutenant," she said, emphasizing his rank.

"Don't 'good morning' me," he said. "What the fuck did you say to my wife?"

She took another step back, hating herself for backing down in the face of his anger. But then again, she wasn't an idiot. He was a stocky man and if he chose to lose his damn mind and take a swing at her, it wasn't going to be because she was an idiot and refused to back away.

"You mean the wife that you cheated on and gave an STD to? That wife?" Laura asked.

"She left me. She fucking left me." He paced the small space like a caged thing.

Laura was grateful for the sounds of soldiers arriving for work in the ops office.

"And how exactly is that my fault?" she asked.

"She said you talked to her." He rounded on her. "That you made her feel bad for fucking lying about your piece of shit husband." A deep flush crawled up Randall's neck, and he ground his teeth until she thought his jaw might fracture from the pressure. "Bitch, you ruined everything. Just like your husband. Always ruining a good thing," he ground out.

"My husband is a better man than you'll ever be," Laura said quietly. "Now get the hell away from me."

Randall stared down at her and, for a flicker of a moment, she thought he might actually hit her. Laura opened her mouth to speak but before she could get any words out Randall was yanked backward, slammed up against the wall. There was a sudden commotion as Trent pressed his elbow to Randall's throat, twisted his fist in the man's collar. "Watch your mouth around my wife, you little shit."

"Trent, I'm thinking this is not a good way to get the charges dropped," Patrick said lightly, glancing over his shoulder as a full colonel Laura didn't recognize stepped out of the conference room. "I'm sure officers at the hearing would much rather see you two discussing your differences of opinion in a more calm, loving way."

Trent's nostrils flared. For a moment, Laura thought she saw his elbow press harder into Randall's skin.

He released his grip and the LT coughed, rubbing his throat.

"Apologize to my wife," Trent said, his words clipped.

"Sorry, ma'am."

"Stay the fuck away from my family," Trent hissed. He released him and Randall stalked off, his expression a hard mask of fury.

Patrick grabbed Trent when he made to follow Randall down the hall. "Unless you want to get deeply acquainted with solo prison sex, keep your damn hands off him."

Trent shrugged Patrick off, irritation vibrating from him in waves. "Got it."

Laura turned, her fingers twining with his, squeezing gently. She smiled up at him, painfully aware of the strength and power of this man. It had twisted up her insides to see evidence of what he was capable of right in front of her. Her hand trembled when he squeezed it back.

"Are you okay?" His voice grated.

"Yes." He couldn't spend the rest of the day this angry. It was bound to go badly for him.

She took a single step closer. Her lips curled into a soft smile. "That was, um," she glanced around, "really sexy."

His expression faltered. "What was?"

She slipped her arms around his waist, not caring that they were in the middle of the hallway. "You threatening him to protect me. I don't usually go for the whole Cro-Magnon man thing. But I liked it."

"Yeah?"

"Yeah." She flicked her tongue over her bottom lip, followed by a quick scrape of her teeth. "It's lunch time."

"It's not even close to lunch time." Trent raised both eyebrows, his jaw tight. She loved that she could still get to him, still see that desire light up his eyes. "What did you have in mind?"

"I was thinking we could sneak out to Belton Dam."

"That might be risky in the middle of the day. There are Blackhawks flying around." His voice sounded harsh. Tight. Erotic.

"When did that ever matter before?"

TRENT WALKED into the ops office. Things were good with Laura. Too good.

He couldn't let himself relax. Couldn't allow the fantasy that they might actually have a chance at beating this thing take hold. There were a few more days until the hearing that would decide his fate, but now, knowing that Randall had lost a key piece of his defense by alienating his wife?

Trent felt hopeful for the first time in a long time.

He was a few minutes early and the office was still empty from lunch. Iaconelli, though, sat at his desk. His shoulders were slumped, his elbows resting on his knees.

"Hey," Trent said, walking over. "You okay?"

Iaconelli looked up, his eyes bleak. There was a Gatorade bottle in one hand that probably didn't have Gatorade in it. He swayed a little in his chair. "Story." He swallowed a long pull from the bottle. "We lost Story."

Trent's skin went cold. He sank into a chair next to Iaconelli. Took the proffered bottle and took a long pull off it himself. The straight vodka burned all the way down and made his eyes water.

At least, that's what he told himself.

~

THE BEDROOM WAS pitch black but for the light from the television. Trent lay in bed, the bottle held loosely in one hand, staring unseeing at the screen. The blankets were tangled around his legs. He hadn't slept.

"How do I fix this? How do I get her to understand that I have to be here?"

Story shook his head. "It doesn't work that way. The old saying that if the Army wanted you to have a family, it would have issued you one …it's a cliché but it's true. And you've chosen the Army a hell of a lot more than you've chosen her lately.

Trent tossed his glasses on the desk, staring at the stark words on the divorce papers in front of him. Reality squeezed around his heart, cutting off his air.

He'd done this. He'd ruined everything with his wife. He'd left her alone to raise the kids, to run their home.

"The wives never understand why we have to go," Story said quietly. "Rebecca won't leave me but we don't have a real marriage. You had that with Laura."

Trent heard what his friend hadn't said. You fucked that up.

"I need to go home," he said, looking at his first sergeant.

Story nodded. "Well, that's about to get a lot easier. We have an appointment with the colonel and sergeant major in an hour." He paused. "We're getting fired."

He shook his head, trying to shake off the memory. Trying to shut down the pain. But it ripped through him, tearing and slashing and slicing. The alcohol did nothing to numb it. Trent took a long pull off the bottle, his throat numb, the rest of his soul not following fast enough. He wanted his heart to stop. Anything to stop the searing pain that threatened to consume him. He stared into the darkness.

He remembered bits and pieces, flashes. Horrible, dark thoughts. An explosion of glass and violence.

Grief filled him. Smothered him.

He started to rise, but her arms tightened around his waist.

He looked down.

He hadn't realized she was sitting with him, his body tucked against her. Warm wetness soaked his thin t-shirt. They were not her tears. He closed his eyes, unable to look at her, unable to pull away, to keep her from seeing this side of him. This terrible grief that made him want to do violence, to rush back to the war and exact vengeance for his friend's death.

Laura's fingers tightened on his waist. He buried his face in her neck and let the grief tear from him.

No words could encompass the emotions surging through his soul. She wrapped him in her arms and simply held him. In the silence, he wept. For every lost soldier. For Story. For Doc. For Ripley and Bull. For Naseem, his terp who'd lost his whole family to Saddam. For Garanji.

He didn't speak. He couldn't. But finally, he wept for the friend he'd lost. And this time, Laura held him when he shattered.

It was a long time before he spoke, his speech slurred. "Did you know that Story saved my life?" he whispered into the darkness.

"No," she said softly.

"It was that day back in '04." He breathed deeply, the sound echoing in his ears. He felt empty, hollowed out. "When I got blown up, he dragged me out of the fight. He thought I was dead, too." He grunted. "We were so inexperienced back in '04. The round got between my body armor and my chest and my heart stopped on impact."

"I'll never forget what it felt like to hear that you'd been killed," she whispered. "It was like the world dropped from underneath me." Her fingers drew gently down his chest. "I didn't know how I was going to go on with my life without you out there in the world somewhere."

Slowly, the force of his grief ebbed, no more a tempest but a trickle. He didn't move, he couldn't. And his wife, his wife was still there.

"You stayed with me," Trent murmured, his voice sore. He cradled her face in his hands.

She sniffed, her hands fluttering over his chest, like she didn't know what to do with them. He lowered his forehead to hers, tears leaking out from behind his closed eyes once more. She simply wrapped her arms around his neck, pressing her body to his.

He paused before speaking again, and when he did it was a whisper more powerful than the loudest shout.

"I was wrong...so goddamned fucking wrong."

Her arms tightened around his neck. "About what?"

"About the war, the Army, fucking everything. Every choice I've made has been wrong. Terribly fucking wrong." He cupped her cheek. "Except the one to come back to you." He lowered his forehead to hers. "I was coming home before I got fired. I was going to figure out how to fix this and then I was going to go back to my boys. But I was wrong about that, too. You're the only thing in the entire world that I've ever gotten right." He ran his fingers over her cheeks. "Regardless of how the hearing turns out, I'm quitting."

"Quitting what?" There was a wariness in her voice. A fear.

"Everything. The Army. The war. I want to stay home and be a dad." His brows drew into another frown. "I want to be here for you."

"I'm not asking you to do that." Her voice was thick with emotion. He hated that he was hurting her all over again.

"You should. You should demand the world from me. You deserve so much better than what I've ever given you." He scraped his fingers over her cheek. "I can't give you your husband back and I can't give you back the time I've spent away from you."

He stroked his thumbs over her cheeks until she opened her eyes and looked at him. He needed her to see him, the truth of the man he was. He couldn't hide that from her. Not anymore. And the truth wasn't something shiny and new. It was badly damaged. It was flawed and broken.

Trent cradled his wife's face in his palms, savoring the soft feel of her skin beneath his fingertips.

"You would really give it all up?" she asked.

Doubt crept in, whispering around his heart. Could he walk away from his troops and the uniform that he'd worn for so long in exchange for runny noses and muddy shoes and PTA meetings? He closed his eyes and felt the little heads resting on his shoulders when he'd read to them at bedtime.

His arms tightened around her. "How did we get to this point?" he asked, brushing his lips over her forehead.

"A LOT OF REASONS." She closed her eyes, wishing the war hadn't chipped away at the foundation of their marriage. Wishing they hadn't spent so much time apart.

Wishing that things weren't so goddamned fragile between them.

Even at that moment, lying in bed, she felt the cloying, clinging fear that the honeymoon was going to end soon. That the strain and the stress were going to slink back into their bed and start chipping the frail thing building between them.

She pressed her lips to his chest, pushing away the worry and the fear and the doubt and deciding for now that she would lie in her husband's arms and simply be.

He shifted so that he was lying between her thighs, and framed her face in his palms. In the pale light, she looked up at him. His eyes were dark and for once uncovered by his glasses. She lifted her knees, resting them against his sides.

"I know...I know the court-martial is a large part of how we ended up here." His voice was a serrated blade. Rusty and dangerous. "But maybe..." He closed his eyes. "Maybe if it forced us together...to be in the same space...maybe it's a good thing?"

Her lips twisted into a wry smile. "So we needed a court-martial to push us back together? Seems a little extreme."

He nibbled on the corner of her mouth before lifting his gaze to hers once more. "I don't want to waste this. This isn't about the court-martial for me anymore, Laura. This isn't just about making things easier for the kids." His thumb stroked her temple. "This is about us now. Maybe it always has been."

She blinked rapidly. He opened his mouth but she pressed her index finger to his lips. "You've been a good soldier. You've gone to war. You should have had a loving wife holding down the home front. And I tried to do that for so long." She stroked his face gently between her fingers. "But you crushed me. You left me alone and empty and I just couldn't do it anymore. I never understood when other wives said they couldn't handle the loneliness anymore." She bit her lips together, needing the pain to ground her. To help her get the words exactly right. "I needed to know you still loved me enough to come back to me. I needed something to hold on to. I had nothing but a memory." Her voice broke. "I'm so sorry it wasn't enough. That I wasn't strong enough to keep waiting."

She swiped at her cheeks, refusing to look at him. She swallowed. "I wasn't strong enough to wait for you." She tried to move away. He panicked. She was leaving him. He was going to have to face this world alone, without her.

He reached for her then, pulling her back, dragging her close and holding her with a quiet urgency that spoke all the things he could not say.

"I left you," she whispered.

"I deserved it." He rested his cheek against her head, holding her. "I never deserved your faith in me."

"I lost it, Trent. I wasn't strong enough to hold on."

He captured her left hand in his. Stroked his thumb over her rings. "This isn't about being strong enough, Laura."

"Then what is it? Failure? Dishonesty? What is it that destroyed us?"

He kissed her gently. "We did. I did. Because I forgot that you were my wife. You needed a husband...You needed me. And I haven't been here for a long time."

The hush fell over them again. A pitch black, deep, abiding calm.

"Are you really getting out of the Army?" she whispered.

"Yes." There was no ambiguity in his voice. "There's nothing left for me. I can't lie to the boys. I can't tell them they're fighting the good fight. I just can't do it anymore." He cleared his throat. "I have to step aside. Let someone who still cares do this."

"It's not that simple." She shook her head. "The Army is part of who you are."

"And it always will be. But you're part of who I am, too."

This was not an argument she wanted to have. She wanted him home with her. She wanted all of this over and done with. But he needed to come to that decision for his own reasons. Not in a moment of grief.

"I'm half a man without you in my life," Trent said after a long moment. "I need you. I need to know you're out there in the world for me to come back to." And at that moment—her mouth beneath his, her fingers brushing the edge of his scar—one more crack was healed, one more wound bandaged.

"I'M AFRAID, Laura. I'm afraid of what I've become. Of what I've brought into our home." He traced the curve of her cheek with the pad of his thumb. "But I still want another chance."

She closed her eyes and Trent felt his fate hanging by the barest thread. He had no hint of how she felt. He didn't know but he had to try. He'd crossed one too many lines in his life that hadn't been worth it. This one was.

She looked up at him, her eyes shining brightly. "I love you. And it took me all of this to remember that 'I love you' doesn't come with a 'but'. Forgiving someone else is easy. Forgiving yourself?" She brushed her lips against his. "That's much harder." She rubbed her cheek against his. "I can't do that for you. But I can walk with you while you work on it."

He rested his cheek against the top of her head. "I haven't been a good husband. I'm not a good man."

She cupped his cheek. "You're wrong." She offered a watery smile. "Well, you're right about the not-being-a-good-husband-thing. But you are a good man. You always have been."

He licked his lips and stroked his thumb over her cheek. He kissed her because he was terrified of losing her again. Terrified because he'd come so close to destroying the one person in his life worth living for. He'd nearly broken her. He could see that clearly now. And while his faith in the system he'd sacrificed everything for was far from restored, his faith in his wife, in their family, was a little more patched up. And lost himself in the taste and touch and love of his wife.

~

"DADDY."

Something poked Trent in the soft spot between his shoulder and his chest. He frowned but tried to ignore it, desperate for a few more minutes of sleep.

"Daddy."

The whisper was more urgent now. A little hand on his shoulder, shoving him from the warm nest of blankets and his wife's soft body.

"Hnnngh." He blinked and opened his eyes. Ethan's face blurred then came back into focus. Trent sat up, the concern etched on Ethan's tiny face cutting through the fog of sleep. "What's wrong?"

"Fluffy's missing." His little voice broke.

"Tell him to go back to bed and we'll find Fluffy in the morning," Laura said, her voice thick with sleep. Then she rolled over and instantly went back to sleep. Trent was envious, but he couldn't shake the idea that he might accidentally squish Fluffy as he stumbled to the bathroom in a couple of hours.

He rubbed his eyes before he reached for his glasses, then slid out of bed and crouched down in front of Ethan. "Okay, buddy. Where does Fluffy usually escape to?"

Ethan shrugged and looked lost and helpless and sad, as though he might never see Fluffy again. Trent brushed his hair out of his face. "Okay, well, let's let Mommy sleep and we'll go find him."

"Her, Daddy. Fluffy's a girl."

Trent frowned, wondering why it mattered. At three in the morning, very little seemed to matter. All that was important at the moment was getting Ethan back to bed.

And, apparently, that involved finding Fluffy. Ethan wrapped his little hand in Trent's and pulled him toward his bedroom. For a moment, the feeling of his son's fingers wrapped around his overwhelmed him. A lump rose in his throat and he brushed his thumb over Ethan's fingers.

He bent and cupped Ethan's face. "Let's go find that rodent."

Forty-five minutes later, Trent was reasonably certain he did not care if Fluffy spent the night in Alcatraz being stalked by a hungry cat. He'd torn apart the back bedroom where the hamsters lived, moved every piece of furniture, lifted every last box, and still there was no Fluffy.

He'd set a trap of peanut butter in the middle of the floor.

No Fluffy.

He'd briefly contemplated a mousetrap, but then remembered his aim wasn't to scar his son for life.

Leaning against the couch in the back bedroom, his arm slung around Ethan's shoulders, Trent looked down at the sleepy boy. "Hey, buddy, why don't we call it a night and we'll find Fluffy in the morning?"

"No, Daddy." Ethan yawned. "If we don't find her tonight, she'll fall asleep during the day and we'll never find her."

"I don't know where else to look."

"The printer! Daddy, I think I just saw her in the printer."

Trent frowned and glanced at the ancient inkjet printer. It looked like something that had come out of the late 1990s. It was actually being used as a stand for the smaller laser printer Laura had bought.

"There's nowhere for a hamster to hide in there."

"Uh huh, Daddy. Fluffy can get into really small spaces."

He looked down at his son. "Define 'really small'."

"Paper towel tube."

There was a tiny hole in the front of the printer, no more than an inch wide. He peered in and could just barely make out her beady black eyes and whiskers. "No way."

It turned out that extracting a hamster from a printer was a delicate operation. More delicate than Trent figured he had the patience for at past-four a.m., but the desire to not drag a bloody mess out of the printer instead of a live rodent gave him a miraculous reserve of patience.

Twenty minutes and twelve pieces of the printer later, Fluffy was successfully extracted from her prison and secured back in her cage with excessive amounts of duct tape sealing any openings and a small suitcase lock securing the door.

Ethan studied Fluffy for a moment, then looked up at Trent like he'd hung the moon. He threw his arms around his father's neck, his breath a huff in Trent's ear. "You're the best daddy in the whole wide world," he whispered.

Trent's heart swelled in his chest as he hugged his son tightly. After a long moment, he eased him back. "I think it's time for you to get back in bed, don't you think?"

Ethan chose that moment to yawn mightily and rub both eyes. Getting him back to sleep turned out to be as much of a production as getting the hamster out of the printer. He had to brush Ethan's teeth again, get him a drink of water, help him go potty, and find his stuffed bear.

It was approaching dawn by the time Trent finally crawled back into bed. Laura made a sleepy sound and he eased in beside her, shifting until her body was nestled against his. He buried his face against her hair and breathed the scent of her in.

She sighed and snuggled closer, pulling his hand up to rest near her heart. "Did you find the rodent?" she mumbled.

"Mmmhmm."

"My hero." Her words were a whisper against his forearm. He kissed her shoulder and closed his eyes. An overwhelming sense of the rightness of things nailed him center mass. He felt. He felt the fear of losing his family, he felt the fatigue of five a.m., he felt the stress of combat that weighed him down. He felt love—an overwhelming love for his wife, for his family.

He felt all of it and the power of the emotions nearly crushed him with their rightness.

He was *home*.

22

———————

Trent stood in the courtroom at the First Cavalry Division headquarters, his hand clasped in his wife's. There was a stubborn set to Laura's jaw as she swiped a piece of lint from his collar. As always, her eyes were what gave away her worry.

He squeezed her hand. "It'll be fine, Laura. Stop fidgeting."

"I can't."

He smiled tightly. "I know."

Patrick walked into the courtroom, a file tucked beneath one arm. Like Trent, he wore his Blues, a sharp dress uniform used for formal occasions. Trent had been to other Article 32 hearings and they'd all been held in the duty uniform of ACUs. Trent assumed that the formal uniforms they were wearing today had been decided by the location.

"You need to pull your shit together," Patrick said by way of greeting.

Trent frowned. "What are you talking about?" His voice was flat.

Patrick gripped his shoulder. "Look, I know Story's death is hitting you hard but you need to put all of that emotion away. I need you to be fully present. Don't bring any baggage into this courtroom."

Trent swallowed and breathed deeply. "Roger."

"I'm serious, Trent. They're going to try to get you to react. You need to dial it back. Just sit there and let me handle this for you."

Laura would help him do that—she was the only person who

could. Her silent, supportive presence wrapped around him like a warm blanket.

She was not just here for show. The rings on her finger meant something. He squeezed her hand tightly.

Laura had dressed sharply today: a neat pencil skirt and a crisp white blouse. Her hair was tied back in a perfect bun. All she was missing was a pair of wire-rimmed glasses and she'd look like a sexy librarian. It dawned on him that he should have told her that.

It wasn't like he was going to jail at the end of the day. But he could have told her how beautiful she looked when they were alone, and he'd missed the opportunity. It was such a little thing, but right now the oversight weighed on him. He squeezed her hand again and then had to let her go so that he could take his seat.

The court started to fill up. Shane and Carponti flanked Laura as everyone filed into their seats. They led her to the row directly behind where Trent would be sitting. They'd only be separated from him by a low wooden wall.

Trent kept his expression carefully blank as Adorno walked into the courtroom. She looked harder than he remembered. Stiffer.

She did not sit with her husband. She didn't even look at him. She stood close to another lawyer, who was having a hushed, intense conversation with Lieutenant Randall. Trent glanced at Patrick, who was watching the interchange with interest.

"What's going on?" he asked as he took a seat next to Patrick.

"I have no idea, but whatever it is, Lieutenant Randall is not happy about it. He's killing that poor piece of gum."

Patrick was right. Randall was doing violence on the gum in his mouth and glaring daggers at his wife, who refused to look at him.

A major walked into the courtroom and leaned across the low barrier separating the counselors from the crowd. He whispered something in Lieutenant Randall's ear, then they both motioned for Patrick, who disappeared into a small room next to the judge's bench.

Trent felt Laura lean in behind him. "What's going on?" she whispered.

He turned around. "No idea."

"Do we want to take bets on whether this is a good thing or a bad thing?" Carponti asked, leaning across the low wall.

"Not particularly a fan of knowing the odds," Trent muttered.

Trent caught his wife staring at the door beyond which Patrick had disappeared with Colonel Pritchard and the unidentified major.

"Sure wish I knew what was going on," Laura said quietly.

"Yeah." Trent leaned one arm on the low wall, capturing her hand in his, needing the comfort of her touch.

An uneasy silence had settled in the courtroom. A stray cough. A rustle of fabric.

The door opened. Patrick stepped through, followed by the other two men.

His friend's expression was polished and unexpressive. But in his eyes Trent saw a glimmer of victory.

He held his breath as Patrick took his seat, turning to talk to him. But he didn't get the chance—he was interrupted by Randall's shout.

"Oh, bullshit!"

"Watch it, lieutenant."

"Fuck you, sir. You were supposed to take care of this."

Randall's lawyer's face flushed. "And you were supposed to keep your dick in your pants. But instead, you went and pissed off the key witness."

The unidentified major was standing next to Adorno. He was clearly her lawyer. She lifted her chin, glaring at her spouse. "The only person I'm willing to testify against is my husband." Her voice was high-pitched and grating but her words were some of the most beautiful words Trent had ever heard.

"You realize I can make her testify about Captain Davila's actions," Randall's lawyer said harshly.

"You could, but that puts your client at risk, as well," the major said, leaning against the low wooden wall. "Or you could cut your losses and we could all just recommend that the charges are dropped given the, ah, recent developments and the witness's unwillingness to cooperate." He grinned. "Unless, of course, you're so vested in this case you want to try the young commander over there without any real evidence."

"Goddamn it, this is bullshit!" Randall exclaimed, his face bright red.

"Lieutenant, one more outburst and I'm going to resign as your attorney."

"You can't do that. The only reason you're still a lawyer is because of my father."

"Yeah, well, putting up with you for the last few months has made me reconsider my debt," his lawyer said calmly. "There's nothing I can do. Even you have to see that."

Adorno leaned forward, barely a foot away from her husband. "I hate you. I hate what you made me become. I lied because of you."

"I didn't make you do anything." He looked down at her with disgust.

Her bottom lip quivered. "I lied because I loved you and you convinced me that Captain Davila was ruining your career." She glanced from Trent to her husband. "Well, I'm done. You'll have the divorce papers tomorrow. And if you really want to move forward with this sham, I'll gladly testify about everything." She smiled coldly. "With proof." She turned to her lawyer. "Sir, can I go? I need to go."

The major grabbed his briefcase. "Call me and we'll figure out how to war game this with the division commander."

When Lieutenant Randall opened his mouth, his lawyer held up his hand. "Not one more word, lieutenant. Go. Now."

The court cleared. Patrick whistled, smiling at his friend. "I think that's a first in my career," he said lightly. "Screw *Days of Our Lives*. The Army has much more in common with the *Springer Show*."

Trent held his breath as Laura spoke from behind him. "Does that mean what I think it means?" she asked.

"Yeah. Yeah, I think it does." Patrick's cell phone vibrated on the desk. He glanced at the text message then looked over at Trent. "Colonel Richter has made some adjustments to the case."

"That was fast," Trent said. "What does that mean?"

"You'll have to talk to him." Patrick's expression revealed nothing.

Trent glanced at his wife, his heart slamming against his ribs. She reached for him, squeezing his fingers gently. "I'll see you in a little bit."

～

TRENT WIPED his palms on his uniform pants and took a deep breath before knocking on
the door of his brigade commander's office.

His pulse pounded in his ears, blocking out all other sound. Laura had wanted to come with him, to hear firsthand what Colonel Richter had decided to do about the charges against him, but one did not take one's spouse to a meeting with the brigade commander. No matter how much he might have wanted her there, it simply wasn't done.

Colonel Richter looked up from where he was placing picture frames in a small box. The big colonel had been a centerpiece of Trent's life for as long as he could remember. The man had even been his battalion commander the first time he deployed.

Now, he stood in his commander's office, unanswered questions on the tip of his tongue. Did Richter think Trent deserved a court-martial? Why hadn't he intervened? As the brigade commander, he had the choice to continue the process started by his battalion commander or stop it.

Trent had chosen not to walk into his commander's office to ask for help. He'd waited, patiently, for a leader he'd trusted to act.

Apparently, now that the evidence against Trent had crumbled, the waiting was over. He had no idea what to expect as he stood on the carpet in front of his brigade commander's desk.

And waited.

"You always think you're ready to change command," Colonel Richter said by way of greeting. "But there are always things you leave undone."

Trent swallowed and said nothing, standing at the position of attention, even as his glasses slid down the bridge of his nose.

"It's hard to believe it's been two years since I took charge of the brigade. But it's time for me to go." Colonel Richter wrapped the photos in an old brown t-shirt and lowered them into the box. Finally, he paused and stared into the box of photographs.

"All charges against you have been dismissed."

Seven simple words that could have been said at any point in the last year and a half. Seven small words that changed Trent's life, lifting the burden from his shoulders.

Why now? He clenched his fists by his sides, anger and frustration clawing at him. *Why did you wait until my life was almost completely destroyed?*

But there were things one simply could not say to a full colonel.

Trent cleared his throat and breathed deeply, trying to rein in his churning emotions.

The charges that had been hanging over his head for the last year were gone. It was over.

Relief, palpable and damn near crushing, washed over him. Absently, he rubbed the aching scar over his heart. It always ached, but lately it didn't seem to be keeping him up at night like it used to.

"You want to ask me why, don't you?" Colonel Richter said, pausing to look at Trent before placing another picture in the box.

"It crossed my mind, sir."

Colonel Richter studied him quietly. "It's purely selfish on my part. I didn't want to leave this unfinished. The new commander has no ties to anyone in this brigade. He doesn't have to live with the decisions you and I have made during this war. He's a Pentagon man." Another picture into the box. The office looked barren, devoid of the passion and intensity Colonel Richter had brought to the brigade. At one time, Trent would have followed him anywhere. He was that kind of leader. One of the few real inspirational leaders among the senior ranks.

"Have a seat." Colonel Richter paused and moved to the small couch. He rubbed his hand over his mouth, his gaze distant and unfocused for a moment. "I had to let this situation develop the way it did for a lot of reasons, none of them good. I know you felt like I left you out in the cold and I'm sorry for that." He cleared his throat. "But the truth is, I could not have acted before now."

"Sir, if I may: What changed?" It was as close to demanding an answer to the question of why that Trent dared to dance.

"Lieutenant Randall's father has been stepping on my neck since this whole thing started. He's a sneaky old bastard, I'll give him that. He had his boss call the division commander and when the chief of staff of the Army calls a division commander, the commander tends to listen." Colonel Richter leaned forward. "I had to play this out the right way or it could have been taken out of my hands. Once Randall's wife changed her story, the case fell apart and I could dismiss the charges."

Trent's career had been sacrificed to placate a spoiled lieutenant's father. He'd known that, of course, but somehow hearing it from Colonel Richter made it sound more calculated.

The brigade commander's expression was grim. "Division is deploying to Afghanistan next spring. I could use a few officers with Afghanistan experience. It's a different fight than Iraq."

Trent had been there almost a decade ago, when special forces was fighting the war from horseback and the conventional forces were attempting to remove a mountain range from the face of the earth at Tora Bora. His first taste of combat had slammed into him like the main gun on his tank. The need for adrenaline had hardwired itself into his bloodstream on that first tour in hell.

He could go back. Back to war. Back to the heady mix of combat and terror.

Away from his family. Away from Laura.

Story had died because he hadn't been able to keep away from the fight. His blood burned with the futility of it all. Everything he'd sacrificed—all the time he'd missed with his family—all of it had been for nothing. He had a long way to go before the grief would not be raw and cutting.

It was a battle he would no longer fight.

Trent swallowed, clenching his fists by his sides.

"I can't go with you, sir." He summoned the energy to meet his commander's gaze, which was filled with resigned disappointment.

"Think about that answer, son."

"Sir, I'm not your son," he said, quietly crossing the line. "I appreciate you dismissing the charges, sir. But my time in the Army is done."

Colonel Richter stood and Trent rose to his feet. "I understand you're upset. Think about this before you make any irrevocable decisions."

Trent bit down on the inside of his cheeks to keep from saying anything else. It took what felt like an act of God, but all he said was, "Roger, sir. But I've given the Army enough. I've done my time in hell." He looked into Colonel Richter's eyes, seeing the disappointment there. It was a terrible thing, to let down someone you admired.

But it was worse, so much worse, to consider his life without his wife and family.

"Are you sure about that?" Colonel Richter asked.

Trent didn't hesitate. He nodded once. And ended his career.

LAURA LOOKED up as her husband stepped into her office, closing the door behind him. An odd expression was twisting his features. Not victory. Not defeat. Fatigue. As if everything over the last few months had slammed into him all at once. She stood, crossing the small space to meet him.

"Okay, you've got to tell me something before I go crazy," she said, a hitch in her voice.

Trent rested his hands on her shoulders, his eyes dark and shadowed behind his glasses. "The charges have been dismissed," he said softly. "He offered me a chance to salvage my career by deploying with division in the spring."

He looked down at her hands where they rested on his chest. "I'm not going." His voice was thick. She said nothing while she listened to him describe his conversation with the colonel. She listened and her heart broke at the stunning lack of loyalty that had been shown to her husband.

The loyalty Trent had given the Army had nearly destroyed their marriage.

She brushed her lips over his as he captured her hands, his big palms rough against hers.

"I screwed up everything with us, Laura." He rubbed his thumbs over the flesh of her knuckles and the sensitive skin near her wedding ring. He sounded so broken. The words were so raw, ripe with his still-fresh grief and the betrayal of the Army, for which he'd sacrificed everything.

"Because you're not a perfect man," she whispered, "but you're a good man." She rubbed the material of his uniform over the scar on his heart. "And you're mine."

She slid her arms around his neck and drew him close. He felt deflated, somehow defeated. She simply held him. It was a long moment before he relaxed and let himself be held. His arms slowly came around her waist.

With a shuddering breath, he exhaled, like he'd been depending on the air in his lungs to keep himself upright. After a long moment, he leaned back. "So I'm going to need some help writing a resume," he said with a twisted smile on his lips.

"You're not making any major life choices right now."

"This is what I want."

"I know you do. But I also want you to make this decision when you're not grieving for a friend."

"Nothing will change my mind. I can't do this anymore. You deserve better."

"So do you."

"No, I don't."

She smiled then. "You're going to argue with me now?"

His answering smile was sad. "Maybe."

"I need you to hear what I'm about to say." Her fingers stroked over the skin of his cheeks, his forehead. Her eyes filled with relief. "I've wanted you home for so long." She rested her forehead against his, savoring the feel and touch of having her husband close enough to touch. "The war almost broke us. But it didn't. It didn't. Now, we need to take some time for us. We need to figure out who we are without the war hanging over our heads."

"Laura, I'm—"

"I'm not actually finished." She pressed her finger over his lips. His eyes were dark with unspoken emotion. "You came home but that's just a start. We've got a long way to go. But we're going to work on that together."

He smiled against her finger. "Can I talk now?"

She closed her eyes, terrified that he would back out, that he would decide to deploy again. And if he did? She would wait. She knew that now. Because these last few weeks had refilled her well. She was no longer empty, no longer pining after a man who didn't know how to be home. It would hurt, but if he decided to stay in the Army, she could do this. She would do this.

But there was fear in her voice when she said, "Depends on what you're going to say."

He brushed his nose against hers. "I don't deserve you." He crushed her to him then, pushing the air from her lungs with the intensity of his embrace. A moment more and he kissed her, pouring a thousand unsaid things into that kiss, that single moment. Her heart blossomed beneath his touch, opening and expanding and making room to love this man again. Not the man who'd left her and gone to war. This man. The man who had come home, a little bit broken, a little bit different, but still the man she loved.

It had taken nearly losing him to see that. She closed her eyes and savored this single moment. Needing it. Needing him.

"I love you." The words tore from his lips, ragged and harsh against her ear. "I'm sorry it took me so long to come home."

The swell of emotion crested and broke and she leaned back, swiping beneath her eyes. "You came back. That's all that matters."

"I'm not the same man I was," he said gently. "I've got a lot of work to do to rewire my normal."

She stroked her hands over his cheeks. "You're right. You are different. But you came

back to me. That's all that matters."

He pulled her against him again, wrapping her tight in his arms. "I was always coming

back to you. It just took me a while to get here."

EPILOGUE

"**A**re you ready for this?" Trent asked, brushing lint from Shane's lapel.

"Honestly?" Shane asked roughly. The crisp blue of their uniforms looked sharp in the setting Texas sun. The warm Sunday afternoon was not oppressively hot and the breeze flowed through the sheer curtains Laura and Nicole had finished hanging that morning. "Yes," he said softly.

"How's Jen feeling?" Trent buffed the U.S. insignia on Shane's collar.

"She's not sick yet. I don't know if that's good or bad."

Carponti adjusted his sleeve. "So what do you want, a boy or a girl?"

"I just want Jen and the baby to be healthy." Shane's voice thickened and he cleared his throat. "I don't care either way."

"I felt the same way," Trent said.

"Oh, I think having a girl would be worse," Carponti said. "I think being sent to the store for tampons at midnight has got to be harder than being sent to the store for a box of condoms."

Trent laughed and shook his head. "There's something wrong with you."

"Come on. You're not going to be embarrassed to go to the store for tampons?"

"I've been married for more than a decade. I've bought tampons before."

"Really? Regular or super?"

Trent laughed and pinched the bridge of his nose before he excused himself and headed toward the house. "None of your damn business."

Trent took in a deep breath and headed into the small bedroom on the first floor, where Shane had spent much of his time recovering from his battle wounds. This was good. Things felt right.

He dug through the small bag he'd brought with him, his hand wrapping around the small orange pill bottle. None of the usual anxiety had started squeezing his heart or shortening his temper but he'd been wary of trying to do too much. He stared down at the bottle, trying to decide if he should take the anxiety med or to run the gauntlet and see what the day brought.

A quiet knock on the door made him tighten his grip on the bottle. He was almost tempted to hide it. Laura slipped in, a warm smile on her face. Her gown looked like it was painted on her body, and her caramel-colored hair was piled high on her head, with just a few stray ringlets dusting over her bare shoulders.

Trent's mouth went dry as she approached him.

"You okay?" Her fingers slid over his where he held the bottle, warm and soft and strong. He swallowed, looking down at their joined hands. "I was, ah, debating whether or not I should take one. Just in case."

Her fingers tightened around his. "Whatever you decide, it's what's best for you. We'll get you through this." She brought her other hand up to cover their hands. "Normal takes time. We'll get you there."

Her smile was brilliant, casting light into the lingering dark corners of his soul. "I didn't think you'd understand."

"I don't," she said honestly. "But that doesn't make it any less real to you. I want you home. The rest will take care of itself." She lifted her chin, meeting his gaze. "And I'll be here to walk through whatever darkness you go through, as long as you'll let me."

He pushed his glasses to the top of his head, then lowered his forehead to hers. "Thanks."

"You're welcome." She brushed her lips across his. "Now, we've got a wedding to attend." She met his gaze. "Are you ready?"

"Yeah. I think I am."

He tucked the pills back into his hygiene bag. They were there if he needed them. For now, that was enough.

LAURA STUCK her head out of the back door and made a motion with her hands.

"Okay, here we go," Shane said roughly from the pergola.

"Take your seats!" Carponti shouted over the crowd.

"This isn't a formation," Trent said. "You don't have to pretend you're the sergeant major."

Carponti adjusted the sleeve of his uniform over his prosthetic hand, his voice unusually gruff. "Yes, I do. Sarn't Major Giles told me to make sure that no one shows their asses today."

The intimate crowd settled into their seats, then silence fell over the small gathering. A light breeze wafted through the sheer curtains around the pergola. Another moment passed and the back door opened.

Ethan and Emma stepped out onto the porch together. Emma wore a tiny silver dress, similar to Laura's and Nicole's, and carried a tiny basket of flowers. She wasn't quite able to master the duties of a flower girl because instead of dropping a few petals here and there, she dropped clumps at random intervals. Ethan carried a small pillow and Trent wondered how Laura had managed to get the rings attached securely enough to keep their son from spilling them.

His son and daughter made their way down the porch steps together, both of them looking far too serious. Trent's heart swelled in his chest as they approached. His little girl looked at him with big eyes filled with trust and love, and his tiny man was trying hard to look grown up and serious. He pointed his little sister toward the chair she was supposed to sit in and then sat in the one next to it. Trent's eyes watered.

Nicole emerged next and Carponti straightened his posture as his wife made her way down the aisle. Nicole looked glamorous as always, but there was something about the way she looked at Carponti that made Trent's heart settle into place. They joked about sex and nothing ever seemed serious between them, but when it mattered, she was there for him.

Then the world tipped beneath his feet as his wife stepped onto the back porch. He'd already seen her in the silver gown, but the light shimmered off her now, making her glow. Seeing her take that first step off the back porch and down the aisle toward him, he felt like he was watching his bride approach all over again. She was more beautiful now, more whole.

More precious. Because they almost hadn't had this day. Or any other days. His mouth went dry and he cleared his throat roughly.

Laura smiled at him like he was the only man in the world, and a fierce swell of emotion ran through him. He swallowed as she stepped onto the pergola. The sunset glinted over her shoulders, framing her in a silver and golden glow. His blood warmed and he wondered how long it would be before he could steal her away for a moment alone.

Then everything stopped as Jen stepped onto the back porch.

Trent felt his throat close as he looked at his best friend's future wife. She wore no veil, just a simple headband glittering with sparkling stones. Her gown swept over her shoulders with the tiniest capped sleeves and sloped gently over her breasts. There was no trace of her scar, no visible proof that she was anything less than perfect. Because she was.

Next to him, Shane cleared his throat. Then coughed and did it again. Trent and Carponti leaned over at the same time.

"Are you crying?" Carponti whispered.

"Fuck off, both of you," Shane mumbled beneath his breath. He exhaled with a rush as she stepped onto the pergola. "Hey."

"Hi." She smiled up at him, her eyes glittering brightly.

"If you go through with this, you're never getting rid of me," he said quietly.

"Chaplain, would you do the honors before he chickens out?" Jen asked.

Chaplain Hobbes smiled. "Of course."

As the ceremony started, a strange sound that faintly resembled a sniffle came from behind him, but he did not turn around. He wasn't sure he could survive seeing Carponti cry. He was pretty sure the world would end if he did.

He met Laura's gaze as Shane took Jen's hands.

And as his long-time friend married the woman of his dreams, Trent stared at the woman of his. There was still a long journey ahead. Many dark nights. Coming home from war was not a single event. It was a process. A journey.

Trent was one of the lucky ones. He'd had a family to come back to. A woman he'd

almost lost.

As Shane kissed his wife, Trent swallowed the hard lump of emotion in his own throat. So many friends lost.

But Shane had made it. So had Carponti.

They'd come home. Back to the families that had waited for them. Back to the families that made it all worthwhile. There was no promise of tomorrow.

But it was a start.

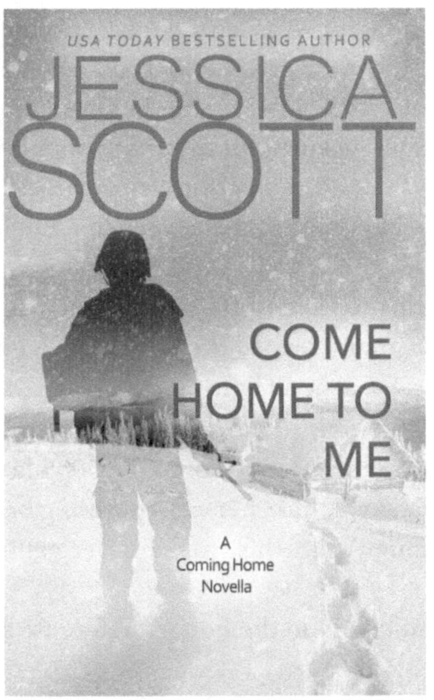

Thank you for reading **BACK TO YOU**. I hope you found Trent & Laura's story as emotionally satisfying as I did. Keep reading to find out what a little girl will do to bring her parents back together. Find out what happens in **COME HOME TO ME!**

All Patrick wanted was his family together for the holidays. But the woman he loves is struggling to leave her memories of the war behind. What will it take for him to finally bring her home?

ONE CLICK COME HOME TO ME, an EMOTIONAL SECOND CHANCE ROMANCE NOW!

EXCERPT FROM COME HOME TO ME

It was hell getting your heart ripped out right before Christmas.

And no matter how much scotch he threw at the problem, Major Patrick MacLean couldn't make the bleeding stop.

Sam was gone. And she'd taken Natalie with her.

Patrick knew all the stages of grief—at least a few of them. The anger. The denial. Maybe not in that order, but he knew how to deal with Seriously Bad Shit.

Except that he hadn't moved—not from the couch or from the bottom of the bottle that he'd crawled into at the start of the holiday half-day schedule.

On the coffee table in front of him, his cell phone vibrated violently.

He blinked rapidly a couple of times. The angry gadget was blurry and out of focus. He was on leave. He didn't have to answer the damn phone if he didn't want to.

At least, he didn't think he did. He *was* on leave, right? He'd signed out, right? He rubbed his temples, trying to think if he'd called the staff duty. Hell, he couldn't remember. He groped in the dark for the bottle as the phone went silent.

Except the damn thing started vibrating again.

Someone didn't know how to take a hint.

He snatched the phone off the table, too irritated to look at the number. "Yeah?"

"Daddy?"

He froze, the haze burning from his brain instantly. The wound Sam had left on his soul ripped open again at the sound of Natalie's voice. He closed his eyes, fighting to breathe against the tightness in his throat. Losing his family was worse, so much worse, than anything Iraq had thrown at him.

"Hey, sugar bear." He cradled his head in his hands, his heart breaking at the sound of her voice.

Natalie wasn't his daughter. Not by blood or legal paperwork.

But he was still her daddy. The only daddy she'd ever known, and in his heart, she was his.

She was his family. Sam was his family.

And they were gone. Just. Gone.

He cleared his throat.

"You're up late," he managed, hoping she didn't hear how bad he sounded to his own ears. "Shouldn't you be sleeping?"

"Something's wrong with Mommy."

Hello, Captain Obvious. He didn't say that, though. He wasn't sure the eight-year-old would appreciate the sarcasm. "Is she hurt?" he asked instead.

"She's crying all the time. And she doesn't talk to me." Her little voice broke. "I don't know how to make her okay."

"Are you okay?"

"No." A tiny, hitched breath. "I want to come home. I want to see you. Mommy... Something is wrong." A sniff, followed by a muffled sob. "Can you come get me?"

"Honey, you're all the way in Maine."

Silence for what felt like an eternity. "Isn't this why they have airplanes?"

He smiled at the deadpan voice. Nat had been working on her repertoire of smartass skills. Any other time, he would have been so proud. Except that his heart hurt at the sound of her voice.

"I—" His voice locked in his throat.

"Daddy, I'm scared." Another quiet sniff. "Please come. This was supposed to be our first Christmas together since you and Mommy came home from Iraq."

Damn. The kid was good at getting what she wanted. He'd told himself that she was too little to remember when he'd kissed her good-bye and gotten on that plane. That she wouldn't remember the phone calls when she'd cried that she wanted him to come home. That she *misted* him when she couldn't say *missed* right.

That maybe she was too little to notice that her mother had packed them off without so much as saying good-bye.

At some level, he'd rationalized that letting Sam go was the right thing to do. That if she wasn't happy anymore, it was better that she left before they started hating each other. That things had changed between them, and he should remember the good times.

It was obvious since she'd come home that something was wrong, but he hadn't pushed. He'd given her space, thinking she needed it to get things sorted in her head.

Except that space, apparently, had been the wrong thing to give.

"Please, Daddy."

He closed his eyes. And made a decision that was either going to damn him to hell or save the little girl and the family that he loved with all his heart.

It was still dark, the moonlight frozen on the path in front of her. The cold penetrated her bones and seeped into her soul. The only sound on the wooded path was the crunch of her boots on the frozen crust. The air froze in her nose and seared her throat, biting at her cheeks as she walked.

Captain Samantha Egan walked through the Maine woods where she'd grown up and felt like she didn't belong there anymore. She didn't belong anywhere. Not at Fort Hood. Not back home.

Everything felt wrong.

And she was cold. But it was more than cold from the temperature. No, it was the cold of something dead in the space where her heart had been. She was more used to the Iraqi heat—even in the dead of what passed for winter there—than the frigid central Maine subarctic temps.

She'd hoped that coming home to Saber Falls might jolt the dead space in her chest back to life. That the darkness would burn away in the bright sunlight sparkling off the frozen trees.

But it hadn't. She'd been home for a few days, back from the war in Iraq for less than a month, and nothing she did felt right. Not being around Natalie. Not being around her mother or her old friends from high school. Especially not being around friends from high school. She'd tried to stop in and see her friends Garrett and Finn Rierson but her lungs had stopped working before she'd even pulled into the police station where Garrett worked. She'd kept driving, avoiding the reality of seeing them. Avoiding the reality of the loss of her best friend that threatened to cut off her air every time she thought about her. She breathed out as she rounded a bend in the snowmobile trail, turning back toward her mother's house, trying to ease the automatic tightness in her chest when she thought about Mel.

The hole in her heart was matched by the hole left in their lives from the war.

Nothing felt right but work. Work and being around the soldiers she'd deployed with were the only things that didn't feel wrong.

Even then, being around the guys from work wasn't the same now that they were all home. She was the odd woman out as the men went home to their wives and the women went home to their husbands and kids.

She pulled her hat down over her ears, trying to keep out the penetrating cold.

Sam had gone home to her daughter. To the man who'd been a part of her life for the last nine years.

And she'd felt nothing.

No joy at seeing Natalie. No happiness at being with Patrick.

Oh, she'd smiled and said all the right things. But inside, something special was broken. There were no words for the utter lack of any feeling. Everything was mechanical and stilted. Off.

Especially with Patrick.

He was a good man. A man she'd loved with everything she was.

But things weren't the same anymore. Something had changed during her deployment. She'd stopped calling as much, unable to bear hearing her daughter's voice on the phone. The pain in her heart when her daughter cried for her ripped out her soul, made her question everything she was doing in the war, in the Army.

But it was different with Patrick. She'd stopped calling him, too; not just Natalie. She hadn't been able to deal with hearing about the homework or dinner or all the other normal things he did while she was deployed. He managed her being gone so much better than she'd done without him.

It wasn't like he hadn't deployed, too. She'd been the worried other half on the other side of the world before.

Maybe the war had taken her ability to feel any happiness at all ever again. The deployment ...the deployment had broken her ability to feel anything for him, and she couldn't say why, only that now she looked at him and felt...nothing. She'd hoped, prayed, that seeing him would make her feel again, would breathe life back into the dead spot in her chest.

But that first night home, when he'd slid into the bed next to her, she'd feigned sleep and denied them both. She sucked in a deep breath, letting the cold burn in her lungs until her eyes watered.

He was no warrior saint. What she'd done—or rather what she hadn't done—had hurt them both. She'd seen his hurt and the anger and frustration just there beneath the surface.

But it hadn't cracked the frozen glass encasing her heart.

She couldn't say what had happened to the love she'd felt for him. But after a week of pretending, she'd broken the news.

"I'm going home for Christmas," she'd said as he'd stripped in the bathroom after PT.

He'd turned slowly, his dark brown eyes filled with expectation and a thousand questions. "Okay?" he'd said cautiously.

"I'm not coming back," she'd said, her voice as flat as the emotions in her chest.

The veins in his neck had bunched, standing out against his skin. "Back to me or back to the Army?"

She looked away from the penetrating concern in his eyes. Patrick was a good man. A strong man. A man who had loved her daughter and who had loved her.

And she wasn't capable of loving him back anymore.

It was better to end it now. Cauterize the wound before it festered and grew in hatred and anger. Maybe they could figure out how to be friends.

Maybe someday, when things weren't all wilted and frayed inside her.

"I'm sorry," was all she had managed.

Walking through the woods now, she couldn't say when things

had gone wrong. She couldn't put a mark on the calendar that she could pinpoint and say *here's when things went to shit* in her life.

She'd hoped coming home would fix things. That the fog would clear away and she'd feel *something* again. But the fog was still there.

And it still felt like she was looking at life from very far away.

So she walked. Through the woods as the sun slid higher over the frozen Maine trees and hills, hoping that something would snap her out of it.

There was no reason for her to feel this way.

She'd made it home from the war when others hadn't. She had a daughter who was healthy and a man who'd taken care of their lives while she was deployed. A career that she was damn good at.

She'd come home.

She just didn't know what that actually felt like.

She didn't know if she'd ever feel again.

But she had to keep going. Had to put one foot in front of the other. She just needed to suck it up and snap herself out of it.

Because she had a daughter to raise. And the war was far from over.

For her, it would never be over. The ghosts would be with her, no matter how far she walked or how hard she tried to pretend they weren't.

Her toes burned from the cold. She needed to get warm. Maybe Mom and Natalie wouldn't be up yet so she could sit by the fire and just let the heat seep into her bones.

Natalie was an early bird, though. All those mornings of getting up for daycare since she was a baby had set the little bugger's internal clock for the ass-crack of dawn. Maybe, though, maybe today she'd sleep in.

It was Christmas, right? Miracles could happen.

Sam had promised her a trip to see Santa. Damn, but she didn't want to drive the hour to Bangor to the mall. She used to love coming home to Central Maine for a visit, but she damn sure hated the thirty-minute drive for the nearest real grocery store or the hour plus to Bangor.

But she'd promised and, well, a promise was a promise.

So if the weather held, she'd bundle her little bear up and head to the mall.

But first she needed to get warm. Badly.

She opened the sliders to her mother's back door. She'd always loved her mom's house. The back of the house faced away from the road and civilization in general. It was peaceful.

She kicked the snow off her boots and slid the door shut behind her.

There was movement in the kitchen. The light was on now. Probably Mom. Guess Natalie's early riser tendencies were genetic. "Mom?"

Silence greeted her question.

She frowned.

Then froze as the shadows near the kitchen sink moved and morphed into the man she'd abandoned.

Patrick stepped into the pale morning light.

"Hi, Sam."

ONE CLICK COME HOME TO ME NOW!

ACKNOWLEDGMENTS

Dear Reader,

This is the most difficult book I've ever written. It's also the one that taught me the value of strong friends to lean on when the going gets really, really rough. I've been working on Laura and Trent's story since 2008 so I'll probably screw this up but anyway, here goes.

Julie Kenner, you kept me sane through long rewrites and many many rounds of edits and revisions. You always gave me straight advice and let me call you in absolute panic. Thanks for being a great mentor and friend. Allison Brennan and Roxanne St Claire, thanks for letting me lean on you when I wanted to quit. Ruthie Knox and Elisabeth Barrett, you are both amazing writers and I am lucky to call you both friend. Not too many folks will come running to a hotel room when there's epic flail going on. Thanks for letting me not have my stuff together all the time. My agent, Donna Bagdasarian, thank you. You know all the thousand reasons why but mostly thanks for believing in me, especially when I don't. And finally to my amazing and talented editor Michele Bidelspach: thank you for pushing me to write this book the way it needed to be written and for having the faith in this story that I sometimes lacked.

A MESSAGE FROM JESSICA SCOTT

Dear Reader,

Thank you so much for reading. If you'd like to make sure you never miss a new release, sign up for my newsletter at http://jessicascott.net/subscribe/ and please like my Facebook page at https://www.facebook.com/JessicaScottAuthor/.

If you enjoyed this story, please consider leaving a review. Word of mouth is incredibly important for helping other readers discover new authors. I appreciate any and all reviews (whether positive or negative or somewhere in between).

Until next time!
Jess

ALSO BY JESSICA SCOTT

THE COMING HOME SERIES

Because of You

I'll Be Home for Christmas: A Coming Home Novella

Anything For You: A Coming Home Short Story

Back to You

Come Home to Me: A Coming Home Novella*

Carry Me Home*

A Place Called Home*

Take Me Home*

Homefront

After The War

Last One Home*

THE FALLING SERIES

Before I Fall

Break My Fall

After I Fall

Catch My Fall

Until We Fall

NONFICTION

To Iraq & Back: On War and Writing

The Long Way Home: One Mom's Journey Home From War

BOOKSHOTS

Dawn's Early Light

Author's Note

The Coming Home series and Homefront series were originally published as separate series. I have rebranded them to get things organized as they were originally intended.

Come Home to Me: A Coming Home Novella* was originally published as part of the Homefront series

Carry Me Home* was originally published as Until There Was You as part of the Coming Home series

A Place Called Home* was originally published as All for You as part of the Coming Home series

Take Me Home* was originally published as It's Always Been You as part of the Coming Home series

Last One Home* was originally published as Find My Way Home as part of the Homefront series

ABOUT THE AUTHOR

Jessica Scott is an Iraq war veteran, an active duty Army officer and the USA Today bestselling author of novels set in the heart of America's Army. She is the mother of two daughters, too many animals, and wife to a retired NCO.

She's also written for the New York Times At War Blog, PBS Point of View Regarding War, and IAVA. She deployed to Iraq in 2009 as part of Operation Iraqi Freedom (OIF)/New Dawn and has had the honor of serving as a company commander at Fort Hood, Texas twice.

She holds a Ph.D. from Duke in sociology and she's been featured as one of Esquire Magazine's Americans of the Year for 2012.

Photo: Courtesy of Buzz Covington Photography

Find her online at http://www.jessicascott.net

For more information,
www.jessicascott.net
jessica@jessicascott.net